THE READER'S LIBRARY

THE works of literature that have been selected and edited for this series are not alone of a character and standard that make them interesting to all readers; they are issued in well made volumes, substantially and attractively bound, so that they may take their place on the library shelves at home, or be carried in the pocket and read at odd moments. They are easily held in the hand. They go naturally into the pocket.

The series contains romances and stories of adventure, poetry and essays, biography and travel, philosophy and science, for the entertainment and instruction of old and young. The type, the size, the weight, the binding, make them available to those who read at all hours of the day or night. They are books to be read, to be used, to be kept close at hand.

To place such literature within everybody's reach under any and all circumstances is the reason for the creation of THE READER'S LIBRARY, to which new titles by famous authors will be constantly added.

LUCAS LEXOW,
Editor.

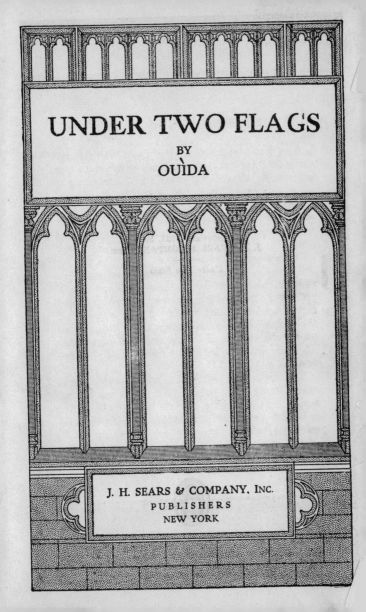

UNDER TWO FLAGS

BY
OUÏDA

J. H. SEARS & COMPANY, Inc.
PUBLISHERS
NEW YORK

Set up, Printed and Bound at the
KINGSPORT PRESS
KINGSPORT TENNESSEE
United States of America

CONTENTS

CONTENTS

UNDER TWO FLAGS.

CHAPTER I.

"BEAUTY OF THE BRIGADES."

A GUARDSMAN at home is always, if anything, rather more luxuriously accommodated than a young Duchess, and Bertie Cecil was never behind his fellows in anything; besides, he was one of the cracks of the Household, and women sent him pretty things enough to fill the Palais Royal. The dressing-table was littered with Bohemian glass and gold-stoppered bottles, and all the perfumes of Araby represented by Breidenback and Rimmel. The dressing-case was of silver, with the name studded on the lid in turquoises; the brushes, bootjack, boot-trees, whip-stands, were of ivory and tortoiseshell. On the softest of sofas, half dressed, and having half an hour before splashed like a water dog out of the bath, as big as a small pond, in the dressing-chamber beyond, was the Hon. Bertie himself, second son of Viscount Royallieu, known generally in the Brigades as "Beauty." The appellative, gained at Eton, was in no way undeserved; when the smoke cleared away that was circling round him out of a great meerschaum bowl, it showed a face of as much delicacy and brilliancy as a woman's; handsome, thoroughbred, languid, nonchalant, with a certain latent recklessness under the impassive calm of habit, and a singular softness given to the large, dark hazel eyes by the unusual length of the lashes over them. His features were exceedingly fair—fair as the fairest girl's; his hair was of the softest, silkiest, brightest chestnut; his mouth very beautifully shaped; on the whole, with a certain gentle, mournful love-me look that his eyes had with them, it was no wonder that great ladies and gay lionnes alike gave him the palm as the handsomest man in all the Household Regiments—not even excepting that splendid golden-haired Colossus, his oldest friend and closest comrade, known as "the Seraph."

He looked at the new tops that Rake, his servant, swung in his hand, and shook his head.

"Better, Rake; but not right yet. Can't you get that tawny color in the tiger's skin there? You go so much to brown."

Rake shook his head in turn, as he set down the incorrigible tops beside six pairs of their fellows, and six times six of every other sort of boots that the covert side, the heather, the flat, or the "sweet shady side of Pall Mall" ever knew.

"Do my best, sir; but Polish don't come nigh Nature, Mr. Cecil."

"Goes beyond it, the ladies say; and to do them justice they favor it much the most," laughed Cecil to himself, floating fresh clouds of Turkish about him. "Willon up?"

"Yes, sir. Come in this minute for orders."

"How'd Forest King stand the train?"

"Bright as a bird, sir; he never mind nothing. Mother o' Pearl she worreted a little, he says; she always do, along of the engine noise; but the King walked in and out just as if the stations were his own stable-yard."

"He gave them gruel and chilled water after the shaking before he let them go to their corn?"

"He says he did, sir."

Rake would by no means take upon himself to warrant the veracity of his sworn foe, the stud-groom; unremitting feud was between them; Rake considered that he knew more about horses than any other man living, and the other functionary proportionately resented back his knowledge and his interference, as utterly out of place in a body-servant.

"To sit wedged in with one's troop for five hours, and in a drizzle too! Houses oughtn't to meet until the day's fine; I'm sure they are in no hurry," said Cecil to himself, as he pocketed a dainty, filmy handkerchief, all perfume, point, and embroidery, with the interlaced B. C., and the crest on the corner, while he looked hopelessly out of the window. He was perfectly happy, drenched to the skin on the moors after a royal, or in a fast thing with the Melton men from Thorpe Trussels to Ranksborough; but three drops of rain when on duty were a totally different matter, to be resented with any amount of dandy's lamentations and epicurean diatribes.

"Ah, young one, how are you? Is the day very bad?" he asked with languid wistfulness as the door opened.

But indifferent and weary—on account of the weather—as the tone was, his eyes rested with a kindly, cordial light on the new-comer, a young fellow of scarcely twenty, like himself in feature, though much smaller and slighter in build; a graceful boy enough, with no fault in his face, except a certain weakness in the mouth, just shadowed only, as yet, with down.

A celebrity, the Zu-Zu, the last coryphée whom Bertie had translated from a sphere of garret bread-and-cheese to a sphere of villa champagne and chicken (and who, of course, in proportion to the previous scarcity of her bread-and-cheese, grew immediately intolerant of any wine less than 90s the dozen), said that Cecil cared for nothing longer than a fortnight, unless it were his horse, Forest King. It was very ungrateful in the Zu-Zu, since he cared for her at the least a whole quarter, paying for his fidelity at the tune of a hundred a month; and, also, it was not true, for, besides Forest King, he loved his young brother Berkeley—which, however, she neither knew nor guessed.

"Beastly!" replied that young gentleman, in reference to the weather, which was indeed pretty tolerable for an English morning in February. "I say, Bertie—are you in a hurry?"

"The very deuce of a hurry, little one; why?" Bertie never was in a hurry, however, and he said this as lazily as possible, shaking the white horsehair over his helmet, and drawing in deep draughts of Turkish Latakia previous to parting with his pipe for the whole of four or five hours.

"Because I am in a hole—no end of a hole—and I thought you'd help me," murmured the boy, half penitently, half caressingly; he was very girlish in his face and his ways. On which confession Rake retired into the bathroom; he could hear just as well there, and a sense of decorum made him withdraw.

"What's up, Berk?"

The boy hung his head, and played a little uneasily with an ormolu terrier-pot, upsetting half the tobacco in it.

Bertie looked at him, and laid his hand gently on the young one's shoulder.

"Come, my boy; out with it! It's nothing very bad, I'll be bound!"

"I want some more money; a couple of ponies," said the boy a little huskily; he did not meet his brother's eyes that were looking straight down on him.

Cecil gave a long, low whistle, and drew a meditative whiff from his meerschaum.

"Très cher, you're always wanting money. So am I. So is everybody. The normal state of man is to want money. Two ponies. What's it for?"

"I lost it at chicken-hazard last night. Poulteney lent it me, and I told him I would send it him in the morning. The ponies were gone before I thought of it, Bertie, and I haven't a notion where to get them to pay him again."

"Heavy stakes, young one, for you," murmured Cecil, while his hand dropped from the boy's shoulder, and a shadow of gravity passed over his face; money was very scarce with himself.

"I couldn't help it," pleaded the lad, with coaxing and almost piteous apology. "I backed Grosvenor's play, and you know he's always the most wonderful luck in the world. I couldn't tell he'd go a crowner and have such cards as he had. How shall I get the money, Bertie? I daren't ask the governor; and besides I told Poulteney he should have it this morning. What do you think if I sold the mare? But then I couldn't sell her in a minute——"

Cecil laughed a little, but his eyes, as they rested on the lad's young, fair, womanish face, were very gentle under the long shade of their lashes.

"Sell the mare! Nonsense! How should anybody live without a hack? I can pull you through, I dare say. Ah! by George, there's the quarters chiming. I shall be too late, as I live."

Not hurried still, however, even by that near prospect, he sauntered to his dressing-table, took up one of the pretty velvet and gold-filigreed absurdities, and shook out all the banknotes there were in it. There were fives and tens enough to count up £45. He reached over and caught up a five from a little heap lying loose on a novel of Du Terrail's, and tossed the whole across the room to the boy.

"There you are, young one! But don't borrow of any but your own people again, Berk. We don't do that. No, no!— no thanks! Shut up all that. If ever you get in a hole, I'll take you out if I can. Good-by—will you go to the Lords? Better not—nothing to see, and still less to hear. All stale. That's the only comfort for us—we are outside!" he said, with something that almost approached hurry in the utterance; so great was his terror of anything approaching a scene, and so eager was he to escape his brother's gratitude.

The boy had taken the notes with delighted thanks indeed, but with that tranquil and unprotesting readiness with which spoiled childishness or unhesitating selfishness accepts gifts and sacrifices from another's generosity, which have been so general that they have ceased to have magnitude. As his brother passed him, however, he caught his hand a second, and looked up with a mist before his eyes, and a flush half of shame, half of gratitude, on his face.

"What a trump you are!—how good you are, Bertie!"

Cecil laughed and shrugged his shoulders.

"First time I ever heard it, my dear boy," he answered, as he lounged down the staircase, his chains clashing and jingling; while, pressing his helmet on to his forehead and pulling the chin scale over his mustaches, he sauntered out into the street where his charger was waiting.

"The deuce!" he thought, as he settled himself in his stirrups, while the raw morning wind tossed his white plume hither and thither. "I never remembered!—I don't believe I've left myself money enough to take Willon and Rake and the cattle down to the Shires to-morrow. If I shouldn't have kept enough to take my own ticket with!—that would be no end of a sell. On my word I don't know how much there's left on the dressing-table. Well! I can't help it; Poulteney had to be paid; I can't have Berk's name show in anything that looks shady."

The £50 had been the last remnant of a bill, done under great difficulties with a sagacious Jew, and Cecil had no more certainty of possessing any more money until next pay day should come round than he had of possessing the moon.

True, the Royallieu Peerage, one of the most ancient and almost one of the most impoverished in the kingdom, could ill afford to maintain its sons in the expensive career on which it had launched them, and the chief there was to spare usually went between the eldest son, a Secretary of Legation in that costly and charming City of Vienna, and the young one, Berkeley, through the old Viscount's partiality; so that, had Bertie ever gone so far as to study his actual position, he would have probably confessed that it was, to say the least, awkward; but then he never did this, certainly never did it thoroughly.

According to all the canons of his Order he was never excited, never disappointed, never exhilarated, never disturbed; and also, of course, never by any chance embarrassed.

This made his reputation on the town; the ladies called it very wicked, but were charmed by the Richelieu-like impudence all the same, and petted the sinner; and from then till now he had held his own with them; dashing through life very fast, as became the first riding man in the Brigades, but enjoying it very fully, smoothly, and softly; liking the world and being liked by it.

To be sure, in the background there was always that ogre of money, and the beast had a knack of growing bigger and darker every year; but then, on the other hand, Cecil never looked at him—never thought about him—knew, too, that he stood just as much behind the chairs of men whom the world accredited as millionaires, and whenever the ogre gave him a cold grip, that there was for the moment no escaping, washed away the touch of it in a warm, fresh draft of pleasure.

CHAPTER II.

LOVE À LA MODE.

LIFE was very pleasant at Royallieu.

It lay in the Melton country, and was equally well placed for Pytchley, Quorn, and Belvoir, besides possessing its own small but very perfect pack of "little ladies," or the "demoiselles," as they were severally nicknamed; the game was closely preserved, pheasants were fed on Indian corn till they were the finest birds in the country, and in the little winding paths of the elder and bilberry coverts thirty first-rate shots, with two loading-men to each, could find flock and feather to amuse them till dinner, with rocketers and warm corners enough to content the most insatiate of knickerbockered gunners. The stud was superb; the cook, a French artist of consummate genius, who had a brougham to his own use and wore diamonds of the first water.

A wintry, watery sun was shining on the terraces as Lord Royallieu paced up and down the morning after the Grand Military; his step and limbs excessively enfeebled, but the carriage of his head and the flash of his dark hawk's eyes as proud and untamable as in his earliest years. He never left his own apartments; and no one, save his favorite "little Berk," ever went to him without his desire. He was too sensitive a man to thrust his age and ailing health in among the young leaders of fashion, the wild men of pleasure, the good wits and the good shots of his son's set.

He looked up suddenly and sharply: coming toward him he saw the figure of the Guardsman. For "Beauty" the Viscount had no love; indeed, well-nigh a hatred, for a reason never guessed by others, and never betrayed by him.

Bertie was not like the Royallieu race; he resembled his mother's family. She, a beautiful and fragile creature whom her second son had loved, for the first years of his life, as he would have thought it now impossible that he could love anyone, had married the Viscount with no affection toward him, while he had adored her with a fierce and jealous passion that her indifference only inflamed. Throughout her married life, however, she had striven to render loyalty and tenderness toward a lord into whose arms she had been thrown, trembling and reluctant; of his wife's fidelity he could not entertain a doubt; though, that he had never won her heart, he could not choose but know. He knew more, too; for she had told it him with a noble candor before he wedded her; knew that the man she did love was a penniless cousin, a cavalry officer, who had made a famous name among the wild mountain tribes of Northern India. This cousin, Alan Bertie—a fearless and chivalrous soldier, fitter for the days of knighthood than for these—had seen Lady Royallieu at Nice, some three years after her marriage; accident had thrown them across each other's path; the old love, stronger, perhaps, now than it had ever been, had made him linger in her presence—had made her shrink from sending him to exile. Evil tongues at last had united their names together; Alan Bertie had left the woman he idolized lest slander should touch her through him, and fallen two years later under the dark dank forests on the desolate moorside of the hills of Hindostan, where long before he had rendered "Bertie's Horse" the most famous of all the wild Irregulars of the East.

After her death, Lord Royallieu found Alan's miniature among her papers, and recalled those winter months by the Mediterranean till he cherished, with the fierce, eager, self-torture of a jealous nature, doubts and suspicions that, during her life, one glance from her eyes would have disarmed and abashed. Her second and favorite child bore her family name—her late lover's name; and, in resembling her race, resembled the dead soldier. It was sufficient to make him hate Bertie with a cruel and savage detestation, which he strove indeed to temper, for he was by nature a just man, and, in his better moments, knew that his doubts wronged both the living and the dead; but which colored, too strongly to be dissembled, all his feelings and his actions toward his son, and might both have soured and wounded any temperament less nonchalantly gentle and supremely careless than Cecil's.

As it was, Bertie was sometimes surprised at his father's dislike to him, but never thought much about it, and attributed it, when he did think of it, to the caprices of a tyrannous old man. To be jealous of the favor shown to his boyish brother could never for a moment have come into his imagination. Lady Royallieu with her last words had left the little fellow, a child of three years old, to the affection and the care of Bertie—himself then a boy of twelve or fourteen—and little as he thought of such things now, the trust of his dying mother had never been wholly forgotten.

A heavy gloom came now over the Viscount's still handsome aquiline, saturnine face, as his second son approached up the terrace; Bertie was too like the cavalry soldier whose form he had last seen standing against the rose light of a Mediterranean sunset. The soldier had been dead eight-and-twenty years; but the jealous hate was not dead yet.

Cecil took off his hunting-cap with a courtesy that sat very well on his habitual languid nonchalance; he never called his father anything but "Royal"; rarely saw, still less rarely consulted him, and cared not a straw for his censure or opinion; but he was too thoroughbred by nature to be able to follow the underbred indecorum of the day which makes disrespect to old age the fashion. "You sent for me?" he asked, taking the cigarette out of his mouth.

"No, sir," answered the old lord curtly; "I sent for your brother. The fools can't take even a message right now, it seems."

"Shouldn't have named us so near alike; it's often a bore!" said Bertie.

"I didn't name you, sir; your mother named you," answered his father sharply; the subject irritated him.

"It's of no consequence which!" murmured Cecil, with an expostulatory wave of his cigar. "We're not even asked whether we like to come into the world; we can't expect to be asked what we like to be called in it. Good-day to you, sir."

And he went without another word. Crossing the length of the old-fashioned Elizabethan terrace, little Berk passed him; he motioned the lad toward the Viscount. "Royal wants to see you, young one."

The boy nodded and went onward; and, as Bertie turned to enter the low door that led out to the stables, he saw his father meet the lad—meet him with a smile that changed the whole character of his face, and pleasant, kindly words of affectionate welcome; drawing his arm about Berkeley's shoulder, and looking with pride upon his bright and gracious youth.

More than an old man's preference would be thus won by the young one; a considerable portion of their mother's fortune, so left that it could not be dissipated, yet could be willed to which son the Viscount chose, would go to his brother by this passionate partiality; but there was not a tinge of jealousy in Cecil; whatever else his faults he had no mean ones, and the boy was dear to him, by a quite unconscious, yet unvarying, obedience to his dead mother's wish.

"Royal hates me as game-birds hate a red dog. Why the deuce, I wonder?" he thought, with a certain slight touch of pain, despite his idle philosophies and devil-may-care indifference. "Well—I am good for nothing, I suppose. Certainly I am not good for much, unless it's riding and making love."

With which summary of his merits, "Beauty," who felt himself to be a master in those two arts, but thought himself a bad fellow out of them, sauntered away to join the Seraph and the rest of his guests; his father's words pursuing him a little, despite his carelessness, for they had borne an unwelcome measure of truth.

"Royal can hit hard," his thoughts continued. "'A pauper and a Guardsman!' By Jove! it's true enough; but he made me so. They brought me up as if I had a million coming to me, and turned me out among the cracks to take my running with the best of them—and they give me just about what pays my groom's book! Then they wonder that a fellow goes to the Jews. Where the deuce else can he go?"

CHAPTER III.

AFTER A RICHMOND DINNER.

It was the height of the season, and the duties of the Household were proportionately and insupportably heavy.

The Brigades were fairly worked to death, and the Indian service, in the heat of the Afghan war, was never more onerous than the campaigns that claimed the Guards from Derby to Ducal.

Escorts to Levees, guards of honor to Drawing rooms, or field-days in the Park and the Scrubs, were but the least portion of it. Far more severe, and still less to be shirked, were the morning exercise in the Ride; the daily parade in the Lady's Mile; the reconnoissances from club windows, the vedettes at Flirtation Corner; the long campaigns at mess-breakfasts, with the study of dice and baccarat tactics, and the fortifications of Strasburg pâté against the invasions of Chartreuse and Chambertin; the breathless, steady charges of Belgravian staircases when a fashionable drum beat the rataplan.

The Household were very hard pressed through the season —a crowded and brilliant one; and Cecil was in request most of all. Bertie, somehow or other, was the fashion—marvelous and indefinable word, that gives a more powerful crown than thrones, blood, beauty, or intellect can ever bestow.

And yet this season, while he made a prima donna by a bravissima, introduced a new tie by an evening's wear, gave a cook the cordon with his praise, and rendered a fresh-invented liqueur the rage by his recommendation, Bertie knew very well that he was ruined.

He knew that a season, a month, a day, might be the only respite left him, the only pause for him 'twixt his glittering, luxurious world and the fiat of outlawry and exile. He knew that the Jews might be down on him any night that he sat at the Guards' mess, flirted with foreign princesses, or laughed at the gossamer gossip of the town over iced drinks in the clubs. His liabilities were tremendous, his resources totally exhausted; but such was the latent recklessness of the careless Royallieu blood, and such the languid devil-may-care of his training and his temper, that the knowledge scarcely ever seriously disturbed his enjoyment of the moment. Somehow, he never realized it.

Yet Cecil lounged out of the club to drive with half a dozen of his set to a water-party at Richmond—a Bacchanalian water-party, with the Zu-Zu and her sisters for the Naiads and the Household for their Tritons.

As they left the Star and Garter, Laura Lelas, the brunette actress, mounted on Cecil's box-seat, remembered she had dropped her cashmere in the dining room. A cashmere is a Parisian's soul, idol, and fetich; servants could not find it; Cecil, who, to do him this justice, was always as courteous to a comédienne as to a countess, went himself. Passing the open windows of another room, he recognized the face of his little brother among a set of young Civil Service fellows, attachés, and cornets. They had no women with them; but they had brought what was perhaps worse—dice for hazard—and were turning the unconscious Star and Garter into an impromptu Crockford's over their wine.

Little Berk's pretty face was very flushed; his lips were set tight, his eyes were glittering; the boy had the gambler's passion of the Royallieu blood in its hottest intensity. He was playing with a terrible eagerness that went to Bertie's heart with the same sort of pang of remorse with which he had looked on him when he had been thrown like dead on his bed at home.

Cecil stopped and leaned over the open window.

"Ah, young one, I did not know you were here. We are going home; will you come?" he asked, with a careless nod to the rest of the young fellows.

Berkeley looked up with a wayward, irritated annoyance.

"No, I can't," he said irritably; "don't you see we are playing, Bertie?"

"I see," answered Cecil, with a dash of gravity, almost of sadness in him, as he leaned farther over the windowsill with his cigar in his teeth.

"Come away," he whispered kindly, as he almost touched the boy, who chanced to be close to the casement. "Hazard is the very deuce for anybody; and you know Royal hates it. Come with us, Berk; there's a capital set here, and I'm going to half a dozen good houses to-night, when we get back. I'll take you with me. Come! you like waltzing, and all that sort of thing, you know."

The lad shook himself peevishly; a sullen cloud over his fair, picturesque, boyish face.

"Let me alone before the fellows," he muttered impatiently. "I won't come, I tell you."

"Soit!"

Cecil shrugged his shoulders, left the window, found the Lelas' cashmere, and sauntered back to the drags without any more expostulation. The sweetness of his temper could never be annoyed, but also he never troubled himself to utter useless words. Moreover, he had never been in his life much in earnest about anything; it was not worth while.

"A pretty fellow I am to turn preacher, when I have sins enough on my own shoulders for twenty," he thought, as he shook the ribbons and started the leaders off to the gay music of Laura Lelas' champagne-tuned laughter.

He went that night, as he had said, to half a dozen good houses, midnight receptions, and after-midnight waltzes; making his bow in a Cabinet Minister's vestibule, and taking up the thread of the same flirtation at three different balls; showing himself for a moment at a Premier's At-home, and looking eminently graceful and pre-eminently weary in an ambassadress' drawing room, and winding up the series by a dainty little supper in the gray of the morning, with a sparkling party of French actresses, as bright as the bubbles of their own Clicquot.

When he went upstairs to his own bedroom, in Piccadilly, about five o'clock, therefore, he was both sleepy and tired, and lamented to that cherished and ever-discreet confidant, a cheroot, the brutal demands of the Service; which would drag him off, in five hours' time, without the slightest regard to his feelings, to take share in the hot, heavy, dusty, scorching work of a field-day up at the Scrubs.

"Here—get me to perch as quick as you can, Rake," he murmured, dropping into an armchair; astonished that Rake did not answer, he saw standing by him instead the boy Berkeley. Surprise was a weakness of raw inexperience that Cecil never felt; his gazette as Commander-in-Chief, or the presence of the Wandering Jew in his lodgings would never have excited it in him. In the first place, he would have merely lifted his eyebrows and said, "Be a fearful bore!" in the second he would have done the same, and murmured, "Queer old cad!"

Surprised, therefore, he was not, at the boy's untimely apparition; but his eyes dwelt on him with a mild wonder, while his lips dropped but one word:

"Amber-Amulet?"

Amber-Amulet was a colt of the most marvelous promise at the Royallieu establishment, looked on to win the next Clearwell, Guineas, and Derby as a certainty. An accident to the young chestnut was the only thing that suggested itself as of possibly sufficient importance to make his brother wait for him at five o'clock on a June morning.

Berkeley looked up confusedly, impatiently:

"You are never thinking but of horses or women," he

said peevishly; "there may be other things in the world, surely."

"Indisputably there are other things in the world, dear boy; but none so much to my taste," said Cecil composedly, stretching himself with a yawn. "With every regard to hospitality and the charms of your society, might I hint that five o'clock in the morning is not precisely the most suitable hour for social visits and ethical questions?"

"For God's sake, be serious, Bertie! I am the most miserable wretch in creation."

Cecil opened his closed eyes, with the sleepy indifference vanished from them, and a look of genuine and affectionate concern on the serene insouciance of his face.

"Ah! you would stay and play that chicken hazard," he thought, but he was not one who would have reminded the boy of his own advice and its rejection; he looked at him in silence a moment, then raised himself with a sigh.

"Dear boy, why didn't you sleep upon it? I never think of disagreeable things till they wake me with my coffee; then I take them up with the cup and put them down with it. You don't know how well it answers; it disposes of them wonderfully."

The boy lifted his head with a quick, reproachful anger, and in the gaslight his cheeks were flushed, his eyes full of tears.

"How brutal you are, Bertie! I tell you I am ruined, and you care no more than if you were a stone. You only think of yourself; you only live for yourself!"

"'Brutal'! What a word, little one. Nobody's brutal now; you never see that form nowadays. Come, what is the worst this time?"

Berkeley looked sullenly down on the table where his elbows leaned; scattering the rose-notes, the French novels, the cigarettes, and the gold essence-bottles with which it was strewn; there was something dogged yet agitated, half-insolent yet half-timidly irresolute, upon him, that was new there.

"The worst is soon told," he said huskily, and his teeth chattered together slightly, as though with cold, as he spoke. "I lost two hundred to-night; I must pay it, or be disgraced forever; I have not a farthing; I cannot get the money for my life; no Jews will lend to me, I am under age; and——and"—his voice sank lower and grew more defiant, for he knew that the sole thing forbidden him peremptorily by both his father and his brothers was the thing he had now to tell—"and—I borrowed three ponies of Granville Lee yesterday, as he came from the Corner with a lot of banknotes after settling-day. I told him I would pay them to-morrow; I made sure I should have won to-night."

Bertie started from his chair, his sleepy languor dissipated; on his face the look that had come there when Lord Royallieu had dishonored his mother's name. In his code there was one shameless piece of utter and unmentionable degradation —it was to borrow of a friend.

"You will bring some disgrace on us before you die, Berkeley," he said, with a keener inflection of pain and contempt than had ever been in his voice. "Have you no common knowledge of honor?"

The lad flushed under the lash of the words, but it was a flush of anger rather than of shame; he did not lift his eyes, but gazed sullenly down on the yellow paper of a Paris romance he was irritably dog-earing.

"You are severe enough," he said gloomily, and yet insolently. "Are you such a mirror of honor yourself? I suppose my debts, at the worst, are about one-fifth of yours."

For a moment even the sweetness of Cecil's temper almost gave way. Be his debts what they would, there was not one among them to his friends, or one for which the law could not seize him. He was silent; he did not wish to have a scene of dissension with one who was but a child to him; moreover, it was his nature to abhor scenes of any sort, and to avert even a dispute, at any cost.

He came back and sat down without any change of expression, putting his cheroot in his mouth.

"Très cher, you are not courteous," he said wearily; "but it may be that you are right. I am not a good one for you to copy from in anything except the fit of my coats; I don't think I ever told you I was. I am not altogether so satisfied with myself as to suggest myself as a model for anything, unless it were to stand in a tailor's window in Bond Street to show the muffs how to dress. That isn't the point, though; you say you want near £300 by to-morrow—to-day rather. I can suggest nothing except to take the morning mail to the Shires, and ask Royal straight out; he never refuses you."

Berkeley looked at him with a bewildered terror that banished at a stroke his sullen defiance; he was irresolute as a girl, and keenly moved by fear.

"I would rather cut my throat," he said, with a wild exaggeration that was but the literal reflection of the trepidation on him; "as I live I would! I have had so much from him lately—you don't know how much—and now of all times, when they threaten to foreclose the mortgage on Royallieu——"

"What? Foreclose what?"

"The mortgage!" answered Berkeley impatiently; to his childish egotism it seemed cruel and intolerable that any extremities should be considered save his own. "You know the lands are mortgaged as deeply as Monti and the entail would allow them. They threatened to foreclose—I think that's the word—and Royal has had God knows what work to stave them off. I no more dare face him, and ask him for a sovereign now than I dare ask him to give me the gold plate off the sideboard."

Cecil listened gravely; it cut him more keenly than he showed to learn the evils and the ruin that so closely menaced his house; and to find how entirely his father's morbid mania against him severed him from all the interests and all the confidence of his family, and left him ignorant of matters even so nearly touching him as these.

"Your intelligence is not cheerful, little one," he said, with a languid stretch of his limbs; it was his nature to glide off painful subjects. "And—I really am sleepy! You think there is no hope Royal would help you?"

"I tell you I will shoot myself through the brain rather than ask him."

Bertie moved restlessly in the soft depths of his lounging-chair.

"It is no use to give you false hopes, young one," he said gently. "I can do nothing! You ought to know me by this time; and if you do, you know too that if the money was mine it should be yours at a word—if you don't, no matter! Frankly, Berk, I am all down-hill; my bills may be called in any moment; when they are I must send in my papers to sell, and cut the country, if my duns don't catch me before, which they probably will; in which event I shall be to all intents and purposes—dead. This is not lively conversation, but you will do me the justice to say that it was not I who introduced it. Only—one word for all, my boy; understand this: if I could help you I would, cost what it might, but as matters stand—I cannot."

"No—yes—I know," Berkeley said hurriedly; "I have no

right to expect it, and have been behaving like a cur, and—and—all that, I know. But—there is one way you could save me, Bertie, if it isn't too much for a fellow to ask."

"I can't say I see the way, little one," said Cecil, with a sigh. "What is it?"

"Why—look here. You see I'm not of age; my signature is of no use; they won't take it; else I could get money in no time on what must come to me when Royal dies; though 'tisn't enough to make the Jews 'melt' at a risk. Now—now —look here. I can't see that there could be any harm in it. You are such chums with Lord Rockingham, and he's as rich as all the Jews put together. What could there be in it if you just asked him to lend you a monkey for me? He'd do it in a minute, because he'd give his head away to you—they all say so—and he'd never miss it. Now, Bertie —will you?"

In his boyish incoherence and its disjointed inelegance the appeal was panted out rather than spoken; and while his head drooped and the hot color burned in his face, he darted a swift look at his brother, so full of dread and misery that it pierced Cecil to the quick as he rose from his chair and paced the room, flinging his cheroot aside; the look disarmed the reply that was on his lips, but his face grew dark.

"What you ask is impossible," he said briefly. "If I did such a thing as that, I should deserve to be hounded out of the Guards to-morrow."

The boy's face grew more sullen, more haggard, more evil, as he still bent his eyes on the table, his glance not meeting his brother's.

"You speak as if it would be a crime," he muttered savagely, with a plaintive moan of pain in the tone; he thought himself cruelly dealt with and unjustly punished.

"It would be the trick of a swindler, and it would be the shame of a gentleman," said Cecil, as briefly still. "That is answer enough."

"Then you will not do it?"

"I have replied already."

There was that in the tone, and in the look with which he paused before the table, that Berkeley had never heard or seen in him before; something that made the supple, childish, petulant, cowardly nature of the boy shrink and be silenced; something for a single instant of the haughty and untamable temper of the Royallieu blood that awoke in the too feminine softness and sweetness of Cecil's disposition.

"You said that you would aid me at any cost, and now that I ask you so wretched a trifle, you treat me as if I were a scoundrel," he moaned passionately. "The Seraph would give you the money at a word. It is your pride—nothing but pride. Much pride is worth to us who are penniless beggars!"

"If we are penniless beggars, by what right should we borrow of other men?"

"You are wonderfully scrupulous, all of a sudden!"

Cecil shrugged his shoulders slightly and began to smoke again. He did not attempt to push the argument. His character was too indolent to defend itself against aspersion, and horror of a quarrelsome scene far greater than his heed of misconstruction.

"You are a brute to me!" went on the lad, with his querulous and bitter passion rising almost to tears like a woman's. "You pretend you can refuse me nothing; and the moment I ask you the smallest thing you turn round on me, and speak as if I were the greatest blackguard on earth. You'll let me go to the bad to-morrow rather than bend your pride to save me; you live like a Duke, and don't care if I should die in a debtor's prison! You only brag about 'honor' when you want to get out of helping a fellow; and if I were to cut my throat to-night you would only shrug your shoulders, and sneer at my death in the clubroom, with a jest picked out of your cursed French novels!"

"Melodramatic, and scarcely correct," murmured Bertie.

"Little one, you are heated, and don't know what you say," he began very gently, a few moments later, as he leaned forward and looked straight in the boy's eyes. "Don't be down about this; you will pull through, never fear. Listen to me; go down to Royal, and tell him all frankly. I know him better than you; he will be savage for a second, but he would sell every stick and stone on the land for your sake; he will see you safe through this. Only bear one thing in mind—tell him all. No half measures, no half confidences; tell him the worst, and ask his help. You will not come back without it."

Berkeley listened; his eyes shunning his brother's, the red color darker on his face.

"Do as I say," said Cecil, very gently still. "Tell him, if you like, that it is through following my follies that you have come to grief; he will be sure to pity you then."

There was a smile, a little sad, on his lips, as he said the last words, but it passed at once as he added:

"Do you hear me? will you go?"

"If you want me—yes."

"On your word, now?"

"On my word."

There was an impatience in the answer, a feverish eagerness in the way he assented that might have made the consent rather a means to evade the pressure than a genuine pledge to follow the advice; that darker, more evil, more defiant look, was still upon his face, sweeping its youth away and leaving in its stead a wavering shadow. He rose with a sudden movement; his tumbled hair, his disordered attire, his bloodshot eyes, his haggard look of sleeplessness and excitement in strange contrast with the easy perfection of Cecil's dress and the calm languor of his attitude. The boy was very young, and was not seasoned to his life and acclimatized to his ruin, like his elder brother. He looked at him with a certain petulant envy; the envy of every young fellow for a man of the world. "I beg your pardon for keeping you up, Bertie," he said huskily. "Good-night."

Cecil gave a little yawn.

"Dear boy, it would have been better if you could have come in with the coffee. Never be impulsive; don't do a bit of good, and is such bad form!"

He spoke lightly, serenely; both because such was as much his nature as it was to breathe, and because his heart was heavy that he had to send away the young one without help, though he knew that the course he had made him adopt would serve him more permanently in the end. But he leaned his hand a second on Berk's shoulder, while for one single moment in his life he grew serious.

"You must know I could not do what you asked; I could not meet any man in the Guards face to face if I sunk myself and sunk them so low. Can't you see that, little one?"

There was a wistfulness in the last words; he would gladly have believed that his brother had at length some perception of his meaning.

"You say so, and that is enough," said the boy pettishly; "I cannot understand that I asked anything so dreadful; but I suppose you have too many needs of your own to have any resources left for mine."

Cecil shrugged his shoulders slightly again, and let him go. But he could not altogether banish a pang of pain at his heart, less even for his brother's ingratitude than at his callousness to all those finer, better instincts of which honor is the concrete name.

For the moment, thought—grave, weary, and darkened—fell on him; he had passed through what he would have suffered any amount of misconstruction to escape—a disagreeable scene; he had been as unable as though he were a Commissionaire in the streets to advance a step to succor the necessities for which his help had been asked; and he was forced, despite all his will, to look for the first time blankly in the face the ruin that awaited him. There was no other name for it: it would be ruin complete and wholly inevitable.

That evening, in the loose-box down at Royallieu, Forest King stood without any body-covering, for the night was close and sultry; a lock of the sweetest hay unnoticed in his rack, and his favorite wheaten-gruel standing uncared-for under his very nose; the King was in the height of excitation, alarm, and haughty wrath. His ears were laid flat to his head, his nostrils were distended, his eyes were glancing uneasily with a nervous, angry fire rare in him, and ever and anon he lashed out his heels with a tremendous thundering thud against the opposite wall, with a force that reverberated through the stables and made his companions start and edge away. It was precisely these companions that the aristocratic hero of the Soldiers' Blue Ribbon scornfully abhorred.

They had just been looking him over—to their own imminent peril; and the patrician winner of the Vase, the brilliant six-year-old of Paris, and Shire and Spa steeple-chase fame, the knightly descendant of the White Cockade blood and of the coursers of Circassia, had resented the familiarity proportionately to his own renown and dignity. The King was a very sweet-tempered horse, a perfect temper, indeed, and ductile to a touch from those he loved; but he liked very few, and would suffer liberties from none. And of a truth his prejudices were very just; and if his clever heels had caught—as it was not his fault that they did not—the heads of his two companions, instead of coming with that ponderous crash into the panels of his box, society would certainly have been no loser, and his owner would have gained more than had ever before hung in the careless balance of his life.

But the iron heels, with their shining plates, only caught the oak of his box-door; and the tête-à-tête in the sultry, oppressive night went on as the speakers moved to a prudent distance; one of them thoughtfully chewing a bit of straw, after the immemorial habit of grooms, who ever seem as if they had been born into this world with a cornstalk ready in their mouths.

"It's a'most a pity—he's in such perfect condition. Tip-top. Cool as a cucumber after the longest pipe-opener; licks his oats up to the last grain; leads the whole string such a rattling spin as never was spun but by a Derby cracker before him. It's a'most a pity," said Willon meditatively, eying his charge, the King, with remorseful glances.

"Prut—tush—tish!" said his companion, with a whistle in his teeth that ended with a "damnation!" "It 'll only knock him over for the race; he'll be right as a trivet after it. What's your little game; coming it soft like that, all of a sudden? You hate that ere young swell like p'ison."

"Aye," assented the head groom with a tigerish energy, viciously consuming his bit of straw. "What for am I—head groom come nigh twenty years; and to Markisses and Wiscounts afore him—put aside in that ere way for a fellow as he's took into his service out of the dregs of a regiment; what was tied up at the triangles and branded D, as I know on, and sore suspected of even worse games than that, and now is that set up with pride and sich-like that nobody's woice ain't heard here except his; I say what am I called on to bear it for?" and the head groom's tones grew hoarse and vehement, roaring louder under his injuries. "A man what's attended a Duke's 'osses ever since he was a shaver, to be put aside for that workhus blackguard! A 'oss has a cold—it's Rake's mash what's to be given. A 'oss is off his feed—it's Rake what's to weigh out the niter and steel. A 'oss is a buck-jumper—it's Rake what's to cure him. A 'oss is entered for a race—it's Rake what's to order his mornin' gallops, and his go-downs o' water. It's past bearin' to have a rascally chap what's been and gone and turned walet, set up over one's head in one's own establishment, and let to ride the high 'oss over one, roughshod like that!"

And Mr. Willon, in his disgust at the equestrian contumely thus heaped on him, bit the straw savagely in two, and made an end of it, with a vindictive "Will yer be quiet there; blow yer," to the King, who was protesting with his heels against the conversation.

"Come, then, no gammon," growled his companion—the "cousin out o' Yorkshire" of the keeper's tree.

"What's yer figure, you say?" relented Willon meditatively.

"Two thousand to nothin'—come!—can't no handsomer," retorted the Yorkshire cousin, with the air of a man conscious of behaving very nobly.

"For the race in Germany?" pursued Mr. Willon, still meditatively.

"Two thousand to nothin'—come!" reiterated the other, with his arms folded to intimate that this and nothing else was the figure to which he would bind himself.

Willon chewed another bit of straw, glanced at the horse as though he were a human thing to hear, to witness, and to judge; grew a little pale; and stooped forward.

"Hush! Somebody'll spy on us. It's a bargain."

"Done! And you'll paint him, eh?"

"Yes—I'll—paint him."

The assent was very husky, and dragged slowly out, while his eyes glanced with a furtive, frightened glance over the loose-box. Then—still with that cringing, terrified look backward to the horse, as an assassin may steal a glance before his deed at his unconscious victim—the head groom and his comrade went out and closed the door of the loose-box and passed into the hot, lowering summer night.

Forest King, left in solitude, shook himself with a neigh; took a refreshing roll in the straw, and turned with an appetite to his neglected gruel. Unhappily for himself, his fine instincts could not teach him the conspiracy that lay in wait for him and his; and the gallant beast, content to be alone, soon slept the sleep of the righteous.

CHAPTER IV.

A STAG HUNT AU CLAIR DE LA LUNE.

"In the case of a Countess, sir, the imagination is more excited," says Dr. Johnson, who had, I suppose, little opportunity of putting that doctrine for amatory intrigues to the test in actual practice. Bertie, who had many opportunities, differed with him. He found love-making in his own polished, tranquil circles apt to become a little dull, and was more amused by Laura Lelas. However, he was sworn to the service of the Guenevere, and he drove his mail-phaeton down that day to another sort of Richmond dinner, of which the lady was the object instead of the Zu-Zu.

She enjoyed thinking herself the wife of a jealous and inexorable lord, and arranged her flirtations to evade him with a degree of skill so great that it was lamentable it should be thrown away on an agricultural husband, who never dreamt that the "Fidelio—III—TstnegeR," which met his eyes in the innocent face of his "Times" referred to an appointment at a Regent Street modiste's, or that the advertisement—"White wins—Twelve," meant that if she wore white camellias in her hair at the opera she would give "Beauty" a meeting after it.

Lady Guenevere was very scrupulous never to violate conventionalities. And yet she was a little fast—very fast, indeed, and was a queen of one of the fastest sets; but then—O sacred shield of a wife's virtue—she could not have borne to lose her very admirable position, her very magnificent jointure, and, above all, the superb Guenevere diamonds!

So, for the sake of the diamonds, she and Bertie had their rendezvous under the rose.

This day she went down to see a dowager Baroness aunt, out at Hampton Court—really went, she was never so imprudent as to falsify her word; and with the Dowager, who was very deaf and purblind, dined at Richmond, while the world thought her dining at Hampton Court. It was nothing to anyone, since none knew it to gossip about, that Cecil joined her there; that over the Star and Garter repast they arranged their meeting at Baden next month; that while the Baroness dozed over the grapes and peaches—she had been a beauty herself, in her own day, and still had her sympathies —they went on the river, in the little toy that he kept there for his fair friends' use; floating slowly along in the coolness of evening, while the stars loomed out in the golden trail of the sunset.

The evening was very hot and soft. There was a low south wind, the water made a pleasant murmur, wending among its sedges. She was very lovely, moreover; lying back there among her laces and Indian shawls, with the sunset in the brown depths of her eyes and on her delicate cheek. And Bertie, as he looked on his liege lady, really had a glow of the old, real, foolish, forgotten feeling stir at his heart, as he gazed on her in the half-light, and thought, almost wistfully, "If the Jews were down on me to-morrow, would she really care, I wonder?"

Really care? Bertie knew his world and its women too well to deceive himself in his heart about the answer. Nevertheless, he asked the question. "Would you care much, chère belle?"

"Care what?"

"If I came to grief—went to the bad, you know; dropped out of the world altogether."

She raised her splendid eyes in amaze, with a delicate shudder through all her laces. "Bertie! you would break my heart! What can you dream of?"

"Oh, lots of us end so! How is a man to end?" answered Bertie philosophically, while his thoughts still ran off in a speculative skepticism. "Is there a heart to break?"

Her ladyship looked at him and laughed.

"A Werther in the Guards! I don't think the rôle will suit either you or your corps, Bertie; but if you do it, pray do it artistically. I remember, last year, driving through Asnières, when they had found a young man in the Seine; he was very handsome, beautifully dressed, and he held fast in his clinched hand a lock of gold hair. Now, there was a man who knew how to die gracefully, and make his death an idyl!"

"Died for a woman?—ah!" murmured Bertie, with the Brummel nonchalance of his order. "I don't think I should do that, even for you—not, at least, while I had a cigar left."

And then the boat drifted backward, while the stars grew brighter and the last reflection of the sun died out; and they planned to meet to-morrow, and talked of Baden, and sketched projects for the winter in Paris, and went in and sat by the window, taking their coffee.

The Dowager went home in her brougham; the Countess drove in his mail-phaeton—objectionable, as she might be seen, but less objectionable than letting her servants know he had met her at Richmond. Besides, she obviated danger by bidding him set her down at a little villa across the park, where dwelt a confidential protégée of hers, whom she patronized; a former French governess, married tolerably well, who had the Countess' confidences, and kept them religiously for sake of so aristocratic a patron, and of innumerable reversions of Spanish point and shawls that had never been worn, and rings, of which her lavish ladyship had got tired.

From here she would take her ex-governess' little brougham, and get quietly back to her own house in Eaton Square, in due time for all the drums and crushes at which she must make her appearance. This was the sort of little device which really make them think themselves in love, and gave the salt to the whole affair. Moreover, there was this ground for it, that had her lord once roused from the straw-yards of his prize cattle, there was a certain stubborn, irrational, old-world prejudice of pride and temper in him that would have made him throw expediency to the winds, then and there, with a blind and brutal disregard to slander and to the fact that none would ever adorn his diamonds as she did. So that Cecil had not only her fair fame, but her still more valuable jewels in his keeping when he started from the Star and Garter in the warmth of the bright summer's evening.

It was a lovely night; a night for lonely highland tarns, and southern shores by Baiæ; without a cloud to veil the brightness of the stars. A heavy dew pressed the odors from the grasses, and the deep glades of the avenues were pierced here and there with a broad beam of silvery moonlight, slanting through the massive boles of the trees, and falling white and serene across the turf. Through the park, with the gleam of the water ever and again shining through the branches of the foliage, Cecil started his horses; his groom he had sent away on reaching Richmond, for the same reason as the Countess had dismissed her barouche, and he wanted no servant, since, as soon as he had set down his liege lady at her protégée's, he would drive straight back to Piccadilly. But he had not noticed what he noted now, that instead of one of his carriage-grays, who had fallen slightly lame, they had put into harness the young one, Maraschino, who matched admirably for size and color, but who, being really a hunter, though he had been broken to shafts as well, was not the horse with which to risk driving a lady.

However, Beauty was a perfect whip and had the pair perfectly in hand, so that he thought no more of the change, as the grays dashed at a liberal half-speed through the park, with their harness flashing in the moonlight, and their scarlet rosettes fluttering in the pleasant air. The eyes besides him, the Titian-like mouth, the rich, delicate cheek, these were, to be sure, rather against the coolness and science that such a five-year-old as Maraschino required; they were distracting even to Cecil, and he had not prudence enough to deny his sovereign lady when she put her hands on the ribbons.

"The beauties! give them to me, Bertie. Dangerous?

How absurd you are; as if I could not drive anything?
Do you remember my four roans at Longchamps?"

She could, indeed, with justice, pique herself on her skill;
she drove matchlessly, but as he resigned them to her, Maraschino and his companion quickened their trot, and tossed their
pretty thoroughbred heads, conscious of a less powerful hand
on the reins.

"I shall let their pace out; there is nobody to run over
here," said her ladyship. "Va-t'en donc, mon beau monsieur."

Maraschino, as though hearing the flattering conjuration,
swung off into a light, quick canter, and tossed his head
again; he knew that, good whip though she was, he could jerk
his mouth free in a second, if he wanted. Cecil laughed—
prudence was at no time his virtue—and leaned back contentedly, to be driven at a slashing pace through the balmy
summer's night, while the ring of the hoofs rang merrily on
the turf, and the boughs were tossed aside with a dewy
fragrance. As they went, the moonlight was shed about their
path in the full of the young night, and at the end of a vista
of boughs, on a grassy knoll were some phantom forms—
the same graceful shapes that stand out against the purple
heather and the tawny gorse of Scottish moorlands, while
the lean rifle-tube creeps up by stealth. In the clear starlight there stood the deer—a dozen of them, a clan of stags
alone—with their antlers clashing like a clash of swords,
and waving like swaying banners as they tossed their heads
and listened.

In an instant the hunter pricked his ears, snuffed the
air, and twitched with passionate impatience at his bit; another instant and he had got his head, and, launching into a
sweeping gallop, rushed down the glade.

Cecil sprang forward from his lazy rest, and seized the
ribbons that in one instant had cut his companion's gloves
to stripes.

"Sit still," he said calmly, but under his breath. "He has
been always ridden with the Buckhounds; he will race the
deer as sure as we live!"

Race the deer he did.

Startled, and fresh for their favorite nightly wandering,
the stags were off like the wind at the noise of alarm, and
the horses tore after them; no skill, no strength, no science
could avail to pull them in; they had taken their bits between
their teeth, and the devil that was in Maraschino lent the
contagion of sympathy to the young carriage mare, who had

never gone at such a pace since she had been first put in her break.

Neither Cecil's hands nor any other force could stop them now; on they went, hunting as straight in line as though staghounds streamed in front of them, and no phaeton rocked and swayed in a dead and dragging weight behind them. In a moment he gauged the closeness and the vastness of the peril; there was nothing for it but to trust to chance, to keep his grasp on the reins to the last, and to watch for the first sign of exhaustion. Long ere that should be given death might have come to them both; but there was a gay excitation in that head-long rush through the summer night; there was a champagne-draught of mirth and mischief in that dash through the starlit woodland; there was a reckless, breathless pleasure in that neck-or-nothing moonlight chase!

Yet danger was so near with every oscillation; the deer were trooping in fast flight, now clear in the moonlight, now lost in the shadow, bounding with their lightning grace over sward and hillock, over briar and brushwood, at that speed which kills most living things that dare to race the "Monarch of the Glens." And the grays were in full pursuit; the hunting fire was in the fresh young horse; he saw the shadowy branches of the antlers toss before him, and he knew no better than to hunt down in their scenting line as hotly as though the field of the Queen's or the Baron's was after them. What cared he for the phaeton that rocked and reeled on his traces; he felt its weight no more than if it were a wicker-work toy, and, extended like a greyhound, he swerved from the road, swept through the trees, and tore down across the grassland in the track of the herd.

As Cecil leaned back, his hands clinched on the reins, his sinews stretched almost to bursting in their vain struggle to recover power over the loosened beasts, the hunting zest woke in him too, even while his eyes glanced on his companion in fear and anxiety for her.

"Tally-ho! hark forward! As I live, it is glorious!" he cried, half unconsciously. "For God's sake, sit still, Beatrice! I will save you."

Inconsistent as the words were, they were true to what he felt; alone, he would have flung himself delightedly into the madness of the chase; for her he dreaded with horror the eminence of their peril.

On fled the deer, on swept the horses; faster in the gleam of the moonlight the antlered troop darted on through the gloaming; faster tore the grays in the ecstasy of their freedom; headlong and heedless they dashed through the thickness of leaves and the weaving of branches; neck to neck, straining to distance each other, and held together by the gall of the harness. The broken boughs snapped, the earth flew up beneath their hoofs; their feet struck scarlet sparks of fire from the stones, the carriage was whirled, rocking and tottering, through the maze of tree-trunks, towering like pillars of black stone up against the steel-blue clearness of the sky. The strain was intense; the danger deadly. Suddenly, straight ahead, beyond the darkness of the foliage, gleamed a line of light; shimmering, liquid, and glassy—here brown as gloom where the shadows fell on it, here light as life where the stars mirrored on it. That trembling line stretched right in their path. For the first time, from the blanched lips beside him a cry of terror rang.

"The river!—oh, heaven!—the river!"

There it lay in the distance, the deep and yellow water, cold in the moon's rays, with its farther bank but a dull gray line in the mists that rose from it, and its swamp a yawning grave, as the horses, blind in their delirium and racing against each other, bore down through all obstacles toward its brink. Death was rarely ever closer; one score yards more, one plunge, one crash down the declivity and against the rails, one swell of the noisome tide above their heads, and life would be closed and passed for both of them. For one breathless moment his eyes met hers—in that moment he loved her, in that moment their hearts beat with a truer, fonder impulse to each other than they had ever done. Before the presence of a threatening death life grows real, love grows precious, to the coldest and most careless.

No aid could come; not a living soul was nigh; the solitude was as complete as though a western prairie stretched around them; there were only the still and shadowy night, the chilly silence, on which the beat of the plunging hoofs shattered like thunder, and the glisten of the flowing water growing nearer and nearer every yard. The tranquillity around only jarred more horribly on ear and brain; the vanishing forms of the antlered deer only gave a weirder grace to the moonlight chase whose goal was the grave. It was like the midnight hunt after Herne the Hunter; but here, behind them, hunted Death.

The animals neither saw nor knew what waited them, as they rushed down on to the broad, gray stream, veiled from them by the slope and the screen of flickering leaves; to save them there was but one chance, and that so desperate that it looked like madness. It was but a second's thought; he gave it but a second's resolve.

The next instant he stood on his feet, as the carriage swayed to and fro over the turf, balanced himself marvelously as it staggered in that furious gallop from side to side, clinched the reins hard in the grip of his teeth, measured the distance with an unerring eye, and, crouching his body for the spring with all the science of the old playing-fields of his Eton days, cleared the dashboard and lighted astride on the back of the hunting five-year-old—how, he could never have remembered or have told.

The tremendous pace at which they went swayed him with a lurch and a reel over the off-side; a woman's cry rang again, clear, and shrill, and agonized on the night; a moment more, and he would have fallen, head downward, beneath the horses' feet. But he had ridden stirrupless and saddleless ere now; he recovered himself with the suppleness of an Arab, and firm-seated behind the collar, with one leg crushed between the pole and Maraschino's flanks, gathering in the ribbons till they were tight-drawn as a bridle, he strained with all the might and sinew that were in him to get the grays in hand before they could plunge down into the water. His wrists were wrenched like pulleys, the resistance against him was hard as iron; but as he had risked life and limb in the leap which had seated him across the harnessed loins of the now terrified beast, so he risked them afresh to get the mastery now; to slacken them, turn them ever so slightly, and save the woman he loved—loved, at least in this hour, as he had not loved her before. One moment more, while the half-maddened beast rushed through the shadows; one moment more, till the river stretched full before them in all its length and breadth, without a living thing upon its surface to break the still and awful calm; one moment—and the force of cool command conquered and broke their wills despite themselves. The hunter knew his master's voice, his touch, his pressure, and slackened speed by an irresistible, almost unconscious habit of obedience; the carriage mare, checked and galled in the full height of her speed, stood erect, pawing the air with her forelegs, and flinging the white froth over her withers, while she plunged blindly in her nervous terror; then with a crash, her feet came down upon the ground, the broken harness shivered together with a sharp, metallic clash; snorting, panting, quivering, trembling, the pair stood passive and vanquished.

The carriage was overthrown; but the high and fearless courage of the peeress bore her unharmed, even as she was flung out on to the yielding fern-grown turf. Fair as she was in every hour, she had never looked fairer than as he swung himself from the now powerless horses and threw himself beside her.

"My love—my love, you are saved!"

The beautiful eyes looked up, half unconscious; the danger told on her now that it was passed, as it does most commonly with women.

"Saved!—lost! All the world must know, now, that you are with me this evening," she murmured with a shudder. She lived for the world, and her first thought was of self.

He soothed her tenderly.

"Hush—be at rest! There is no injury but what I can repair, nor is there a creature in sight to have witnessed the accident. Trust in me; no one shall ever know of this. You shall reach town safely and alone."

And, while he promised, he forgot that he thus pledged his honor to leave four hours of his life so buried that, however much he needed, he neither should nor could account for them.

CHAPTER V.

THE PAINTED BIT.

BADEN was at its brightest. The Victoria, the Badischer Hof, the Stephanie Bauer were crowded. The Kurliste had a dazzling string of names. Imperial grandeur sauntered in slippers; chiefs, used to be saluted with "Ave Cæsar Imperator," smoked a papelito in peace over "Galignani."

Baden was full. The supreme empires of demi-monde sent their sovereigns, diamond-crowned and resistless, to outshine all other principalities and powers, while in breadth of marvelous skirts, in costliness of cobweb laces, in unapproachability of Indian shawls and gold embroideries, and mad fantasies and Cleopatra extravagances, and jewels fit for a Maharajah, the Zu-Zu was distanced by none.

Among the kings and heroes and celebrities who gathered

under the pleasant shadow of the pine-crowned hills, there was not one in his way greater than the steeple-chaser, Forest King—certes, there was not one half so honest.

The Guards' Crack was entered for the Prix de Dames, the sole representative of England. There were two or three good things out of French stables,—specially a killing little bay, L'Etoile,—and there was an Irish sorrel, the property of an Austrian of rank, of which fair things were whispered; but it was scarcely possible that anything could stand against the King and that wonderful stride of his which spread-eagled his field like magic, and his countrymen were well content to leave their honor and their old renown to "Beauty" and his six-year-old.

Forest King champed his bit between his teeth a little; it tasted bitter; he tossed his head and licked it with his tongue impatiently; the taste had got down his throat and he did not like its flavor; he turned his deep, lustrous eyes with a gentle patience on the crowd about him, as though asking them what was the matter with him. No one moved his bit; the only person who could have had such authority was busily giving the last polish to his coat with a fine handkerchief—that glossy neck which had been so dusted many a time with the cobweb coronet-broidered handkerchiefs of great ladies—and his instincts, glorious as they were, were not wise enough to tell him to kick his head groom down, then and there, with one mortal blow, as his poisoner and betrayer.

The King chafed under the taste of that "painted quid"; he felt a nausea as he swallowed, and he turned his handsome head with a strange, pathetic astonishment in his glance. At that moment a familiar hand stroked his mane, a familiar foot was put into his stirrup, Bertie threw himself into saddle; the lightest weight that ever gentleman-rider rode, despite his six-foot length of limb. The King, at the well-known touch, the well-loved voice, pricked his delicate ears, quivered in all his frame with eager excitation, snuffed the air restlessly through his distended nostrils, and felt every vein under his satin skin thrill and swell with pleasure; he was all impatience, all power, all longing, vivid intensity of life. If only that nausea would go! He felt a restless sickliness stealing on him that his young and gallant strength had never known since he was foaled. But it was not in the King to yield to a little; he flung his head up, champing angrily at the bit, then walked down to the starting-post with his old calm, collected grace; and Cecil, looking at the glossy bow of the neck, and feeling the width of the magnificent ribs beneath him, stooped from his saddle a second as he rode out of the inclosure and bent to the Seraph.

"Look at him, Rock! the thing's as good as won."

The day was very warm and brilliant; all Baden had come down to the race-course; continuous strings of carriages, with their four or six horses and postilions, held the line far down over the plains; mob there was none, save of women in matchless toilets, and men with the highest names in the "Almanac de Gotha"; the sun shone cloudlessly on the broad, green plateau of Iffesheim, on the white amphitheater of chalk hills, and on the glittering, silken folds of the flags of England, France, Prussia, and of the Grand Duchy itself, that floated from the summits of the Grand Stand, Pavilion, and Jockey Club.

The ladies, descending from the carriages, swept up and down on the green course that was so free from "cads" and "legs"; their magnificent skirts trailing along without the risk of a grain of dust; their costly laces side by side with the Austrian uniforms of the military men from Rastadt. The betting was but slight; the Paris formulas, "Combien contre l'Étoile?" "Six cents francs sur le cheval Anglais?" echoing everywhere in odd contrast with the hubbub and striking clamor of English betting rings; the only approach to anything like "real business" being transacted between the members of the Household and those of the Jockey Clubs. Iffesheim was pure pleasure, like every other item of Baden existence, and all aristocratic, sparkling, rich, amusement-seeking Europe seemed gathered there under the sunny skies, and on everyone's lips in the titled throng was but one name—Forest King's. Even the coquettish bouquet-sellers, who remembered the dresses of his own colors which Cecil had given them, last year when he had won the Rastadt, would sell nothing except little twin scarlet and white moss rosebuds; of which thousands were gathered and died that morning in honor of the English Guards' champion.

A slender event usually, the presence of the renowned crack of the Household Cavalry made the Prix de Dames the most eagerly watched-for entry on the card; and the rest of the field were scarcely noticed as the well-known gold-embroidered jacket came up at the starting-post.

The King saw that blaze of light and color over course and stands that he knew so well by this time; he felt the pressure round him of his foreign rivals as they reared and pulled and

fretted and passaged; the old longing quivered in all his eager
limbs, the old fire wakened in all his dauntless blood; like the
charger at sound of the trumpet-call, he lived in his past vic-
tories, and was athirst for more. But yet—between him and
the sunny morning there seemed a dim, hazy screen; on his
delicate ear the familiar clangor smote with something dulled
and strange; there seemed a numbness stealing down his
frame; he shook his head in an unusual and irritated impatience; he did not know what ailed him. The hand he loved
so loyally told him the work that was wanted of him; but he
felt its guidance dully too, and the dry, hard, hot earth, as he
struck it with his hoof, seemed to sway and heave beneath
him; the opiate had stolen into his veins and was creeping
stealthily and surely to the sagacious brain, and over the
clear, bright senses.

The signal for the start was given; the first mad headlong
rush broke away with the force of a pent-up torrent suddenly
loosened; every instinct of race and custom, and of that
obedience which rendered him flexible as silk to his rider's
will, sent him forward with that stride which made the
Guards' Crack a household word in all the Shires. For a moment he shook himself clear of all his horses, and led off in
the old grand sweeping canter before the French bay three
lengths in the one single effort.

Then into his eyes a terrible look of anguish came; the
numb and sickly nausea was upon him, his legs trembled,
before his sight was a blurred, whirling mist; all the strength
and force and mighty life within him felt ebbing out, yet he
struggled bravely. He strained, he panted, he heard the
thundering thud of the first flight gaining nearer and nearer
upon him; he felt his rivals closing hotter and harder in on
him; he felt the steam of his opponent's smoking, foam-
dashed withers burn on his own flanks and shoulders; he felt
the maddening pressure of a neck-to-neck struggle; he felt
what in all his victorious life he had never known—the
paralysis of defeat.

The glittering throngs spreading over the plains gazed at
him in the sheer stupor of amazement; they saw that the
famous English hero was dead-beat as any used-up knacker.

One second more he strove to wrench himself through the
throng of his horses, through the headlong crushing press,
through—worst foe of all!—the misty darkness curtaining his
sight! one second more he tried to wrestle back the old life
into his limbs, the unworn power and freshness into nerve

and sinew. Then the darkness fell utterly; the mighty heart failed; he could do no more—and his rider's hand slackened and turned him gently backward; his rider's voice sounded very low and quiet to those who, seeing that every effort was hopeless, surged and clustered round his saddle.

"Something ails the King," said Cecil calmly; "he is fairly knocked off his legs. Some Vet must look to him; ridden a yard farther he will fall."

Words so gently spoken!—yet in the single minute that alone had passed since they had left the Starter's Chair, a lifetime seemed to have been centered, alike to Forest King and to his owner.

The field swept on with a rush, without the favorite; and the Prix de Dames was won by the French bay L'Étoile.

CHAPTER VI.

"PETITE REINE."

WHEN a young Prussian had shot himself the night before for roulette losses, the event had not thrilled, startled, and impressed the gay Baden gathering one tithe so gravely and so enduringly as did now the unaccountable failure of the great Guards' Crack.

Men could make nothing of it save the fact that there was "something dark" somewhere. The "painted quid" had done its work more thoroughly than Willon and the welsher had intended; they had meant that the opiate should be just sufficient to make the favorite off his speed, but not to take effects so palpable as these. It was, however, so deftly prepared that under examination no trace could be found of it, and the result of veterinary investigation, while it left unremoved the conviction that the horse had been doctored, could not explain when or how, or by what medicines. Forest King had simply "broken down"; favorites do this on the flat and over the furrow from an overstrain, from a railway journey, from a touch of cold, from a sudden decay of power, from spasm, or from vertigo; those who lose by them may think what they will of "roping," or "painting," or "nobbling," but what can they prove?

Even in the great scandals that come before the autocrats of the Jockey Club, where the tampering is clearly known, can the matter ever be really proven and sifted? Very rarely. The trainer affects stolid unconsciousness or unimpeachable respectability; the hapless stable-boy is cross-examined, to protest innocence and ignorance, and most likely protest them rightly; he is accused, dismissed, and ruined; or some young jock has a "caution" out everywhere against him, and never again can get a mount even for the commonest handicap; but, as a rule, the real criminals are never unearthed, and by consequence are never reached and punished.

The Household, present and absent, were heavily hit. They cared little for the "crushers" they incurred, but their champion's failure, when he was in the face of Europe, cut them more terribly. The fame of the English riding-men had been trusted to Forest King and his owner, and they, who had never before betrayed the trust placed in them, had broken down like any screw out of a livery stable; like any jockey bribed to "pull" at a suburban selling-race. It was fearfully bitter work; and, unanimous to a voice, the indignant murmur of "doctored" ran through the titled, fashionable crowds on the Baden course in deep and ominous anger.

The Seraph's grand wrath poured out fulminations against the wicked-doer whosoever he was, or wheresoever he lurked.

Cecil alone, amid it all, was very quiet; he said scarcely a word, nor could the sharpest watcher have detected an alteration in his countenance. Only once, when they talked around him of the investigations of the Club, and of the institution of inquiries to discover the guilty traitor, he looked up with a sudden, dangerous lighting of his soft, dark, hazel eyes, under the womanish length of their lashes: "When you find him, leave him to me."

The light was gone again in an instant; but those who knew the wild strain that ran in the Royallieu blood knew by it that, despite his gentle temper, a terrible reckoning for the evil done his horse might come some day from the Quietist.

He said little or nothing else, and to the sympathy and indignation expressed for him on all sides he answered with his old, listless calm. But, in truth, he barely knew what was saying or doing about him; he felt like a man stunned and crushed with the violence of some tremendous fall; the excitation, the agitation, the angry amazement around him (growing as near clamor as was possible in those fashionable betting-circles, so free from roughs and almost free from book-makers), the conflicting opinions clashing here and there—even, indeed, the graceful condolence of the brilliant women

—were insupportable to him. He longed to be out of this world which had so well amused him; he longed passionately, for the first time in his life, to be alone.

For he knew that with the failure of Forest King had gone the last plank that saved him from ruin; perhaps the last chance that stood between him and dishonor. The blow fell with crashing force; the fiercer because his indolence had persisted in ignoring his danger, and because his whole character was so naturally careless and so habituated to ease and to enjoyment.

For the first time in his life the society of his troops of acquaintance became intolerably oppressive; for the first time in his life he sought refuge from thought in the stimulus of drink, and dashed down neat Cognac as though it were iced Badminton, as he drove with his set off the disastrous plains of Iffesheim. He shook himself free of them as soon as he could; he felt the chatter round him insupportable; the men were thoroughly good-hearted, and though they were sharply hit by the day's issue, never even by implication hinted at owing the disaster to their faith in him, but the very cordiality and sympathy they showed cut him the keenest—the very knowledge of their forbearance made his own thoughts darkest.

Far worse to Cecil than the personal destruction the day's calamity brought him was the knowledge of the entire faith these men had placed in him, and the losses which his own mistaken security had caused them. Granted he could neither guess nor avert the trickery which had brought about his failure; but none the less did he feel that he had failed them; none the less did the very generosity and magnanimity they showed him sting him like a scourge.

He got away from them at last, and wandered out alone into the gardens of the Stephanien, till the green trees of an alley shut him in in solitude, and the only echo of the gay world of Baden was the strain of a band, the light mirth of a laugh, or the roll of a carriage sounding down the summer air.

Where he had thrown himself on a bench beneath a mountain-ash, trying vainly to realize this thing which had come upon him—and to meet which not training, nor habit, nor a moment's grave reflection had ever done the slightest to prepare him; gazing, blankly and unconsciously, at the dense pine woods and rugged glens of the Forest that sloped upward and around above the green and leafy nest of Baden—he watched mechanically the toiling passage of a charcoal-burner going up the hillside in distance through the firs.

A soft touch came on his arm as he sat there; he looked up, surprised. Before him stood a dainty, delicate little form, all gay with white lace, and broideries, and rose ribbons, and floating hair fastened backward with a golden fillet; it was that of the little Lady Venetia,—the only daughter of the House of Lyonnesse, by a late marriage of his Grace,—the eight-year-old sister of the colossal Seraph; the plaything of a young and lovely mother, who had flirted in Belgravia with her future stepson before she fell sincerely and veritably in love with the gallant and still handsome Duke.

Cecil roused himself and smiled at her; he had been by months together at Lyonnesse most years of the child's life, and had been gentle to her as he was to every living thing, though he had noticed her seldom.

"Well, Petite Reine," he said kindly, bitter as his thoughts were; calling her by the name she generally bore. "All alone? Where are your playmates?"

"Petite Reine," who, to justify her sobriquet, was a grand, imperial little lady, bent her delicate head—a very delicate head, indeed, carrying itself royally, young though it was.

"Ah! you know I never care for children!"

It was said so disdainfully, yet so sincerely, without a touch of affection, and so genuinely, as the expression of a matured and contemptuous opinion, that even in that moment it amused him. She did not wait an answer, but bent nearer, with an infinite pity and anxiety in her pretty eyes.

"I want to know—you are so vexed; are you not? They say you have lost all your money!"

"Do they? They are not far wrong then. Who are 'they,' Petite Reine?"

"Oh! Prince Alexis, and the Duc de Lorance, and mamma, and everybody. Is it true?"

"Very true, my little lady."

"Ah!" She gave a long sigh, looking pathetically at him, with her head on one side, and her lips parted; "I heard the Russian gentleman saying that you were ruined. Is that true, too?"

"Yes, dear," he answered wearily, thinking little of the child in the desperate pass to which his life had come.

Petite Reine stood by him silent; her proud, imperial young ladyship had a very tender heart, and she was very sorry; she had understood what had been said before her of him vaguely indeed, and with no sense of its true meaning, yet still with the quick perception of a brilliant and petted child. Looking at her, he saw with astonishment that her eyes were filled with tears. He put out his hand and drew her to him.

"Why, little one, what do you know of these things? How did you find me out here?"

She bent nearer to him, swaying her slender figure, with its bright gossamer muslins, like a dainty hare-bell, and lifting her face to his—earnest, beseeching, and very eager.

"I came—I came—please don't be angry—because I heard them say you had no money, and I want you to take mine. Do take it! Look, it is all bright gold, and it is my own, my very own. Papa gives it to me to do just what I like with. Do take it; pray do!"

Coloring deeply, for the Petite Reine had that true instinct of generous natures,—a most sensitive delicacy for others,— but growing ardent in her eloquence and imploring in her entreaty, she shook on to Cecil's knee, out of a little enamel sweetmeat box, twenty bright Napoleons that fell in a glittering shower on the grass.

He started, and looked at her in a silence that she mistook for offense. She leaned nearer, pale now with her excitement, and with her large eyes gleaming and melting with passionate entreaty.

"Don't be angry; pray take it; it is all my own, and you know I have bonbons, and books, and playthings, and ponies, and dogs till I am tired of them; I never want the money; indeed I don't. Take it, please take it; and if you will only let me ask Papa or Rock they will give you thousands and thousands of pounds, if that isn't enough. Do let me!"

Cecil, in silence still, stooped and drew her to him. When he spoke his voice shook ever so slightly, and he felt his eyes dim with an emotion that he had not known in all his careless life; the child's words and action touched him deeply, the caressing, generous innocence of the offered gift, beside the enormous extravagance and hopeless bankruptcy of his career, smote him with a keen pang, yet moved him with a strange pleasure.

"Petite Reine," he murmured gently, striving vainly for his old lightness, "Petite Reine, how some man will love you one day! Thank you from my heart, my little innocent friend."

Her face flushed with gladness; she smiled with all a child's unshadowed joy.

"Ah! then you will take it! and if you want more only let me ask them for it; papa and Philip never refuse me anything!"

His hand wandered gently over the shower of her hair, as he put back the Napoleons that he had gathered up into her azure bonbonnière.

"Petite Reine, you are a little angel; but I cannot take your money, my child, and you must ask for none for my sake from your father or from Rock. Do not look so grieved, little one; I love you none the less because I refuse it."

Petite Reine's face was very pale and grave; a delicate face, in its miniature feminine childhood almost absurdly like the Seraph's; her eyes were full of plaintive wonder and of pathetic reproach.

"Ah!" she said, drooping her head with a sigh; "it is no good to you because it is such a little; do let me ask for more!"

He smiled, but the smile was very weary.

"No, dear, you must not ask for more; I have been very foolish, my little friend, and I must take the fruits of my folly; all men must. I can accept no one's money, not even yours; when you are older and remember this, you will know why. But I do not thank you the less from my heart."

She looked at him, pained and wistful.

"You will not take anything, Mr. Cecil?" she asked with a sigh, glancing at her rejected Napoleons.

He drew the enamel bonbonnière away.

"I will take that if you will give it me, Petite Reine, and keep it in memory of you."

As he spoke, he stooped and kissed her very gently; the act had moved him more deeply than he thought he had it in him to be moved by anything, and the child's face turned upward to him was of a very perfect and aristocratic loveliness, far beyond her years.

He took the pretty Palais Royal gold-rimmed sweetmeat box, and slipped it into his waistcoat pocket. It was only a child's gift, a tiny Paris toy; but it had been brought to him in a tender compassion, and he did keep it; kept it through dark days and wild nights, through the scorch of the desert and the shadows of death, till the young eyes that questioned him now with such innocent wonder had gained the grander luster of their womanhood and had brought him a grief wider than he knew now.

At that moment, as the child stood beside him under the

drooping acacia boughs, one of the men of the Stephanien approached him with an English letter, which, as it was marked "instant," they had laid apart from the rest of the visitors' pile of correspondence. Cecil took it wearily— nothing but fresh embarrassments could come to him from England—and looked at the little Lady Venetia.

"Will you allow me?"

She bowed her graceful head; with all the naïf unscious-ness of a child, she had all the manner of the veille cour; together they made her enchanting.

He broke the envelope and read—a blurred, scrawled, miserable letter; the words erased with passionate strokes, and blotted with hot tears, and scored out in impulsive misery. It was long, yet at a glance he scanned its message and its meaning; at the first few words he knew its whole as well as though he had studied every line.

A strong tremor shook him from head to foot, a tremor at once of passionate rage and of as passionate pain; his face blanched to a deadly whiteness; his teeth clinched as though he were restraining some bodily suffering, and he tore the letter in two and stamped it down into the turf under his heel, with a gesture as unlike his common serenity of man-ner as the fiery passion that darkened in his eyes was un-like the habitual softness of his too pliant and too unresentful temper.

The child watched him, startled and awed. She touched his hand softly.

"What is it? Is it anything worse?"

He turned his eyes on her with a dry, hot, weary anguish in them; he was scarcely conscious what he said or what he answered.

"Worse—worse?" he repeated mechanically, while his heel still ground down in loathing the shattered paper into the grass. "There can be nothing worse! It is the vilest, black-est shame."

He spoke to his thoughts, not to her; the words died in his throat; a bitter agony was on him; all the golden sum-mer evening, all the fair green world about him, were in-distinct and unreal to his senses; he felt as if the whole earth were of a sudden changed; he could not realize that this thing could come to him and his—that this foul dis-honor could creep up and stain them—that this infamy could ever be of them and upon them. All the ruin that before had fallen on him to-day was dwarfed and banished;

it looked nothing beside the unendurable horror that reached him now.

Petite Reine lingered wistfully; she did not like to leave him.

"Let me stay with you," she pleaded caressingly. "You are vexed at something; I cannot help you, but Rock will—the Duke will. Do let me ask them?"

He laid his hand on her shoulder; his voice, as he answered, was hoarse and unsteady.

"No; go, dear. You will please me best by leaving me. Ask none—tell none; I can trust you to be silent, Petite Reine."

She gave him a long, earnest look.

"Yes," she answered simply and gravely, as one who accepts, and not lightly, a trust.

Then she went slowly and lingeringly, with the sun on the gold fillet binding her hair, but the tears heavy on the shadow of her silken lashes. When next they met again the luster of a warmer sun, that once burned on the white walls of the palaces of Phœnicia and the leaping flames of the Temple of the God of Healing, shone upon them; and through the veil of those sweeping lashes there gazed the resistless sovereignty of a proud and patrician womanhood.

Alone, his head sank down upon his hands; he gave reins to the fiery scorn, the acute suffering which turn by turn seized him with every moment that seared the words of the letter deeper and deeper down into his brain. Until this he had never known what it was to suffer; until this his languid creeds had held that no wise man feels strongly, and that to glide through life untroubled and unmoved is as possible as it is politic. Now he suffered, he suffered dumbly as a dog, passionately as a barbarian; now he was met by that which, in the moment of its dealing, pierced his panoplies of indifference, and escaped his light philosophies.

"Oh, God!" he thought, "if it were anything—anything—except Disgrace!"

In a miserable den, an hour or so before—there are miserable dens even in Baden, that gold-decked rendezvous of princes, where crowned heads are numberless as couriers, and great ministers must sometimes be content with a shakedown—two men sat in consultation. Though the chamber was poor and dark, their table was loaded with various expensive wines and liqueurs. Of a truth they were flush of money, and selected this poor place from motives of concealment rather than of necessity. One of them was the "welsher," Ben Davis; the other, a smaller, quieter man, with a keen, vivacious Hebrew eye and an olive-tinted skin, a Jew, Ezra Baroni. The Jew was cool, sharp, and generally silent; the "welsher," heated, eager, flushed with triumph, and glowing with a gloating malignity. Excitement and the fire of very strong wines, of whose vintage brandy formed a large part, had made him voluble in exultation; the monosyllabic sententiousness that had characterized him in the loose-box at Royallieu had been dissipated under the ardor of success; and Ben Davis, with his legs on the table, a pipe between his teeth, and his bloated face purple with a brutal contentment, might have furnished to a Teniers the personification of culminated cunning and of delighted tyranny.

"That precious Guards' swell!" he muttered gloatingly, for the hundredth time. "I've paid him out at last! He won't take a 'walk over' again in a hurry. Cuss them swells! they allays die so game; it aint half a go after all, giving 'em a facer; they just come up to time so cool under it all, and never show they are down, even when their backers throw up the sponge. You can't make 'em give in, not even when they're mortal hit; that's the crusher of it."

"Vell, vhat matter that ven you have hit 'em?" expostulated the more philosophic Jew.

"Why, it is a fleecin' of one," retorted the welsher savagely, even amid his successes. "A clear fleecin' of one. If one gets the better of a dandy chap like that, and brings him down neat and clean, one ought to have the spice of it. One ought to see him wince and—cuss 'em all!—that's just what they'll never do. No! not if it was ever so. You may pitch into 'em like Old Harry, and those d——d fine gentlemen'll just look as if they liked it. You might strike 'em dead at your feet, and it's my belief, while they was cold as stones they'd manage to look not beaten yet. It's a fleecin' of one—a fleecin' of one!" he growled afresh.

The Jew laughed a little.

"Vot a shild you are, you Big Ben! Vot matter how he look, so long as you have de success and pocket de monish?"

Big Ben gave a long growl, like a mastiff tearing to reach a bone just held above him.

"Hang the blunt! The yellows aint a quarter worth to me what it 'ud be to see him just look as if he knew he was knocked over. Besides, laying agin' him by that ere commission's piled up hatsful of the ready, to be sure; I don't say it haint; but there's two thou' knocked off for Willon, and the fool don't deserve a tizzy of it. He went and put the paint on so thick that, if the Club don't have a flare-up about the whole thing——"

"Let dem!" said the Jew serenely. "Dey can do vot dey like; dey von't get to de bottom of de vell. Dat Villon is sharp; he vill know how to keep his tongue still; dey can prove nothin'; dey may give de sack to a stable-boy, or dey may tink demselves mighty bright in seein' a mare's nest, but dey vill never come to us."

The welsher gave a loud, hoarse guffaw of relish and enjoyment.

"No! We know the ins and outs of Turf Law a trifle too well to be caught napping. A neater thing weren't ever done, if it hadn't been that the paint was put a trifle too thick. The 'oss should have just run ill, and not knocked over, clean out o' time like that. However, there aint no odds a-cryin' over spilt milk. If the Club do come a inquiry, we'll show 'em a few tricks that'll puzzle 'em. But it's my belief they'll let it off on the quiet; there aint a bit of evidence to show the 'oss was doctored, and the way he went stood quite as well for having been knocked off his feet and off his legs by the woyage and sich like. And now you go and put that swell to the grindstone for Act 2 of the comedy; will yer?"

Ezra Baroni smiled, where he leaned against the table, looking over some papers.

"Dis is a delicate matter; don't you come putting your big paw in it—you'll spoil it all."

Ben Davis growled afresh:

"No, I aint a-goin'. You know as well as me I can't show in the thing. Hanged if I wouldn't a'most lief risk a lifer out at Botany Bay for the sake o' wringin' my fine-feathered bird myself, but I daresn't. If he was to see me in it, all 'ud be up. You must do it. Get along; you look uncommon respectable. If your coat-tails was a little bit longer, you might right and away be took for a parson."

The Jew laughed softly, the welsher grimly, at the compliment they paid the Church; Baroni put up his papers into a neat Russia letter book. Excellently dressed, without a touch of flashiness, he did look eminently respectable— and lingered a moment.

"I say, dear shild; vat if de Marquis vant to buy off and hush up? Ten to von he vill; he care no more for monish than for dem macaroons, and he love his friend, dey say."

Ben Davis took his legs off the table with a crash, and stood up, flushed, thirstily eager, almost aggressive in his peremptory excitement.

"Without wringing my dainty bird's neck? Not for a million paid out o' hand! Without crushing my fine gentleman down into powder? Not for all the blunt of every one o' the Rothschilds! Curse his woman's face! I've got to keep dark now; but when he's crushed, and smashed, and ruined, and pilloried, and druv' out of this fine world, and warned off of all his aristocratic race-courses, then I'll come in and take a look at him; then I'll see my brilliant gentleman a worn-out, broken-down swindler, a-dyin' in a bagnio!"

The intense malignity, the brutal hungry lust for vengeance that inspired the words, lent their coarse vulgarity something that was for the moment almost tragical in its strength; almost horrible in its passion. Ezra Baroni looked at him quietly, then without another word went out—to a congenial task.

"Dat big shild is a fool," mused the subtler and gentler Jew. "Vengeance is but de breath of de vind; it blow for you one day, it blow against you de next; de only real good is monish."

The Seraph had ridden back from Iffesheim to the Bad in company with some Austrian officers, and one or two of his own comrades. He had left the Course late, staying to exhaust every possible means of inquiry as to the failure of Forest King, and to discuss with other members of the New-market and foreign jockey clubs the best methods—if method there were—of discovering what foul play had been on foot with the horse. That there was some, and very foul too, the testimony of men and angels would not have dissuaded the Seraph; and the event had left him most unusually grave and regretful.

As he swung himself out of saddle, a well-dressed, quiet, rather handsome little man drew near respectfully, lifting his hat—it was M. Baroni. The Seraph had never seen the man in his life that he knew of, but he was himself naturally frank, affable, courteous, and never given to hedging himself behind the pale of his high rank; provided you did not bore him, you might always get access to him easily enough—the Duke used to tell him, too easily.

Therefore, when Ezra Baroni deferentially approached with, "The Most Noble the Marquis of Rockingham, I think?" the Seraph, instead of leaving the stranger there discomfited, nodded and paused with his inconsequent good nature; thinking how much less bosh it would be if everybody could call him, like his family and his comrades, "Rock."

"That is my name," he answered. "I do not know you. Do you want anything of me?"

The Seraph had a vivid terror of people who "wanted him," in the subscription, not the police, sense of the word; and had been the victim of frauds innumerable.

"I wished," returned Baroni respectfully, but with sufficient independence to conciliate his auditor, whom he saw at a glance cringing subservience would disgust, "to have the opportunity of asking your lordship a very simple question."

The Seraph looked a little bored, a little amused.

"Well, ask it, my good fellow; you have your opportunity!" he said impatiently, yet good-humored still.

"Then would you, my lord," continued the Jew with his strong Hebrew-German accent, "be so good as to favor me by saying whether this signature be your own?"

The Jew held before him a folded paper, so folded that one line only was visible, across which was dashed in bold characters, "Rockingham."

The Seraph put up his eye-glass, stooped, and took a steadfast look; then shook his head.

"No; that is not mine; at least, I think not. Never made my R half a quarter so well in my life."

"Many thanks, my lord," said Baroni quietly. "One question more and we can substantiate the fact. Did your lordship indorse any bill on the 15th of last month?"

The Seraph looked surprised, and reflected a moment. "No, I didn't," he said, after a pause. "I have done it for men, but not on that day; I was shooting at Hornsey Wood most of it, if I remember right. Why do you ask?"

"I will tell you, my lord, if you grant me a private interview."

The Seraph moved away. "Never do that," he said briefly; "private interviews," thought he, acting on past experience, "with women always mean proposals, and with men always mean extortion."

Baroni made a quick movement toward him.

"An instant, my lord! This intimately concerns yourself. The steps of an hotel are surely not the place in which to speak of it?"

"I wish to hear nothing about it," replied Rock, putting him aside; while he thought to himself regretfully, "That is 'stiff,' that bit of paper; perhaps some poor wretch is in a scrape. I wish I hadn't so wholly denied my signature. If the mischief's done, there's no good in bothering the fellow."

The Seraph's good nature was apt to overlook such trifles as the Law.

Baroni kept pace with him as he approached the hotel door, and spoke very low.

"My lord, if you do not listen, worse may befall the reputation both of your regiment and your friends."

The Seraph swung round; his careless, handsome face set stern in an instant; his blue eyes grave, and gathering an ominous fire.

"Step yonder," he said curtly, signing the Hebrew toward the grand staircase. "Show that person to my rooms, Alexis."

But for the publicity of the entrance of the Badischer Hof the mighty right arm of the Guardsman might have terminated the interview then and there, in different fashion. Baroni had gained his point, and was ushered into the fine chambers set apart for the future Duke of Lyonnesse. The Seraph strode after him, and as the attendant closed the door and left them alone in the first of the great lofty suite, all glittering with gilding, and ormolu, and malachite, and rose velvet, and Parisian taste, stood like a tower above the Jew's small, slight form; while his words came curtly, and only by a fierce effort through his lips.

"Substantiate what you dare to say, or my grooms shall throw you out of that window! Now?"

Baroni looked up, unmoved; the calm, steady, undisturbed glance sent a chill over the Seraph; he thought if this man came but for purposes of extortion, and were not fully sure that he could make good what he had said, this was not the look he would give.

"I desire nothing better, my lord," said Baroni quietly, "though I greatly regret to be the messenger of such an errand. This bill, which in a moment I will have the honor of showing you, was transacted by my house (I am one of the partners of a London discounting firm), indorsed thus by your celebrated name. Moneys were lent on it, the bill was made payable at two months' date; it was understood that you accepted it; there could be no risk with such a signature as yours. The bill was negotiated; I was in Leyden, Lubeck, and other places at the period; I heard nothing of the matter. When I returned to London, a little less than a week ago, I saw the signature for the first time. I was at once aware that it was not yours, for I had some paid bills, signed by you, at hand, with which I compared it. Of course, my only remedy was to seek you out, although I was nearly certain, before your present denial, that the bill was a forgery."

He spoke quite tranquilly still, with a perfectly respectful regret, but with the air of a man who has his title to be heard, and is acting simply in his own clear right. The Seraph listened, restless, impatient, sorely tried to keep in the passion which had been awakened by the hint that this wretched matter could concern or attaint the honor of his corps.

"Well! speak out!" he said impatiently. "Details are nothing. Who drew it? Who forged my name, if it be forged? Quick! give me the paper."

"With every trust and every deference, my lord, I cannot let the bill pass out of my own hands until this unfortunate matter be cleared up—if cleared up it can be. Your lordship shall see the bill, however, of course, spread here upon the table; but first, let me warn you, my Lord Marquis, that the sight will be intensely painful to you.

"Very painful, my lord," added Baroni impressively. "Prepare yourself for——"

Rock dashed his hand down on the marble table with a force that made the lusters and statuettes on it ring and tremble.

"No more words! Lay the bill there."

Baroni bowed and smoothed out upon the console the crumpled document, holding it with one hand, yet leaving visible with the counterfeited signature one other, the name of the forger in whose favor the bill was drawn; that other signature was—"Bertie Cecil."

"I deeply regret to deal you such a blow from such a friend, my lord," said the Jew softly. The Seraph stooped and gazed—one instant of horrified amazement kept him dumb there, staring at the written paper as at some ghastly thing; then all the hot blood rushed over his fair, bold face; he flung himself on the Hebrew, and, ere the other could have breath or warning, tossed him upward to the painted ceiling and hurled him down again upon the velvet carpet, as lightly as a retriever will catch up and let fall a wild duck or a grouse, and stood over Baroni where he lay.

"You hound!"

Baroni, lying passive and breathless with the violence of the shock and the surprise, yet kept, even amid the hurricane of wrath that had tossed him upward and downward as the winds toss leaves, his hold upon the document, and his clear, cool, ready self-possession.

"My lord," he said faintly, "I do not wonder at your excitement, aggressive as it renders you; but I cannot admit that false which I know to be a for——"

"Silence! Say that word once more, and I shall forget myself and hurl you out into the street like the dog of a Jew you are!"

"Have patience an instant, my lord. Will it profit your friend and brother-in-arms if it be afterward said that when this charge was brought against him, you, my Lord Rockingham, had so little faith in his power to refute it that you bore down with all your mighty strength in a personal assault upon one so weakly as myself, and sought to put an end to the evidence against him by bodily threats against my safety, and by—what will look legally, my lord, like—an attempt to coerce me into silence and to obtain the paper from my hands by violence?"

He stood silent, overwhelmed with the intensity of his own passion, baffled by the ingenuity of a serpent-wisdom he could not refute.

Ezra Baroni saw his advantage. He ventured to raise himself slightly.

"My lord, since your faith in your friend is so perfect, send for him. If he be innocent, and I a liar, with a look I shall be confounded."

The tone was perfectly impassive, but the words expressed a world. For a moment the Seraph's eyes flashed on him with a look that made him feel nearer his death than he had been near to it in all his days; but Rockingham restrained himself from force.

"I will send for him," he said briefly; in that answer there was more of menace and of meaning than in any physical action.

He moved and let Baroni rise; shaken and bruised, but otherwise little seriously hurt, and still holding, in a tenacious grasp, the crumpled paper. He rang; his own servant answered the summons.

"Go to the Stephanien and inquire for Mr. Cecil. Be quick; and request him, wherever he be, to be so good as to come to me instantly—here."

The servant bowed and withdrew; a perfect silence followed between these two so strangely assorted companions; the Seraph stood with his back against the mantelpiece, with every sense on the watch to catch every movement of the Jew's, and to hear the first sound of Cecil's approach. The minutes dragged on; the Seraph was in an agony of probation and impatience. Once the attendants entered to light the chandeliers and candelabra; the full light fell on the dark, slight form of the Hebrew, and on the superb attitude and the fair, frank, proud face of the standing Guardsman; neither moved—once more they were left alone.

The moments ticked slowly away one by one, audible in the silence. Now and then the quarters chimed from the clock; it was the only sound in the chamber.

CHAPTER VII.

FOR A WOMAN'S SAKE.

THE door opened—Cecil entered.

The Seraph crossed the room, with his hand held out; not for his life in that moment would he have omitted that gesture of friendship. Involuntarily he started and stood still one instant in amaze; the next, he flung thought away and dashed into swift, inconsequent words.

"Cecil, my dear fellow! I'm ashamed to send for you on such a blackguard errand. Never heard of such a swindler's trick in all my life; couldn't pitch the fellow into the street because of the look of the thing, and can't take any other measures without you, you know. I only sent for you to expose the whole abominable business, never because I believe—— Hang it! Beauty, I can't bring myself to say it even! If a sound thrashing would have settled the matter, I wouldn't have bothered you about it, nor told you a syllable. Only you are sure, Bertie, aren't you, that I never listened to this miserable outrage on us both with a second's thought there could be truth in it? You know me? you trust me too well not to be certain of that?"

The incoherent address poured out from his lips in a breathless torrent; he had never been so excited in his life; and he pleaded with as imploring an earnestness as though he had been the suspected criminal, not to be accused with having one shadow of shameful doubt against his friend. His words would have told nothing except bewilderment to one who should have been a stranger to the subject on which he spoke; yet Cecil never asked even what he meant. There was no surprise upon his face, no flush of anger, no expression of amaze or indignation; only the look which had paralyzed Rock on his entrance; he stood still and mute.

The Seraph looked at him, a great dread seizing him lest he should have seemed himself to cast this foul thing on his brother-in-arms; and in that dread all the fierce fire of his freshly-loosened passion broke its bounds.

"Damnation! Cecil, can't you hear me? A hound has brought against you the vilest charge that ever swindlers framed: an infamy that he deserves to be shot for, as if he were a dog. He makes me stand before you as if I were your accuser; as if I doubted you; as if I lent an ear one second to his loathsome lie. I sent for you to confront him, and to give him up to the law. Stand out, you scoundrel, and let us see how you dare look at us now!"

He swung round at the last words, and signed to Baroni to rise from the couch where he sat. The Jew advanced slowly, softly.

"If your lordship will pardon me, you have scarcely made it apparent what the matter is for which this gentleman is wanted. You have scarcely explained to him that it is on a charge of forgery."

The Seraph's eyes flashed on him with a light like a lion's, and his right hand clinched hard.

"By my life! if you say that word again you shall be flung in the street like the cur you are, let me pay what I will for it! Cecil, why don't you speak?"

Bertie had not moved; not a breath escaped his lips. He stood like a statue, deadly pale in the gaslight; when the figure of Baroni rose up and came before him, a great darkness stole on his face—it was a terrible bitterness, a great horror, a loathing disgust; but it was scarcely criminality, and it was not fear. Still he stood perfectly silent—a guilty man, any other than his loyal friend would have said: guilty, and confronted with a just accuser. The Seraph saw that look, and a deadly chill passed over him, as it had done at the Jew's first charge—not doubt; such heresy to his creeds, such shame to his comrade and his corps could not be in him; but a vague dread hushed his impetuous vehemence. The dignity of the old Lyonnesse blood asserted its ascendency.

"M. Baroni, make your statement. Later on Mr. Cecil can avenge it."

Cecil never moved; once his eyes went to Rockingham with a look of yearning, grateful, unendurable pain; but it was repressed instantly; a perfect passiveness was on him. The Jew smiled.

"My statement is easily made, and will not be so new to this gentleman as it was to your lordship. I simply charge the Honorable Bertie Cecil with having negotiated a bill with my firm for £750, on the 15th of last month, drawn in his own favor, and accepted at two months' date by your lordship. Your signature you, my Lord Marquis, admit to be a forgery—with that forgery I charge your friend!"

"The 15th!"

The echo of those words alone escaped the dry, white lips of Cecil; he showed no amaze, no indignation; once only, as the charge was made, he gave a sudden gesture, with a sudden gleam, so dark, so dangerous, in his eyes, that his comrade thought and hoped that with one moment more the Jew would be dashed down at his feet with the lie branded on his mouth by the fiery blow of a slandered and outraged honor. The action was repressed; the extraordinary quiescence, more hopeless because more resigned than any sign of pain or of passion, returned either by force of self-control or by the stupor of despair.

The Seraph gazed at him with a fixed, astounded horror; he could not believe his senses; he could not realize what he saw. His dearest friend stood mute beneath the charge of lowest villainy—stood powerless before the falsehoods of a Jew extortioner!

"Bertie! Great Heaven!" he cried, well-nigh beside himself, "how can you stand silent there? Do you hear—do you hear aright? Do you know the accursed thing this conspiracy has tried to charge you with? Say something, for the love of God! I will have vengeance on your slanderer, if you take none."

Still—Cecil stood silent; there was a strange, set, repressed anguish on his face that made it chill as stone; there was an unnatural calm upon him; yet he lifted his head with a gesture haughty for the moment as any action that his defender could have wished.

"I am not guilty," he said simply.

The Seraph's hands were on his own in a close, eager grasp almost ere the words were spoken.

"Beauty, Beauty! never say that to me. Do you think I can ever doubt you?"

For a moment Cecil's head sank; the dignity with which he had spoken remained on him, but the scorn of his defiance and his denial faded.

"No; you cannot; you never will."

The words were spoken almost mechanically, like a man in a dream. Ezra Baroni, standing calmly there with the tranquillity that an assured power alone confers, smiled slightly once more.

"You are not guilty, Mr. Cecil? I shall be charmed if we can find it so. Your proofs?"

"Proof? I give you my word."

Baroni bowed, with a sneer at once insolent but subdued.

"We men of business, sir, are—perhaps inconveniently for gentlemen—given to a preference in favor of something more substantial. Your word, doubtless, is your bond among your acquaintance; it is a pity for you that your friend's name should have been added to the bond you placed with us. Business men's pertinacity is a little wearisome, no doubt, to officers and members of the aristocracy like yourself; but all the same I must persist—how can you disprove this charge?"

The Seraph turned on him with the fierceness of a bloodhound.

"You dog! If you use that tone again in my presence, I will double-thong you till you cannot breathe!"

Baroni laughed a little; he felt secure now, and could not resist the pleasure of braving and of torturing the "aristocrats."

"I don't doubt your will or your strength, my lord; but neither do I doubt the force of the law to make you account for any brutality of the prize-ring your lordship may please to exert on me."

The Seraph ground his heel into the carpet.

"We waste words on that wretch," he said abruptly to

Cecil. "Prove his insolence the lie it is, and we will deal with him later on."

"Precisely what I said, my lord," murmured Baroni. "Let Mr. Cecil prove his innocence."

Into Bertie's eyes came a hunted, driven desperation. He turned them on Rockingham with a look that cut him to the heart; yet the abhorrent thought crossed him—was it thus that men guiltless looked?

"Mr. Cecil was with my partner at 7.50 on the evening of the 15th. It was long over business hours, but my partner to oblige him stretched a point," pursued the soft, bland, malicious voice of the German Jew. "If he were not at our office—where was he? That is simple enough."

"Answered in a moment!" said the Seraph, with impetuous certainty. "Cecil!—to prove this man what he is, not for an instant to satisfy me—where were you at that time on the 15th?"

"The 15th!"

"Where were you?" pursued his friend. "Were you at mess? at the clubs? dressing for dinner?—where—where? There must be thousands of ways of remembering—thousands of people who'll prove it for you?"

Cecil stood mute still; his teeth clinched on his under lip. He could not speak—a woman's reputation lay in his silence.

"Can't you remember?" implored the Seraph. "You will think—you must think!"

There was a feverish entreaty in his voice. That hunted helplessness with which a question so slight yet so momentous was received, was forcing in on him a thought that he flung away like an asp.

Cecil looked both of them full in the eyes—both his accuser and his friend. He was held as speechless as though his tongue were paralyzed; he was bound by his word of honor; he was weighted with a woman's secret.

"Don't look at me so, Bertie, for mercy's sake! Speak! where were you?"

"I cannot tell you; but I was not there."

The words were calm; there was a great resolve in them, moreover; but his voice was hoarse and his lips shook. He paid a bitter price for the butterfly pleasure of a summer-day love.

"Cannot tell me?—cannot? You mean you have forgotten!"

"I cannot tell you; it is enough."

There was an almost fierce and sullen desperation in the answer; its firmness was not shaken, but the ordeal was terrible. A woman's reputation—a thing so lightly thrown away with an idler's word, a Lovelace's smile!—that was all he had to sacrifice to clear himself from the toils gathering around him. That was all! And his word of honor.

Baroni bent his head with an ironic mockery of sympathy. "I feared so, my lord. Mr. Cecil 'cannot tell.' As it happens, my partner can tell. Mr. Cecil was with him at the hour and on the day I specify; and Mr. Cecil transacted with him the bill that I have had the honor of showing you——"

"Let me see it."

The request was peremptory to imperiousness, yet Cecil would have faced his death far sooner than he would have looked upon that piece of paper.

Baroni smiled.

"It is not often that we treat gentlemen under misfortune in the manner we treat you, sir; they are usually dealt with more summarily, less mercifully. You must excuse altogether my showing you the document; both you and his lordship are officers skilled, I believe, in the patrician science of fist-attack."

He could not deny himself the pleasure and the rarity of insolence to the men before him, so far above him in social rank, yet at that juncture so utterly at his mercy.

"You mean that we should fall foul of you and seize it?" thundered Rockingham in the magnificence of his wrath. "Do you judge the world by your own wretched villainies? Let him see the paper; lay it there, or, as there is truth on earth, I will kill you where you stand."

The Jew quailed under the fierce flashing of those leonine eyes. He bowed with that tact which never forsook him.

"I confide it to your honor, my Lord Marquis," he said, as he spread out the bill on the console. He was an able diplomatist.

Cecil leaned forward and looked at the signatures dashed across the paper; both who saw him saw also the shiver, like a shiver of intense cold, that ran through him as he did so, and saw his teeth clinch tight, in the extremity of rage, in the excess of pain, or—to hold in all utterance that might be on his lips.

"Well?" asked the Seraph, in a breathless anxiety. He knew not what to believe, what to do, whom to accuse of, or how to unravel this mystery of villainy and darkness; but he felt, with a sickening reluctance which drove him wild, that his friend did not act in this thing as he should have acted; not as men of assured innocence and secure honor act beneath such a charge. Cecil was unlike himself, unlike every deed and word of his life, unlike every thought of the Seraph's fearless expectance, when he had looked for the coming of the accused as the signal for the sure and instant unmasking, condemnation, and chastisement of the false accuser.

"Do you still persist in denying your criminality in the face of that bill, Mr. Cecil?" asked the bland, sneering, courteous voice of Ezra Baroni.

"I do. I never wrote either of these signatures; I never saw that document until to-night."

The answer was firmly given, the old blaze of scorn came again in his weary eyes, and his regard met calmly and unflinchingly the looks fastened on him; but the nerves of his lips twitched, his face was haggard as by a night's deep gambling; there was a heavy dew on his forehead—it was not the face of a wholly guiltless, of a wholly unconscious man; often even as innocence may be unwittingly betrayed into what wears the semblance of self-condemnation.

"And yet you equally persist in refusing to account for your occupation of the early evening hours of the 15th? Unfortunate!"

"I do; but in your account of them you lie!"

There was a sternness inflexible as steel in the brief sentence. Under it for an instant, though not visibly, Baroni flinched; and a fear of the man he accused smote him, more deep, more keen than that with which the sweeping might of the Seraph's fury had moved him. He knew now why Ben Davis had hated with so deadly a hatred the latent strength that slept under the quietest languor and nonchalance of "the d——d Guards' swell."

What he felt, however, did not escape him by the slightest sign.

"As a matter of course you deny it!" he said, with a polite wave of his hand. "Quite right; you are not required to criminate yourself. I wish sincerely we were not compelled to criminate you."

The Seraph's grand, rolling voice broke in; he had stood chafing, chained, panting, in agonies of passion and of misery.

"M. Baroni!" he said hotly, the furious vehemence of his anger and his bewilderment obscuring in him all memory of either law or fact, "you have heard his signature and your statements alike denied once for all by Mr. Cecil. Your document is a libel and a conspiracy, like your charge; it is false, and you are swindling; it is an outrage, and you are a scoundrel; you have schemed this infamy for the sake of extortion; not a sovereign will you obtain through it. Were the accusation you dare to make true, I am the only one whom it can concern, since it is my name which is involved. Were it true—could it possibly be true—I should forbid any steps to be taken in it; I should desire it ended once and forever. It shall be so now, by God!"

"My lord," Baroni said softly, "you have called me by many epithets, and menaced me with many threats since I have entered this chamber; it is not a wise thing to do with a man who knows the law. However, I can allow for the heat of your excitement. As regards the rest of your speech, you will permit me to say that its wildness of language is only equaled by the utter irrationality of your deductions and your absolute ignorance of all legalities. Were you alone concerned and alone the discoverer of this fraud, you could prosecute or not as you please; but we are the subjects of its imposition, ours is the money that he has obtained by that forgery, and we shall in consequence open the prosecution."

"Prosecution?" The echo rang in an absolute agony from his hearers; he had thought of it as, at its worst, only a question between himself and Cecil.

The accused gave no sign, the rigidity and composure he had sustained throughout did not change; but at the Seraph's accent the hunted and pathetic misery which had once before gleamed in his eyes came there again; he held his comrade in a loyal and exceeding love. He would have let all the world stone him, but he could not have borne that his friend should cast even a look of contempt.

"Prosecution!" replied Baroni quietly. "It is a matter of course, my lord, that Mr. Cecil denies the accusation; it is very wise; the law specially cautions the accused to say nothing to criminate themselves. But we waste time in words; and, pardon me, if you have your friend's interest at heart, you will withdraw this very stormy championship; this utterly useless opposition to an inevitable line of action. I must arrest Mr. Cecil; but I am willing—for I know to

high families these misfortunes are terribly distressing—
to conduct everything with the strictest privacy and delicacy.
In a word, if you and he consult his interests, he will accompany me unresistingly; otherwise I must summon legal
force. Any opposition will only compel a very unseemly
encounter of physical force, and with it the publicity I am
desirous, for the sake of his relatives and position, to spare
him."

"Cecil, tell me—what is to be done? This infamous outrage cannot pass! cannot go on! I will send for the Duke,
for——"

"Send for no one."

Bertie's voice was slightly weaker, like that of a man exhausted by a long struggle, but it was firm and very quiet.
Its composure fell on Rockingham's tempestuous grief and
rage with a sickly, silencing awe, with a terrible sense of
some evil here beyond his knowledge and ministering, and
of an impotence alike to act and to serve, to defend and
to avenge—the deadliest thing his fearless life had ever
known.

"Pardon me, my lord," interposed Baroni, "I can waste
time no more. You must be now convinced yourself of your
friend's implication in this very distressing affair."

"I!" The Seraph's majesty of haughtiest amaze and scorn
blazed from his azure eyes on the man who dared say this
thing to him. "I! If you dare hint such a damnable shame
to my face again, I will wring your neck with as little
remorse as I would a kite's. I believe in his guilt? Forgive me, Cecil, that I can even repeat the word! I believe
in it? I would as soon believe in my own disgrace—in
my father's dishonor!"

"How will your lordship account, then, for Mr. Cecil's
total inability to tell us how he spent the hours between six
and nine on the 15th?"

"Unable? He is not unable; he declines! Bertie, tell me
what you did that one cursed evening? Whatever it was,
wherever it was, say it for my sake, and shame this devil."

Cecil would more willingly have stood a line of leveled
rifle-tubes aimed at his heart than that passionate entreaty
from the man he loved best on earth. He staggered slightly,
as if he were about to fall, and a faint white foam came
on his lips; but he recovered himself almost instantly. It
was so natural to him to repress every emotion that it was
simply old habit to do so now.

"I have answered," he said very low, each word a pang—
"I cannot."

Baroni waved his hand again with the same polite, significant gesture.

"In that case, then, there is but one alternative. Will you
follow me quietly, sir, or must force be employed?"

"I will go with you."

The reply was very tranquil, but in the look that met his
own as it was given, Baroni saw that some other motive
than that of any fear was its spring; that some cause
beyond the mere abhorrence of "a scene" was at the root
of the quiescence.

"It must be so," said Cecil huskily to his friend. "This
man is right, so far as he knows. He is only acting on
his own convictions. We cannot blame him. The whole is
—a mystery, an error. But, as it stands, there is no
resistance."

"Resistance! By God! I would resist if I shot him dead,
or shot myself. Stay—wait—one moment! If it be an error
in the sense you mean, it must be a forgery of your name
as of mine. You think that?"

"I did not say so."

The Seraph gave him a rapid, shuddering glance; for once
the suspicion crept in on him—was this guilt? Yet even now
the doubt would not be harbored by him.

"Say so—you must mean so! You deny them as yours;
what can they be but forgeries? There is no other ex-
planation. I think the whole matter a conspiracy to extort
money; but I may be wrong—let that pass. If it be, on
the contrary, an imitation of both our signatures that has
been palmed off upon these usurers, it is open to other
treatment. Compensated for their pecuniary loss, they can
have no need to press the matter further, unless they find
out the delinquent. See here"—he went to a writing-cabinet
at the end of the room, flung the lid back, swept out a
heap of papers, and wrenching a blank check from its book,
threw it down before Baroni—"here! fill it up as you like,
and I will sign it in exchange for the forged sheet."

Cecil, ere the Hebrew could speak, leaned forward, took
the check and tore it in two.

"God bless you, Rock," he said, so low that it only reached
the Seraph's ear, "but you must not do that."

"Beauty, are you mad?" cried the Marquis passionately.
"If this villainous thing be a forgery, you are its victim as

much as I—tenfold more than I. If this Jew choose to sell
the paper to me, naming his own compensation, whose affair
is it except his and mine? They have been losers, we in-
demnify them. It rests with us to find out the criminal.
M. Baroni, there are a hundred more checks in that book;
name your price, and you shall have it; or, if you prefer
my father's, I will send to him for it. His Grace will sign
one without a question of its errand, if I ask him. Come!
your price?"

Baroni had recovered the momentary temptation, and was
strong in the austerity of virtue, in the unassailability of
social duty.

"You behave most nobly, most generously by your friend,
my lord," he said politely. "I am glad such friendship ex-
ists on earth. But you really ask me what is not in my
power. In the first place, I am but one of the firm, and
have no authority to act alone; in the second, I most certainly, were I alone, should decline totally any pecuniary
compromise. A great criminal action is not to be hushed
up by any monetary arrangement. You, my Lord Marquis,
may be ignorant in the Guards of a very coarse term used
in law, called 'compounding a felony.' That is what you
tempt me to now."

The Seraph, with one of those oaths that made the
Hebrew's blood run cold, though he was no coward, opened
his lips to speak; Cecil arrested him with that singular impassiveness, that apathy of resignation which had characterized his whole conduct throughout, save at a few brief
moments.

"Make no opposition. The man is acting but in his own
justification. I will wait for mine. To resist would be to
degrade us with a bully's brawl; they have the law with
them. Let it take its course."

The Seraph dashed his hand across his eyes; he felt blind
—the room seemed to reel with him.

"Oh, God! that you——"

He could not finish the words. That his comrade, his
friend, one of his own corps, of his own world, should
be arrested like the blackest thief in Whitechapel or in the
Rue du Temple!

Cecil glanced at him, and his eyes grew infinitely yearning
—infinitely gentle; a shudder shook him all through his
limbs. He hesitated a moment; then he stretched out his
hand.

"Will you take it—still?"

Almost before the words were spoken, his hand was held in both of the Seraph's.

"Take it? Before all the world—always, come what will."

His eyes were dim as he spoke, and his rich voice rang clear as the ring of silver, though there was the tremor of emotion in it. He had forgotten the Hebrew's presence; he had forgotten all save his friend and his friend's extremity. Cecil did not answer; if he had done so, all the courage, all the calm, all the control that pride and breeding alike sustained in him, would have been shattered down to weakness; his hand closed fast in his companion's, his eyes met his once in a look of gratitude that pierced the heart of the other like a knife; then he turned to the Jew with a haughty serenity.

"M. Baroni, I am ready."

Another moment, and the door had closed; Cecil had gone out to his fate, and the Seraph, with no eyes on him, bowed down his head upon his arms where he leaned against the marble table, and, for the first time in all his life, felt the hot tears roll down his face like rain, as the passion of a woman mastered and unmanned him—he would sooner a thousand times have laid his friend down in his grave than have seen him live for this.

They walked out into the evening air unnoticed; Cecil had given his consent to follow the bill-discounter without resistance, and he had no thought to break his word; he had submitted himself to the inevitable course of this fate that had fallen on him, and the whole tone of his temper and his breeding lent him the quiescence, though he had none of the doctrine of a supreme fatalist. There were carriages standing before the hotel, waiting for those who were going to the ball-room, to the theater, to an archduke's dinner, to a princess' entertainment; he looked at them with a vague, strange sense of unreality—these things of the life from which he was now barred out forever. The sparkling tide of existence in Baden was flowing on its way, and he went out an accused felon, branded, and outlawed, and dishonored from all place in the world that he had led, and been caressed by and beguiled with for so long.

To-night, at this hour, he should have been among all that was highest and gayest and fairest in Europe at the banquet of a Prince—and he went by his captor's side, a convicted criminal.

Once out in the air, the Hebrew laid his hand on his arm. He started—it was the first sign that his liberty was gone! He restrained himself from all resistance still, and passed onward, down where Baroni motioned him out of the noise of the carriages, out of the glare of the light, into the narrow, darkened turning of a side street. He went passively; for this man trusted to his honor.

In the gloom stood three figures, looming indistinctly in the shadow of the houses. One was a Huissier of the Staats-Procurator, beside whom stood the Commissary of Police of the district; the third was an English detective. Ere he saw them their hands were on his shoulders, and the cold chill of steel touched his wrists. The Hebrew had betrayed him, and arrested him in the open street. In an instant, all the wild blood of his race, all the pride of his breeding, all the honor of his service, flashed into fire and leaped into action. Trusted, he would have been true to his accuser; deceived, the chains of his promise were loosened, and all he thought, all he felt, all he knew were the lion impulses, the knightly instincts, the resolute choice to lose life rather than to lose freedom, of a soldier and a gentleman. All he remembered was that he would fight to the death rather than be taken alive; that they should kill him where he stood, in the starlight, rather than lead him in the sight of men as a felon.

With the strength that lay beneath all the gentle languor of his habits and with the science of the Eton Playing Fields of his boyhood, he wrenched his wrist free ere the steel had closed, and with the single straightening of his left arm felled the detective to earth like a bullock, with a crashing blow that sounded through the stillness like some heavy timber stove in; flinging himself like lightning on the Huissier, he twisted out of his grasp the metal weight of the handcuffs, and wrestling with him was woven for a second in that close-knit struggle which is only seen when the wrestlers wrestle for life and death. The vise-like pressure of the stalwart arms of his opponent crushed him in till his ribs seemed to bend and break under the breathless oppression, the iron force; but desperation nerved him, the Royallieu blood, that never took defeat, was roused now, for the first time in his careless life; his skill and his nerve were unrivaled, and with a last effort he dashed the Huissier off him, and lifting him up—he never knew how—as he would have lifted a log of wood, hurled him down in the white streak of moonlight that alone slanted through the peaked roofs of the crooked by-street.

The cries of Baroni had already been heard; a crowd, drawn by their shrieking appeals, were bearing toward the place in tumult. The Jew had the quick wit to give them, as call-word, that it was a croupier who had been found cheating and fled; it sufficed to inflame the whole mob against the fugitive. Cecil looked round him once—such a glance as a Royal gives when the gaze-hounds are panting about him and the fangs are in his throat; then, with the swiftness of the deer itself, he dashed downward into the gloom of the winding passage at the speed which had carried him, in many a foot-race, victor in the old green Eton meadows.

Flight!—for the instant the word thrilled through him with a loathing sense.

"It is for her sake—and his," he thought; and without a moment's pause, without a backward look, he ran, as the stag runs with the bay of the pack behind it, down into the shadows of the night.

The hue and cry was after him; the tumult of a crowd's excitement, raised it knows not why or wherefore, was on his steps, joined with the steadier and keener pursuit of men organized for the hunter's work, and trained to follow the faintest track, the slightest clew. The moon was out, and they saw him clearly, though the marvelous fleetness of his stride had borne him far ahead in the few moments' start he had gained. He heard the beat of their many feet on the stones, the dull thud of their running, the loud clamor of the mob, the shrill cries of the Hebrew offering gold with frantic lavishness to whoever should stop his prey. All the breathless excitement, all the keen and desperate straining, all the tension of the neck-and-neck struggle that he had known so often over the brown autumn country of the Shires at home, he knew now, intensified to horror, made deadly with despair, changed into a race for life and death.

A gay burst of music broke on the stillness from the distance; he had left the brilliance of the town behind him, and was now in its by-streets and outskirts. The sound seemed to thrill him to the bone; it was like the echo of the lost life he was leaving forever.

The by-lanes he took were deserted, and he was now well-nigh out of the town, with the open country and forest

lying before him. He never looked back; but he could
tell that the pursuit was falling farther and farther behind him; that the speed at which he went was breaking the
powers of his hunters; fresh throngs added indeed to
the first pursuers as they tore down through the starlit night,
but none had the science with which he went, the trained,
matchless skill of the university foot-race. He left them more
and more behind him each second of the breathless chase,
that, endless as it seemed, had lasted bare three minutes.
If the night were but dark! The silver glory of the
radiance was shed on every rood of ground; one hour of a
winter night, one hour of the sweeping ink-black rain of
an autumn storm, and he could have made for shelter as
the stag makes for it across the broad, brown Highland
water.

Before him stretched indeed the gloom of the masses of
pine, the upward slopes of tree-stocked hills, the vastness of
the Black Forest; but they were like the mirage to a man
who dies in a desert; he knew, at the pace he went, he
could not live to reach them.

But he would go till he died; go till they fired on him;
go, though the skies felt swirling round like a sea of fire,
and the hard, hot earth beneath his feet jarred his whole
frame as his feet struck it flying.

The angle of an old wood house, with towering roof and
high-peaked gables, threw a depth of shadow at last across
his road; a shadow black and rayless, darker for the white
glisten of the moon around. Built more in the Swiss
than the German style, a massive balcony of wood ran round
it, upon and beneath which in its heavy shade was an
impenetrable gloom, while the twisted wooden pillars ran
upward to the gallery, loggia-like. With rapid perception
and intuition he divined rather than saw these things, and,
swinging himself up with noiseless lightness, he threw himself full-length down on the rough flooring of the balcony.
If they passed he was safe, for a brief time more at least;
if they found him—his teeth clinched like a mastiff's where
he lay—he had the strength in him still to sell his life dearly.

The pursuers came closer and closer, and by the clamor
that floated up in indistinct and broken fragments, he knew
that they had tracked him. He heard the tramp of their
feet as they came under the loggia; he heard the click of
the pistols—they were close upon him at last in the blackness of night.

CHAPTER VIII.

THE KING'S LAST SERVICE.

"Is he up there?" asked a voice in the darkness.

"Not likely. A cat couldn't scramble up that woodwork," answered a second.

"Send a shot, and try," suggested a third.

There he lay, stretched motionless on the flat roof of the veranda. He heard the words as the thronging mob surged, and trampled, and swore, and quarreled, beneath him, in the blackness of the gloom; balked of their prey, and savage for some amends. There was a moment's pause —a hurried, eager consultation; then he heard the well-known sound of a charge being rammed down, and the sharp drawing out of a ramrod; there was a flash, a report, a line of light flamed a second in his sight; a ball hissed past him with a loud, singing rush, and bedded itself in the timber, a few inches above his uncovered hair. A dead silence followed; then the muttering of many voices broke out afresh.

"He's not there, at any rate," said one, who seemed the chief; "he couldn't have kept as still as that with a shot so near him. He's made for the open country and the forest, I'll take my oath."

Then the treading of many feet trampled their way out from beneath the loggia; their voices and their rapid steps grew fainter and fainter as they hurried away through the night. For a while, at least, he was safe.

For some moments he lay prostrated there; the rushing of the blood on his brain, the beating of his heart, the panting of his breath, the quivering of his limbs after the intense muscular effort he had gone through, mastered him and flung him down there, beaten and powerless. He felt the foam on his lips, and he thought with every instant that the sur-charged veins would burst; hands of steel seemed to crush in upon his chest, knotted cords to tighten in excruciating pain about his loins; he breathed in short, convulsive gasps; his eyes were blind, and his head swam. A dreaming fancy that this was death vaguely came on him, and he was glad it should be so.

How long he lay there he never knew; when conscious-ness returned to him all was still; the moon was shining down clear as the day, the west wind was blowing softly among his hair. He staggered to his feet and leaned against the timber of the upper wall; the shelving, impenetrable darkness sloped below; above were the glories of a summer sky at midnight, around him the hills and woods were bathed in the silver light; he looked, and he remembered all.

He had escaped his captors; but for how long? While yet there were some hours of the night left, he must find some surer refuge, or fall into their hands again. Yet it was strange that in this moment his own misery and his own peril were less upon him than a longing to see once more— and for the last time—the woman for whose sake he suffered this. Their love had had the lightness and the languor of their world, and had had but little depth in it; yet, in that hour of his supreme sacrifice to her, he loved her as he had not loved in his life.

The dare-devil wildness and the cool quietude that were so intimately and intricately mingled in his nature could alone have prompted and projected such a thought and such an action as suggested themselves to him now; in the moment of his direst extremity, of his utter hopelessness, of his most imminent peril, he went—to take a last look at his mistress! Baden, for aught he knew, might be but one vast network to mesh in and to capture him; yet he ran the risk with the dauntless temerity that had ever lain underneath the in-differentism and the indolence of his habits.

Keeping always in the shadow, and moving slowly, so as to attract no notice from those he passed, he made his way deliberately, straight toward the blaze of light where all the gayety of the town was centered; he reckoned, and rightly, as it proved, that the rumor of his story, the noise of his pursuit, would not have penetrated here as yet; his own world would be still in ignorance. A moment, that was all he wanted, just to look upon a woman's beauty; he went forward daringly and tranquilly to the venture. If any had told him that a vein of romance was in him, he would have stared and thought them madmen; yet something almost as wild was in his instinct now. He had lost so much to keep her honor from attainder; he wished to meet the gaze of her fair eyes once more before he went out to his exile.

In one of the string of waiting carriages he saw a loose domino lying on the seat; he knew the liveries and the foot-men, and he signed them to open the door. "Tell Count

Carl I have borrowed these," he said to the servant, as he sprang into the vehicle, slipped the scarlet-and-black domino on, took the mask, and left the carriage. The man touched his hat and said nothing; he knew Cecil well, as an intimate friend of his young Austrian master. In that masquerade guise he was safe; for the few minutes, at least, which were all he dared take.

He went on, mingled among the glittering throng, and pierced his way to the ballroom, the Venetian mask covering his features; many spoke to him; by the scarlet-and-black colors they took him for the Austrian; he answered none, and treaded his way among the blaze of hues, the joyous echoes of the music, the flutter of the silk and satin dominoes, the mischievous challenge of whispers. His eyes sought only one; he soon saw her, in the white and silver mask-dress, with the spray of carmine-hued eastern flowers, by which he had been told, days ago, to recognize her. A crowd of dominoes were about her, some masked, some not. Her eyes glanced through the envious disguise and her lips were laughing. He approached her with all his old tact in the art d'arborer le cotillon; not hurriedly, so as to attract notice, but carefully, so as to glide into a place near her.

"You promised me this waltz," he said very gently in her ear. "I have come in time for it."

She recognized him by his voice, and turned from a French prince to rebuke him for his truancy, with gay raillery and mock anger.

"Forgive me, and let me have this one waltz—please do!" She glanced at him a moment, and let him lead her out.

"No one has my step as you have it, Bertie," she murmured, as they glided into the measure of the dance.

She thought his glance fell sadly on her as he smiled.

"No?—but others will soon learn it."

Yet he had never treaded more deftly the maze of the waltzers, never trodden most softly, more swiftly, or with more science, the polished floor. The waltz was perfect; she did not know it was also a farewell. The delicate perfume of her floating dress, the gleam of the scarlet flower-spray, the flash of the diamonds studding her domino, the fragrance of her lips as they breathed so near his own; they haunted him many a long year afterward.

His voice was very calm, his smile was very gentle, his step, as he swung easily through the intricacies of the circle, was none the less smooth and sure for the race that had so late strained his sinews to bursting; the woman he loved saw no change in him; but as the waltz drew to its end, she felt his heart beat louder and quicker on her own; she felt his hand hold her own more closely, she felt his head drooped over her till his lips almost touched her brow;— it was his last embrace; no other could be given here, in the multitude of these courtly crowds. Then, with a few low-murmured words that thrilled her in their utterance, and echoed in her memory for years to come, he resigned her to the Austrian Grand Duke who was her next claimant, and left her silently—forever.

Less heroism has often proclaimed itself, with blatant trumpet to the world—a martyrdom.

He looked back once as he passed from the ballroom— back to the sea of colors, to the glitter of light, to the moving hues, amid which the sound of the laughing, intoxicating music seemed to float; to the glisten of the jewels and the gold and the silver—to the scene, in a word, of the life that would be his no more. He looked back in a long, lingering look, such as a man may give the gladness of the earth before the gates of a prison close on him; then he went out once more into the night, threw the domino and the mask back again into the carriage, and took his way, alone.

He passed along till he had gained the shadow of a by-street, by a sheer unconscious instinct; then he paused, and looked round him—what could he do? He wondered vaguely if he were not dreaming; the air seemed to reel about him, and the earth to rock; the very force of control he had sustained made the reaction stronger; he began to feel blind and stupefied. How could he escape? The railway station would be guarded by those on the watch for him; he had but a few pounds in his pocket, hastily slipped in as he had won them, "money-down," at écarté that day; all avenues of escape were closed to him, and he knew that his limbs would refuse to carry him with any kind of speed farther. He had only the short, precious hours remaining of the night in which to make good his flight—and flight he must take to save those for whom he had elected to sacrifice his life. Yet how? and where?

A hurried, noiseless footfall came after him; Rake's voice came breathless on his ear, while the man's hand went up in the unforgotten soldier's salute—

"Sir! no words. Follow me, and I'll save you."

The one well-known voice was to him like water in a desert

land; he would have trusted the speaker's fidelity with his life. He asked nothing, said nothing, but followed rapidly and in silence; turning and doubling down a score of crooked passages, and burrowing at the last like a mole in a still, deserted place on the outskirts of the town, where some close-set trees grew at the back of stables and out-buildings.

In a streak of the white moonlight stood two hunters, saddled; one was Forest King. With a cry, Cecil threw his arms round the animal's neck; he had no thought then except that he and the horse must part.

"Into the saddle, sir! quick as your life!" whispered Rake. "We'll be far away from this d——d den by morning."

Cecil looked at him like a man in stupor—his arm still over the gray's neck.

"He can have no stay in him! He was dead-beat on the course."

"I know he was, sir; but he aint now; he was pisined; but I've a trick with a 'oss that'll set that sort o' thing—if it aint gone too far, that is to say—right in a brace of shakes. I doctored him; he's hisself agen; he'll take you till he drops."

The King thrust his noble head closer in his master's bosom, and made a little murmuring noise, as though he said, "Try me!"

"God bless you, Rake!" Cecil said huskily. "But I cannot take him; he will starve with me. And—how did you know of this?"

"Beggin' your pardon, your honor, he'll eat chopped furze with you better than he'll eat oats and hay along of a new master," returned Rake rapidly, tightening the girths. "I don't know nothin', sir, save that I heard you was in a strait; I don't want to know nothin'; but I sees them cursed cads a-runnin' of you to earth, and thinks I to myself, 'Come what will, the King will be the ticket for him.' So I ran to your room unbeknown, packed a little valise, and got out the passports; then back again to the stables, and saddled him like lightnin', and got 'em off—nobody knowing but Bill there. I seed you go by into the Kursaal, and laid in wait for you, sir. I made bold to bring Mother o' Pearl for myself."

And Rake stopped, breathless and hoarse with passion and grief that he would not utter. He had heard more than he said.

"For yourself?" echoed Cecil. "What do you mean? My good fellow, I am ruined. I shall be beggared from to-night—utterly. I cannot even help you or keep you; but Lord Rockingham will do both for my sake."

The ci-devant soldier struck his heel into the earth with a fiery oath.

"Sir, there aint time for no words. Where you goes I go. I'll follow you while there's a drop o' blood in me. You was good to me when I was a poor devil that everyone scouted; you shall have me with you to the last, if I die for it. There!"

Cecil's voice shook as he answered. The fidelity touched him as adversity could not do.

"Rake, you are a noble fellow. I would take you, were it possible; but—in an hour I may be in a felon's prison. If I escape that, I shall lead a life of such wretchedness as——"

"That's not nothing to me, sir."

"But it is much to me," answered Cecil. "As things have turned—life is over with me, Rake. What my own fate may be I have not the faintest notion—but let it be what it will, it must be a bitter one. I will not drag another into it."

"If you send me away, I'll shoot myself through the head, sir; that's all."

"You will do nothing of the kind. Go to Lord Rockingham, and ask him from me to take you into his service. You cannot have a kinder master."

"I don't say nothing agen the Marquis, sir," said Rake doggedly; "he's a right-on generous gentleman, but he aren't you. Let me go with you, if it's just to rub the King down. Lord, sir! you don't know what straits I've lived in—what a lot of things I can turn my hand to—what a one I am to fit myself into any rat-hole, and make it spicy. Why, sir, I'm that born scamp, I am—I'm a deal happier on the cross and getting my bread just anyhow, than I am when I'm in clover like you've kep' me."

Rake's eyes looked up wistfully and eager as a dog's when he prays to be let out of kennel to follow the gun; his voice was husky and agitated with a strong excitement. Cecil stood a moment, irresolute, touched and pained at the man's spaniel-like affection—yet not yielding to it.

"I thank you from my heart, Rake," he said at length, "but it must not be. I tell you my future life will be beggary——"

"You'll want me anyways, sir," retorted Rake, ashamed of the choking in his throat. "I ask your pardon for interruptin', but every second's that precious like. Besides, sir, I've got to cut and run for my own sake. I've laid Willon's head open, down there in the loose box; and when he's come to himself a pretty hue and cry he'll raise after me. He painted the King, that's what he did; and I told him so, and I gev' it to him—one—two—amazin'! Get into saddle, sir, for the Lord's sake! and here, Bill—you run back, shut the door, and don't let nobody know the 'osses are out till the mornin'. Then look like a muff as you are, and say nothin'!"

The stable-boy stared, nodded assent, and sloped off. Rake threw himself across the brown mare.

"Now, sir! a steeple-chase for our lives! We'll be leagues away by the day-dawn, and I've got their feed in the saddle-bags, so that they'll bait in the forests. Off, sir, for God's sake, or the blackguards will be down on you again!"

As he spoke the clamor and tread of men of the town racing to the chase were wafted to them on the night wind, drawing nearer and nearer; Rake drew the reins tight in his hand in fury.

"There they come—the d——d beaks! For the love of mercy, sir, don't check now. Ten seconds more and they'll be on you; off, off!—or by the Lord Harry, sir, you'll make a murderer of me, and I'll kill the first man that lays his hand on you!"

Far and fast they rode through the night, never drawing rein. The horses laid well to their work; their youth and their mettle were roused, and they needed no touch of spur, but neck-and-neck dashed down through the sullen gray of the dawn and the breaking flush of the first sunrise. On the hard, parched earth, on the dew-laden moss, on the stretches of wayside sward, on the dry white dust of the ducal roads, their hoofs thundered, unfollowed, unechoed; the challenge of no pursuit stayed them, and they obeyed the call that was made on their strength with good and gallant willingness.

They had raced nigh twenty English miles by the time the chimes of a village were striking six o'clock; it was the only group of dwellings they had ventured near in their flight; the leaded lattices were thrust open with a hasty clang, and women's heads looked out as the iron tramp of the hunters' feet struck fire from the stones. A few cries were raised; one burgher called them to know their errand; they answered nothing, but traversed the street with lightning speed, gone from sight almost ere they were seen. A league farther on was a wooded bottom, all dark and silent, with a brook murmuring through it under the leafy shade of lilies and the tangle of water-plants; there Cecil checked the King and threw himself out of saddle.

"He is not quite himself yet," he murmured, as he loosened the girths and held back the delicate head from the perilous cold of the water to which the horse stretched so eagerly; he thought more of Forest King than he thought, even in that hour, of himself. He did all that was needed with his own hands; fed him with the corn from the saddle-bags, cooled him gently, led him to drink a cautious draught from the bubbling little stream, then let him graze and rest under the shade of the aromatic pines and the deep bronze leaves of the copper beeches; it was almost dark, so heavy and thickly laced were the branches, and exquisitely tranquil in the heart of the hilly country, in the peace of the early day, with the rushing of the forest brook the sole sound that was heard, and the everlasting sighing of the pine-boughs overhead.

Cecil leaned a while silently against one of the great gnarled trunks, and Rake affected to busy himself with the mare; in his heart was a tumult of rage, a volcano of curiosity, a pent-up storm of anxious amaze, but he would have let Mother o' Pearl brain him with a kick of her iron plates rather than press a single look that should seem like doubt, or seem like insult in adversity to his fallen master.

Cecil's eyes, drooped and brooding, gazed a long half-hour down in silence into the brook bubbling at his feet; then he lifted his head and spoke—with a certain formality and command in his voice, as though he gave an order on parade.

"Rake, listen, and do precisely what I bid you; neither more nor less. The horses cannot accompany me, nor you either; I must go henceforth where they would starve, and you would do worse. I do not take the King into suffering, nor you into temptation."

Rake, who at the tone had fallen unconsciously into the attitude of "attention," giving the salute with his old military instinct, opened his lips to speak in eager protestation; Cecil put up his hand.

"I have decided; nothing you can say will alter me. We are near a by-station now; if I find none there to prevent me, I shall get away by the first train; to hide in these woods is out of the question. You will return by easy stages to Baden, and take the horses at once to Lord Rockingham. They are his now. Tell him my last wish was that he should take you into his service; and he will be a better master to you than I have ever been. As for the King"—his lips quivered, and his voice shook a little, despite himself—"he will be safe with him. I shall go into some foreign service—Austrian, Russian, Mexican, whichever be open to me. I would not risk such a horse as mine to be sold, ill-treated, tossed from owner to owner, sent in his old age to a knacker's yard, or killed in a skirmish by a cannon-shot. Take both him and the mare back, and go back yourself. Believe me, I thank you from my heart for your noble offer of fidelity, but accept it I never shall."

A dead pause came after his words; Rake stood mute; a curious look—half-dogged, half-wounded, but very resolute—had come on his face.

Rake was silent a moment; then his hand touched his cap again.

"Very well, sir," and without opposition or entreaty, he turned to resaddle the mare.

Alone, Cecil flung himself full-length down on the turf beneath the beech woods; his arms thrown forward, his face buried in the grass, all gay with late summer forest blossoms; for the first time the whole might of the ruin that had fallen on him was understood by him; for the first time it beat him down beneath it, as the overstrained tension of nerve and of self-restraint had their inevitable reaction. He knew what this thing was which he had done—he had given up his whole future.

For a while he lay there like a drunken man, heavy and motionless; he had parted more easily with the woman he loved than he had parted with Forest King. The chimes of some far-off monastery, or castle-campanile, swung lazily in the morning stillness; the sound revived him, and recalled to him how little time there was if he would seek the flight that had begun on impulse and was continued in a firm, unshrinking resolve; he must go on, and on, and on.

He rose slowly, staggering a little, and feeling blinded and dazzled with the blaze of the morning sun as he went out of the beech wood. There were the marks of the hoofs on the damp, dewy turf; his lips trembled a little as he saw them—he would never ride the horse again!

Some two miles, more or less, lay between him and the

railway. He was not certain of his way, and he felt a sickening exhaustion on him; he had been without food since
his breakfast before the race. A gamekeeper's hut stood
near the entrance of the wood; he had much recklessness
in him, and no caution. He entered through the half-open
door, and asked the keeper, who was eating his sausage and
drinking his lager, for a meal.

"I'll give you one if you'll bring me down that hen-
harrier," growled the man in south German; pointing to
the bird that was sailing far off, a mere speck in the sunny
sky.

Cecil took the rifle held out to him, and without seeming
even to pause to take aim, fired. The bird dropped like a
stone through the air into the distant woods. There was no
tremor in his wrist, no uncertainty in his measure. The
keeper stared; the shot was one he had thought beyond
any man's range, and he set food and drink before his
guest with a crestfallen surprise, oddly mingled with ven-
eration.

"You might have let me buy my breakfast, without making
me do murder," said Bertie quietly, as he tried to eat. The
meal was coarse—he could scarcely touch it; but he drank
the beer down thirstily, and took a crust of bread. He
slipped his ring, a great sapphire graven with his crest,
off his finger, and held it out to the man.

"That is worth fifty double-Fredericks. Will you take it
in exchange for your rifle and some powder and ball?"

The German stared again, open-mouthed, and clinched the
bargain eagerly. He did not know anything about gems,
but the splendor of this dazzled his eye, while he had guns
more than enough, and could get many others at his lord's
cost. Cecil fastened a shot-belt round him, took a powder-
flask and cartridge-case, and with a few words of thanks,
went on his way.

Now that he held the rifle in his hand, he felt ready for
the work that was before him; if hunted to bay, at any
rate he could now have a struggle for his liberty. He
walked on through the still summer dawn, with the width
of the country stretching sun-steeped around him. The
sleeplessness, the excitement, the misery, the wild running of
the past night had left him strengthless and racked with
pain, but he knew that he must press onward or be caught,
sooner or later, like netted game in the poacher's silken
mesh. He had no conception what to do; he had but one

resolve—to keep his secret; if, to do it, he killed himself
with the rifle his sapphire ring had bought.

Carelessly daring always, he sauntered now into the station
for which he had made, without a sign on him that could
attract observation; he wore still the violet velvet Spanish-
like dress, the hessians, and the broad-leafed felt hat with
an eagle's feather fastened in it, that he had worn at the
races; and with the gun in his hand there was nothing to distinguish him from any tourist "milor," except that in one
hand he carried his own valise. He cast a rapid glance
around; no warrant for his apprehension, no announcement
of his personal appearance had preceded him here; he was
safe—safe in that; safer still in the fact that the train rushed
in so immediately on his arrival there, that the few people
about had no time to notice or speculate upon him. The
coupé was empty, by a happy chance; he took it, throwing
his money down with no heed that when the little he had
left was once expended he would be penniless, and the train
whirled on with him, plunging into the heart of forest and
mountain, and the black gloom of tunnels, and the golden seas
of corn-harvest. When he had taken his ticket and they had
asked him to where it should be, he had answered to their
amaze, "to the farthest place it goes," and he was borne on
now unwitting where it went; on and on, on and on, while he
knew nothing, as the opium-like sleep of intense weariness
held him in its stupor.

He awoke at last with a start; it was evening; the stilly
twilight was settling over all the land, and the train was
still rushing onward, fleet as the wind. His eyes, as they
opened dreamily, fell on a face half obscured in the gloaming; he leaned forward, bewildered and doubting his senses.

"Rake!"

Rake gave a salute hurriedly and in embarrassment.

"It's I, sir!—yes, sir."

Cecil thought himself dreaming still.

"You! You had my orders?"

"Yes, sir; I had your orders," murmured the ex-soldier,
more confused than he had ever been in the whole course of
his audacious life, "and they was the first I ever disobeyed—
they was. You see, sir, they was just what I couldn't swallow nohow—that's the real, right-down fact! Send me to
the devil, Mr. Cecil, for you, and I'll go at the first biddin',
but leave you just when things are on the cross for you,
damn me if I will!—beggin' your pardon, sir!"

And Rake, growing fiery and eloquent, dashed his cap down on the floor of the coupé with an emphatic declaration of resistance. Cecil looked at him in silence; he was not certain still whether this were not a fantastic folly he was dreaming.

"Damn me if I will, Mr. Cecil! You won't keep me— very well; but you can't prevent me follerin' of you, and foller you I will; and so there's no more to be said about it, sir; but just to let me have my own lark, as one may say. You said you'd go to the station, I went there; you took your ticket, I took my ticket. I've been traveling behind you till about two hours ago, then I looked at you; you was asleep, sir. 'I don't think my master's quite well,' says I to Guard; 'I'd like to get in there along of him.' 'Get in with you, then,' says he (only we was jabbering that willainous tongue o' theirs), for he sees the name on my traps is the same as that on your traps—and in I get. Now, Mr. Cecil, let me say one word for all, and don't think I'm a insolent, ne'er-do-well for having been and gone and disobeyed you; but you was good to me when I was sore in want of it; you was even good to my dog— rest his soul, the poor beast! there never were a braver!— and stick to you I will till you kick me away like a cur. The truth is, it's only being near of you, sir, that keeps me straight; if I was to leave you I should become a bad 'un again, right and away. Don't send me from you, sir, as you took mercy on me once!"

Rake's voice shook a little toward the close of his harangue, and in the shadows of evening light, as the train plunged through the gathering gloom, his ruddy, bright, bronzed face looked very pale and wistful.

Cecil stretched out his hand to him in silence that spoke better than words.

Rake hung his head.

"No, sir; you're a gentleman, and I've been an awful scamp! It's enough honor for me that you would do it. When I'm more worth it, perhaps—but that won't never be."

"You are worth it now, my gallant fellow." His voice was very low; the man's loyalty touched him keenly. "It was only for yourself, Rake, that I ever wished you to leave me."

"God bless you, sir!" said Rake passionately; "them words are better nor ten tosses of brandy!"

Cecil sat silent a while, his head drooped down on his

hands, while the evening deepened to night. At last he looked up.

"The King? Where is he?"

Rake flushed shamefacedly under his tanned skin.

"Beggin' your pardon, sir; behind you."

"Behind me?"

"Yes, sir; him and the brown mare. I couldn't do nothin' else with 'em, you see, sir, so I shipped him along with us. You can easily send 'em on to England from Paris, if you're determined to part with 'em; but you know the King always was fond of drums and trumpets and that like. You remember, sir, when he was a colt we broke him into it and taught him a bit of maneuvering; 'cause, till you found what pace he had in him, you'd thought of makin' a charger of him. He loves the noise of soldiering—he do; and if he thought you was goin' away without him, he'd break his heart, Mr. Cecil, sir. It was all I could do to keep him from follerin' of you this morning; he sawed my arms off a'most."

With which, Rake, conscious that he had been guilty of unpardonable disobedience and outrageous interference, hung his head over the gun; a little anxious and a good deal ashamed.

Cecil smiled a little, despite himself.

"Rake, you will do for no service, I am afraid; you are terribly insubordinate!"

He had not the heart to say more; the man's fidelity was too true to be returned with rebuke; and stronger than all surprise and annoyance was a strange mingling of pain and pleasure in him to think that the horse he loved so well was still so near him, the comrade of his adversity as he had been the companion of his happiest hours.

"These things will keep him a few days," he thought, as he looked at his hunting-watch, and the priceless pearl in each of his wristband-studs. He would have pawned every atom he had about him to have had the King with him a week longer.

The night fell, the stars came out, the storm-rack of a coming tempest drifted over the sky, the train rushed onward through the thickening darkness, through the spectral country—it was like his life, rushing headlong down into impenetrable gloom. The best, the uttermost, that he could look for was a soldier's grave, far away under some foreign soil.

A few evenings later the Countess Guenevere stood alone in her own boudoir in her Baden suite; she was going to dine with an Archduchess of Russia, and the splendid jewels of her House glittered through the black shower of her laces, and crowned her beautiful glossy hair, her delicate imperial head. In her hands was a letter—oddly written in pencil on a leaf torn out of a betting-book, but without a tremor or a change in the writing itself. And as she stood a shiver shook her frame; in the solitude of her lighted and luxurious chamber her cheek grew pale, her eyes grew dim.

"To refute the charge," ran the last words of what was at best but a fragment, "I must have broken my promise to you, and have compromised your name. Keeping silence myself, but letting the trial take place, law-inquiries so execrable and so minute, would soon have traced through others that I was with you that evening. To clear myself I must have attainted your name with public slander, and drawn this horrible ordeal on you before the world. Let me be thought guilty. It matters little. Henceforth I shall be dead to all who know me, and my ruin would have exiled me without this. Do not let an hour of grief for me mar your peace, my dearest; think of me with no pain, Beatrice; only with some memory of our past love. I have not strength yet to say—forget me; and yet,—if it be for your happiness,—blot out from your remembrance all thought of what we have been to one another; all thought of me and of my life, save to remember now and then that I was dear to you."

The words grew indistinct before her sight, they touched the heart of the world-worn coquette, of the victorious sovereign, to the core; she trembled greatly as she read them. For—in her hands was his fate. Though no hint of this was breathed in his farewell letter, she knew that with a word she could clear him, free him, and call him back from exile and shame, give him once more honor and guiltlessness in the sight of the world. With a word she could do this: his life was in the balance that she held as utterly as though it were now hers to sign, or to destroy, his death-warrant. It rested with her to speak and to say he had no guilt.

But to do this she must sacrifice herself. She stood mute, irresolute, a shudder running through her till her diamonds shook in the light; the heavy tears stole slowly down, one by one, and fell upon the blurred and blackened paper; her heart ached with an exceeding bitterness. Then shudderingly still, and as though there were a coward crime in the action, her hand unclosed and let the letter fall into the spirit flame of a silver lamp, burning by; the words that were upon it merited a better fate, a fonder cherishing, but—they would have compromised her. She let them fall, and burn, and wither. With them she gave up his life to its burden of shame, to its fate of exile.

She would hear his crime condemned, and her lips would not open; she would hear his name aspersed, and her voice would not be raised; she would know that he dwelt in misery, or died under foreign suns unhonored and unmourned, while tongues around her would babble of his disgrace—and she would keep her peace.

She loved him—yes; but she loved better the dignity in which the world held her, and the diamonds from which the law would divorce her if their love were known.

She sacrificed him for her reputation and her jewels; the choice was thoroughly a woman's.

CHAPTER IX.

IN THE CAFÉ OF THE CHASSEURS.

THE red-hot light of the after-glow still burned on the waters of the bay, and shed its Egyptian-like luster on the city that lies in the circle of the Sahel, with the Mediterranean so softly lashing with its violet waves the feet of the white, sloping town. The sun had sunk down in fire—the sun that once looked over those waters on the legions of Scipio and the iron brood of Hamilcar, and that now gave its luster on the folds of the French flags as they floated above the shipping of the harbor, and on the glitter of the French arms, as a squadron of the army of Algeria swept back over the hills to their barracks.

In one of the cafés there, a mingling of all the nations under the sun was drinking demi-tasses, absinthe, vermouth, or old wines. Half a dozen of that famous regiment the Chasseurs d'Afrique were gathered together, some with their feet resting on the little marble-topped tables, some reading the French papers, all smoking their inseparable companions

—the brûles-gueles; fine, stalwart, sun-burned fellows, with faces and figures that the glowing colors of their uniform set off to the best advantage.

"Loo-Loo was in fine voice to-night," said one.

"Yes; she took plenty of cognac before she sang; that always clears her voice," said a second.

"And I think that did her spirits good, shooting that Kabyl," said a third. "By the way, did he die?"

"N'sais pas," said the third, with a shrug of his shoulders; "Loo-Loo's a good aim."

"Sac à papier, yes! Rire-pour-tout taught her."

"You have much of such sharp service here, I suppose?" asked a voice in very pure French. The speaker was leaning against the open door of the café; a tall, lightly built man, dressed in a velvet shooting tunic, much the worse for wind and weather, a loose shirt, and jack-boots splashed and worn out.

"When we are at it, monsieur," returned the Chasseur. "I only wish we had more."

"Of course. Are you in need of recruits?"

"They all want to come to us and to the Zouaves," smiled Chanrellon, surveying the figure of the one who addressed him, with a keen sense of its symmetry and its sinew. "Still, a good sword brings its welcome. Do you ask seriously, monsieur?"

He did not answer the question literally, but came over from the doorway and seated himself at the little marble table opposite Claude, leaning his elbows on it.

"I have a doubt," he said. "I am more inclined to your foes."

"Dieu de Dieu!" ejaculated Chanrellon, pulling at his tawny mustaches. "A bold thing to say before five Chasseurs."

He smiled, a little contemptuously, a little amusedly.

"I am not a croc-mitaine, perhaps; but I say what I think, with little heed of my auditors, usually."

Chanrellon bent his bright brown eyes curiously on him. "He is a croc-mitaine," he thought. "He is not to be lost."

"I prefer your foes," went on the other, quite quietly, quite listlessly, as though the glittering, gas-lit café were not full of French soldiers. "In the first place, they are on the losing side; in the second, they are the lords of the soil; in the third, they live as free as air; and in the fourth, they have undoubtedly the right of the quarrel!"

"Monsieur!" cried the Chasseurs, laying their hands on their swords, fiery as lions. He looked indolently and wearily up from under the long lashes of his lids, and went on, as though they had not spoken.

"I will fight you all, if you like, but I don't think it's worth while," he said carelessly, where he leaned over the marble table. "Brawling's bad style; we don't do it. I was saying, I like your foes best; mere matter of taste; no need to quarrel over it—that I see. I shall go into their service or into yours, monsieur—will you play a game of dice to decide!"

"Decide?—but how?"

"Why—this way," said the other, with the weary listlessness of one who cares not two straws how things turn. "If I win, I go to the Arabs; if you win, I come to your ranks."

"Mort de Dieu! it is a droll gambling," murmured Chanrellon. "But—if you do win, do you think we shall let you go off to our enemies? Pas si bête, monsieur!"

"Yes, you will," said the other quietly. "Men who knew what honor meant enough to redeem Rire-pour-tout's pledge of safety to the Bedouins, will not take advantage of an openly confessed and unarmed adversary."

A murmur of ratification ran through his listeners.

Chanrellon swore a mighty oath.

"Pardieu, no. You are right. If you want to go, you shall go. Holà there! bring the dice. Champagne, monsieur? Vermouth? cognac?"

"Nothing, I thank you."

He leaned back with an apathetic indolence and indifference oddly at contrast with the injudicious daring of his war-provoking words and the rough campaigning that he sought. The assembled Chasseurs eyed him curiously; they liked his manner and they resented his first speeches; they noted every particular about him—his delicate white hands, his weather-worn and travel-stained dress, his fair, aristocratic features, his sweeping, abundant beard, his careless, cool, tired, reckless way; and they were uncertain what to make of him.

The dice were brought.

"What stakes, monsieur?" asked Chanrellon.

"Ten napoleons a side—and—the Arabs."

He set ten napoleons down on the table; they were the only coins he had in the world; it was very characteristic that he risked them.

They threw the main—two sixes.

"You see," he murmured, with a half smile, "the dice know it is a drawn duel between you and the Arabs."

"C'est un drôle, c'est un brave!" muttered Chanrellon; and they threw again.

The Chasseur cast a five; his was a five again.

"The dice cannot make up their minds," said the other listlessly, "they know you are Might and the Arabs are Right."

The Frenchmen laughed; they could take a jest goodhumoredly, and alone amid so many of them, he was made sacred at once by the very length of odds against him.

They rattled the boxes and threw again—Chanrellon's was three; his two.

"Ah!" he murmured. "Right kicks the beam and loses; it always does, poor devil!"

The Chasseur leaned across the table, with his brown, fearless, sunny eyes full of pleasure.

"Monsieur! never lament such good fortune for France. You belong to us now; let me claim you!"

He bowed more gravely than he had borne himself hitherto.

"You do me much honor; fortune has willed it so. One word only in stipulation."

Chanrellon assented courteously.

"As many as you choose."

"I have a companion who must be brigaded with me, and I must go on active service at once."

"With infinite pleasure. That doubtless can be arranged. You shall present yourself to-morrow morning; and for to-night, this is not the season here yet; and we are triste à faire frémir; still I can show you a little fun, though it is not Paris!"

But he rose and bowed again.

"I thank you, not to-night. You shall see me at your barracks with the morning."

"Ah, ah! monsieur!" cried the Chasseur eagerly, and a little annoyed. "What warrant have we that you will not dispute the decree of the dice, and go off to your favorites, the Arabs?"

He turned back and looked full in Chanrellon's face, his own eyes a little surprised, and infinitely weary.

"What warrant? My promise."

Then, without another syllable, he lounged slowly out through the soldiers and the idlers, and disappeared in the confused din and chiar-oscuro of the gas-lit street without, through the press of troopers, grisettes, merchants, beggars, sweetmeat-sellers, lemonade-sellers, curaçoa sellers, gaunt Bedouins, negro boys, shrieking muleteers, laughing lorettes, and glittering staff officers.

"That is done!" he murmured to his own thoughts. "Now for life under another flag!"

Claude de Chanrellon sat mute and amazed a while, gazing at the open door; then he drank a fourth beaker of champagne and flung the emptied glass down with a mighty crash.

"Ventre bleu! whoever he is, that man will eat fire, bons garçons!"

CHAPTER X.

"L'AMIE DU DRAPEAU."

"Did I not say he would eat fire?"

"Pardieu! c'est un brave."

"Rides like an Arab."

"Smokes like a Zouave."

"Cuts off a head with that back circular sweep—ah—h——h! magnificent!"

"And dances like an Aristocrat; not like a tipsy Spahi!"

The last crown to the chorus of applause, and insult to the circle of applauders, was launched with all the piquance of inimitable canteen-slang and camp-assurance, from a speaker who had perched astride on a broken fragment of wall, with her barrel of wine set up on end on the stones in front of her, and her six soldiers, her gros bébées, as she was given maternally to calling them, lounging at their ease on the arid, dusty turf below. She was very pretty, audaciously pretty, though her skin was burned to a bright sunny brown, and her hair was cut as short as a boy's, and her face had not one regular feature in it. But then—regularity! who wanted it, who would have thought the most pure classic type a change for the better, with those dark, dancing, challenging eyes; with that arch, brilliant, kitten-like face, so sunny, so mignon, and those scarlet lips like a bud of camellia that were never so handsome as when a cigarette was between them, or sooth to say, not seldom a brûle guele itself?"

She was pretty, she was insolent, she was intolerably coquettish, she was mischievous as a marmoset; she would swear, if need be, like a Zouave: she could fire galloping, she could toss off her brandy or her vermouth like a trooper; she would on occasion clinch her little brown hand and deal a blow that the recipient would not covet twice; she was an enfant de Paris and had all its wickedness at her fingers; she would sing you guinguette songs till you were suffocated with laughter, and she would dance the cancan at the Salle de Mars, with the biggest giant of a Cuirassier there. And yet with all that, she was not wholly unsexed; with all that she had the delicious fragrance of youth, and had not left a certain feminine grace behind her, though she wore a vivan-dière's uniform, and had been born in a barrack, and meant to die in a battle; it was the blending of the two that made her piquante, made her a notoriety in her own way; known at pleasure, and equally, in the Army of Africa as "Cig-arette," and "L'Amie du Drapeau."

"Not like a tipsy Spahi!" It was a cruel cut to her gros bébées, mostly Spahis, lying there at her feet, or rather at the foot of the wall, singing the praises—with magnanimity beyond praise—of a certain Chasseur d'Afrique.

"Ho, Cigarette!" growled a little Zouave, known as Tata Leroux. "That is the way thou forsakest thy friends for the first fresh face."

"Well, it is not a face like a tobacco-stopper, as thine is, Tata!" responded Cigarette, with a puff of her namesake; the repartee of the camp is apt to be rough. "He is Bel-à-faire-peur, as you nickname him."

"A woman's face!" growled the injured Tata; whose own countenance was of the color and well-nigh of the flatness of one of the red bricks of the wall.

"Ouf!" said the Friend of the Flag, with more expression in that single ejaculation than could be put in a volume. "He does woman's deeds, does he? He has woman's hands, but they can fight, I fancy? Six Arabs to his own sword the other day in that skirmish! Superb!"

"Sapristi! And what did he say, this droll, when he looked at them lying there? Just shrugged his shoulders and rode away. 'I'd better have killed myself; less mischief, on the whole!' Now who is to make anything of such a man as that?"

"Ah! he did not stop to cut their gold buttons off, and steal their cangiars, as thou wouldst have done, Tata? Well! he has not learned la guerre," laughed Cigarette. "It was a waste; he should have brought me their sashes, at least. By the way—when did he join?"

"Ten—twelve—years ago, or thereabouts."

"He should have learned to strip Arabs by this time, then," said the Amie du Drapeau, turning the tap of her barrel to replenish the wine-cup; "and to steal from them too, living or dead. Thou must take him in hand, Tata!"

"Sacré bleu!" grumbled Tata, "thy heart is all gone to the Englishman."

"My heart is a reveil matin, Tata; it wakes fresh every day. An Englishman, perdie! Why dost thou think him that?"

"Because he is a giant," said Tata.

Cigarette snapped her fingers:

"I have danced with grenadiers and cuirassiers quite as tall, and twice as heavy. Après?"

"Because he bathes—splash! like any water-dog."

"Because he is silent."

"Because he rises in his stirrups."

"Because he likes the sea."

"Because he knows le boxe."

"Because he is so quiet, and blazes like the devil underneath."

Under which mass of overwhelming proofs of nationality the Amie du Drapeau gave in.

"Yes, like enough. Besides, the other one is English. Lour-i-loo, of the Chasses-marais, tells me that the other one waits on him like a slave when he can—cleans his harness, litters his horse, saves him all the hard work, when he can do it without being found out. Where did they come from?"

"They will never tell."

Cigarette tossed her nonchalant head. She had never shed tears in her life. A dashing, dauntless, vivacious life, just in its youth, loving plunder, and mischief, and mirth; caring for nothing; and always ready with a laugh, a song, a slang repartee, or a shot from the dainty pistols thrust in her sash, that a general of division had given her, whichever best suited the moment.

Her mother a camp-follower, her father nobody knew who; a spoiled child of the Army from her birth, with a heart as bronzed as her cheek, and her respect for the laws of meum and tuum nil; yet with odd, stray, nature-sown instincts here and there, of a devil-may-care nobility, and of a wild grace that nothing could kill—Cigarette was the pet of the Army of Africa, and was as lawless as most of her patrons.

Of course, she was a little Amazon; of course, she was a

little Guerrilla; of course, she did not know what a blush
meant; of course, her thoughts were as slang and as riotous
as her mutinous mischief was in its act; but she was "bon
soldat," as she was given to say, with a toss of her curly
head; and she had some of the virtues of soldiers. Soldiers
had been about her ever since she first remembered having
a wooden casserole for a cradle, and sucking down red wine
through a pipe-stem. Soldiers had been her books, her
teachers, her models, her guardians, and, later on, her lovers,
all the days of her life. She had had no guiding-star, except
the eagles on the standards; she had had no cradle-song,
except the rataplan and the réveillé; she had had no sense
of duty taught her, except to face fire boldly, never to
betray a comrade, and to worship but two deities, "la Gloire"
and "la France."

Yet there were tales told in the barrack-yards and under
canvas of the little Amie du Drapeau that had a gentler side.
Of how softly she would touch the wounded; of how deftly
she would cure them. Of how carelessly she would dash
through under a raking fire, to take a draught of water to a
dying man.

On she dashed now, swift as a greyhound, light as a
hare; glancing here and glancing there as she bounded over
the picturesque desolation of the Cashbah; it was just noon,
and there were few could brave the noon-heat as she did; it
was very still; there was only from a little distance the
roll of the French kettle-drums where the drummers of
the African regiments were practicing. "Holà! le v'la!" cried
Cigarette to herself, as her falcon-eyes darted right and
left; and, like a chamois, she leaped down over the great
masses of Turkish ruins, cleared the channel of a dry water-
course, and alighted just in front of a Chasseur d'Afrique,
who was sitting alone on a broken fragment of white
marble, relic of some Moorish mosque, whose delicate columns, crowned with wind-sown grasses, rose behind him,
against the deep intense blue of the cloudless sky.

He was sitting thoughtfully enough, almost wearily, trac-
ing figures in the dry sand of the soil with the point of his
scabbard; yet he had all the look about him of a brilliant
French soldier, of one who, morever, had seen hot and stern
service. He was bronzed, but scarcely looked so after the
red, brown, and black of the Zouaves and the Turcos, for
his skin was naturally very fair, the features delicate, the
eyes very soft.

"Ah, ha, mon Roumi! Tata Leroux says you are English; by the faith, he must be right, or you would never sit musing there like an owl in the sunlight! Take a draught of my burgundy; bright as rubies. I never sell bad wines—not I! I know better than to drink them myself."

He started and rose; and, before he took the bidon, bowed to her, raising his cap with a grave, courteous obeisance; a bow that had used to be noted in throne-rooms for its perfection of grace.

"Ah, ma belle, is it you?" he said wearily. "You do me much honor."

"Morbleu!" she said pettishly. "You are too fine for us, mon brave. In what country, I should wonder, does one learn such dainty ceremony as that?"

"Where should one learn courtesies, if not in France?" he answered wearily. He had danced with this girl-soldier the night before at a guinguette ball, seeing her for the first time, for it was almost the first time he had been in the city since the night when he had thrown the dice, and lost ten Napoleons and the Bedouins to Claude de Chanrellon; but his thoughts were far from her in this moment.

"Ouf! you have learnt carte and tierce with your tongue!" cried Cigarette, provoked to receive no more compliment than that. "They say you are English, but I don't believe it; you speak too soft, and you sound the double L's too well. A Spaniard, eh?"

"Do you find me so devout a Catholic that you think so?"

She laughed. "A Greek, then?"

"Still worse. Have you seen me cheat at cards?"

"An Austrian? You waltz like a White Coat?"

He shook his head.

She stamped her little foot into the ground—a foot fit for a model, with its shapely military boot; spurred, too, for Cigarette rode like a circus-rider.

"Bécasse! say what you are, then, at once."

"A soldier of France. Can you wish me more?"

For the first time her eyes flashed and softened—her one love was the tricolor.

"True!" she said simply. "But you were not always a soldier of France? You joined, they say, twelve years ago? What were you before then?"

She here cast herself down in front of him, and, with her elbows on the sand, and her chin on her hands, watched him with all the frank curiosity and unmoved nonchalance imaginable, as she launched the question point-blank.

"Before!" he said slowly. "Well—a fool."

"You belonged to the majority, then!" said Cigarette, with a piquance made a thousand times more piquant by the camp slang she spoke in. "You should not have had to come into the ranks, mon ami; majorities—specially that majority—have very smooth sailing generally!"

He looked at her more closely, though she wearied him.

"Where have you got your ironies, Cigarette? You are so young."

She shrugged her shoulders.

"Bah! one is never young, and always young in camps. Young? Pardieu! When I was four I could swear like a grenadier, plunder like a préfet, lie like a priest, and drink like a bohemian."

Yet—with all that—and it was the truth, the brow was so open under the close rings of the curls, the skin so clear under the sun-tan, the mouth so rich and so arch in its youth!

"Why did you come into the service?" she went on, before he had a chance to answer her. "You were born in the Noblesse—bah! I know an aristocrat at a glance! Ceux qui ont pris la peine de naître!—don't you like 'Figaro'? My men played it last winter, and I was Figaro myself. Now many of those aristocrats come; shoals of them; but it is always for something. They all come for something; most of them have been ruined by the lionnes, a hundred million of francs gone in a quarter! Ah, bah! what blind bats the best of you are! They have gambled, or bet, or got into hot water, or fought too many duels, or caused a court scandal, or something; all the aristocrats that come to Africa are ruined. What ruined you, M. l'Aristocrat?"

"Aristocrat? I am none. I am a Corporal of the Chasseurs."

"Diable! I have known a Duke a Corporal! What ruined you?"

"What ruins most men, I imagine—folly."

"Folly, sure enough!" retorted Cigarette, with scornful acquiescence. She had no patience with him. He danced so deliciously, he looked so superb, and he would give her nothing but these absent answers. "Wisdom don't bring men who look as you look into the ranks of the volunteers for Africa. Besides, you are too handsome to be a sage!"

He laughed a little.

"I never was one, that's certain. And you are too pretty to be a cynic."

"A what?" She did not know the word. "Is that a good cigar you have? Give me one. Do women smoke in your old country?"

"Oh, yes—many of them."

"Where is it, then?"

"I have no country—now."

"But the one you had?"

"I have forgotten I ever had one."

"Did it treat you ill, then?"

"Not at all."

"Had you anything you cared for in it?"

"Well—yes."

"What was it? A woman?"

"No—a horse."

He stooped his head a little as he said it, and traced more figures slowly in the sand.

"Ah!"

She drew a short, quick breath. She understood that; she would only have laughed at him had it been a woman; Cigarette was more veracious than complimentary in her estimate of her own sex.

"There was a man in the Cuirassiers I knew," she went on softly, "loved a horse like that;—he would have died for Cossack;—but he was a terrible gambler, terrible. Not but what I like play myself. Well, one day he played and played till he was mad, and everything was gone; and then in his rage he staked the only thing he had left. Staked and lost the horse! He never said a word; but he just slipped a pistol in his pocket, went to the stable, kissed Cossack one—twice—thrice—and shot himself through the heart."

"Poor fellow!" murmured the Chasseur d'Afrique, in his chestnut beard.

Cigarette was watching him with all the keenness of her falcon eyes; "he has gambled away a good deal too," she thought. "It is always the same old story with them."

And with a bound to which indignation lent wings like a swallow's, the Friend of the Flag, insulted and amazed at the apathy with which her advances to friendship had been received, dashed off at her topmost speed, singing all the louder out of bravado. "To have nothing more to say to me after dancing with me all night!" thought Cigarette, with fierce wrath at such contumely, the first neglect the pet of the Spahis had ever experienced.

Meanwhile, where she had left him among the stones of the ruined mosque, the Chasseur, whom they nicknamed Bel-à-faire-peur, in a double sense, because of his "woman's face," as Tata Leroux termed it, and because of the terror his sword had become through North Africa, sat motionless with his right arm resting on his knee, and his spurred heel thrust into the sand; the sun shining down unheeded in its fierce, burning glare on the chestnut masses of his beard and the bright glitter of his uniform.

He was a dashing cavalry soldier, who had had a dozen wounds cut over his body by the Bedouin swords, in many and hot shirmishes; who had waited through sultry African nights for the lion's tread, and had fought the desert-king and conquered; who had ridden a thousand miles over the great sand waste, and the boundless arid plains, and slept under the stars with the saddle beneath his head, and his rifle in his hand, all through the night; who had served, and served well, in fierce, arduous, unremitting work, in trying campaigns and in close discipline; who had blent the verve, the brilliance, the daring, the eat-drink-and-enjoy-for-to-morrow-we-die of the French Chasseur, with something that was very different, and much more tranquil.

Yet, though as bold a man as any enrolled in the French Service, he sat alone here in the shadow of the column, thoughtful, motionless, lost in silence.

In his left hand was a Galignani, six months old, and his eyes rested on a line in the obituary:

"On the 10th ult., at Royallieu, suddenly, the Right Hon. Denzil, Viscount Royallieu; aged 90."

CHAPTER XI.

UNDER THE HOUSES OF HAIR.

It was just sunset.

Camped on one of the bare stretches above the Mustapha Road was a circle of Arab tents.

The encampment stretched far over the level, arid earth, and there was more than one tent where the shadowing folds of the banner marked the abode of some noble Djied.

In the central tent, tall and crimson-stripped, with its mighty standard reared in front, and its opening free to the night, sat the Khalifa, the head of the tribe, with a circle of Arabs about him. He was thrown on his cushions, rich enough for a seraglio, while the rest squatted on the morocco carpet that covered the bare ground, and that was strewn with round brass Moorish trays and little cups emptied of their coffee.

Beneath its light, which fell full on him, flung down upon another pile of cushions facing the open front of the tent, was a guest whom the Khalifa delighted to honor. Only a Corporal of Chasseurs, and once a foe, yet one with whom the Arab found the brotherhood of brave men, and on whom he lavished, in all he could, the hospitalities and honors of the desert.

The story of their friendship ran thus:

The tribe was now allied with France, or, at least, had accepted French sovereignty, and pledged itself to neutrality in the hostilities still rife; but a few years before, far in the interior and leagued with the Kabaïles, it had been one of the fiercest and most dangerous among the enemies of France.

Through four or five seasons of warfare, the Sheik and the Chasseur had encountered each other, till each had grown to look for the other's face as soon as the standards of the Bedouins flashed in the sunshine opposite the guidons of the Imperial forces; till each had watched and noted the other's unmatched prowess, and borne away the wounds of the other's home-strokes, with the admiration of a bold soldier for a bold rival's dauntlessness and skill; till each had learned to long for an hour, hitherto always prevented by waves of battle that had swept them too soon asunder, when they should meet in a duello once for all, and try their strength together till one bore off victory and one succumbed to death.

At last it came to pass that, after a lengthened term of this chivalrous antagonism, the tribe were sorely pressed by the French troops, and could no longer mass its fearless front to face them, but had to flee southward to the desert, and encumbered by its flocks and its women, was hardly driven and greatly decimated. Now among those women was one whom the Sheik held above all earthly things except his honor in war; a beautiful antelope-eyed creature, lithe and graceful as a palm, and the daughter of a pure Arab

race, on whom he could not endure for any other sight
than his own to look, and whom he guarded in his tent as the
chief pearl of all his treasures; herds, flocks, arms, even his
horses, all save the honor of his tribe, he would have surrendered rather than surrender Djelma.

One day the Chasseurs had pitched their camp where a few
barren, withered trees gave a semblance of shelter, and a
little thread of brackish water oozed through the yellow earth.

Suddenly the noon lethargy of the camp was broken; a
trumpet-call rang through the stillness; against the amber
transparency of the horizon line the outlines of half a dozen
horsemen were seen looming nearer and nearer with every
moment; they were some Spahis who had been out "sondant
le terrain aux environs." The mighty frame of Châteauroy,
almost as unclothed as an athlete's, started from its slumberous, panting rest; his eyes lightened hungrily; he muttered
a fiery oath: "Mort de Dieu!—they have the woman!"

They had the woman. She had been netted near a water-
spring, to which she had wandered too loosely guarded, and
too far from the Bedouin encampment. The delight of the
haughty Sidi's eyes was borne off to the tents of his foes, and
the Colonel's face flushed darkly with an eager, lustful
warmth, as he looked upon his captive. Rumor had not out-
boasted the Arab girl's beauty; it was lustrous as ever was
that when, far yonder to the eastward, under the curled palms
of Nile, the sorceress of the Cæsars swept through her rose-
strewn palace chambers. Only Djelma was as innocent as
the gazelle, whose grace she resembled, and loved her lord
with a great love.

Of her suffering her captor took no more heed than if she
were a young bird dying of shot-wounds; but, with one tri-
umphant, admiring glance at her, he wrote a message in
Arabic, to send to the Khalifa, ere her loss was discovered—
a message more cruel than iron. He hesitated a second,
where he lay at the opening of his tent, whom he should
send with it. His men were almost all half-dead with the
sun-blaze. His glance chanced to light in the distance on a
soldier to whom he bore no love—causelessly, but bitterly all
the same. He had him summoned, and eyed him with a
curious amusement—Châteauroy treated his squadrons with
much the same sans-façon familiarity and brutality that a
chief of filibusters uses to his.

"So! you heed the heat so little, you give up your turn
of water to a drummer, they say?"

The Chasseur gave the salute with a calm deference. A faint flush passed over the sun-bronze of his forehead. He had thought the Sidney-like sacrifice had been unobserved.

"The drummer was but a child, mon Commandant."

"Be so good as to give us no more of those melodramatic acts!" said M. le Marquis contemptuously. "You are too fond of trafficking in those showy fooleries. You bribe your comrades for their favoritism too openly. Ventre bleu! I forbid it—do you hear?"

"I hear, mon Colonel."

The assent was perfectly tranquil and respectful. He was too good a soldier not to render perfect obedience, and keep perfect silence, under any goad of provocation to break both.

"Obey, then!" said Châteauroy savagely. "Well, since you love heat so well, you shall take a flag of truce and my scroll to the Sidi Ilderim. But tell me, first, what do you think of this capture?"

"It is not my place to give opinions, M. le Colonel."

"Pardieu! it is your place when I bid you. Speak, or I will have the matraque cut the words out of you!"

"I may speak frankly?"

"Ten thousand curses—yes!"

"Then, I think that those who make war on women are no longer fit to fight with men."

For a moment the long, sinewy, massive form of Châteauroy started from the skins on which he lay at full length, like a lion started from its lair. His veins swelled like black cords; under the mighty muscle of his bare chest his heart beat visibly in the fury of his wrath.

"By God! I have a mind to have you shot like a dog!"

The Chasseur looked at him carelessly, composedly, but with a serene deference still, as due from a soldier to his chief.

"You have threatened it before, M. le Colonel. It may be as well to do it, or the army may think you capricious."

Raoul de Châteauroy crushed a blasphemous oath through his clenched teeth, and laughed a certain short, stern, sardonic laugh, which his men dreaded more than his wrath.

"No; I will send you instead to the Khalifa. He often saves me the trouble of killing my own curs. Take a flag of truce and this paper, and never draw rein till you reach him, if your beast drop dead at the end."

The Chasseur saluted, took the paper, bowed with a certain

languid, easy grace that camp life never cured him of, and went. He knew that the man who should take the news of his treasure's loss to the Emir Ilderim would, a thousand to one, perish by every torture desert cruelty could frame, despite the cover of the white banner.

Châteauroy looked after him, as he and his horse passed from the French camp in the full burning tide of noon.

"If the Arabs kill him," he thought, "I will forgive Ilderim five seasons of rebellion."

The Chasseur, as he had been bidden, never drew rein across the scorching plateau. At last, ere he reached the Bedouin tents, that were still but slender black points against the horizon, he saw the Sheik and a party of horsemen returning from a foraging quest, and in ignorance as yet of the abduction of Djelma. He galloped straight to them, and halted across their line of march, with the folds of the little white flag fluttering in the sun. The Bedouins drew bridle, and Ilderim advanced alone. He was a magnificent man, of middle age, with the noblest type of the eagle-eyed, aquiline desert beauty. He was a superb specimen of his race, without the lean, withered, rapacious, vulture look which often mars it. His white haik floated round limbs fit for a Colossus; and under the snowy folds of his turban the olive-bronze of his bold forehead, the sweep of his jet-black beard, and the piercing luminance of his eyes had a grand and kingly majesty.

A glance of recognition flashed from him on the Lascar, who had so often crossed swords with him; and he waved back the scroll with dignified courtesy.

"Read it me."

It was read. Bitterly, blackly shameful, the few brutal words were. They netted him as an eagle is netted in a shepherd's trap.

The moment that he gave a sign of advancing against his ravishers, the captive's life would pay the penalty; if he merely remained in arms, without direct attack, she would be made the Marquis' mistress, and abandoned later to the army. The only terms on which he could have her restored were instant submission to the Imperial rule, and personal homage of himself and all his Djouad to the Marquis as the representative of France—homage in which they should confess themselves dogs and the sons of dogs.

So ran the message of peace.

The Chasseur read on to the end calmly. Then he lifted

his gaze, and looked at the Emir—he expected fifty swords to
be buried in his heart.

With a wild, shrill yell, the Bedouins whirled their naked
sabers above their heads, and rushed down on the bearer of
this shame to their chief and their tribe. The Chasseur did
not seek to defend himself. He sat motionless. He thought
the vengeance just.

The Sheik raised his sword, and signed them back, as he
pointed to the white folds of the flag. Then his voice rolled
out like thunder over the stillness of the plains:

"But that you trust yourself to my honor I would rend you
limb from limb. Go back to the tiger who rules you, and tell
him that—as Allah liveth—I will fall on him and smite him
as he hath never been smitten. Dead or living, I will have
back my own. If he take her life, I will have ten thousand
lives to answer it; if he deal her dishonor, I will light such
a holy war through the length and breadth of the land that his
nation shall be driven backward like choked dogs into the sea,
and perish from the face of the earth for evermore. And
this I swear by the Law and the Prophet!"

The menace rolled out, imperious as a monarch's, thrilling
through the desert hush. The Chasseur bent his head, as the
words closed. His own teeth were tightly clinched, and his
face was dark.

"Emir, listen to one word," he said briefly. "Shame has
been done to me as to you. Had I been told what words I
bore, they had never been brought by my hand. You know
me. You have had the marks of my steel, as I have had
the marks of yours. Trust me in this, Sidi. I pledge you my
honor that, before the sun sets, she shall be given back to you
unharmed, or I will return here myself, and your tribe shall
slay me in what fashion they will. So alone can she be
saved uninjured. Answer, will you have faith in me?"

The desert chief looked at him long; sitting motionless as
a statue on his stallion, with the fierce gleam of his eyes
fixed on the eyes of the man who so long had been his
foe in contests whose chivalry equaled their daring. The
Chasseur never wavered once under the set, piercing, ruthless gaze.

Then the Emir pointed to the sun, that was not at its
zenith:

"You are a great warrior: such men do not lie. Go, and
if she be borne to me before the sun is half-way sunk toward
the west, all the branches of the tribes of Ilderim shall be

as your brethren, and bend as steel to your bidding. If not
—as God is mighty—not one man in all your host shall
live to tell the tale!"

The Chasseur bowed his head to his horse's mane; then,
without a word, wheeled round, and sped back across the
plain.

When he reached his own cavalry camp, he went straight-
way to his chief. What passed between them none ever
knew. The interview was brief; it was possibly as stormy.
Pregnant and decisive it assuredly was; and the squadrons of
Africa marveled that the man who dared beard Raoul de
Châteauroy in his lair came forth with his life. Whatever
the spell he used, the result was a marvel.

At the very moment that the sun touched the lower half
of the western heavens, the Sheik Ilderim, where he sat in his
saddle, with all his tribe stretching behind him, full-armed,
to sweep down like falcons on the spoilers, if the hour passed
with the pledge unredeemed, saw the form of the Chasseur
reappear between his sight and the glare of the skies; nor
did he ride alone. That night the Pearl of the Desert lay
once more in the mighty, sinuous arms of the great Emir.

But, with the dawn, his vengeance fell in terrible fashion
on the sleeping camp of the Franks; and from that hour
dated the passionate, savage, unconcealed hate of Raoul de
Châteauroy for the most daring soldier of all his fiery Horse,
known in his troop as "Bel-à-faire-peur."

It was in the tent of Ilderim now that he reclined, looking
outward at the night where flames were leaping ruddily under
a large caldron, and far beyond was the dark immensity of
the star-studded sky; the light of the moon strayed in and
fell on the chestnut waves of his beard, out of which the long
amber stem of an Arab pipe glittered like a golden line, and
on the delicate, feminine cast of his profile, which, with the
fairness of the skin—fair, despite a warm hue of bronze—
and the long, slumberous softness of the hazel eyes, were
in so marked a contrast of race with the eagle outlines of
the Bedouins around.

From the hour of the restoration of his treasure the Sheik
had been true to his oath; his tribe in all its branches had
held the French lascar in closest brotherhood. Through him
their alliance, or more justly to speak, their neutrality, was
secured to France, and the Bedouin Chief loved him with
a great, silent, noble love that was fast rooted in the granite
of his nature. Between them there was a brotherhood that

beat down the antagonism of race, and was stronger than the instinctive hate of the oppressed for all who came under the abhorred standard of the usurpers. He liked the Arabs, and they liked him; a grave courtesy, a preference for the fewest words and least demonstration possible, a marked opinion that silence was golden, and that speech was at best only silver-washed metal, an instinctive dread of all discovery of emotion, and a limitless power of resisting and suppressing suffering, were qualities the nomads of the desert and the lion of the Chasseurs d'Afrique had in common; as they had in unison a wild passion for war, a dauntless zest in danger, and a love for the hottest heat of fiercest battle.

The night was someway spent when the talk of wild-pigeon-blue mares and sorrel stallions closed between the Djied and his guest; and the French soldier, who had been sent hither from the Bureau Arabe with another of his comrades, took his way through the now still camp where the cattle were sleeping, and the fires were burning out, and the banner-folds hung motionless in the luster of the stars, to the black-and-white tent prepared for him.

As he opened the folds and entered, his fellow-soldier, who was lying on his back, with his heels much higher than his head, and a short pipe in his teeth, tumbled himself up with a rapid somersault, and stood bolt upright, giving the salute; a short, sturdy little man, with a skin burnt like a coffee-berry, that was in odd contrast with his light, dancing blue eyes, and his close, matted curls of yellow hair.

"Beg pardon, sir! I was half asleep!"

The Chasseur laughed a little.

"Don't talk English; somebody will hear you one day."

"What's the odds if they do, sir?" responded the other. "It relieves one's feelin's a little. All of 'em know I'm English, but never a one of 'em know what you are. The name you was enrolled by won't really tell 'em nothing. They guess it aint yours. That cute little chap, Tata, he says to me yesterday, 'you're always a-treatin' of your galonné like as if he was a prince.' 'Damme!' says I, 'I'd like to see the prince as would hold a candle to him.' 'You're right there,' says the little 'un. 'There aint his equal for takin' off a beggar's head with a back sweep.'"

The Corporal laughed a little again, as he tossed himself down on the carpet.

"Well, it's something to have one virtue! But have a care what those chatter-boxes get out of you."

"Lord, sir! Aint I been a-takin' care these ten years? It comes quite natural now. I couldn't keep my tongue still; that wouldn't be in anyways possible. So I've let it run on oiled wheels on a thousand rum tracks and doublings."

"You are happy enough in Algeria—eh?" asked the one he served.

"I, sir? Never was so happy in my life, sir. I'd be discontented indeed if I wasn't. Always some spicy bit of fighting. If there aren't a fantasia, as they call it, in the field, there's always somebody to pot in a small way; and, if you're lying by in barracks, there's always a scrimmage hot as pepper to be got up with fellows that love the row just as well as you do. It's life, that's what it is; it aint rustin'."

"Then you prefer the French service?"

"Right and away, sir."

Then he paused. "Won't there never be no hope, sir?" he whispered, while his voice trembled a little under the long, fierce "Zephyr" sweep of his yellow mustaches.

The Chasseur rallied himself with a slight, careless laugh; the laugh with which he had met before now the onslaught of charges ferocious as those of the magnificent day of Mazagran.

"Whom for? Both of us? Oh, yes; very likely we shall achieve fame, and die sous-officers or gardes-champêtres! A splendid destiny."

"No, sir," said the other, with the hesitation still in the quiver of his voice. "You know I meant, no hope of your ever being again——"

He stopped; he scarcely knew how to phrase the thoughts he was thinking.

The other moved with a certain impatience.

"How often must I tell you to forget that I was ever anything except a soldier of France?—forget as I have forgotten it!"

The audacious irrepressible "Crache-au-nez-d'la-Mort," whom nothing could daunt and nothing could awe, looked penitent and ashamed as a chidden spaniel.

"I know, sir. I have tried, many a year; but I thought, perhaps, as how his lordship's death——"

"No life and no death can make any difference to me, except the death that some day an Arbico's lunge will give me; and that is a long time coming."

"Ah, for God's sake, Mr. Cecil, don't talk like this!"

The Chasseur gave a short, sharp shiver, and started at the name, as if a bullet had struck him.

"Never say that again!"

Rake, Algerian-christened "Crache-au-nez-d'la-Mort," stammered a contrite apology.

"I never have done, sir—not for never a year; but it wrung it out of me like—you talking of wanting death in that way——"

"Oh, I don't want death!" laughed the other, with a low, indifferent laughter, that had in it a singular tone of sadness all the while. "I am of our friends the Spahis' opinion— that life is very pleasant with a handsome, well-chosen harem, and a good horse to one's saddle. Unhappily harems are too expensive for Roumis! Yet I am not sure that I am not better amused in the Chasseurs than I was in the Household— specially when we are at war. I suppose we must be wild animals at the core, or we should never find such an infinite zest in the death grapple. Good-night!"

Long after his comrade had slept soundly, and the light in the single bronze Turkish candle-branch had flickered and died away, the Chasseur d'Afrique lay wakeful; looking outward through the folds of the tent at the dark and silent camp of the Arabs, and letting his memory drift backward to a time that had grown to be to him as a dream—a time when another world than the world of Africa had known him as Bertie Cecil.

He was "dead"; therein had lain all his security; thereby had "Beauty of the Brigades" been buried beyond all discovery in "Bel-à-faire-peur" of the 2d Chasseurs d'Afrique. When, on the Marseilles rails, the maceration and slaughter of as terrible an accident as ever befell a train rushing through midnight darkness, at headlong speed, had left himself and the one man faithful to his fortunes unharmed by little less than a miracle; he had seen in the calamity the surest screen from discovery or pursuit.

Leaving the baggage where it was jammed among the débris, he had struck across the country with Rake for the few leagues that still lay between them and the city, and had entered Marseilles as weary foot travelers, before half the ruin on the rails had been seen by the full noon sun.

As it chanced a trading yawl was loading in the port, to run across to Algiers that very day. The skipper was short of men, and afraid of the Lascars, who were the only sailors that he seemed likely to find to fill up the vacant places in his small crew.

Cecil offered himself and his comrade for the passage. He had only a very few gold pieces on his person, and he was willing to work his way across, if he could.

"But you're a gentleman," said the skipper, doubtfully eying him, and his velvet dress, and his black sombrero with its eagle's plume. "I want a rare, rough, able seaman, for there'll be like to be foul weather. She looks too fair to last," he concluded, with a glance upward at the sky.

He was a Liverpool man, master and owner of his own rakish-looking little black-hulled craft, that, rumor was wont to say, was not averse to a bit of slaving, if she found herself in far seas, with a likely run before her.

"You're a swell, that's what you are," emphasized the skipper. "You bean't no sort of use to me."

"Wait a second," answered Cecil. "Did you ever chance to hear of a schooner called 'Regina'?"

The skipper's face lighted in a moment.

"Her as was in the Biscay, July come two years? her as druv' through the storm like a mad thing, and flew like a swallow, when everything was splittin' and founderin', and shipping seas around her? her as was the first to bear down to the great 'Wrestler,' a-lyin' there hull over in water, and took aboard all as ever she could hold o' the passengers; a-pitchin' out her own beautiful cabin fittin's to have as much room for the poor wretches as ever she could? Be you a-meanin' her?"

Cecil nodded assent.

"She was my yacht, that's all; and I was without a captain through that storm. Will you think me a good enough sailor now?"

The skipper wrung his hand till he nearly wrung it off.

"Good enough! Blast my timbers! there aren't one will beat you in any waters. Come on, sir, if so be as you wishes it; but never a stroke of work shall you do atween my decks. I never did think as how one of your yachting-nobs could ever be fit to lay hold of a tiller; but, hang me, if the Club make such sailors as you it's a rare 'un! Lord a mercy! why, my wife was in the 'Wrestler.' I've heard her tell scores of times as how she was a'most dead when that little yacht came through a swaling sea, that was all heavin' and roarin' round the wreck, and as how the swell what owned it gev' his cabin up to the womenkind, and had his swivel guns and his handsome furniture pitched overboard, that he might be able to carry more passengers, and fed 'em, and gev' 'em champagne all around, and treated 'em like a prince, till he ran 'em straight into Brest Harbor. But, damn me! that ever a swell like you should——"

"Let's weigh anchor," said Bertie quietly.

And so he crossed unnoticed to Algeria, while through Europe the tidings went that the mutilated form, crushed between iron and wood, on the Marseilles line, was his, and that he had perished in that awful, ink-black, sultry southern night, when the rushing trains had met, as meet the thunderclouds. The world thought him dead; as such the journals recorded him, with the shameful outlines of imputed crime, to make the death the darker; as such his name was forbidden to be uttered at Royallieu; as such the Seraph mourned him with passionate, loving force, refusing to the last to accredit his guilt:—and he, leaving them in their error, was drafted into the French army under two of his Christian names, which happily had a foreign sound—Louis Victor—and laid aside forever his identity as Bertie Cecil.

He went at once on service in the interior, and had scarcely come in any of the larger towns since he had joined.

From the extremes of luxury, indolence, indulgence, pleasure, and extravagance, Cecil came to the extremes of hardship, poverty, discipline, suffering, and toil. The first years were, it is true, years of intense misery to him. He suffered acutely many times; suffered till he was heart-sick of his life; but he never sought to escape the slightest penalty or hardship, and not even Rake ever heard from him a single syllable of irritation or of self-pity.

Moreover, the war-fire woke in him.

CHAPTER XII.

THE IVORY SQUADRONS.

THE Chambrée of the Chasseurs was bright and clean in the morning light; in common with all Algerian barrack rooms as unlike the barrack rooms of the ordinary army as Cigarette, with her debonnaire devilry, smoking on a gun-wagon, was unlike a trim Normandy soubrette, sewing on a bench in the Tuileries gardens.

Disorder reigned supreme; but Disorder, although a disheveled goddess, is very often a picturesque one, and more of an artist than her better-trained sisters; and the disorder was brightened with a thousand vivid colors and careless touches that blent in confusion to enchant a painter's eyes. The room was crammed with every sort of spoil that the adventurous, pillaging temper of the troopers could forage from Arab tents, or mountain caves, or river depths, or desert beasts and birds.

Ignorance jostled art, and bizarrerie ran hand in hand with talent, in all the products of the Chasseurs' extemporized studio; but nowhere was there ever clumsiness, and everywhere was there an industry, gay, untiring, accustomed to make the best of the worst; the workers laughing, chattering, singing, in all good-fellowship, while the fingers that gave the dead thrust held the carver's chisel, and the eyes that glared blood-red in the heat of battle twinkled mischievously over the meerschaum bowl, in whose grinning form some great chief of the Bureaucratie had just been sculptured in audacious parody.

In the midst sat Rake, tattooing with an eastern skill the skin of a great lion, that a year before he had killed in single combat in the heart of Oran, having watched for the beast twelve nights in vain, high perched on a leafy crest of rock, above a water-course.

The laughter, the work, and the clatter of conflicting tongues were at their height; Cecil sat, now listening, now losing himself in thought, while he gave the last touch to the carvings before him. They were a set of chessmen which it had taken him years to find materials for and to perfect; the white men were in ivory, the black in walnut, and were two opposing squadrons of French troops and of mounted Arabs. Beautifully carved, with every detail of costume rigid to truth, they were his masterpiece, though they had only been taken up at any odd ten minutes that had happened to be unoccupied during the last three or four years. The chessmen had been about with him in so many places and under canvas so long, from the time that he chipped out their first Zouave pawn, as he lay in the broiling heat of Oran prostrate by a dry brook's stony channel, that he scarcely cared to part with them, and had refused to let Rake offer them for sale, with all the rest of the carvings. Stooping over them, he did not notice the doors open at the end of the Chambrée until a sudden silence that fell on the babble and uproar round him made him look up; then he rose and gave the salute with the rest of his discomfited and awe-stricken troopers. Châteauroy with a brilliant party had entered.

The Colonel flashed an eagle glance round.

"Fine discipline! You shall go and do this pretty work at Beylick!"

The soldiers stood like hounds that see the lash; they knew that he was like enough to carry out his threat; though they were doing no more than they had always tacit, if not open, permission to do. Cecil advanced, and fronted him.

"Mine is the blame, mon Commandant!"

The Marquis gave a grim, significant smile, that cut like so much cord of the scourge.

"Ca va sans dire! Wherever there is insubordination in the regiment, the blame is very certain to be yours! Corporal Victor, if you allow your Chambrée to be turned into the riot of a public fair, you will soon find yourself degraded from the rank you so signally contrive to disgrace."

The words were far less than the tone they were spoken in, that gave them all the insolence of so many blows, as he swung on his heel and bent to the ladies of the party he escorted. Cecil stood mute; bearing the rebuke as it became a Corporal to bear his Commander's anger; a very keen observer might have seen that a faint flush rose over the sun tan of his face, and that his teeth clinched under his beard; but he let no other sign escape him.

The very self-restraint irritated Châteauroy, who would have been the first to chastise the presumption of a reply, had any been attempted.

"Back to your place, sir!" he said, with a wave of his hand, as he might have waved back a cur. "Teach your men the first formula of obedience, at any rate!"

Cecil fell back in silence. He went to his place at the farther end of the chamber and stood, keeping his eyes on the chess carvings, lest the control which was so bitter to retain should be broken if he looked on at the man who had been the curse and the antagonist of his whole life in Algeria.

A voice woke him from his reverie.

"Are those beautiful carvings yours?"

He looked up, and in the gloom of the alcove where he

stood, where the sun did not stray, and two great rugs of
various skins, with some conquered banners of Bedouins,
hung like a black pall, he saw a woman's eyes resting on
him; proud, lustrous eyes, a little haughty, very thoughtful,
yet soft withal, as the deepest hue of deep waters. He
bowed to her with the old grace of manner that had so
amused and amazed the little vivandière.

"Yes, madame; they are mine."

"Ah?—what wonderful skill!"

She took the White King, an Arab Sheik on his charger,
in her hand, and turned to those about her, speaking of its
beauties and its workmanship in a voice low, very melodious,
ever so slightly languid, that fell on Cecil's ear like a chime
of long-forgotten music. Twelve years had drifted by since
he had been in the presence of a high-bred woman, and
those lingering, delicate tones had the note of his dead past.

"You have an exquisite art. They are for sale?" she asked
him. She spoke with the careless, gracious courtesy of a
grande dame to a Corporal of Chasseurs; looking little at
him, much at the ivory Kings and their mimic hosts of
Zouaves and Bedouins.

"They are at your service, madame."

"And their price?" She had been purchasing largely of
the men on all sides as she had swept down the length of
the Chambrée, and she drew out some French banknotes as
she spoke. Never had the bitterness of poverty smitten him
as it smote him now when this young patrician offered him
her gold! Old habits vanquished; he forgot who and where
he now was; he bowed as in other days he had used to bow
in the circle of St. James'.

"Is—the honor of your acceptance, if you will deign to
give that."

He forgot that he was not as he once had been. He forgot that he stood but as a private of the French army before
an aristocrat whose name he had never heard.

She turned and looked at him, which she had never done
before, so absorbed had she been in the chessmen, and so
little did a Chasseur of the ranks pass into her thoughts.
There was an extreme of surprise, there was something of
offense, and there was still more of coldness in her glance;
a proud, languid, astonished coldness of regard, though it
softened slightly as she saw that he had spoken in all courtesy
of intent.

She bent her graceful, regal head.

"I thank you. Your very clever work can, of course, only be mine by purchase."

And with that she laid aside the White King among his little troop of ivory Arabs and floated onward with her friends. Cecil's face paled slightly under the mellow tint left there by the desert sun and the desert wind; he swept the chessmen into their walnut case and thrust them out of sight under his knapsack.

"What a fool I am still!" he thought, as he made his way out of the barrack room. "I might have fairly forgotten by this time that I ever had the rights of a gentleman."

CHAPTER XIII.

CIGARETTE EN CONSEIL ET CACHETTE.

"CORPORAL VICTOR, M. le Commandant desires you to present yourself at his campagne to-night, at ten precisely, with all your carvings; above all, with the chessmen."

The swift, sharp voice of a young officer of his regiment wakened Cecil from his musing, as he went on his way down the crowded, tortuous, stifling street. He had scarcely time to catch the sense of the words, and to halt, giving the salute, before the Chasseur's skittish little Barbary mare had galloped past him.

Cecil involuntarily stood still. His face darkened. All orders that touched on the service, even where harshest and most unwelcome, he had taught himself to take without any hesitation, till he now scarcely felt the check of the steel curb; but to be ordered thus like a lackey—to take his wares thus like a hawker!

"Ah, ma cantche! We are soldiers, not traders—aren't we? You don't like that, M. Victor? You are no peddler—eh? And you think you would rather risk being court-martialed and shot than take your ivory toys for the Black Hawk's talons?"

Cecil glanced up in astonishment at the divination and translation of his thoughts, to encounter the bright, falcon eyes of Cigarette looking down on him from a little oval casement above, dark as pitch within, and whose embrasure, with its rim of gray stone coping, set off like a picture-frame, with a heavy background of unglazed Rembrandt shadow, the piquant head of the Friend of the Flag.

"You will go to your Colonel's to-night?" she said questioningly.

She repeated her question imperiously, as Cecil kept silent: "You will go to-night?"

He shrugged his shoulders. He did not care to discuss his Colonel's orders with this pretty little Bacchante.

"Oh, a chief's command, you know——"

"A fico for a chief!" retorted Cigarette impatiently. "Why don't you say the truth? You are thinking you will disobey, and risk the rest!"

"Well, why not? I grant his right in barrack and field, but——"

"But?" echoed Cigarette, leaning out of her oval hole, perched in the quaint, gray Moresco wall, parti-colored with broken encaustics of varied hues. "Chut, bon camerade! that little word has been the undoing of the world ever since the world began. 'But' is a blank cartridge, and never did anything but miss fire yet. Shoot dead, or don't aim at all, whichever you like; but never make a coup manqué with 'but'! So you won't obey Châteauroy in this?"

He was silent again. He would not answer falsely, and he did not care to say his thoughts to her.

"'No,'" pursued Cigarette, translating his silence at her fancy, "you say to yourself, 'I am an aristocrat—I will not be ordered in this thing'—you say, 'I am a good soldier; I will not be sent for like a hawker'—you say, 'I was noble once; I will show my blood at last, if I die!' Ah!—you say that!"

He laughed a little as he looked up at her.

"Not exactly that, but something as foolish, perhaps. Are you a witch, my pretty one?"

"I am a witch! That is, I can put two and two together, and read men, though I don't read the alphabet. Well, one reading is a good deal rarer than the other. So you mean to disobey the Hawk to-night? I like you for that."

"But if you mutiny once, they will shoot you, and you will die."

"Well," he answered her slowly, "why not? Death is no great terror; I risk it every day for the sake of a common soldier's rations; why should I not chance it for the sake and in the defense of my honor?"

"Bah! men sell their honor for their daily bread all the world over!" said Cigarette, with the satire that had treble raciness from the slang in which she clothed it. "But it is not you alone. See here—one example set on your part, and half your regiment will mutiny too. It is bitter work to obey the Black Hawk, and if you give the signal of revolt, three parts of your comrades will join you. Now what will that end in, beau lion—eh?"

"Tell me—you are a soldier yourself, you say."

"Yes, I am a soldier!" said Cigarette between her tight-set teeth, while her eyes brightened, and her voice sank down into a whisper that had a certain terrible meaning in it, like the first dropping of the scattered, opening shots in the distance before a great battle commences; "and I have seen war, not holiday war, but war in earnest. Oh, yes! I am a soldier, and I will tell you one thing I have seen. I have seen soldiers mutiny, a squadron of them, because they hated their chief and loved two of their sous-officers; and I have seen the end of it all—a few hundred men, blind and drunk with despair, at bay against as many thousand, and walled in with four lines of steel and artillery, and fired on from a score of cannon-mouths—volley on volley, like the thunder—till not one living man was left, and there was only a shapeless, heaving, moaning mass, with the black smoke over all. That is what I have seen; you will not make me see it again?"

Her face was very earnest, very eloquent, very dark, and tender with thought; there was a vein of grave, even of intense feeling, that ran through the significant words to which tone and accent lent far more meaning than lay in their mere phrases; the little bohemian lost her insolence when she pleaded for her "children," her comrades; and the mischievous pet of the camp never treated lightly what touched the France that she loved—the France that, alone of all things in her careless life, she held in honor and reverence.

"You will not make me see it again?" she said, once more leaning out, with her eyes, that were like a brown brook sparkling deep, yet bright in the sun, fixed on him. "They would rise at your bidding, and they would be mowed down like corn. You will not?"

"Never! I give you my word."

The promise was from his heart.

"C'est ça, tu es bon soldat!"

He bent over the hand she held to his in the courtesy natural with him to all her sex, and touched it lightly with his lips.

"Thank you, my little comrade," he said simply, with the graver thought still on him that her relation and her entreaty had evoked; "you have given me a lesson that I shall not be quick to forget."

Cecil thought that a gallant boy was spoiled in this eighteen-year-old brunette of a campaigner; he might have gone further and said that a hero was lost.

"Voilà!" said Cigarette between her little teeth.

She stood in the glittering Algerine night, brilliant with a million stars, and balmy with a million flowers, before the bronze trellised gate of the villa on the Sahel, where Châteauroy, when he was not on active service indemnified himself, with the magnificence that his private fortune enabled him to enjoy, for the unsparing exertions and the rugged privations that he always shared willingly with the lowest of his soldiers.

To-night the windows of the pretty, low, snow-white, far-stretching building were lighted and open.

"Ah, bah!" she muttered as she pressed her pretty lips to the lattice-work.

She looked a moment longer through the gilded scroll-work; then, as she had done once before, thrust her pistols well within her sash that they should not catch upon the boughs, and pushing herself through the prickly cactus hedge, impervious to anything save herself or a Barbary marmoset, twisted with marvelous ingenuity through the sharp-pointed leaves, and the close barriers of spines, and launched herself with inimitable dexterity on to the other side of the cacti.

She crossed the breadth of the grounds under the heavy shade of arbutus trees with a hare's fleetness, and stood a second looking at the open windows and the terraces that lay before them, brightly lighted by the summer moon and by the lamps that sparkled among the shrubs.

"Ah!" she said, quickly and sharply, with a deep-drawn breath.

Yet all she saw was a small and brilliant group sauntering to and fro before the open windows, after dinner, listening to the bands, which, through dinner, had played to them, and laughing low and softly; and, at some distance from them, beneath the shade of a cedar, the figure of a Corporal of Chasseurs,—calm, erect, motionless,—as though he were the figure of a soldier cast in bronze. The scene was simple enough, though very picturesque; but it told, by its vivid force of contrast, a whole history to Cigarette.

"A true soldier!" she muttered, where she lay among the rhododendrons, while her eyes grew very soft, as she gave the highest word of praise that her whole range of language held. "A true soldier! How he keeps his promise! But it must be bitter!"

She looked a while, very wistfully, at the Chasseur, where he stood under the Lebanon boughs; then her glance swept bright as a hawk's over the terrace, and lighted with a prescient hatred on the central form of all—a woman's. There were two other great ladies there; but she passed them, and darted with unerring instinct on that proud, fair, patrician head, with its haughty, stag-like carriage and the crown of its golden hair.

Crouched there among the rhododendrons, she lay as still as a mouse, moving nearer and nearer, until her ear, quick and unerring as an Indian's, could detect the sense of the words spoken by that group, which so aroused all the hot ire of her warrior's soul and her democrat's impatience. Châteauroy himself was bending his fine, dark head toward the patrician on whom her instinct of sex had fastened her hatred.

"You expressed your wish to see my Corporal's little sculptures again, madame," he was murmuring now, as Cigarette got close enough under her flower shadows to catch the sense of the words. "To hear was to obey with me. He waits your commands yonder."

"Mille tonneres! It was you, was it, brought him here?" muttered the Friend of the Flag to herself, with the passion in her burning more hotly against that "silver pheasant," whose delicate train was sweeping the white marbles of Châteauroy's terraces, and whose reply, "with fashion, not with feeling, softly freighted," she lost, though she could guess what it had been, when a lackey crossed the lawn, and summoned the Chasseur from his waiting-place beneath the cedars.

Cecil obeyed, passed up the terrace stairs, and stood before his Colonel, giving the salute.

Châteauroy spoke with a carelessness as of a man to a dog, turning to his Corporal.

"Victor, Mme. la Princesse honors you with the desire to see your toys again. Spread them out."

The savage authority of his general speech was softened

for sake of his guest's presence, but there was a covert tone in the words that made Cigarette murmur to herself:

"If he forget his promise, I will forgive him!"

Cecil had not forgotten it; neither had he forgotten the lesson that this fair aristocrate had read him in the morning. He saluted his chief silently, set the chessbox down upon the ledge of the marble balustrade, and stood silent, without once glancing at the fair and haughty face that was more brilliant still in the African starlight than it had been in the noon sun of the Chasseurs' Chambrée.

The carvings were passed from hand to hand as the Marquis' six or eight guests, listlessly willing to be amused in the warmth of the evening after their dinner, occupied themselves with the ivory chess armies, cut with a skill and a finish worthy a Roman studio. Praise enough was awarded to the art, but none of them remembered the artist, who stood apart, grave, calm, with a certain serene dignity that could not be degraded because others chose to treat him as the station he filled gave them fit right to do.

Only one glanced at him with a touch of wondering pity, softening her pride; she who had rejected the gift of those mimic squadrons.

"You were surely a sculptor once?" she asked him with that graceful, distant kindness which she might have shown some Arab outcast.

"Never, madame."

"Indeed! Then who taught you such exquisite art?"

"It cannot claim to be called art, madame."

She looked at him with an increased interest: the accent of his voice told her that this man, whatever he might be now, had once been a gentleman.

"Oh, yes; it is perfect of its kind. Who was your master in it?"

"A common teacher, madame—Necessity."

There was a very sweet gleam of compassion in the luster of her dark, dreaming eyes.

"Does necessity often teach so well?"

"In the ranks of our army, madame, I think it does—often, indeed, much better."

Châteauroy had stood by and heard, with as much impatience as he cared to show before guests whose rank was precious to the man who had still weakness enough to be ashamed that his father's brave and famous life had first been cradled under the thatch roof of a little posting-house.

"Victor knows that neither he nor his men have any right to waste their time on such trash," he said carelessly; "but the truth is they love the canteen so well that they will do anything to add enough to their pay to buy brandy."

She whom he had called Mme. la Princesse looked with a doubting surprise at the sculptor of the white Arab King she held.

"That man does not carve for brandy," she thought.

"It must be a solace to many a weary hour in the barracks to be able to produce such beautiful trifles as these?" she said aloud. "Surely you encourage such pursuits, monsieur?"

"Not I," said Châteauroy, with a dash of his camp tone that he could not withhold. "There are but two arts or virtues for a trooper to my taste—fighting and obedience."

"You should be in the Russian service, M. de Châteauroy," said the lady with a smile, that, slight as it was, made the Marquis' eyes flash fire.

"Almost I wish I had been," he answered her; "men are made to keep their grades there, and privates who think themselves fine gentlemen receive the lash they merit."

"How he hates his Corporal!" thought Miladi, while she laid aside the White King once more.

"Nay," interposed Châteauroy, recovering his momentary self-abandonment, "since you like the bagatelles, do me honor enough to keep them."

"Oh, no! I offered your soldier his own price for them this morning, and he refused any."

Châteauroy swung round.

"Ah, sacripant! you dared refuse your bits of ivory when you were honored by an offer for them."

Cecil stood silent; his eyes met his chief's steadily; Châteauroy had seen that look when his Chasseur had bearded him in the solitude of his tent, and demanded back the Pearl of the Desert.

The Princess glanced at both; then she stooped her elegant head slightly to the Marquis.

"Do not blame your Corporal unjustly through me, I pray you. He refused any price, but he offered them to me very gracefully as a gift, though of course it was not possible that I should accept them so."

"The man is the most insolent larron in the service," muttered her host, as he motioned Cecil back off the terrace. "Get you gone, sir, and leave your toys here, or I will have them broken up by a hammer."

The words were low, that they should not offend the ears of the great ladies who were his listeners; but they were coarsely savage in their whispered command, and the Princess heard them.

"He has brought his Chasseur here only to humiliate him," thought Miladi, with the same thought that flashed through the mind of the little Friend of the Flag where she hid among her rhododendrons. Now the dainty aristocrat was very proud, but she was not so proud but that justice was stronger in her than pride; and a noble, generous temper mellowed the somewhat too cold and languid negligence of one of the fairest and haughtiest women that ever adorned a court.

"Wait," she said, while she let her eyes rest on the carver of the sculptures with a grave compassion, though she addressed his chief. "You wholly mistake me. I laid no blame whatever on your Corporal. Let him take the chessmen back with him; I would on no account rob him of them. I can well understand that he does not care to part with such masterpieces of his art; and that he would not appraise them by their worth in gold only shows that he is a true artist, as doubtless also he is a true soldier."

The words were spoken with a gracious courtesy; the clear, cold tone of her habitual manner just marking in them still the difference of caste between her and the man for whom she interceded, as she would equally have interceded for a dog who should have been threatened with the lash because he had displeased her. That very tone struck a sharper blow to Cecil than the insolence of his commander had power to deal him. His face flushed a little; he lifted his cap to her with a grave reverence, and moved away.

"I thank you, madame. Keep them, if you will so far honor me."

The words reached only her ear. In another instant he had passed away down the terrace steps, obedient to his chief's dismissal.

"Ah! have no kind scruples in keeping them, madame," Châteauroy laughed to her, as she still held in her hand, doubtfully, the White Sheik of the chess Arabs; "I will see that Bel-à-faire-peur, as they call him, does not suffer by losing these trumperies, which, I believe, old Zist-et-Zest, a veteran of ours and a wonderful carver, had really far more to do with producing than he. You must not let your gracious pity be moved by such fellows as these troopers of mine; they are the most ingenious rascals in the world, and know as well how to produce a dramatic effect in your presence as they do how to drink and to swear when they are out of it."

"Very possibly," she said, with an indolent indifference; "but that man was no actor, and I never saw a gentleman if he have not been one."

"Like enough," answered the Marquis. "I believe many 'gentlemen' come in our ranks who have fled their native countries and broken all laws from the Decalogue to the Code Napoleon. So long as they fight well, we don't ask their past criminalities. We cannot afford to throw away a good sabreur because he has made his own land too hot to hold him."

"Of what country is your Corporal, then?"

"I have not an idea. I imagine his past must have been something very black indeed, for the slightest trace of it has never, that I know of, been allowed to let slip from him. He encourages the men in every insubordination, buys their favor with every sort of stage trick, thinks himself the finest gentleman in the whole brigades of Africa, and ought to have been shot long ago, if he had had his real deserts."

She let her glance dwell on him with a contemplation that was half contemptuous amusement, half unexpressed dissent.

"I wonder he has not been, since you have the ruling of his fate," she said, with a slight smile lingering about the proud, rich softness of her lips.

"So do I."

There was a gaunt, grim, stern significance in the three monosyllables that escaped him unconsciously; it made her turn and look at him more closely.

"How has he offended you?" she asked.

Châteauroy laughed off the question.

"In a thousand ways, madame. Chiefly because I received my regimental training under one who followed the traditions of the Armies of Egypt and the Rhine, and have, I confess, little tolerance, in consequence, of a rebel who plays the martyr, and a soldier who is too effeminate an idler to do anything except attitudinize in interesting situations to awaken sympathy."

She listened with something of distaste upon her face where she still leaned against the marble balustrade, toying with the ivory Bedouins.

"I am not much interested in military discussions," she said coldly, "but I imagine—if you will pardon me for saying so—that you do your Corporal some little injustice here. I should not fancy he 'affects' anything, to judge from the very good tone of his manners. For the rest, I shall not keep the chessmen without making him fitting payment for them; since he declines money, you will tell me what form that had better take to be of real and welcome service to a Chasseur d'Afrique."

Châteauroy, more incensed than he chose or dared to show, bowed courteously, but with a grim, ironic smile.

"If you really insist, give him a Napoleon or two whenever you see him; he will be very happy to take it and spend it au cabaret, though he played the aristocrat to-day. But you are too good to him, he is one of the very worst of my pratiques; and you are as cruel to me in refusing to deign to accept my trooper's worthless bagatelles at my hands."

She bent her superb head silently, whether in acquiescence or rejection he could not well resolve with himself, and turned to the staff officers, among them the heir of a princely semi-royal French House, who surrounded her, and sorely begrudged the moments she had given to those miniature carvings and the private soldier who had wrought them. She was no coquette; she was of too imperial a nature, had too lofty a pride, and was too difficult to charm or to enchain; but those meditative, brilliant, serene eyes had a terrible gift of wakening without ever seeking love, and of drawing without ever recompensing homage.

Crouched down among her rose-hued covert, Cigarette had watched and heard; her teeth set tightly, her breath coming and going swiftly, her hand clinched close on the butts of her pistols; fiery curses, with all the infinite variety in cursing of a barrack répertoire, chasing one another in hot, fast mutterings off those bright lips, that should have known nothing except a child's careless and innocent song.

"Comme elle est belle! comme elle est belle!" she whispered every now and then to herself, with a new, bitter, serious meaning in the whisper that had, with all its hate, something pathetic too.

"I know what he meant now!" she pondered, and her spirited, sparkling, brunette face was dark and weary, like a brown, sun-lightened brook over whose radiance the heavy shadow of some broad-spread eagle's wings hovers, hiding the sun.

She looked once, twice, thrice, more inquiringly, envyingly, thirstily; then, as the band under the cedars rolled out their music afresh, and light laughter echoed to her from the terrace, she turned and wound herself back under the cover of the shrubs; not joyously and mischievously as she had come, but almost as slowly, almost as sadly, as a hare that the greyhounds have coursed drags itself through the grasses and ferns.

Once through the cactus hedge her old spirit returned; she shook herself angrily with petulant self-scorn; she swore a little, and felt that the fierce, familiar words did her good like brandy poured down her throat; she tossed her head like a colt that rebels against the gall of the curb; then, fleet as a fawn, she dashed down the moonlit road at topmost speed. "Diantre! she can't do what I do!" she thought.

And she ran the faster, and sang a drinking-song of the Spahis all the louder, because still at her heart a dull pain was aching.

CHAPTER XIV.

THE MISTRESS OF THE WHITE KING.

CECIL, having watered, fed, and littered down his tired horse, made his way to a little café he commonly frequented, and spent the few sous he could afford on an iced draught of lemon-flavored drink. Eat he could not; overfatigue had given him a nausea for food. He could not stay in the café; it was the hour of dinner for many, and the odors, joined with the noise, were insupportable to him.

A few doors farther in the street, which was chiefly of Jewish and Moslem shops, there was a quaint place kept by an old Moor, who had some of the rarest and most beautiful treasures of Algerian workmanship in his long, dark, silent chambers. With this old man Cecil had something of a friendship; he had protected him one day from the mockery and outrage of some drunken Indigènes, and the Moor, warmly grateful, was ever ready to give him a cup of coffee and a hubble-bubble in the stillness of his dwelling. Its resort was sometimes welcome to him as the one spot, quiet and noiseless, to which he could escape out of the continuous turmoil of street and of barrack, and he went thither now. He found the old man sitting cross-legged behind his counter; a noble-looking, aged Mussulman, with a long beard like white silk, with cashmeres and broidered stuffs of peerless texture hanging above his head, and all around him things of silver, of gold, of ivory, of amber, of feathers, of bronze, of emeralds, of ruby, of beryl, whose rich colors glowed through the darkness.

"No coffee, no sherbet; thanks, good father," said Cecil, in answer to the Moor's hospitable entreaties. "Give me only license to sit in the quiet here. I am very tired."

"Sit and be welcome, my son," said Ben Arsli. "Whom should this roof shelter in honor, if not thee? Musjid shall bring thee the supreme solace."

The supreme solace was a nargilé, and its great bowl of rose-water was soon set down by the little Moorish lad at Cecil's side. Whether fatigue really weighted his eyes with slumber, or whether the soothing sedative of the pipe had its influence, he had not sat long in the perfect stillness of the Moor's shop before the narrow view of the street under the awning without was lost to him, the luster and confusion of shadowy hues swam a while before his eyes, the throbbing pain in his temples grew duller, and he slept—the heavy, dreamless sleep of intense exhaustion.

Ben Arsli glanced at him, and bade Musjid be very quiet. Half an hour or more passed; none had entered the place. The grave old Moslem was half slumbering himself, when there came a delicate odor of perfumed laces, a delicate rustle of silk swept the floor; a lady's voice asked the price of an ostrich-egg superbly mounted in gold. Ben Arsli opened his eyes—the Chasseur slept on; the newcomer was one of those great ladies who now and then winter in Algeria.

Her carriage waited without; she was alone, making purchase of those innumerable splendid trifles with which Algiers is rife, while she drove through the town in the cooler hour before the sun sank into the western sea.

The Moor rose instantly, with profound salaams, before her, and began to spread before her the richest treasures of his stock. Under plea of the light, he remained near the entrance with her; money was dear to him, and must not be lost, but he would make it, if he could, without awakening the tired soldier.

A roll of notes had passed from her hand to the Moslem's, and she was about to glide out to her carriage, when a lamp which hung at the farther end caught her fancy. It was very singular; a mingling of colored glass, silver, gold, and ivory being wrought in with much beauty in its formation.

"Is that for sale?" she inquired.

As he answered in the affirmative, she moved up the shop, and, her eyes being lifted to the lamp, had drawn close to Cecil before she saw him. When she did so, she paused near in astonishment.

"Is that soldier asleep?"

"He is, madame," softly answered the old man, in his slow, studied French. "He comes here to rest sometimes out of the noise; he was very tired to-day, and I think ill, would he have confessed it."

"Indeed!" Her eyes fell on him with compassion.

"He is a Chasseur d'Afrique?" she asked the Moslem.

"Yes, madame. I think—he must have been something very different some day."

She did not answer; she stood with her thoughtful eyes gazing on the worn-out soldier.

"He saved me once, madame, at much risk to himself, from the savagery of some Turcos," the old man went on. "Of course he is always welcome under my roof. The companionship he has must be bitter to him, I fancy; they do say he would have had his officer's grade, and the cross, too, long before now, if it were not for his Colonel's hatred."

"Ah! I have seen him before now; he carves in ivory. I suppose he has a good sale for those things with you?"

The Moor looked up in amazement.

"In ivory, madame?—he? Allah-il-Allah! I never heard of it. It is strange——"

"Very strange. Doubtless you would have given him a good price for them?"

"Surely I would; any price he should have wished. Do I not owe him my life?"

At that moment little Musjid let fall a valuable coffee-tray, inlaid with amber; his master, with muttered apology, hastened to the scene of accident; the noise startled Cecil, and his eyes unclosed to all the dreamy, fantastic colors of the place, and met those bent on him in musing pity—saw that lustrous, haughty, delicate head bending slightly down through the many-colored shadows.

He thought he was dreaming, yet on instinct he rose, staggering slightly, for sharp pain was still darting through his head and temples.

"Madame! pardon me! Was I sleeping?"

"You were, and rest again. You look ill," she said gently, and there was, for a moment, less of that accent in her voice, which the night before had marked so distinctly, so pointedly, the line of demarcation between a Princess of Spain and a soldier of Africa.

"I thank you; I ail nothing."

He had no sense that he did, in the presence of that face which had the beauty of his old life; under the charm of that voice which had the music of his buried years.

"I fear that is scarcely true!" she answered him. "You look in pain; though as a soldier, perhaps, you will not own it?"

"A headache from the sun—no more, madame."

He was careful not again to forget the social gulf which yawned between them.

"That is quite bad enough! Your service must be severe?"

"In Africa, Miladi, one cannot expect indulgence."

"I suppose not. You have served long?"

"Twelve years, madame."

"And your name?"

"Louis Victor."

She entered it in the little book from which she had taken her banknotes.

"I may be able to serve you," she said, as she wrote. "I will speak of you to the Marshal; and when I return to Paris, I may have an opportunity to bring your name before the Emperor. He is as rapid as his uncle to reward military merit; but he has not his uncle's opportunities for personal observation of his soldiers."

The color flushed his forehead.

"You do me much honor," he said rapidly, "but if you would gratify me, madame, do not seek to do anything of the kind."

"And why? Do you not even desire the cross?"

"I desire nothing, except to be forgotten."

"You seek what others dread then?"

"It may be so. At any rate, if you would serve me, madame, never say what can bring me into notice."

She regarded him with much surprise, with some slight sense of annoyance; she had bent far in tendering her influence at the French court to a private soldier, and his rejection of it seemed as ungracious as it was inexplicable.

At that moment the Moor joined them.

"Miladi was about to purchase that lamp?" asked Cecil. "Her Highness will not find anything like it in all Algiers."

The lamp was taken down, and the conversation turned from himself.

"May I bear it to your carriage, madame?" he asked, as she moved to leave, having made it her own, while her footman carried out the smaller articles she had bought to the equipage. She bowed in silence; she was very exclusive, she was not wholly satisfied with herself for having conversed thus with a Chasseur d'Afrique in a Moor's bazaar. Still, she vaguely felt pity for this man; she equally vaguely desired to serve him.

"Wait, M. Victor!" she said, as he closed the door of her carriage. "I accepted your chessmen last night, but you are very certain that it is impossible I can retain them on such terms."

A shadow darkened his face.

"Let your dogs break them then, madame. They shall not come back to me."

"You mistake—I did not mean that I would send them back. I simply desire to offer you some equivalent for them. There must be something that you wish for?—something which would be acceptable to you in the life you lead?"

"I have already named the only thing I desire."

He had been solicitous to remember and sustain the enormous difference in their social degrees; but at the offer of her gifts, of her patronage, of her recompense, the pride of his old life rose up to meet her own.

"To be forgotten? A sad wish! Nay, surely life in a regiment of Africa cannot be so cloudless that it can create in you no other?"

"It is not. I have another."

"Then tell it to me; it shall be gratified."

"It is to enjoy a luxury long ago lost forever. It is—to be allowed to give the slight courtesy of a gentleman without being tendered the wage of a servant."

She understood him; she was moved, too, by the inflexion of his voice. She was not so cold, not so negligent, as the world called her.

"I had passed my word to grant it; I cannot retract," she answered him, after a pause. "I will press nothing more on you. But—as an obligation to me—can you find no way in which a rouleau of gold would benefit your men?"

"No way that I can take it for them. But, if you care indeed to do them a charity, a little wine, a little fruit, a few flowers (for there are those among them who love flowers), sent to the hospital, will bring many benedictions on your name, madame. They lie in infinite misery there!"

"I will remember," she said simply, while a thoughtful sadness passed over her brilliant face. "Adieu, M. le Caporal; and if you should think better of your choice, and will allow your name to be mentioned by me to his Majesty, send me word through my people. There is my card."

The carriage whirled away down the crooked street. He stood under the tawny awning of the Moorish house, with the thin, glazed card in his hand. On it was printed:

"Mme. la Princesse Corona d'Amagüe,
"Hôtel Corona, Paris."

In the corner was written, "Villa Aïaussa, Algiers." He thrust it in the folds of his sash, and turned within.

"Do you know her?" he asked Ben Arsli.

The old man shook his head.

"She is the most beautiful of thy many fair Frankish women. I never saw her till to-day. She seemed to have an interest in thee, my son. But listen here. Touching these ivory toys—if thou dost not bring henceforth to me all the work in them that thou doest, thou shalt never come here more to meet the light of her eyes."

Cecil smiled and pressed the Moslem's hand.

"I kept them away because you would have given me a hundred piasters for what had not been worth one. As for her eyes, they are stars that shine on another world than an African trooper's. So best!"

Mme. la Princesse passed from her carriage to her own morning room and sank down on a couch.

She took the White King in her hand and gazed at it with a certain interest.

"That man has been noble once," she thought. "What a fate—what a cruel fate! How bitter his life must be!" she mused. "When Philip comes, perhaps he will show some way to aid him. And yet—who can serve a man who only desires to be forgotten?"

Then, with a certain impatient sense of some absurd discrepancy, of some unseemly occupation, in her thus dwelling on the wishes and the burdens of a sous-officier of Light Cavalry, she laughed a little, and put the White Chief back once more in his place.

She left the chess-table and went onward to the dressing and bath and bed chambers, which opened in one suite from her boudoir, and resigned herself to the hands of her attendants for her dinner toilet.

The Moslem had said aright of her beauty; and now, as her splendid hair was unloosened and gathered up afresh with a crescent-shaped comb of gold that was not brighter than the tresses themselves, the brilliant, haughty, thoughtful face was of a truth, as he had said, the fairest that had ever come from the Frankish shores to the hot African sea-board. Many beside the old Moslem had thought it "the fairest that e'er the sun shone on," and held one grave, lustrous glance of the blue imperial eyes above aught else on earth. Many had loved her—all without return. Yet, although only twenty years had passed over her proud head, the Princess Corona d'Amagüe had been wedded and been widowed.

Wedded, with no other sentiment than that of a certain pity and a certain honor for the man whose noble Spanish name she took. Widowed, by a death that was the seal of her marriage sacrament, and left her his wife only in name and law.

The marriage had left no chain upon her; it had only made her mistress of wide wealth, of that villa on the Sicilian Sea, of that light, spacious palace-dwelling in Paris that bore her name, of that vast majestic old castle throned on brown Estremaduran crags, and looking down on mighty woods of cork and chestnut, and flashing streams of falling water hurling through the gorges. The death had left no regret upon her; it only gave her for a while a graver shadow over the brilliancy of her youth and of her beauty, and gave her for always—or for so long, at least, as she so chose to use it —a plea for that indifference to men's worship of her which their sex called heartlessness; which her own sex thought an ultra-refined coquetry; and which was, in real truth, neither the one nor the other, but simply the negligence of a woman very difficult to touch, and, as it had seemed, impossible to charm.

A great French painter once, in Rome, looking on her from a distance, shaded his eyes with his hand, as if her beauty, like the sun, dazzled him. "Exquisite—superb!" he muttered; and he was a man whose own ideals were so matchless that living women rarely could wring out his praise. "She is nearly perfect, your Princess Corona!"

"Nearly!" cried a Roman sculptor. "What, in Heaven's name, can she want?"

"Only one thing!"

"And that is——"

"To have loved."

Wherewith he turned into the Greco.

He had found the one flaw—and it was still there. What he missed in her was still wanting.

CHAPTER XV.

"MILADI AUX BEAUX YEUX BLEUS."

EARLY the next morning Cecil, with some of the rough-riders of his regiment, was sent far into the interior to bring in a string of colts, bought of a friendly desert tribe, and destined to be shipped to France for the Imperial Haras. The mission took two days; early on the third day they returned with the string of wild young horses, whom it had taken not a little exertion and address to conduct successfully through the country into Algiers.

Châteauroy was himself present when the colts were taken into the stable-yard; and himself inquired, without the medium of any third person, the whole details of the sale and of the transit. It was impossible, with all his inclination, to find any fault either with the execution of the errand or with the brief, respectful answers by which his corporal replied to his rapid and imperious cross-questionings. There were a great number of men within hearing, many of them the most daring and rebellious pratiques of the regiment; and Cecil would have let the coarsest upbraidings scourge him rather than put the temptation to mutiny in their way which one insubordinate or even not strictly deferential word from him would have given. Hence the inspection passed off peaceably; as the Marquis turned on his heel, however, he paused a moment.

"Victor!"

"Mon Commandant?"

"I have not forgotten your insolence, with those ivory toys. But Mme. la Princesse herself has deigned to solicit that it shall be passed over unpunished. She cannot, of course, yield to your impertinent request to remain also unpaid for them. I charged myself with the fulfillment of her wishes. You deserve the matraque, but since Miladi herself is lenient enough to pardon you, you are to take this instead. Hold your hand, sir!"

Cecil put out his hand; he expected to receive a heavy blow from his commander's saber, that possibly might break the wrist. These little trifles were common in Africa.

Instead, a rouleau of Napoleons was laid on his open palm. Châteauroy knew the gold would sting more than the blow.

For the moment Cecil had but one impulse—to dash the pieces in the giver's face. In time to restrain the impulse, he caught sight of the wild, eager hatred gleaming in the eyes of Rake, of Petit Picpon, of a score of others, who loved him and cursed their Colonel, and would at one signal from him have sheathed their swords in the mighty frame of the Marquis, though they should have been fired down the next moment themselves for the murder. The warning of Cigarette came to his memory; his hand clasped on the gold; he gave the salute calmly as Châteauroy swung himself away.

Rather unconsciously than by premeditation his steps turned through the streets that led to his old familiar haunt, the As de Pique; and dropping down on a bench under the awning, he asked for a draught of water. It was brought him at once; the hostess, a quick, brown little woman from Paris, whom the lovers of Eugène Sue called Rigolette, adding of her own accord a lump of ice and a slice or two of lemon, for which she vivaciously refused payment, though generosity was by no means her cardinal virtue.

He did not look at the newspapers she offered him; but sat gazing out from the tawny awning, like the sail of a Neapolitan felucca, down the checkered shadows and the many-colored masses of the little, crooked, rambling, semi-barbaric alley. He was thinking of the Napoleons in his sash and of the promise he had pledged to Cigarette. That he would keep it he was resolved.

The heavy folds of a Bedouin's haick, brushing the papers off the bench, broke the thread of his musings. As he stooped for them, he saw that one was an English journal some weeks old. His own name caught his eye—the name buried so utterly, whose utterance in the Sheik's tent had struck him like a dagger's thrust. The flickering light and

darkness, as the awning waved to and fro, made the lines
move dizzily upward and downward as he read—read the
short paragraph touching the fortunes of the race that had
disowned him:

"The Royallieu Succession.—We regret to learn that the
Rt. Hon. Viscount Royallieu, who so lately succeeded to the
family title on his father's death, has expired at Mentone,
whither his health had induced him to go some months
previous. The late Lord was unmarried. His next brother
was, it will be remembered, many years ago, killed on a
southern railway. The title, therefore, now falls to the
third and only remaining son, the Hon. Berkeley Cecil, who,
having lately inherited considerable properties from a distant
relative, will, we believe, revive all the old glories of this
Peerage, which have, from a variety of causes, lost somewhat
of their ancient brilliancy."

Cecil sat quite still, as he had sat looking down on the
record of his father's death, when Cigarette had rallied him
with her gay challenge among the Moresco ruins. His face
flushed hotly under the warm, golden hue of the desert
bronze, then lost all its color as suddenly, till it was as pale
as any of the ivory he carved. The letters of the paper
reeled and wavered, and grew misty before his eyes; he lost
all sense of the noisy, changing, polyglot crowd thronging
past him; he, a common soldier in the Algerian Cavalry, knew
that, by every law of birthright, he was now a Peer of
England.

He rose with a sudden impulse, with a proud, bold instinct
of birth and freedom. Let him stand here in what grade
he would, with the badge of a Corporal of the Army of
Africa on his arm, this inheritance that had come to him
was his; he bore the name and the title of his house as
surely as any had ever borne it since the first of the Norman
owners of Royallieu had followed the Bastard's banner

His hand touched the thirty gold pieces in his sash.

He started, as the recollection of the forgotten insult came
back on him. He stood a while in thought; then he took
his resolve.

A half hour of quick movement, for he had become used
to the heat as an Arab and heeded it as little, brought him
before the entrance-gates of the Villa Aïoussa. A native of
Soudan, in a rich dress, who had the office of porter, asked

him politely his errand. Every indigène learns by hard experience to be courteous to a French soldier. Cecil simply asked, in answer, if Mme. la Princesse were visible. The negro returned cautiously that she was at home, but doubted her being accessible. "You come from M. le Marquis?" he inquired.

"No; on my own errand."

"You!" Not all the native African awe of a Roumi could restrain the contemptuous amaze in the word.

"I. Ask if Corporal Victor, of the Chasseurs, can be permitted a moment's interview with your mistress. I come by permission," he added, as the native hesitated between his fear of a Roumi and his sense of the appalling unfittingness of a private soldier seeking audience of a Spanish princess. The message was passed about between several of the household; at last a servant of higher authority appeared:

"Madame permitted Corporal Victor to be taken to her presence. Would he follow?"

He uncovered his head and entered, passing through several passages and chambers, richly hung and furnished. A singular sensation came on him, half of familiarity, half of strangeness, as he advanced along them; for twelve years he had seen nothing but the bare walls of barrack rooms, the goat-skin of douars, and the canvas of his own camp-tent. To come once more, after so long an interval, amid the old things of luxury and grace that had been so long unseen wrought curiously on him. He could not fairly disentangle past and present.

His spur caught in the yielding carpet, and his saber clashed slightly against it; as the rentrée au caserne had done an hour before, the sound recalled the actual present to him. He was but a French soldier, who went on sufferance into the presence of a great lady. All the rest was dead and buried.

Some half dozen apartments, large and small, were crossed; then into that presence he was ushered.

She moved forward as her servant announced him.

"You have come, I trust, to withdraw your prohibition? Nothing will give me greater pleasure than to bring his Majesty's notice to one of the best soldiers his Army holds."

There was that in the words, gently as they were spoken, that recalled him suddenly to himself; they had that negligent, courteous pity she would have shown to some colon begging at her gates! He forgot—forgot utterly—that he was only an African trooper. He only remembered that he had once been a gentleman, that—if a life of honor and of self-negation can make any so—he was one still. He advanced and bowed with the old serene elegance that his bow had once been famed for; and she, well used to be even over-critical in such trifles, thought, "That man has once lived in courts!"

"Pardon me, madame, I do not come to trespass so far upon your benignity," he answered, as he bent before her. "I come to express, rather, my regret that you should have made one single error."

"Error!"—a haughty surprise glanced from her eyes as they swept over him. Such a word had never been used to her in the whole course of her brilliant and pampered life of sovereignty and indulgence.

"One common enough, madame, in your Order. The error to suppose that under the rough cloth of a private trooper's uniform there cannot possibly be such aristocratic monopolies as nerves to wound."

"I do not comprehend you." She spoke very coldly; she repented profoundly of her concession in admitting a Chasseur d'Afrique to her presence.

"Possibly not. Mine was the folly to dream that you would ever do so. I should not have intruded on you now, but for this reason: the humiliation you were pleased to pass on me I could neither refuse nor resent to the dealer of it. Had I done so, men who are only too loyal to me would have resented with me, and been thrashed or been shot, as payment. I was compelled to accept it, and to wait until I could return your gift to you. I have no right to complain that you pained me with it, since one who occupies my position ought, I presume, to consider remembrance, even by an outrage, an honor done to him by the Princess Corona."

As he said the last words he laid on a table that stood near him the gold of Châteauroy's insult. She had listened with a bewildering wonder, held in check by the haughtier impulse of offense, that a man in this grade could venture thus to address, thus to arraign her. His words were totally incomprehensible to her, though, by the grave rebuke of his manner, she saw that they were fully meant, and, as he considered, fully authorized by some wrong done to him. As he laid the gold pieces down upon her table, an idea of the truth came to her.

"I know nothing of what you complain of; I sent you no money. What is it you would imply?" she asked him, looking up from where she leaned back in the low couch into whose depth she had sunk as he had spoken.

"You did not send me these? Not as payment for the chess service?"

"Assuredly not. After what you said the other day, I should have scarcely been so ill-bred and so heedless of inflicting pain. Who used my name thus?"

His face lightened with a pleasure and a relief that changed it wonderfully; that brighter look of gladness had been a stranger to it for so many years.

"You give me infinite happiness, madame. You little dream how bitter such slights are where one has lost the power to resent them! It was M. de Châteauroy, who this morning——"

"Dared to tell you I sent you those coins?"

The serenity of a courtly woman of the world was unbroken, but her blue and brilliant eyes darkened and gleamed beneath the sweep of their lashes.

"Perhaps I can scarcely say so much. He gave them, and he implied that he gave them from you. The words he spoke were these."

He told her them as they had been uttered, adding no more; she saw the construction they had been intended to bear, and that which they had borne naturally to his ear; she listened earnestly to the end. Then she turned to him with the exquisite softness of grace which, when she was moved to it, contrasted so vividly with the haughty and almost chill languor of her habitual manner.

"Believe me, I regret deeply that you should have been wounded by this most coarse indignity; I grieve sincerely that through myself in any way it should have been brought upon you. As for the perpetrator of it, M. de Châteauroy will be received here no more; and it shall be my care that he learns not only how I resent his unpardonable use of my name, but how I esteem his cruel outrage to a defender of his own Flag. You did exceedingly well and wisely to acquaint me; in your treatment of it as an affront that I was without warrant to offer you, you showed the just indignation of a soldier, and—of what I am very sure you are—a gentleman."

He bowed low before her.

"Madame, you have made me the debtor of my enemy's outrage. Those words from you are more than sufficient compensation for it."

"A poor one, I fear! Your Colonel is your enemy, then? And wherefore?"

He paused a moment.

"Why, at first, I scarcely know. We are antagonistic, I suppose."

"But is it usual for officers of his high grade to show such malice to their soldiers?"

"Most unusual. In this service especially so; although officers rising from the ranks themselves are more apt to contract prejudices and ill feeling against, as they are to feel favoritism to, their men, than where they enter the regiment in a superior grade at once. At least, that is the opinion I myself have formed; studying the working of the different systems."

"You know the English service, then?"

"I know something of it."

"And still, though thinking this, you prefer the French?"

"I distinctly prefer it, as one that knows how to make fine soldiers and how to reward them; as one in which a brave man will be valued, and a worn-out veteran will not be left to die like a horse at a knacker's."

"A brave man valued, and yet you are a corporal!" thought Miladi, as he pursued:

"Since I am here, madame, let me thank you, in the Army's name, for your infinite goodness in acting so munificently on my slight hint. Your generosity has made many happy hearts in the hospital."

"Generosity! Oh, do not call it by any such name! What did it cost me? We are terribly selfish here. I am indebted to you that for once you made me remember those who suffered."

She spoke with a certain impulse of candor and of self-accusation that broke with great sweetness the somewhat careless coldness of her general manner; it was like a gleam of light that showed all the depth and the warmth that in truth lay beneath that imperious languor of habit. It broke further the ice of distance that severed the grande dame from the cavalry soldier.

At last the conversation turned back to his Chief.

"You seem to be aware of some motive for your commandant's dislike?" she asked him. "Tell me to what you attribute it?"

"It is a long tale, madame."

"No matter; I would hear it."

"I fear it would only weary you."

"Do not fear that. Tell it me?"

He obeyed, and told to her the story of the Emir and of the Pearl of the Desert; and Venetia Corona listened, as she had listened to him throughout, with an interest that she rarely vouchsafed to the recitals and the witticisms of her own circle. He gave to the narrative a soldierly simplicity and a picturesque coloring that lent a new interest to her; and she was of that nature which, however, it may be led to conceal feeling from pride and from hatred, never fails to awaken to indignant sympathy at wrong.

"This barbarian is your chief!" she said, as the tale closed. "His enmity is your honor! I can well credit that he will never pardon your having stood between him and his crime."

"He has never pardoned it yet, of a surety."

"I will not tell you it was a noble action," she said, with a smile sweet as the morning—a smile that few saw light on them. "It came too naturally to a man of honor for you to care for the epithet. Yet it was a great one, a most generous one. But I have not heard one thing: what argument did you use to obtain her release?"

"No one has ever heard it," he answered her, while his voice sank low. "I will trust you with it; it will not pass elsewhere. I told him enough of—of my own past life to show him that I knew what his had been, and that I knew, moreover, though they were dead to me now, men in that greater world of Europe who would believe my statement if I wrote them this outrage on the Emir, and would avenge it for the reputation of the Empire. And unless he released the Emir's wife, I swore to him that I would so write, though he had me shot on the morrow; and he knew I should keep my word."

She was silent some moments, looking on him with a musing gaze, in which some pity and more honor for him were blended.

"You told him your past. Will you confess it to me?"

"I cannot, madame."

"And why?"

"Because I am dead! Because, in your presence, it becomes more bitter to me to remember that I ever lived."

"You speak strangely. Cannot your life have a resurrection?"

"Never, madame. For a brief hour you have given it one —in dreams. It will have no other."

"But surely there may be ways—such a story as you have told me brought to the Emperor's knowledge, you would see your enemy disgraced, yourself honored?"

"Possibly, madame. But it is out of the question that it should ever be so brought. As I am now, so I desire to live and die."

"You voluntarily condemn yourself to this?"

"I have voluntarily chosen it. I am well sure that the silence I entreat will be kept by you?"

"Assuredly; unless by your wish it be broken. Yet—I await my brother's arrival here; he is a soldier himself; I shall hope that he will persuade you to think differently of your future. At any rate, both his and my own influence will always be exerted for you, if you will avail yourself of it."

"You do me much honor, madame. All I will ever ask of you is to return those coins to my Colonel, and to forget that your gentleness has made me forget, for one merciful half hour, the sufferance on which alone a trooper can present himself here."

He swept the ground with his képi as though it were the plumed hat of a Marshal, and backed slowly from her presence, as he had many a time long before backed out of a throne-room.

As he went, his eyes caught the armies of the ivory chessmen; they stood under glass, and had not been broken by her lapdog.

Miladi, left alone there in her luxurious morning room, sat a while lost in thought. He attracted her; he interested her; he aroused her sympathy and her wonder as the men of her own world had failed to do—aroused them despite the pride which made her impatient of lending so much attention to a mere Chasseur d'Afrique. She had seen much of the world, and was naturally far more penetrative and more correct in judgment than are most women. She discovered the ring of true gold in his words, and the carriage of pure breeding in his actions.

"Such a man as that buried in the ranks of this brutalized army!" she mused. "What fatal chance could bring him here? Misfortune, not misconduct, surely. I wonder if Lyon could learn? He shall try."

"Your Chasseur has the air of a Prince, my love," said a voice behind her.

"Equivocal compliment! A much better air than most

Princes," said Mme. Corona, glancing up with a slight shrug of her shoulders, as her guest and traveling companion, the Marquise de Rénardière, entered.

"Indeed! I saw him as he passed out; and he saluted me as if he had been a Marshal. Why did he come?"

Venetia Corona pointed to the Napoleons, and told the story; rather listlessly and briefly.

"Ah! The man has been a gentleman, I dare say. So many of them come to our army. I remember General Ville-fleur's telling me—he commanded here a while—that the ranks of the Zephyrs and Zouaves were full of well-born men, utterly good-for-nothing, the handsomest scoundrels possible; who had every gift and every grace, and yet come to no better end than a pistol-shot in a ditch or a mortal thrust from Bedouin steel. I dare say your Corporal is one of them."

"It may be so."

"But you doubt it, I imagine."

"I am not sure now that I do. But this person is certainly unlike a man to whom disgrace has ever attached."

"You think your protégé, then, has become what he is through adversity, I suppose? Very interesting!"

"I really can tell you nothing of his antecedents. Through his skill at sculpture, and my notice of it, considerable indignity has been brought upon him; and a soldier can feel, it seems, though it is very absurd that he should! That is all my concern with the matter, except that I have to teach his commander not to play with my name in his barrack yard."

She spoke with that negligence which always sounded very cold, though the words were so gently spoken. Her best and most familiar friends always knew when, with that courtly chillness, she had signed them their line of demarcation.

And the Marquise de Rénardière said no more, but talked of the Ambassador's poems.

CHAPTER XVI.

ZARAILA.

The African day was at its noon.

From the first break of dawn the battle had raged; now, at midday, it was at its height. Far in the interior, almost on the edge of the great desert, in that terrible season when air that is flame by day is ice by night, and when the scorch of a blazing sun may be followed in an hour by the blinding fury of a snow-storm, the slaughter had gone on, hour through hour, under a shadowless sky, blue as steel, hard as a sheet of brass. The Arabs had surprised the French encampment, where it lay in the center of an arid plain that was called Zaraila. Hovering like a cloud of hawks on the entrance of the Sahara, massed together for one mighty, if futile, effort—with all their ancient war-lust, and with a new despair—the tribes who refused the yoke of the alien empire were once again in arms; were once again combined in defense of those limitless kingdoms of drifting sand, of that beloved belt of bare and desolate land so useless to the conqueror, so dear to the nomad. When they had been, as it had been thought, beaten back into the desert wilderness; when, without water and without cattle, it had been calculated that they would, of sheer necessity, bow themselves in submission, or perish of famine and of thirst; they had recovered their ardor, their strength, their resistance, their power to harass without ceasing, if they could never arrest, the enemy. They had cast the torch of war afresh into the land, and here, southward, the flame burned bitterly, and with a merciless tongue devoured the lives of men, licking them up as a forest fire the dry leaves and the touchwood.

Circling, sweeping, silently, swiftly, with that rapid spring, that marvelous whirlwind of force, that is of Africa, and of Africa alone, the tribes had rushed down in the darkness of night, lightly as a kite rushes through the gloom of the dawn. For once the vigilance of the invader served him naught; for once the Frankish camp was surprised off its guard. While the air was still chilly with the breath of the night, while the first gleam of morning had barely broken through the mists of the east, while the picket-fires burned through the dusky gloom, and the sentinels and vedettes paced slowly to and fro, and circled round, hearing nothing worse than the stealthy tread of the jackal, or the muffled flight of a night-bird, afar in the south a great dark cloud had risen, darker than the brooding shadows of the earth and sky.

The cloud swept onward, like a mass of cirrhi, in those shadows shrouded. Fleet as though wind-driven, dense as though thunder-charged, it moved over the plains. As it grew nearer and nearer, it grew grayer, a changing mass of white and black that fused, in the obscurity, into a shadow color; a dense array of men and horses flitting noiselessly like spirits, and as though guided alone by one rein and moved alone by one breath and one will; not a bit champed, not a linen-fold loosened, not a shiver of steel was heard; as silently as the winds of the desert sweep up northward over the plains, so they rode now, host upon host of the warriors of the soil.

The outlying vedettes, the advancing sentinels, had scrutinized so long through the night every wavering shade of cloud and moving form of buffalo in the dim distance, that their sleepless eyes, strained and aching, failed to distinguish this moving mass that was so like the brown plains and starless sky that it could scarce be told from them. The night, too, was bitter; northern cold cut hardly chillier than this that parted the blaze of one hot day from the blaze of another. The sea-winds were blowing cruelly keen, and men who at noon gladly stripped to their shirts, shivered now where they lay under canvas.

Awake while his comrades slept around him, Cecil was stretched, half unharnessed.

Flick-Flack—coiled asleep in his bosom—thrilled, stirred, and growled. He rose, and, with the little dog under his arm, looked out from the canvas. He knew that the most vigilant sentry in the service had not the instinct for a foe afar off that Flick-Flack possessed. He gazed keenly southward, the poodle growling on; that cloud so dim, so distant, caught his sight. Was it a moving herd, a shifting mist, a shadow-play between the night and dawn?

For a moment longer he watched it; then, what it was he knew, or felt by such strong instinct as makes knowledge; and, like the blast of a clarion, his alarm rang over the unarmed and slumbering camp.

An instant, and the hive of men, so still, so motionless, broke into violent movement; and from the tents the half-clothed sleepers poured, wakened, and fresh in wakening as hounds. Perfect discipline did the rest. With marvelous,

with matchless swiftness and precision they harnessed and
got under arms. They were but fifteen hundred or so in all
—a single squadron of Chasseurs, two battalions of Zouaves,
half a corps of Tirailleurs, and some Turcos; only a branch
of the main body, and without artillery. But they were some
of the flower of the army of Algiers, and they roused in a
second, with the vivacious ferocity of the bounding tiger,
with the glad, eager impatience for the slaughter of the unloosed hawk. Yet, rapid in its wondrous celerity as their
united action was, it was not so rapid as the downward
sweep of that war-cloud that came so near, with the tossing
of white draperies and the shine of countless sabers, now
growing clearer and clearer out of the darkness, till, with a
whir like the noise of an eagle's wings, and a swoop like an
eagle's seizure, the Arabs whirled down upon them, met a
few yards in advance by the answering charge of the Light
Cavalry.

There was a crash as if rock were hurled upon rock, as the
Chasseurs, scarce seated in saddle, rushed forward to save
the pickets; to encounter the first blind force of the attack,
and to give the infantry, further in, more time for harness
and defense. Out of the caverns of the night an armed multitude seemed to have suddenly poured.

It was not a battle; it was a frightful tangling of men
and brutes. No contest of modern warfare, such as commences and conquers by a duel of artillery, and, sometimes,
gives the victory to whosoever has the superiority of ordnance, but a conflict, hand to hand, breast to breast, life
for life; a Homeric combat of spear and of sword even while
the first volleys of the answering musketry pealed over the
plain.

The Chasseurs could not charge; they were hemmed in,
packed between bodies of horsemen that pressed them together
as between iron plates; now and then they could cut their
way through, clear enough to reach their comrades of the
demie cavalerie, but as often as they did so, so often the
overwhelming numbers of the Arabs surged in on them afresh
like a flood, and closed upon them, and drove them back.

Every soldier in the squadron that lived kept his life by
sheer, breathless, ceaseless, hand-to-hand sword-play, hewing
right and left, front and rear, without pause, as, in the great
tangled forests of the west, men hew aside branch and brushwood ere they can force one step forward.

It was bitter, stifling, cruel work. The answering fire of

the Zouaves and Tirailleurs kept the Arabs further at bay, and mowed them faster down; but in the Chasseurs' quarter of the field—parted from the rest of their comrades as they had been by the rush of that broken charge with which they had sought to save the camp and arrest the foe—the worst pressure of the attack was felt, and the fiercest of the slaughter fell.

The Chef d'Escadron had been shot dead as they had first swept out to encounter the advance of the desert horsemen; one by one the officers had been cut down, singled out by the keen eyes of their enemies, and throwing themselves into the deadliest of the carnage with the impetuous self-devotion characteristic of their service. At the last there remained but a mere handful out of all the brilliant squadron that had galloped down in the gray of the dawn to meet the whirlwind of Arab fury. At their head was Cecil.

Two horses had been killed under him, and he had thrown himself afresh across unwounded chargers, whose riders had fallen in the mêlée, and at whose bridles he had caught as he shook himself free of the dead animals' stirrups. His head was uncovered; his uniform, hurriedly thrown on, had been torn aside, and his chest was bare to the red folds of his sash; he was drenched with blood, not his own, that had rained on him as he fought; and his face and his hands were black with smoke and with powder. He could not see a yard in front of him; he could not tell how the day went anywhere, save in that corner where his own troop was hemmed in. As fast as they beat the Arabs back, and forced themselves some clearer space, so fast the tribes closed in afresh. No orders reached him from the General of Brigade in command; except for the well-known war-shouts of the Zouaves that ever and again rang above the din, he could not tell whether the French battalions were not cut utterly to pieces under the immense numerical superiority of their foes. All he could see was that every officer of Chasseurs was down, and that, unless he took the vacant place, and rallied them together, the few score troopers that were still left would scatter, confused and demoralized, as the best soldiers will at times when they can see no chief to follow.

He spurred the horse he had just mounted against the dense crowd opposing him, against the hard, black wall of dust, and smoke, and steel, and savage faces, and lean, swarthy arms, which were all that his eyes could see, and that seemed impenetrable as granite, moving and changing though it was.

He thrust the gray against it, while he waved his sword above his head.

"En avant, mes fréres! France! France! France!"

His voice—well known, well loved—thrilled the hearts of his comrades, and brought them together like a trumpet-call. They had gone with him many a time into the hell of battle, into the jaws of death. They surged about him now; striking, thrusting, forcing, with blows of their sabers or their lances and blows of their beasts' fore-feet, a passage one to another, until they were reunited once more as one troop, while their shrill shouts, like an oath of vengeance, echoed after him in the defiance that has pealed victorious over so many fields from the soldiery of France. They loved him; he had called them his brethren. They were like lambs for him to lead, like tigers for him to incite.

He glanced back on them, guarding his head the while from the lances that were rained on him; and he lifted the guidon higher and higher, till, out of the ruck and the throng, the brazen bird caught afresh the rays of the rising sun.

"Suivez-moi!" he shouted.

Then, like arrows launched at once from a hundred bows, they charged; he still slightly in advance of them, the bridle flung upon his horse's neck, his head and breast bare, one hand striking aside with his blade the steel shafts as they poured on him, the other holding high above the press the Eagle of the Bonapartes.

The effort was superb.

Dense bodies of Arabs parted them in the front from the camp where the battle raged, harassed them in the rear with flying shots and hurled lances, and forced down on them on either side like the closing jaws of a trap. The impetuosity of their onward movement was, for the moment, irresistible; it bore headlong all before it; the desert horses recoiled, and the desert riders themselves yielded—crushed, staggered, trodden aside, struck aside, by the tremendous impetus with which the Chasseurs were thrown upon them. For the moment the Bedouins gave way, shaken and confused, as at the head of the French they saw this man, with his hair blowing in the wind, and the sun on the fairness of his face, ride down on them thus unharmed, though a dozen spears were aimed at his naked breast; dealing strokes sure as death, right and left as he went, with the light from the hot, blue skies on the ensign of France that he bore.

They knew him; they had met him in many conflicts; and

wherever the "fair Frank," as they called him, came, there they knew of old the battle was hard to win; bitter to the bitterest end, whether that end were defeat, or victory costly as defeat in its achievement.

And for the moment they recoiled under the shock of that fiery onslaught; for the moment they parted and wavered and oscillated beneath the impetus with which he hurled his hundred Chasseurs on them, with that light, swift, indescribable rapidity and resistlessness of attack characteristic of the African Cavalry.

Cecil held the Eagle still, and looked round on the few left to him.

"You are sons of the Old Guard; die like them."

They answered with a pealing cry, terrible as the cry of the lion in the hush of night, but a shout that had in it assent, triumph, fealty, victory, even as they obeyed him and drew up to die.

There was nothing for them but to draw up thus, and await their butchery, defending the Eagle to the last; looking till the last toward that "woman's face of their leader," as they had often termed it, that was to them now as the face of Napoleon was to the soldiers who loved him.

There was a pause, brief as is the pause of the lungs to take a fuller breath. The Arabs honored these men, who alone and in the midst of the hostile force, held their ground and prepared thus to be slaughtered one by one, till of all the squadron that had ridden out in the darkness of the dawn there should be only a black, huddled, stiffened heap of dead men and of dead beasts. The chief who led them pressed them back, withholding them from the end that was so near to their hands when they should stretch that single ring of horsemen all lifeless in the dust.

"You are great warriors," he cried, in the Sabir tongue; "surrender; we will spare!"

Cecil looked back once more on the fragment of his troop, and raised the Eagle higher aloft where the wings should glisten in the fuller day. Half naked, scorched, blinded; with an open gash in his shoulder where the lance had struck, and with his brow wet with the great dews of the noon-heat and the breathless toil; his eyes were clear as they flashed with the light of the sun in them; his mouth smiled as he answered:

"Have we shown ourselves cowards, that you think we shall yield?"

A hurrah of wild delight from the Chasseurs he led greeted

and ratified the choice. "On meurt—on ne se rend pas!" they shouted in the words which, even if they be but legendary, are too true to the spirit of the soldiers of France not to be as truth in their sight. Then, with their swords above their heads, they waited for the collision of the terrible attack which would fall on them upon every side, and strike all the sentient life out of them before the sun should be one point higher in the heavens. It came: with a yell as of wild beasts in their famine, the Arabs threw themselves forward, the chief himself singling out the "fair Frank" with the violence of a lion flinging himself on a leopard. One instant longer, one flash of time, and the tribes pressing on them would have massacred them like cattle driven into the pens of slaughter. Ere it could be done, a voice like the ring of a silver trumpet echoed over the field:

"En avant! En avant! Tue, tue, tue!"

Above the din, the shouts, the tumult, the echoing of the distant musketry, that silvery cadence rung; down into the midst, with the Tricolor waving above her head, the bridle of her fiery mare between her teeth, the raven of the dead Zouave flying above her head, and her pistol leveled in deadly aim, rode Cigarette.

Behind her, by scarcely a length, galloped three squadrons of Chasseurs and Spahis; trampling headlong over the corpse-strewn field, and breaking through the masses of the Arabs as though they were seas of corn.

She wheeled her mare round by Cecil's side at the moment when, with six swift passes of his blade, he had warded off the Chief's blows and sent his own sword down through the chest-bones of the Bedouin's mighty form.

"Well struck! The day is turned! Charge!"

She gave the order as though she were a Marshal of the Empire, the sun-blaze full on her where she sat on the rearing, fretting, half-bred gray, with the Tricolor folds above her head, and her teeth tight gripped on the chain-bridle, and her face all glowing and warm and full of the fierce fire of war—a little Amazon in scarlet and blue and gold; a young Jeanne d'Arc, with the crimson fez in lieu of the silvered casque, and the gay broideries of her fantastic dress instead of the breastplate of steel. And with the Flag of her idolatry, the Flag that was as her religion, floating back as she went, she spurred her mare straight against the Arabs, straight over the lifeless forms of the hundreds slain; and after her poured the fresh squadrons of cavalry, the ruby burnous of the Spahis streaming on the wind as their darling led them on to retrieve the day for France.

Not a bullet struck, not a saber grazed her; but there, in the heat and the press of the worst of the slaughter, Cigarette rode hither and thither, to and fro, her voice ringing like a bird's song over the field, in command, in applause, in encouragement, in delight; bearing her standard aloft and untouched; dashing heedless through a storm of blows; cheering on her "children" to the charge again and again; and all the while with the sunlight full on her radiant, spirited head, and with the grim, gray raven flying above her, shrieking shrilly its "Tue, tue, tue!" The Army believed with superstitious faith in the potent spell of that veteran bird, and the story ran that, whenever he flew above a combat, France was victor before the sun set. The echo of the raven's cry, and the presence of the child who, they knew, would have a thousand musket-balls fired in her fair young breast rather than live to see them defeated, made the fresh squadrons sweep in like a whirlwind, bearing down all before them.

Cigarette saved the day.

CHAPTER XVII.

THE LOVE OF THE AMAZON.

BEFORE the sun had declined from his zenith the French were masters of the field, and pursued the retreat of the Arabs till, for miles along the plain, the line of their flight was marked with horses that had dropped dead in the strain, and with the motionless forms of their desert-riders, their cold hands clinched in the loose, hot sands, and their stern faces turned upward to the cloudless scorch of their native skies, under whose freedom they would never again ride forth to the joyous clash of the cymbals and the fierce embrace of the death-grapple.

When at length she returned, coming in with her ruthless Spahis, whose terrible passions she feared no more than Vergil's Volscian huntress feared the beasts of the forest and plain, the raven still hovered above her exhausted mare, the torn flag was still in her left hand; and the bright laughter, the flash of ecstatic triumph, was still in her face as she sang the last lines of her own war-chant. The leopard nature was roused in her. She was a soldier; death had been about her from her birth; she neither feared to give nor to receive it; she was proud as ever was young Pompeius flushed with the glories of his first eastern conquests; she was happy as such elastic, sun-lit, dauntless youth as hers alone can be, returning in the reddening after-glow, at the head of her comrades, to the camp that she had saved.

Cruelty, heroism, vanity, and bravery were all on fire, and all fed to their uttermost, most eager, most ardent flame, now that she came back at the head of her Spahis; while all who remained of the soldiers who, but for her, would have been massacred long ere then, without one spared among them, threw themselves forward, crowded round her, caressed, and laughed, and wept, and shouted with all the changes of their intense mercurial temperaments; kissed her boots, her sash, her mare's drooping neck, and, lifting her, with wild vivas that rent the sky, on to the shoulders of the two tallest men among them, bore her to the presence of the only officer of high rank who had survived the terrors of the day, a Chef de Bataillon of the Zouaves.

And he, a grave and noble-looking veteran, uncovered his head and bowed before her as courtiers bow before their queens.

"Mademoiselle, you saved the honor of France. In the name of France, I thank you."

The tears rushed swift and hot into Cigarette's bright eyes —tears of joy, tears of pride. She was but a child still in much, and she could be moved by the name of France as other children by the name of their mothers.

"Chut! I did nothing," she said rapidly. "I only rode fast."

The frenzied hurrahs of the men who heard her drowned her words. They loved her for what she had done; they loved her better still because she set no count on it.

"The Empire will think otherwise," said the Major of the Zouaves. "Tell me, my Little One, how did you do this thing?"

Cigarette, balancing herself with a foot on either shoulder of her supporters, gave the salute, and answered:

"Simply, mon Commandant—very simply. I was alone, riding midway between you and the main army—three leagues, say, from each. I was all alone; only Vole-qui-veut flying with me for fun. I met a colon. I knew the man.

For the matter of that, I did him once a service—saved his geese and his fowls from burning, one winter's day, in their house, while he wrung his hands and looked on. Well, he was full of terror, and told me there was fighting yonder—here he meant—so I rode nearer to see. That was just upon sunrise. I dismounted, and ran up a palm there." And Cigarette pointed to a far-off slope crowned with the remains of a once-mighty palm forest. "I got up very high. I could see miles round. I saw how things were with you. For the moment I was coming straight to you. Then I thought I should do more service if I let the main army know, and brought you a re-enforcement. I rode fast. Dieu! I rode fast. My horse dropped under me twice; but I reached them at last, and I went at once to the General. He guessed at a glance how things were, and I told him to give me my Spahis and let me go. So he did. I got on a mare of his own staff, and away we came. Ma foi! it was a near thing. If we had been a minute later, it had been all up with you."

"True, indeed," muttered the Zouave in his beard. "A superb action, my Little One. If all soldiers were like you, to command a battalion would be paradise!"

"All soldiers would do anything I have done," retorted Cigarette, who never took a compliment at the expense of her "children." "They do not all get the opportunity, look you; c'est tout! Opportunity is a little angel; some catch him as he goes, some let him pass by forever. You must be quick with him, for he is like an eel to wriggle away. If you want a good soldier, take that aristocrat of the Chasse-Marais— that beau Victor. Pouf! all his officers were down; and how splendidly he led the troop! He was going to die with them rather than surrender. Napoleon"—and Cigarette uncovered her curly head reverentially as at the name of a deity—"Napoleon would have given him his brigade ere this. If you had seen him kill the chief!"

"He will have justice done him, never fear. And for you —the Cross shall be on your breast, Cigarette, if I live over to-night to write my dispatches."

And the Chef de Bataillon saluted her once more, and turned away to view the carnage-strewn plain, and number the few who remained out of those who had been wakened by the clash of the Arab arms in the gray of the earliest dawn.

Cigarette's eyes flashed like sun playing on water, and her flushed cheeks grew scarlet. Since her infancy it had been her dream to have the Cross, to have the Grande Croix to lie above her little lion's heart; it had been the one longing, the one ambition, the only undying desire of her soul; and lo! she touched its realization!

The wild, frantic, tumultuous cheers and caresses of her soldiery, who could not triumph in her and triumph with her enough to satiate them, recalled her to the actual moment. She sprang down from her elevation, and turned on them with a rebuke. "Ah! you are making this fuss about me while hundreds of better soldiers than I lie yonder. Let us look to them first; we will play the fool afterward."

And, though she had ridden fifty miles that day, if she had ridden one—though she had eaten nothing since sunrise, and had only had one draught of bad water—though she was tired, and stiff, and bruised, and parched with thirst, Cigarette dashed off as lightly as a young goat to look for the wounded and the dying men who strewed the plain far and near.

She remembered one whom she had not seen after that first moment in which she had given the word to the squadrons to charge.

It was a terrible sight—the arid plain, lying in the scarlet glow of sunset, covered with dead bodies, with mutilated limbs, with horses gasping and writhing, with men raving like mad creatures in the torture of their wounds.

"Is he killed? Is he killed?" she thought, as she bent over each knot of motionless bodies, where, here and there, some faint, stifled breath, or some moan of agony, told that life still lingered beneath the huddled, stiffening heap. And a tightness came at her heart, an aching fear made her shrink, as she raised each hidden face, that she had never known before. "What if he be?" she said fiercely to herself. "It is nothing to me. I hate him, the cold aristocrat! I ought to be glad if I see him lie here."

A dog's moan caught her ear; she turned and looked across. Upright, among a ghastly pile of men and chargers, sat the small, snowy poodle of the Chasseurs, beating the air with its little paws, as it had been taught to do when it needed anything, and howling piteously as it begged.

"Flick-Flack? What it is, Flick-Flack?" she cried to him, while, with a bound, she reached the spot. The dog leaped on her, rejoicing. The dead were thick there—ten or twelve deep—French trooper and Bedouin rider flung across each other, horribly entangled with the limbs, the manes, the shattered bodies of their own horses. Among them she saw the face she sought, as the dog eagerly ran back, caressing the hair of a soldier who lay underneath the weight of his gray charger, that had been killed by a musket-ball.

Cigarette grew very pale. For a moment she thought him dead; then, as she drew him out where the cooled breeze of the declining day could reach him, a slow breath, painfully drawn, moved his chest; she saw that he was unconscious from the stifling oppression under which he had been buried since the noon; an hour more without the touch of fresher air, and life would have been extinct.

Cigarette had with her the flask of brandy that she always brought on such errands as these; she forced the end between his lips, and poured some down his throat; her hand shook slightly as she did so, a weakness the gallant little campaigner never before then had known.

It revived him in a degree; he breathed more freely, though heavily, and with difficulty still; but gradually the deadly, leaden color of his face was replaced by the hue of life, and his heart began to beat more loudly. Consciousness did not return to him; he lay motionless and senseless, with his head resting on her lap, and with Flick-Flack, in eager affection, licking his hands and his hair.

"He was as good as dead, Flick-Flack, if it had not been for you and me," said Cigarette, while she wetted his lips with more brandy. "Ah, bah! and he would be more grateful, Flick-Flack, for a scornful scoff from Miladi!"

Still, though she thought this, she let his head lie on her lap, and, as she looked down on him, there was the glisten as of tears in the brave, sunny eyes of the little Friend of the Flag.

"Il est si beau, si beau, si beau!" she muttered in her teeth, drawing the silk-like locks of his hair through her hands. She loved to see him lie there as though he were asleep, to cheat herself into the fancy that she watched his rest to wake it with a kiss on his lips. In that unconsciousness, in that abandonment, he seemed wholly her own; passion which she could not have analyzed made her bend above him with a half-fierce, half-dreamy delight in that solitary possession of his beauty, of his life.

The restless movements of little Flick-Flack detached a piece of twine passed round his favorite's throat; the glitter of gold arrested Cigarette's eyes. She caught what the poodle's impatient caress had broken from the string. It was a small, blue-enamel medallion bonbon-box, with a hole through it by which it had been slung—a tiny toy once costly, now tarnished, for it had been carried through many rough scenes and many years of hardship; had been bent by blows struck at the breast against which it rested, and was clotted now with blood. Inside it was a woman's ring, of sapphires and opals.

She looked at both close, in the glow of the setting sun; then passed the string through and fastened the box afresh. It was a mere trifle, but it sufficed to banish her dream; to arouse her to contemptuous, impatient bitterness with that new weakness that had for the hour broken her down to the level of this feverish folly. He was beautiful—yes! She could not bring herself to hate him; she could not help the brimming tears blinding her eyes when she looked at him, stretched senseless thus. But he was wedded to his past; that toy in his breast, whatever it might be, whatever tale might cling to it, was sweeter to him than her lips would ever be. Bah! there were better men than he; why had she not let him lie and die as he might, under the pile of dead?

Bah! she could have killed herself for her folly! She, who had scores of lovers, from princes to piou-pious, and never had a heartache for one of them, to go and care for a silent "cidevant," who had never even noticed that her eyes had any brightness or her face had any charm!

"You deserve to be shot—you!" said Cigarette, fiercely abusing herself as she put his head off her lap, and rose abruptly and shouted to a Tringlo, who was at some distance searching for the wounded. "Here is a Chasse-Marais with some breath in him," she said curtly, as the man with his mule-cart and its sad burden of half-dead, moaning, writhing frames drew near to her summons. "Put him in. Soldiers cost too much training to waste them on jackals and kites, if one can help it. Lift him up—quick!"

"He is badly hurt?" said the Tringlo.

She shrugged her shoulders.

"Oh, no! I have had worse scratches myself. The horse fell on him, that was the mischief. Most of them here have swallowed the 'petite pilule d'oubli' once and for all. I never saw a prettier thing—every Lascar has killed his own little knot of Arbicos. Look how nice and neat they lie."

She was not going to have him imagine she cared for that Chasseur whom he lifted up on his little wagon with so kindly a care—not she! Cigarette was as proud in her way as was ever the Princess Venetia Corona.

Nevertheless, she kept pace with the mules, carrying little Flick-Flack, and never paused on her way, though she passed scores of dead Arabs, whose silver ornaments and silk embroideries, commonly after such a fantasia, replenished the knapsack and adorned in profusion the uniform of the young filibuster; being gleaned by her, right and left, as her lawful harvest after the fray.

"Leave him there. I will have a look at him," she said, at the first empty tent they reached. The camp had been the scene of as fierce a struggle as the part of the plain which the cavalry had held, and it was strewn with the slaughter of Zouaves and Tirailleurs. The Tringlo obeyed her, and went about his errand of mercy. Cigarette, left alone with the wounded man, lying insensible still on a heap of forage, ceased her song and grew very quiet. She had a certain surgical skill, learned as her untutored genius learned most things, with marvelous rapidity, by observation and intuition; and she had saved many a life by her knowledge and her patient attendance on the sufferers.

The tent had been a scullion's tent; the poor marmiton had been killed; his fire had gone out, but his brass pots and pans, his jar of fresh water, and his various preparations for the General's dinner were still there. The General was dead also. The soup stood unserved; the wild plovers were taken by Flick-Flack; the empty dishes waited for the viands which there were no hands to prepare and no mouths to eat. Cigarette glanced round, and saw all with one flash of her eyes; then she knelt down beside the heap of forage, and, for the first thing, dressed his wounds with the cold, clear water, and washed away the dust and the blood that covered his breast.

Cecil had been stunned by a stroke from his horse's hoof as the poor beast fell beneath and rolled over him. His wounds were slight—marvelously so, for the thousand strokes that had been aimed at him; but it was difficult to arouse him from unconsciousness, and his face was white as death where he lay on the heap of dry reeds and grasses. She began to feel fear of that lengthened syncope; a chill, tight, despairing fear that she had never known in her life before. She knelt silent a moment, drawing through her hand the wet locks of his hair with the bright threads of gold gleaming in it.

Then she started up, and, leaving him, found a match, and lighted the died-out wood afresh; the fire soon blazed up, and she warmed above it the soup that had grown cold, poured into it some red wine that was near, and forced some, little by little, down his throat. It was with difficulty at first that she could pass any through his tightly locked teeth; but by degrees she succeeded, and, only half-conscious still, he drank it faster; the heat and the strength reviving him as its stimulant warmed his veins. His eyes did not unclose, but he stirred, moved his limbs, and, with some muttered words she could not hear, drew a deeper breath and turned.

"He will sleep now—he is safe," she thought to herself, while she stood watching him with a curious conflict of pity, impatience, anger, and relief at war within her.

Silence settled over the camp; half the slain could not be buried, and the clear, luminous stars rose on the ghastly plateau. All that were heard were the challenge of sentinels, the tramp of patrols. The guard visited her once. "C'est Cigarette," she said briefly, and she was left undisturbed.

Every now and then, four or five times in an hour, she gave him whom she tended the soup or the wine that she kept warmed for him over the embers. He took it without knowledge, sunk half in lethargy, half in sleep; but it kept the life glowing in him which, without it, might have perished of cold and exhaustion as the chills and northerly wind of the evening succeeded to the heat of the day, and pierced through the canvas walls of the tent.

"I have saved his life twice," she thought, looking at him; "beware of the third time, they say!"

He moved restlessly, and she went to him. His face was flushed now; his breath came rapidly and shortly; there was some fever on him. The linen was displaced from his wounds; she dipped it again in water, and laid the cooled bands on them. "Ah, bah! If I were not unsexed enough for this, how would it be with you now?" she said in her teeth. He tossed wearily to and fro; detached words caught her ear as he muttered them.

"Let it be, let it be—he is welcome! How could I prove it at his cost? I saved him—I could do that. It was not much——"

She listened with intent anxiety to hear the other whispers ending the sentence, but they were stifled and broken.

"Tiens!" she murmured below her breath. "It is for some other he has ruined himself."

She could not catch the words that followed. They were in an unknown language to her, for she knew nothing of English, and they poured fast and obscure from his lips as he moved in feverish unrest; the wine that had saved him from exhaustion inflaming his brain in his sleep. Now and then French phrases crossed the English ones; she leaned down to seize their meaning till her cheek was against his forehead, till her lips touched his hair; and at that half caress her heart beat, her face flushed, her mouth trembled with a too vivid joy, with an impulse, half fear and half longing, that had never so moved her before.

"If I had my birthright," he muttered in her own tongue. "If I had it—would she look so cold then? She might love me—women used once. O God! if she had not looked on me, I had never known all I had lost!"

Cigarette started as if a knife had stabbed her, and sprang up from her rest beside him.

"She—she—always she!" she muttered fiercely, while her face grew duskily scarlet in the fire-glow of the tent; and she went slowly away, back to the low wood fire.

This was to be ever her reward!

Her eyes glistened and flashed with the fiery, vengeful passions of her hot and jealous instincts. Cigarette had in her the violence, as she had the nobility, of a grand nature that has gone wholly untutored and unguided; and she had the power of southern vengeance in her, though she had also the swift and rapid impulse to forgiveness of a generous and sunlit temper. It was bitter, beyond any other bitterness that could have wounded her, for the spoilt, victorious, imperious, little empress of the Army of Algeria to feel that, though she had given his life twice back to this man, she was less to him than the tiny white dog that nestled in his breast; that she, who never before had endured a slight, or known what neglect could mean, gave care, and pity, and aid, and even tenderness, to one whose only thought was for a woman who had accorded him nothing but a few chill syllables of haughty condescension!

He lay there unconscious of her presence, tossing wearily to and fro in fevered, unrefreshing sleep, murmuring incoherent words of French and English strangely mingled; and Cigarette crouched on the ground, with the firelight playing all over her picturesque, childlike beauty, and her large eyes strained and savage, yet with a strange, wistful pain in them.

Yet she did not leave him.

She was too generous for that. "What is right is right.

He is a soldier of France," she muttered, while she kept her
vigil. She felt no want of sleep; a hard, hateful wakefulness
seemed to have banished all rest from her! she stayed there
all the night through. Whenever she could ease or aid him
she rose and did so, with the touch of water on his forehead,
or of cooled wine to his lips, by the alteration of the linen
on his wounds, or the shifting of the rough forage that made
his bed. But she did it without anything of that loving,
lingering attendance she had given before; she never once
drew out the task longer than it needed, or let her hands
wander among his hair, or over his lips, as she had done
before.

And he never once was conscious of it; he never once knew
that she was near. He did not waken from the painful,
delirious, stupefied slumber that had fallen on him; he only
vaguely felt that he was suffering pain; he only vaguely
dreamed of what he murmured of—his past, and the beauty
of the woman who had brought all the memories of that past
back on him.

And this was Cigarette's reward—to hear him mutter
wearily of the proud eyes and of the lost smile of another!

The dawn came at last; her constant care and the skill with
which she had cooled and dressed his wounds had done him
infinite service; the fever had subsided, and toward morning
his incoherent words ceased, his breathing grew calmer and
more tranquil; he fell asleep—sleep that was profound,
dreamless, and refreshing.

She looked at him with a tempestuous shadow darkening
her face, that was soft with a tenderness that she could not
banish. She hated him; she ought to have stabbed or shot
him rather than have tended him thus; he neglected her, and
only thought of that woman of his old Order. As a daughter
of the People, as a child of the Army, as a soldier of France,
she ought to have killed him rather than have caressed his
hair and soothed his pain! Pshaw! She ground one in another her tiny white teeth, that were like a spaniel's.

Then gently, very gently, lest she should waken him, she
took her tunic skirt with which she had covered him from the
chills of the night, put more broken wood on the fading fire,
and with a last, lingering look at him where he slept, passed
out from the tent as the sun rose in a flushed and beautiful
dawn. He would never know that she had saved him thus:
he never should know it, she vowed in her heart.

CHAPTER XVIII.

BY THE BIVOUAC FIRE.

THE camp was large, and a splendid picture of color, movement, picturesque combination, and wonderful light and shadow, as the sun-glow died out and the fires were lighted; for the nights were now intensely cold—cold with the cutting, icy, withering bise, and clear above as an Antarctic night, though the days were still hot and dry as flame.

On the left were the Tirailleurs, the Zouaves, the Zephyrs; on the right were the Cavalry and the Artillery; in the center of all was the tent of the Chief. Everywhere, as evening fell, the red warmth of fires rose; the caldron of soup or of coffee simmered, gypsy-like, above; the men lounged around, talking, laughing, cooking, story-telling at their pleasure; after the semi-starvation of the last week, the abundance of stores that had come in with other Tringlos besides poor Biribi caused a universal hilarity.

Cecil sat now, having recovered from the effects of the day of Zaraila within a little distance of the fire at which his men were stewing some soup in the great simmering copper bowl. They had eaten nothing for nigh a week, except some moldy bread, with a chance of a stray cat or a shot bird to flavor it. Hunger was a common thorn in Algerian warfare, since not even the matchless intendance of France could regularly supply the troops across those interminable breadths of arid land, those sun-scorched plains, swept by Arab foragers.

"Beau Victor! you took their parts well," said a voice behind him, as Cigarette vaulted over a pile of knapsacks and stood in the glow of the fire, with a little pipe in her pretty rosebud mouth and her cap set daintily on one side of her curls.

He looked up, and smiled.

"Not so well as your own clever tongue would have done. Words are not my weapons."

"No! You are as silent as the grave commonly; but when you do speak, you speak well," said the vivandière-Demosthenes condescendingly. "I hate silence myself! Thoughts are very good grain, but if they are not whirled round, round, round, and winnowed and ground in the millstones of talk, they keep little, hard, useless kernels, that not a soul can digest."

With which metaphor Cigarette blew a cloud of smoke into the night air, looking the prettiest little genre picture in the ruddy firelight that ever was painted on such a background of wavering shadow and undulating flame.

"Will your allegory hold good, petite?" smiled Cecil, thinking but little of his answer or of his companion, of whose service to him he remained utterly ignorant. "I fancy speech is the chaff most generally, little better. So, they talk of you for the Cross? No soldier ever, of a surety, more greatly deserved it."

Her eyes gleamed with a luster like the African planets above her; her face caught all the fire, the light, the illumination of the flames flashing near her.

"I did nothing," she said curtly. "Any man on the field would have done the same."

"That is easy to say; not so easy to prove. In all great events there may be the same strength, courage, and desire to act greatly in those who follow as in the one that leads; but it is only in that one that there is also the daring to originate, the genius to seize aright the moment of action and of success."

He looked at her, and for the hour understood her aright; he saw that there was the love for her country and the power of sacrifice of a Viriathus or an Arminius in this gay-plumaged and capricious little hawk of the desert.

"You have a noble nature, Cigarette," he said, with an earnest regard at her. "My poor child, if only——" He paused. He was thinking what it was hard to say to her—if only the accidents of her life had been different, what beauty, grace, and genius might have been developed out of the untamed, untutored, inconsequent, but glorious nature of the child-warrior.

"Holà!" she cried, suddenly. "There is one of your countrymen. I detest your country, but, ma foi! I must confess she breeds uncommonly handsome men."

She was a dilettante in handsome men; she nodded her head now to where, some yards off, at another of the campfires, stood, with some officers of the regiment, one of the tourists; a very tall, very fair man, with a gallant bearing, and a tawny beard that glittered to gold in the light of the flames.

Cecil's glance followed Cigarette's. With a great cry he sprang to his feet and stood entranced, gazing at the stranger. She saw the startled amaze, the longing love, the agony of

recognition, in his eyes; she saw the impulse in him
to spring forward, and the shuddering effort with which
the impulse was controlled. He turned to her almost
fiercely.

"He must not see me! Keep him away—away, for God's
sake!"

He could not leave his men; he was fettered there where
his squadron was camped. He went as far as he could from
the flame-light into the shadow, and thrust himself among
the tethered horses. Cigarette asked nothing; comprehended at a
glance with all the tact of her nation; and sauntered forward
to meet the officers of the regiment as they came up to the
picket-fire with the yellow-haired English stranger. She
knew how charming a picture there, with her hands lightly
resting on her hips, and her bright face danced on by the
ruddy fire-glow, she made; she knew she could hold thus the
attention of a whole brigade. The eyes of the stranger
lighted on her, and his voice laughed in mellow music to his
companions and ciceroni.

"Your intendance is perfect; your ambulance is perfect;
your camp-cookery is perfect, messieurs; and here you have
even perfect beauty, too! Truly, campaigning must be pleasant work in Algeria!"

Then he turned to her with compliments frank and gay,
and full of a débonnaire grace that made her doubt he could
be of Albion.

It was a fantastic picture by the bright scarlet light of the
camp-fire, with the Little One in her full glory of mirth and
mischief, and her circle of officers laughing on her with admiring eyes; nearest her the towering height of the English
stranger, with the gleam of the flame in the waves of his
leonine beard.

From the darkness, where the scores of gray horses were
tethered, Cecil's eyes were riveted on it. There were none
near to see him; had there been, they would have seen an
agony in his eyes that no physical misery, no torture of the
battlefield, had brought there. His face was bloodless, and
his gaze strained through the gleam on to the fire-lit group
with a passionate intensity of yearning—he was well used to
pain, well used to self-control, well used to self-restraint, but
for the first time in his exile the bitterness of a struggle
almost vanquished him. All the old love of his youth went
out to this man, so near beside him, yet so hopelessly severed
from him; looking on the face of his friend, a violence of

longing shook him. "O God, if I were dead!" he thought, "they might know then——"

He would have died gladly to have had that familiar hand once more touch his; those familiar eyes once more look on him with the generous, tender trust of old.

His brain reeled, his thoughts grew blind, as he stood there among his horses, with the stir and tumult of the bivouac about him. There was nothing simpler, nothing less strange, than that an English soldier should visit the Franco-Arab camp; but to him it seemed like the resurrection of the dead.

A while, and the group broke up and was scattered. When they were quite gone, Cigarette came softly to him; she could not see him well in the gloom, but she touched his hand.

"Dieu! how cold you are! He is gone."

He could not answer her to thank her, but he crushed in his the little, warm, brown palm. She felt a shiver shake his limbs.

"Is he your enemy?" she asked.

"No."

"What, then?"

"The man I love best on earth."

"Ah!" She had felt a surprise she had not spoken that he should flee thus from any foe. "He thinks you dead, then?"

"Yes."

"And must always think so?"

"Yes." He held her hand still, and his own wrung it hard —the grasp of comrade to comrade, not of man to woman. "Child, you are bold, generous, pitiful; for God's sake, get me sent out of this camp to-night. I am powerless."

There was that in the accent which struck his listener to the heart. He was powerless, fettered hand and foot as though he were a prisoner; a night's absence, and he would be shot as a deserter. He had grown accustomed to this rendering up of all his life to the rules of others; but now and then the galled spirit chafed, the netted stag strained at the bonds.

"I will try," said Cigarette simply, without anything of her audacity or of her vanity in the answer. "Go you to the fire; you are cold."

"Are you sure he will not return?"

"Not he. They are gone to eat and drink; I go with them. What is it you fear?"

"My own weakness."

"You are a fine soldier," said Cigarette musingly; "such men are not weak."

"Why? We are only strong as tigers are strong—just the strength of the talon and fang. I do not know. I was weak as water once; I may be again, if—if——"

He scarcely knew that he was speaking aloud; he had forgotten her! His whole heart seemed burned as with fire by the memory of that one face so familiar, so well loved, yet from which he must shrink as though some cowardly sin were between them. The wretchedness on him seemed more than he could bear; to know that this man was so near that the sound of his voice raised could summon him, yet that he must remain as dead to him—remain as one dead after a craven and treacherous guilt.

He turned suddenly, almost violently, upon Cigarette.

"You have surprised my folly from me; you know my secret so far; but you are too brave to betray me, you are too generous to tell of this? I can trust you to be silent?"

Her face flushed scarlet with astonished anger; her little, childlike form grew instinct with haughty and fiery dignity.

"Monsieur, that question from one soldier of France to another is insult. We are not dastards!"

There was a certain grave reproach that mingled with the indignant scorn of the answer, and showed that her own heart was wounded by the doubt, as well as her military pride by the aspersion. Even amid the conflict of pain at war in him he felt that, and hastened to soothe it.

"Forgive me, my child; I should not have wronged you with the question. It is needless, I know. Men can trust you to the death, they say."

"To the death—yes."

The answer was thoughtful, dreamy, almost sad, for Cigarette. His thoughts were too far from her in their tumult of awakened memories to note the tone as he went rapidly on:

"You have ingenuity, compassion, tact; you have power here, too, in your way. For the love of Heaven get me sent out on some duty before dawn! There is Biribi's murder to be avenged—would they give the errand to me?"

She thought a moment.

"We will see," she said curtly. "I think I can do it. But go back, or you will be missed. I will come to you soon."

She left him then, rapidly; drawing her hand quickly out of the clasp of his.

Cecil mechanically returned to the fire at which the men of

his tribu were cooking their welcome supper, and set down near them.

He sat like a man in a dream, while the loosened tongues of the men ran noisily on a hundred themes as they chaffed each other, exchanged a fire of bivouac jokes more racy than decorous, and gave themselves to the enjoyment of their rude meal, that had to them that savor which long hunger alone can give.

"He said once that he would take my hand before all the world always, come what would," he thought. "Would he take it now, I wonder? Yes; he never believed against me."

"How weak I am!" he thought bitterly. "What does it matter? Life is so short, one is a coward indeed to fret over it. I cannot undo what I did. I cannot, if I would. To betray him now! God! not for a kingdom, if I had the chance! Besides, she may live still; and, even were she dead, to tarnish her name to clear my own would be a scoundrel's baseness—baseness that would fail as it merited; for who could be brought to believe me now?"

As he sat with his head bent down and his forehead leaning on his arm, while the hard biscuit that served for a plate stood unnoticed beside him, with the food that the soldiers had placed on it, he did not hear Cigarette's step till she touched him on the arm. Then he looked up; her eyes were looking on him with a tender, earnest pity.

"Hark! I have done it," she said gently. "But it will be an errand very close to death that you must go on——"

He raised himself erect, eagerly.

"No matter that! Ah, mademoiselle, how I thank you!"

"Chut! I am no Paris demoiselle!" said Cigarette, with a dash of her old acrimony. "Ceremony in a camp—pouf! You must have been a court chamberlain once, weren't you? Well, I have done it. Your officers were talking yonder of a delicate business; they were uncertain who best to employ. I put in my speech—it was dead against military etiquette, but I did it. I said to M. le Général: 'You want the best rider, the most silent tongue, and the surest steel in the squadrons? Take Bel-à-faire-peur, then.' 'Who is that?' asked the general; he would have sent out of camp anybody but Cigarette for the interruption. 'Mon Général,' said I, 'the Arabs asked that, too, the other day, at Zaraila.' 'What!' he cried, 'the man Victor—who held the ground with his Chasseurs? I know—a fine soldier. M. le Colonel, shall we send him?' The Black Hawk scowled thunder on you. Then he laughed.

'Yes, mon Général,' he answered him, 'take him, if you like. It is fifty to one whoever goes on that business will not come back alive, and you will rid me of the most insolent fine gentleman in my squadrons.' The general hardly heard him; he was deep in thought; but he asked a good deal about you from the Hawk, and Châteauroy spoke for your fitness for the errand they are going to send you on, very truthfully, for a wonder. I don't know why; but he wants you to be sent, I think; most likely that you may be cut to pieces. And so they will send for you in a minute. I have done it as you wished, 'le diable prend le fruit.'"

Cecil grasped both her hands in his with warm gratitude, that was still, like the touch of his hands, the gratitude of comrade to comrade, not of man to woman.

"God bless you, Cigarette! You are a true friend, my child. You have done me immeasurable benefits——"

"Oh, hé! I am a true friend," said the Little One, somewhat pettishly. She would have preferred another epithet.

She drew her hands away from him.

"A great thing I have done, certainly! Got you permission to go and throw a cartel at old King Death; that is all! There! Loup-à-griffes-de-fer is coming to you. That is your summons."

The orderly so nicknamed approached, and brought the bidding of the general in command of the Cavalry for Cecil to render himself at once to his presence. These things brook no second's delay in obedience; he went with a quick adieu to Cigarette, and the little Friend of the Flag was left in his vacant place beside the fire.

And there was a pang at her heart.

"Ten to one he goes to his death," she thought. But Cigarette, volage little mischief though she was, could reach very high in one thing; she could reach a love that was unselfish, and one that was heroic.

A few moments, and Cecil returned.

"Rake," he said rapidly, in the French he habitually used, "saddle my horse and your own. I am allowed to choose one of you to accompany me."

Rake, in paradise, and the envied of every man in the squadrons, turned to his work—with him a task of scarce more than a second; and Cecil approached his little Friend of the Flag.

"My child, I cannot attempt to thank you. But for you, I

should have been tempted to send my lance through my own heart."

"Keep its lunge for the Arbicos, mon ami," said Cigarette brusquely—the more brusquely because that new and bitter pang was on her. "As for me, I want no thanks."

"No; you are too generous. But not the less do I wish I could render them more worthily than by words. If I live, I will try; if not, keep this in my memory. It is the only thing I have."

He put into her hand the ring she had seen in the little bon-bonnière; a ring of his mother's that he had saved when he had parted with all else, and had put off his hand and into the box of Petite Reine's gift the day he entered the Algerian army.

Cigarette flushed scarlet with passions he could not under-stand, and she could not have disentangled.

"The ring of your mistress! Not for me, if I know it! Do you think I want to be paid?"

"The ring was my mother's," he answered her simply. "And I offer it only en souvenir."

She lost all her hot color and all her fiery wrath; his grave and gentle courtesy always strangely stilled and rebuked her; but she raised the ring off the ground where she had flung it, and placed it back in his hand.

"If so, still less should you part with it. Keep it; it will bring you happiness one day. As for me, I have done nothing!"

"You have done what I value the more for that noble dis-claimer. May I thank you thus, Little One?"

He stooped and kissed her; a kiss that the lips of a man will always give to the bright, youthful lips of a woman, but a kiss, as she knew well, without passion, even without tender-ness in it.

With a sudden impetuous movement, with a shyness and a refusal that had never been in her before, she wrested herself from him, her face burning, her heart panting, and plunged away from him into the depth of the shadow; and he never sought to follow her, but threw himself into saddle as his gray was brought up. Another instant, and, armed to the teeth, he rode out of the camp into the darkness of the silent, melan-choly, lonely Arab night.

CHAPTER XIX.

SEUL AU MONDE.

THE errand on which he went was one, as he was well aware, from which it were a thousand chances to one that he ever issued alive.

It was to reach a distant branch of the Army of Occupation with dispatches for the chief in command there, and to do this he had to pass through a fiercely hostile region, occupied by Arabs with whom no sort of peace had ever been made, the most savage as well as the most predatory of the wandering tribes. His knowledge of their tongue, and his friendship with some men of their nation, would avail him nothing here; for their fury against the Franks was intense, and it was said that all prisoners who had fallen into their hands had been put to death with merciless barbarities. This might be true or untrue; wild tales were common among Algerian campaigners; whichever it were, he thought little of it as he rode out on to the lonely plains. Every kind of hazardous adventure and every variety of peril had been familiar with him in this African life; and now there were thoughts and memories on him which deadened every recollection of merely physical risk.

"We must ride as hard and as fast as we can, and as silently," were the only words he exchanged with Rake, as he loosened his gray to a hand-gallop.

"All right, sir," answered the trooper, whose warm blood was dancing, and whose blue eyes were alive like fire with delight.

They had two hundred miles to traverse, and had received only the command he had passed to Rake, to ride "hard, fast, and silently."

It was just nightfall; the after-glow had faded only a few moments before. Giving their horses, which they were to change once, ten hours for the distance, and two for bait and for rest, he reckoned that they would reach the camp before the noon of the coming day, as the beasts, fresh and fast in the camp, flew like greyhounds beneath them.

Another night ride that they had ridden together came to the minds of both; but they spoke not a word as they swept on, their sabers shaken loose in their sheaths, their lances well gripped, and the pistols with which they had been supplied sprung in their belts, ready for instant action if a call should come for it.

The first five-and-twenty miles passed without interruption, and the horses lay well and warmly to their work. They halted to rest and bait the beasts in a rocky hollow, sheltered from the blasts of the bise, and green with short, sweet grass, sprung up afresh after the summer drought.

They were before long in saddle again and off, the country growing wilder at each stride the horses took.

"It is all alive with Arabs for the next ten leagues," said Cecil, as he settled himself in his saddle. "They have come northward and been sweeping the country like a locust-swarm, and we shall blunder on some of them sooner or later. If they cut me down, don't wait; but slash my sabertasche loose and ride off with it."

"All right, sir," said Rake obediently; but he thought to himself, "Leave you alone with them demons? Damn me if I will!"

And away they went once more, in speed and in silence, the darkness of full night closing in on them, the skies being black with the heavy drift of rising storm-clouds.

Meantime Cigarette was feasting with the officers of the regiment. The dinner was the best that the camp-scullions could furnish in honor of the two or three illustrious tourists who were on a visit to the headquarters of the Algerian Army; and the Little One, the heroine of Zaraila, and the toast of every mess throughout Algeria, was as indispensable as the champagnes.

Not a word escaped her that could have given a clew to the secret with which he had involuntarily weighted her; she only studied with interest and keenness the face and the words of this man whom he had loved, and from whom he had fled as criminals flee from their accusers.

"What is your name?" she asked him curtly, in one of the pauses of the amorous and witty nonsense that circulated in the tent in which the officers of Chasseurs were entertaining him.

"Well—some call me Seraph."

"Ah! you have petits noms, then, in Albion? I should have thought she was too somber and too stiff for them. Besides?"

"Lyonnesse."

"What a droll name! What are you?"

"A soldier."

"Good! What grade?"

"A Colonel of Guards."

Cigarette gave a little whistle to herself; she remembered that a Marshal of France had once said of a certain Chasseur, "He has the seat of the English Guards."

"My pretty catechist, M. le Duc does not tell you his title," cried one of the officers.

Cigarette interrupted him with a toss of her head.

"Ouf! Titles are nothing to me. I am a child of the People. So you are a Duke, are you, M. le Seraph? Well, that is not much, to my thinking. Bah! there is Fialin made a Duke in Paris, and there are aristocrats here wearing privates' uniforms, and littering down their own horses. Bah! Have you that sort of thing in Albion?"

"Attorneys throned on high, and gentlemen glad to sweep crossings? Oh, yes!" laughed her interlocutor. "But you speak of aristocrats in your ranks—that reminds me. Have you not in this corps a soldier called Louis Victor?"

He had turned as he spoke to one of the officers, who answered him in the affirmative; while Cigarette listened with all her curiosity and all her interest, that needed a deeper name, heightened and tight-strung.

"A fine fellow," continued the Chef d'Escadron to whom he had appealed. "He behaved magnificently the other day at Zaraila; he must be distinguished for it. He is just sent on a perilous errand, but though so quiet he is a croc-mitaine, and woe to the Arabs who slay him! Are you acquainted with him?"

"Not in the least. But I wished to hear all I could of him. I have been told he seems above his present position. Is it so?"

"Likely enough, monsieur; he seems a gentleman. But then we have many gentlemen in the ranks, and we can make no difference for that. Cigarette can tell you more of him; she used to complain that he bowed like a Court chamberlain."

"Oh, hé!—I did!" cried Cigarette, stung into instant irony because pained and irritated by being appealed to on the subject. "And, of course, when so many of his officers have the manners of Pyrenean bears, it is a little awkward for him to bring us the manners of a Palace!"

Which effectually chastised the Chef d'Escadron, who was one of those who had a ton de garnison of the roughest, and piqued himself on his powers of fence much more than on his habits of delicacy.

"Has this Victor any history?" asked the English Duke.

"He has written one with his sword; a fine one," said Cigarette curtly. "We are not given here to care much about any other."

"Quite right; I asked because a friend of mine who had seen his carvings wished to serve him, if it were possible; and——"

"Ho! That is Miladi, I suppose?" Cigarette's eyes flashed fire instantly, in wrath and suspicion. "What did she tell you about him, la belle dédaigneuse?"

"I am ignorant of whom you speak?" he answered, with something of surprise and annoyance.

"Are you?" said Cigarette, in derision. "I doubt that. Of whom should I speak but of her? Bah! She insulted him, she offered him gold, she sent my men the spoils of her table, as if they were paupers, and he thinks it all divine because it is done by Mme. la Princesse Corona d'Amague! Faugh! when he was delirious, the other night, he could babble of nothing but of her—of her!"

The jealous, fiery impatience in her vanquished every other thought; she was a child in much, she was untutored in all; she had no thought that by her scornful vituperation of "Miladi" she could either harm Cecil or betray herself. But she was amazed to see the English guest change color with a haughty anger that he strove to subdue as he half rose and answered her with an accent in his voice that reminded her—she knew not why—of Bel-à-faire-peur and of Marquise.

"Mme. la Princesse Corona d'Amague is my sister; why do you venture to couple the name of this Chasseur with hers?"

Cigarette sprang to her feet, vivacious, imperious, reckless, dared to anything by the mere fact of being publicly arraigned.

"Pardieu! Is it insult to couple the silver pheasant with the Eagles of France?—a pretty idea, truly! So she is your sister, is she? Miladi? Well, then, tell her from me to think twice before she outrages a soldier with 'patronage'; and tell her, too, that had I been he I would have ground my ivory toys into powder before I would have let them become the playthings of a grande dame who tendered me gold for them!"

The Englishman looked at her with astonishment that was mingled with a vivid sense of intense annoyance and irritated pride, that the name he cherished closest should be thus brought in, at a camp dinner, on the lips of a vivandière and in connection with a trooper of Chasseurs.

"I do not understand your indignation, mademoiselle," he said, with an impatient stroke to his beard. "There is no occasion for it. Mme. Corona d'Amagüe, my sister," he continued, to the officers present, "became accidentally acquainted with the skill at sculpture of this Corporal of yours; he appeared to her a man of much refinement and good breeding. She chanced to name him to me, and feeling some pity——"

"M. le Duc!" cried the ringing voice of Cigarette, loud and startling as a bugle-note, while she stood like a little lioness, flushed with the draughts of champagne and with the warmth of wrath at once jealous and generous, "keep your compassion until it is asked of you. No soldier of France needs it; that I promise you. I know this man that you talk of 'pitying.' Well, I saw him at Zaraila three weeks ago; he had drawn up his men to die with them rather than surrender and yield up the guidon; I dragged him half dead, when the field was won, from under his horse, and his first conscious act was to give the drink that I brought him to a wretch who had thieved from him. Our life here is hell upon earth to such as he, yet none ever heard a lament wrung out of him; he is gone to the chances of death to-night as most men go to their mistresses' kisses; he is a soldier Napoleon would have honored. Such a one is not to have the patronage of a Miladi Corona, nor the pity of a stranger of England. Let the first respect him; let the last imitate him!"

And Cigarette, having pronounced her defense and her eulogy with the vibrating eloquence of some orator from a tribune, threw her champagne goblet down with a crash, and, breaking through the arms outstretched to detain her, forced her way out despite them, and left her hosts alone in their lighted tent.

"C'est Cigarette!" said the Chef d'Escadron, with a shrug of his shoulders, as of one who explained, by that sentence, a whole world of irreclaimable eccentricities.

"A strange little Amazon!" said their guest. "Is she in love with this Victor, that I have offended her so much with his name?"

The Major shrugged his shoulders.

"I don't know that, monsieur," answered one. "She will defend a man in his absence, and rate him to his face most soundly. Cigarette whirls about like a little paper wind-mill, just as the breeze blows; but, as the windmill never leaves its stick, so she is always constant to the Tricolor."

Their guest said little more on the subject; in his own thoughts he was bitterly resentful that, by the mention of this Chasseur's fortunes, he should have brought in the name he loved so well—the purest, fairest, haughtiest name in Europe—into a discussion with a vivandière at a camp dinner.

Châteauroy, throughout, had said nothing; he had listened in silence, the darkness lowering still more heavily upon his swarthy features; only now he opened his lips for a few brief words:

"Mon cher Duc, tell Madame not to waste the rare balm of her pity. The fellow you inquire for was an outcast and an outlaw when he came to us. He fights well—it is often a blackguard's virtue!"

His guest nodded and changed the subject; his impatience and aversion at the introduction of his sister's name into the discussion made him drop the theme unpursued, and let it die out forgotten.

While the Seraph slept dreamlessly, with the tents of the French camp around him, and the sleepless eyes of Cigarette watched afar off the dim, distant forms of the vedettes as they circled slowly round at their outpost duty—eight leagues off, through a vast desert of shadow and silence, the two horsemen swept swiftly on. Not a word had passed be-tween them; they rode close together in unbroken stillness; they were scarcely visible to each other, for there was no moon, and storm-clouds obscured the skies. Now and then their horses' hoofs struck fire from a flint-stone, and the flash sparkled through the darkness; often not even the sound of their gallop was audible on the gray, dry, loose soil.

Every rood of the road was sown thick with peril. No frowning ledge of rock, with pine-roots in its clefts, but might serve as the barricade behind which some foe lurked; no knot of cypress-shrubs, black even on that black sheet of shadow, but might be pierced with the steel tubes of lev-eled, waiting muskets.

They had reached the center of the plain when the sound they had long looked for rang on their ears, piercing the heavy, breathless stillness of the night. It was the Allah-il-Allah of their foes, the war-cry of the Moslem. Out of the gloom—whether from long pursuit or some near hiding-place they could not tell—there broke suddenly upon them the fury of an Arab onslaught.

How they were attacked, how they resisted, how they struck, how they were encompassed, how they thrust back those who were hurled on them in the black night, with the north sea-wind like ice upon their faces, and the loose African soil drifting up in clouds of sand around them, they could never have told. Nor how they strained free from the armed ring that circled them, and beat aside the shafts of lances and the blades of swords, and forced their chargers breast to breast against the fence of steel, and through the tempest of rage, and blows, and shouts, and wind, and driven sand, cut their way through the foe whose very face they scarce could see, and plunged away into the shadows across the desolation of the plain, pursued, whether by one or by a thousand they could not guess; for the gallop was noiseless on the powdered soil, and the Arab yell of baffled passion and slaughterous lust was half drowned in the rising of the windstorm. Had it been day, they would have seen their passage across the level table-land traced by a crimson stream upon the sand, in which the blood of Frank and Arab blended equally.

As it was, they dashed headlong down through the darkness that grew yet denser and blacker as the storm rose. For miles the ground was level before them, and they had only to let the half-maddened horses, that had as by a miracle escaped all injury, rush on at their own will through the whirl of the wind that drove the dust upward in spiral columns and brought icy breaths of the north over the sear, sun-burned, southern wastes.

For a long space they had no sense but that of rapid, cease-less motion through the thick gloom and against the pressure of the violent blasts. The need of their gallop and the strength of the currents of air were like some narcotic that drowned and that dizzied perception. In the intense dark-ness neither could see, neither hear, the other; the instinct of the beasts kept them together, but no word could be heard above the roar of the storm, and no light broke the somber veil of shadow through which they passed as fast as leop-ards course through the night. The first faint streak of dawn grew gray in the east when Cecil felt his charger stagger and sway beneath him, and halt, worn out and quivering in every sinew with fatigue. He threw himself off the animal in time to save himself from falling with it as it reeled and sank to the ground.

"Massena cannot stir another yard," he said. "Do you think they follow us still?"

There was no reply.

He strained his sight to pierce the darkness, but he could distinguish nothing; the gloom was still too deep. He spoke more loudly; still there was no reply. Then he raised his voice in a shout; it rang through the silence, and, when it ceased, the silence reigned again.

A deadly chill came on him. How had he missed his comrade? They must be far apart, he knew, since no response was given to his summons; or—the alternative rose before him with a terrible foreboding.

That intense quiet had a repose as of death in it, a ghastly loneliness that seemed filled with desolation. His horse was stretched before him on the sand, powerless to rise and drag itself a rood onward, and fast expiring. From the plains around him not a sound came, either of friend or foe. The consciousness that he was alone, that he had lost forever the only friend left to him, struck on him with that conviction which so often foreruns the assurance of calamity. Without a moment's pause he plunged back in the direction he had come, leaving the charger on the ground to pant its life out as it must, and sought to feel his way along, so as to seek as best he could the companion he had deserted. He had re-passed the ground already traversed by some hundred yards or more, which seemed the length of many miles in the hurricane that was driving over the earth and sky, when some outline still duskier than the dusky shadow caught his sight; it was the body of a horse, standing on guard over the fallen body of a man.

Another moment and he was beside them.

"My God! Are you hurt?"

He could see nothing but an indistinct and shapeless mass, without form or color to mark it out from the brooding gloom and from the leaden earth. But the voice he knew so well answered him with the old love and fealty in it; eager with fear for him.

"When did you miss me, sir? I didn't mean you to know; I held on as long as I could; and when I couldn't no longer, I thought you was safe not to see I'd knocked over, so dark as it was."

"Great Heavens! You are hurt, then?"

"Just finished, sir. Lord! it don't matter. Only you ride
on, Mr. Cecil; ride on, I say. Don't mind me."

"What is it? When were you struck? O Heaven! I never
dreamt——"

Cecil hung over him, striving in vain through the shadows
to read the truth from the face on which he felt by instinct
the seal of death was set.

"I never meant you should know, sir. I meant just to drop
behind and die on the quiet. You see, sir, it was just this
way; they hit me as we forced through them. There's the
lance-head in my loins now. I pressed it in hard, and kept
the blood from flowing, and thought I should hold out so till
the sun rose. But I couldn't do it so long; I got sick and
faint after a while, and I knew well enough it was death.
So I dropped down while I'd sense left to check the horse
and get out of saddle in silence. I hoped you wouldn't miss
me, in the darkness and the noise the wind was making; and
you didn't hear me then, sir. I was glad."

His voice was checked in a quick, gasping breath; his only
thought had been to lie down and die in solitude so that
his master might be saved.

A great sob shook Cecil as he heard; no false hope came
to him; he felt that this man was lost to him forever, that
this was the sole recompense which the cruelty of Africa
would give to a fidelity passing the fidelity of woman; these
throes of dissolution the only payment with which fate would
ever requite a loyalty that had held no travail weary, no
exile pain, and no danger worthy counting, so long as they
were encountered and endured in his own service.

"Don't take on about it, sir," whispered Rake, striving to
raise his head that he might strain his eyes better through
the gloom to see his master's face. "It was sure to come
some time; and I ain't in no pain—to speak of. Do leave
me, Mr. Cecil—leave me, for God's sake, and save yourself!"

"Did you leave me?"

The answer was very low, and his voice shook as he uttered it; but through the roar of the hurricane Rake heard it.

"That was different, sir," he said simply. "Let me lie
here, and go you on. It'll soon be over, and there's naught
to be done."

"O God! is no help possible?"

"Don't take on, sir; it's no odds. I allays was a scamp,
and scamps die game, you know. My life's been a rare spree,
count it all and all; and it's a great, good thing, you see,

sir, to go off quick like this. I might have been laid in hospital. If you'd only take the beast and ride on, sir——"

"Hush! hush! Would you make me coward, or brute, or both?" The words broke in an agony from him.

His grief fell dully on ears half deafened already to the sounds of the living world. The exhaustion that follows on great loss of blood was upon the soldier who for the last half hour had lain there in the darkness and the stillness, quietly waiting death, and not once seeking even to raise his voice for succor lest the cry should reach and should imperil his master.

The morning had broken now, but the storm had not lulled. By the fitful gleams of day he could see the blood slowly ebbing out from the great gap where the lance-head was still bedded with its wooden shaft snapped in two; he could see the drooped head that he had raised upon his knee, with the yellow, northern curls that no desert suns had darkened; and Rake's eyes, smiling so brightly and so bravely still, looked up from under their weary lids to his.

"I'd never let you take my hand before, sir; just take it once now—will you?—while I can see you still."

Their hands met as he asked it, and held each other close and long; all the loyal service of the one life, and all the speechless gratitude of the other, told better than by all words in that one farewell.

A light that was not from the stormy, dusky morning shone over the soldier's face.

"Time was, sir," he said, with a smile, "when I used to think as how, some day or another, when I should have done something great and grand, and you was back among your own again, and they here had given me the Cross, I'd have asked you to have done that before all the Army, and just to have said to 'em, if so you'd liked, 'He was a scamp, and he wasn't thought good for naught; but he kep' true to me, and you see it made him go straight, and I aren't ashamed to call him my friend.' I used to think that, sir, though 'twas silly, perhaps. But it's best as it is—a deal best, no doubt. If you was only back safe in camp——"

"O God! cease! I am not worthy one thought of love like yours."

"Yes, you are, sir—leastways, you was to me. When you took pity on me, it was just a toss-up if I didn't go right to the gallows. Don't grieve that way, Mr. Cecil. If I could just have seen you home again in your place, I should have been glad—that's all. You'll go back one day, sir; when you do, tell the King I ain't never forgot him."

His voice grew faint as the last sentence stole from his lips; he lay quite still, his head leaned back against his master; and the day came, with the north winds driving over the plains, and the gray mists tossed by them to and fro like smoke.

There was a long silence, a pause in which the windstorm ceased, and the clouds of the loosed sands sunk. In that awful stillness, in that sudden lull in the madness of the hurricane, death had a horror which it never wore in the riot of the battlefield, in the intoxication of the slaughter. There was no pity in earth or heaven; the hard, hot ground sucked down its fill of blood; the icy air enwrapped them like a shroud.

The faithfulness of love, the strength of gratitude, were of no avail; the one perished in agony, the other was powerless to save.

In that momentary hush, as the winds sank low, the heavy eyes, half sightless now, sought with their old wistful, dog-like loyalty the face to which so soon they would be blind forever.

"Would you tell me once, sir—now? I never asked—I never would have done—but may be I might know in this last minute. You never sinned that sin you bear the charge on?"

"God is my witness, no."

The light, that was like sunlight, shone once more in the aching, wandering eyes.

"I knew, I knew! It was——"

Cecil bowed his head over him, lower and lower.

"Hush! He was but a child; and I——"

With a sudden and swift motion, as though new life were thrilling in him, Rake raised himself erect, his arms stretched outward to the east, where the young day was breaking.

"I knew, I knew! I never doubted. You will go back to your own some day, and men shall learn the truth—thank God! thank God!"

Then, with that light still on his face, his head fell backward; and with one quick, brief sigh his life fled out forever.

The time passed on; the storm had risen afresh; the violence of the gusts blew yellow sheets of sand whirling over

the plains. Alone, with the dead across his knees, Cecil sat
motionless as though turned to stone. His eyes were dry
and fixed; but ever and again a great, tearless sob shook
him from head to foot. The only life that linked him with
the past, the only love that had suffered all things for his
sake, were gone, crushed out as though they never had been,
like some insect trodden in the soil.

He was alone on earth; and the solitudes around him were
not more desolate than his own fate.

Instinctively, he moved to carry out the duty trusted to
him. He looked east and west, north and south; there was
nothing in sight that could bring him aid; there were only
the dust-clouds hurled in billows hither and thither by the
bitter winds still blowing from the sea. All that could be
done had to be done by himself alone. His own safety hung
on the swiftness of his flight: for aught he knew, at every
moment, out of the mist and the driven sheets of sand there
might rush the desert-horses of his foes. But this memory
was not with him; all he thought of was that burden stretched
across his limbs, which, laid down one hour here unwatched,
would be the prey of the jackal and the vulture. He raised
it reverently in his arms, and with long, laborious effort
drew its weight up across the saddle of the charger which
stood patiently waiting by, turning its docile eyes with a
plaintive, wondering sadness on the body of the rider it had
loved. Then he mounted himself; and with the head of his
lost comrade borne up upon his arm, and rested gently on
his breast, he rode westward over the great plain to where
his mission lay.

CHAPTER XX.

"JE VOUS ACHÈTE VOTRE VIE."

THUS burdened, he made his way for over two leagues.
The hurricane never abated, and the blinding dust rose around
him in great waves. The horse fell lame; he had to dis-
mount, and move slowly and painfully over the loose, heavy
soil on foot, raising the drooping head of the lifeless rider.
It was bitter, weary, cruel travail, of an intolerable labor, of
an intolerable pain.

At last he drew near the caravanserai where he had been
directed to obtain a change of horses. As a man walks

in a dream, he led the sinking beast toward its shelter, as
its irregular corner towers became dimly perceptible to him
through the dizzy mists that had obscured his sight. By
sheer instinct he found his route straight toward the open
arch of its entrance-way, and into the square courtyard
thronged with mules and camels and horses. The groups
in the court paused in their converse and in their occupa-
tions, and looked in awe at the gray charger with its strange
burden, and the French Chasseur who came so blindly forward like a man feeling his passage through the dark.
There was something in the sight that had a vague terror
for them before they clearly saw what this thing was which
was thus brought into their presence. Cecil moved slowly
on into their midst, his hand on the horse's rein; then a
great darkness covered his sight; he swayed to and fro, and
fell senseless on the gray stone of the paved court, while
the muleteers and the camel-drivers, the Kabyls and the
French, who were mingled there, crowded around him in fear
and in wonder. When consciousness returned to him he
was lying on a stone bench in the shadow of the wall, with
the coolness of the fountain water bubbling near, and a throng
of lean, bronzed, eager faces about him in the midday sunlight which had broken through the windstorm.

Instantly he remembered all.

"Where is he?" he asked.

They knew that he meant the dead man, and answered
him in a hushed murmur of many voices. They had placed
the body gently down within, in a darkened chamber.

A shiver passed over him; he stretched his hand out for
water that they held to him.

"Saddle me a fresh horse; I have my work to do."

He knew that for no friendship, or grief, or suffering, or
self-pity might a soldier pause by the wayside while his errand
was still undone, his duty unfulfilled.

He drank the water thirstily; then, reeling slightly still,
from the weakness that was still upon him, he rose, rejecting
their offers of aid. "Take me to him," he said simply. They
understood him; there were French soldiers among them, and
they took him, without question or comment, across the court
to the little square stone cell within one of the towers, where
they had laid the corpse.

He motioned them all back with his hand, and went into
the gloom of the chamber alone. Not one among them followed.

When he came forth again the reckless and riotous fantas-
sins of France turned silently and reverentially away, so
that they should not look upon his face. For it was well
known throughout the army that no common tie had bound
together the exiles of England, and the fealty of comrade
to comrade was sacred in their sight.

The fresh animal, saddled, was held ready outside the gates.
He crossed the court, moving still like a man without sense
of what he did; he had the instinct to carry out the mission
trusted to him, instantly and accurately, but he had no distinct perception or memory of aught else, save of those long-
familiar features of which, ere he could return, the cruel
sun of Africa would not have spared one trace.

He passed under the shadow of the gateway arch—a
shadow black and intense against the golden light which, with
the ceasing of the storm, flooded the land in the full morning.
There were movement, noise, change, haste in the entrance.
Besides the arrival of the detachment of the line and a
string of northward-bound camels, the retinue of some travelers of rank was preparing for departure, and the resources
of the humble caravanserai were taxed beyond their powers.
The name that some of the hurrying grooms shouted loudly
in their impatience broke through his stupor and reached him.
It was that of the woman whom, however madly, he loved
with all the strength of a passion born out of utter hopelessness. He turned to the outrider nearest him:

"You are of the Princess Corona's suite? What does
she do here?"

"Madame travels to see the country and the war."

"The war? This is no place for her. The land is alive
with danger—rife with death."

"Miladi travels with M. le Duc, her brother. Miladi does
not know what fear is."

"But——"

The remonstrance died on his lips; he stood gazing out
from the gloom of the arch at a face close to him, on which
the sun shone full, a face unseen for twelve long years, and
which, a moment before laughing and careless in the light,
changed, and grew set, and rigid, and pale with the pallor
of an unutterable horror. His own flushed, and moved, and
altered with a wholly different emotion—emotion that was,
above all, of an intense and yearning tenderness. For a
moment both stood motionless and speechless; then, with a
marvelous self-command and self-restraint, Cecil brought his

hand to his brow in military salute, passed with the impassiveness of a soldier who passed a gentleman, reached his charger, and rode away upon his errand over the brown and level ground.

He had known his brother in that fleeting glance, but he hoped that his brother would see no more in him than a French trooper who bore resemblance by a strange hazard to one long believed to be dead and gone.

Full remembrance, full consideration of what he had done, never came to him as he dashed on across the many leagues that still lay between him and his goal. His one impulse had been to spare the other from the knowledge that he lived; his one longing was to have the hardness and the bitterness of his own life buried in the oblivion of a soldier's grave.

Within six-and-thirty hours the instructions he bore were in the tent of the Chef du Bataillon whom they were to direct, and he himself returned to the caravanserai to fulfill with his own hand to the dead those last offices which he would delegate to none. It was night when he arrived; all was still and deserted. He inquired if the party of tourists was gone; they answered him in the affirmative; there only remained the detachment of the French infantry, which were billeted there for a while.

It was in the coolness and the hush of the night, with the great stars shining clearly over the darkness of the plains, that they made the single grave, under a leaning shelf of rock, with the somber fans of a pine spread above it, and nothing near but the sleeping herds of goats. The sullen echo of the soldiers' muskets gave its only funeral requiem.

When all was over, and the startled flocks had settled once again to rest and slumber, Cecil still remained there alone. Thrown down upon the grave, he never moved as hour after hour went by. In the stillness that had succeeded to the storm of the past day there was not a sound except the bleating of the young goats straying from the herd. He lay prostrate under the black boughs of the pine; the exhaustion of great fatigue was on him; a grief, acute as remorse, consumed him for the man who, following his fate, had only found at the end a nameless and lonely grave in the land of his exile.

He started with a thrill of almost superstitious fear as through the silence he heard a name whispered—the name of his childhood. of his past.

He sprang to his feet, and as he turned in the moonlight he saw once more his brother's face, pale as the face of the dead, and strained with an agonizing dread. Concealment was no longer possible. The younger man knew that the elder lived; knew it by a strange and irresistible certainty that needed no proof, that left no place for hope or fear in its chill, leaden, merciless conviction.

For some moments neither spoke. A flood of innumerable memories choked thought or word in both. They knew each other—all was said in that.

Cecil was the first to break the silence. He moved nearer with a rapid movement, and his hand fell heavily on the other's shoulder.

"Have you lived stainlessly since?"

The question was stern as the demand of a judge. His brother shuddered beneath this touch, and covered his face with his hands.

"God is my witness, yes! But you—you—they said that you were dead!"

Cecil's hand fell from his shoulder. There was that in the words which smote him more cruelly than any Arab steel could have done; there was the accent of regret.

"I am dead," he said simply; "dead to the world and you." He who bore the title of Royallieu covered his face. "How have you lived?" he whispered hoarsely.

"Honorably. Let that suffice. And you?"

The other looked up at him with a piteous appeal—the old, timorous, terrified appeal that had been so often seen on the boy's face, strangely returning on the gracious and mature beauty of the man.

"In honor too, I swear! That was my first disgrace, and my last. You bore the weight of my shame? Good God, what can I say? Such nobility, such sacrifice——"

He would have said enough, more than enough, to satisfy the one who had lost all for his sake, had there but been once in his voice no fear, but only love. While crushed with the weight of his brother's surpassing generosity, he still was filled with only one thought that burned through the darkness of his bewildered horror, and that thought was his own jeopardy. Even in the very first hours of his knowledge that the man whom he had believed dead was living—living and bearing the burden of the guilt he should have borne —what he was filled with was the imminence of his own peril.

Cecil stood in silence, looking at him. He saw that life had gone softly, smoothly, joyously, with this weak and feminine nature; and that, in the absence of temptation to evil, its career had been fair and straight in the sight of the world. He saw that his brother had been, in one word, happy. He saw that happiness had done for this character what adversity had done for his own. He saw that by it had been saved a temperament that calamity would have wrecked. He stood and looked at him, but he spoke not one word; whatever he felt, he restrained from all expression.

The younger man still hid his face upon his hands, as if, even in those pale, gray moonbeams, he shunned the light that was about him.

"We believed you were dead," he murmured wildly. "They said so; there seemed every proof. But when I saw you yesterday, I knew you—I knew you, though you passed me as a stranger. I stayed on here; they told me you would return. God! what agony this day and night have been!"

Cecil was silent still; he knew that this agony had been the dread lest he should be living.

The younger man stood half stupefied, half maddened.

"Bertie—Bertie!" he stammered, in hurried appeal—and the name of his youth touched the hearer of it strangely, making him for the moment forget all save that he looked once more upon one of his own race—"on my soul, I never doubted that the story of your death was true. No one did. All the world believed it. If I had known you lived, I would have said that you were innocent; I would—I would have told them how I forged your friend's name and your own when I was so desperate that I scarce knew what I did. But they said that you were killed, and I thought then—then—it was not worth while; it would have broken my father's heart. God help me! I was a coward!"

He spoke the truth; he was a coward; he had ever been one.

"I am in your power—utterly in your power," he moaned in his fear. "I stand in your place; I bear your title; you know that our father and our brother are dead? All that I have inherited is yours. Do you know that, since you have never claimed it?"

"I know it."

"And you have never come forward to take your rights?"

"What I did not do to clear my own honor, I was not likely to do merely to hold a title."

The meaning of his answer drifted beyond the ear on which his words fell; it was too high to be comprehended by the lower nature. The man who lived in prosperity and peace, and in the smile of the world, and the purple of power, looked bewildered at the man who led the simple, necessitous, perilous, semi-barbaric existence of an Arab-Franco soldier.

"But—great Heaven!—this life of yours? It must be wretchedness?"

"Perhaps. It has at least no disgrace in it."

The reply had the only sternness of contempt that he had suffered himself to show. It stung down to his listener's soul.

"No—no!" he murmured. "You are happier than I. You have no remorse to bear! And yet—to tell the world that I am guilty——"

"You need never tell it; I shall not."

He spoke quite quietly, quite patiently. Yet he well knew, and had well weighed, all he surrendered in that promise— the promise to condemn himself to a barren and hopeless fate forever.

"You will not?"

The question died almost inaudible on his dry, parched tongue. The one passion of fear upon him was for himself; even in that moment of supplication his disordered thoughts hovered wildly over the chances of whether, if his elder brother even now asserted his innocence and claimed his birthright, the world and its judges would ever believe him. Cecil for a while again was silent, standing there by the newly made grave of the soldier who had been faithful as those of his own race and of his own Order never had been. His heart was full. The ingratitude and the self-absorption of this life for which his own had been destroyed smote him with a fearful suffering. And only a few hours before he had looked once more on the face of the beloved friend of his youth; a deadlier sacrifice than to lay down wealth, and name, and heritage, and the world's love, was to live on, leaving that one comrade of his early days to believe him dead after a deed of shame.

"Do not fear me," he said, gently and very gravely. "I have kept your secret twelve years; I will keep it still. Be happy—be as happy as you can. All I bid of you in return is so to live that in your future your past shall be redeemed."

"My God! You cannot mean it! And you——"

"I shall lead the life fittest for me. I am content in it. It is enough."

The answer was very calm, but it choked him in its utterance. Before his memory rose one fair, proud face. "Content!" Ah, Heaven! It was the only lie that had ever passed his lips.

His hand lay still upon his brother's shoulder, leaning more heavily there, in the silence that brooded over the hushed plains.

"Let us part now, and forever. Leave Algeria at once. That is all I ask."

Then, without another word that could add reproach or seek for gratitude, he turned and went away over the great, dim level of the African waste while the man whom he had saved sat as in stupor; gazing at the brown shadows, and the sleeping herds, and the falling stars that ran across the sky, and doubting whether the voice he had heard and the face upon which he had looked were not the visions of a waking dream.

CHAPTER XXI.

"VENETIA."

How that night was spent Cecil could never recall in full. Vague memories remained with him of wandering over the shadowy country, of seeking by bodily fatigue to kill the thoughts rising in him, of drinking at a little water-channel in the rocks as thirstily as some driven deer, of flinging himself down at length, worn out, to sleep under the hanging brow of a mighty wall of rock; of waking, when the dawn was reddening the east, with the brown plains around him, and far away under a knot of palms was a goatherd with his flock, like an idyl from the old pastoral life of Syria.

He had come so far out of the ordinary route across the plains that it was two hours or more before he saw the dark, gray square of the caravanserai walls, and to its left that single, leaning pine growing out of a cleft within the rock that overhung the spot where the keenest anguish all his life had known had been encountered and endured— the spot which yet, for sake of the one laid to rest there beneath the somber branches, would be forever dearer to him than any other place in the soil of Africa.

While yet the caravanserai was distant, the piteous cries of a mother-goat caught his ear. She was bleating beside a water-course, into which her kid of that spring had fallen, and whose rapid swell, filled by the recent storm, was too strong for the young creature. Absorbed as he was in his own thoughts, the cry reached him and drew him to the spot. It was not in him willingly to let any living thing suffer, and he was always gentle to all animals. He stooped, and, with some little difficulty, rescued the little goat for its delighted dam.

As he bent over the water he saw something glitter beneath it. He caught it in his hand and brought it up. It was the broken half of a chain of gold, with a jewel in each link. He changed color as he saw it; he remembered it as one that Venetia Corona had worn on the morning that he had been admitted to her. It was of peculiar workmanship, and he recognized it at once. He stood with the toy in his hand, looking long at the shining links, with their flashes of precious stones. They seemed to have voices that spoke to him of her about whose beautiful white throat they had been woven—voices that whispered incessantly in his ear, "Take up your birthright, and you will be free to sue to her at least, if not to win her." No golden and jeweled plaything ever tempted a starving man to theft as this tempted him now to break the pledge he had just given.

His birthright! He longed for it for this woman's sake —for the sake, at least, of the right to stand before her as an equal, and to risk his chance with others who sought her smile—as he had never done for any other thing which, with that heritage, would have become his.

It was almost noon when Cecil approached the gates of the Algerine house-of-call. He went within, and bathed, and dressed, and drank some of the thin, cool wine that found its way thither in the wake of the French army. Then he sat down for a while at one of the square, cabin-like holes which served for casements in the tower he occupied, and, looking out into the court, tried to shape his thoughts and plan his course.

The trampling of horses on the pavement below roused his attention. A thrill of hope went through him that his brother might have lingering conscience, latent love enough, to have made him refuse to obey the bidding to leave Africa. He rose and leaned out. Amid the little throng of riding-horses, grooms, and attendants who made an open way through the polyglot crowd of an Algerian caravanserai at noon, he saw the one dazzling face of which he had so lately dreamed by the water-freshet in the plains. It was but a moment's glance, for she had already dismounted from her mare, and was passing within with two other ladies of her party; but in that one glance he knew her. His discovery of the chain gave him a plea to seek her. Should he avail himself of it? He hesitated a while. It would be safest, wisest, best, to deliver up the trinket to her courier, and pass on his way without another look at that beauty which could never be his, which could never lighten for him even with the smile that a woman may give her equal or her friend. He knew that; but he longed to indulge the madness, despite it; and he did so. He went down into the court below, and found her suite.

"Tell your mistress that I, Louis Victor, have some jewels which belong to her, and ask her permission to restore them to her hands," he said to one of her equerries.

"Give them to me, if you have picked them up," said the man, putting out his hand for them.

Cecil closed his own upon them.

"Go and do as I bid you."

The equerry paused, doubtful whether or no to resist the tone and the words. A Frenchman's respect for the military uniform prevailed. He went within.

In the best chamber of the caravanserai Venetia Corona was sitting, listless in the heat, when her attendant entered. She was lost in thought. She had heard, the day before, a story that had touched her—of a soldier who had been slain crossing the plains, and had been brought, through the hurricane and the sandstorm, at every risk, by his comrade, who had chosen to endure all peril and wretchedness rather than leave the dead body to the vultures and the kites. It was a nameless story to her—the story of two obscure troopers, who, for aught she knew, might have been two of the riotous and savage brigands that were common in the Army of Africa. But the loyalty and the love shown in it had moved her.

When her servant approached her now with Cecil's message she hesitated some few moments in surprise. She had not known that he was in her vicinity. The story she had heard had been simply of two unnamed Chasseurs d'Afrique, and he himself might have fallen on the field weeks before, for aught that she had heard of him. Some stray rumors of his defense of the encampment of Zaraila, and of the fine prowess shown in his last charge, alone had drifted to her. He was but a trooper; and he fought in Africa. The world had no concern with him, save the miniature world of his own regiment.

She hesitated some moments; then gave the required permission.

The room was darkened from the piercing light without; and in its gloom, as he was ushered in, the scarlet of her cashmere and the gleam of her fair hair was all that, for the moment, he could see. He bowed very low that he might get his calmness back before he looked at her; and her voice in its lingering music came on his ear.

"You have found my chain, I think? I lost it in riding yesterday. I am greatly indebted to you for taking care of it."

"It is I, madame, who am the debtor of so happy an accident."

His words were very low, and his voice shook a little over them; he was thinking not of the jeweled toy that he came here to restore, but of the inheritance that had passed away from him forever, and which, possessed, would have given him the title to seek what his own efforts could do to wake a look of tenderness in those proud eyes which men ever called so cold, but which he felt might still soften, and change, and grow dark with the thoughts and the passions of love, if the soul that gazed through them were but once stirred from its repose.

"Your chain is here, madame, though broken, I regret to see," he continued, as he took the little box from his coat and handed it to her. She took it, and thanked him, without, for the moment, opening the enamel case as she motioned him to a seat at a little distance from her own.

"You have been in terrible scenes since I saw you last," she continued. "The story of Zaraila reached us. Surely they cannot refuse you the reward of your service now?"

"It will make little difference, madame, whether they do or not."

"Little difference! How is that?"

"To my own fate, I meant. Whether I be captain or a corporal cannot alter——"

He paused; he dreaded lest the words should escape him which should reveal to her that which she would regard as such intolerable offense, such insolent indignity, when felt for her by a soldier in the grade he held.

"No? Yet such recognition is usually the ambition of every military life."

A very weary smile passed over his face.

"I have no ambition, madame. Or, if I have, it is not a pair of epaulettes that will content it."

She understood him; she comprehended the bitter mockery that the tawdry, meretricious rewards of regimental decoration seemed to the man who had waited to die at Zaraila as patiently and as grandly as the Old Guard at Waterloo.

"I understand! The rewards are pitifully disproportionate to the services in any army. Yet how magnificently you and your men, as I have been told, held your ground all through that fearful day!"

"We did our duty—nothing more."

"Well! is not that the rarest thing among men?"

"Not among soldiers, madame."

"Then you think that every trooper in a regiment is actuated by the finest and most impersonal sentiment that can actuate human beings!"

"I will not say that. Poor wretches! they are degraded enough, too often. But I believe that more or less in every good soldier, even when he is utterly unconscious of it, is an impersonal love for the honor of his Flag, an uncalculating instinct to do his best for the reputation of his corps. We are called human machines; we are so, since we move by no will of our own; but the lowest among us will at times be propelled by one single impulse—a desire to die greatly. It is all that is left to most of us to do."

She looked at him with that old look which he had seen once or twice before in her, of pity, respect, sympathy, and wonder, all in one.

"Yes," she said thoughtfully, while over the brilliancy of her face there passed a shadow. "There must be infinite nobility among these men, who live without hope—live only to die. That soldier, a day or two ago, who brought his dead comrade through the hurricane, risking his own death rather than leave the body to the carrion-birds—you have heard of him? What tenderness, what greatness there must have been in that poor fellow's heart!"

"Oh, no! That was nothing."

"Nothing! They have told me he came every inch of the way in danger of the Arabs' shot and steel. He had suffered so much to bring the body safe across the plains, he fell down insensible on his entrance here."

"You set too much store on it. I owed him a debt far greater than any act like that could ever repay."

"You! Was it you?"

"Yes, madame. He who perished had a thousandfold more of such nobility as you have praised than I."

"Ah! Tell me of him," she said simply; but he saw that the lustrous eyes bent on him had a grave, sweet sadness in them that was more precious and more pitiful than a million utterances of regret could ever have been.

Her hands toyed listlessly with the enamel bonbonnière, whose silver had lost all its bright enameling, and was dinted and dulled till it looked no more than lead. The lid came off at her touch as she musingly moved it round and round; the chain and the ring fell into her lap; the lid remained in her hand, its interior unspoiled and studded in its center with one name in turquoise letters—"Venetia."

She started as the word caught her eye; the color came warmer into her cheek; she looked closer and closer at the box; then, with a rapid movement, turned her head and gazed at her companion.

"How did you obtain this?"

"The chain, madame? It had fallen in the water."

"The chain! No! the box!"

He looked at her in surprise.

"It was given me very long ago."

"And by whom?"

"By a young child, madame."

Her lips parted slightly, the flush on her cheeks deepened; the beautiful face, which the Roman sculptor had said only wanted tenderness to make it perfect, changed, moved, was quickened with a thousand shadows of thought.

"The box is mine! I gave it! And you?"

He rose to his feet, and stood entranced before her, breathless and mute.

"And you?" she repeated.

He was silent still, gazing at her. He knew her now—how had he been so blind as never to guess the truth before, as never to know that those imperial eyes and that diadem of golden hair could belong alone but to the women of one race?

"And you?" she cried once more, while she stretched her hand out to him. "And you—you are Philip's friend? you are Bertie Cecil?"

Silently he bowed his head; not even for his brother's sake, or for the sake of his pledged word, could he have lied to her.

But her outstretched hands he would not see, he would not take. The shadow of an imputed crime was stretched between them.

"Petite Reine!" he murmured. "Ah, God! how could I be so blind?"

She grew very pale as she sank back again upon the couch from which she had risen. It seemed to her as though a thousand years had drifted by since she had stood beside this man under the summer leaves of the Stephanien, and he had kissed her childish lips, and thanked her for her loving gift. And now—they had met thus!

He said nothing. He stood paralyzed, gazing at her. There had been no added bitterness needed in the cup which he drank for his brother's sake, yet this bitterness surpassed all others; it seemed beyond his strength to leave her in the belief that he was guilty. She in whom all fair and gracious things were met; she who was linked by her race to his past and his youth; she whose clear eyes in her childhood had looked upon him in that first hour of the agony that he had suffered then, and still suffered on, in the cause of a coward and an ingrate.

She was pale still; and her eyes were fixed on him with a gaze that recalled to him the look with which "Petite Reine" had promised that summer day to keep his secret, and tell none of that misery of which she had been witness.

"They thought that you were dead," she said at length, while her voice sank very low. "Why have you lived like this?"

He made no answer.

"It was cruel to Philip," she went on, while her voice still shook. "Child though I was, I remember his passion of grief when the news came that you had lost your life. He has never forgotten you. So often now he will still speak of you! He is in your camp. We are traveling together. He will be here this evening. What delight it will give him to know his dearest friend is living! But why—why—have kept him ignorant, if you were lost to all the world beside?"

Still he answered her nothing. The truth he could not tell; the lie he would not. She paused, waiting reply. Receiving none, she spoke once more, her words full of that exquisite softness which was far more beautiful in her than in women less tranquil, less chill, and less negligent in ordinary moments.

"Mr. Cecil, I divined rightly! I knew that you were far higher than your grade in Africa; I felt that in all things, save in some accident of position, we were equals. But why have you condemned yourself to this misery? Your life is brave, is noble, but it must be a constant torture to such as you? I remember well what you were—so well, that I wonder we have never recognized each other before now. The existence you lead in Algeria must be very terrible to you, though it is greater, in truth, than your old years of indolence."

He sank down beside her on a low seat, and bowed his head on his hands for some moments. He knew that he must leave this woman whom he loved, and who knew him now as one whom in her childhood she had seen caressed and welcomed by all her race, to hold him guilty of this wretched, mean, and fraudulent thing, under whose charge he had quitted her country. Great dews of intense pain gathered on his forehead; his whole mind, and heart, and soul revolted against this brand of a guilt not his own that was stamped on him; he could have cried out to her the truth in all the eloquence of a breaking heart.

But he knew that his lips had been sealed by his own choice forever; and the old habits of his early life were strong upon him still. He lifted his head and spoke gently, and very quietly, though she caught the tremor that shook through the words.

"Do not let us speak of myself. You see what my life is; there is no more to be said. Tell me rather of your own story—you are no longer the Lady Venetia? You have been wedded and widowed, they say?"

"The wife of an hour—yes! But it is of yourself that I would hear. Why have left the world, and, above all, why have left us, to think you dead? I was not so young when we last saw you, but that I remember well how all my people loved you."

"Leave my life alone, for God's sake!" he said passionately. "Tell me of your own—tell me, above all, of his. He loved me, you say?—O Heaven! he did. Better than any creature that ever breathed; save the man whose grave lies yonder."

"He does so still," she answered eagerly. "Philip's is not a heart that forgets. It is a heart of gold, and the name of his earliest friend is graven on it as deeply now as ever. He thinks you dead; to-night will be the happiest hour he has ever known when he shall meet you here."

He rose hastily, and moved thrice to and fro the narrow floor whose rugged earth had been covered with furs and rugs lest it should strike a chill to her as she passed over it; the torture grew unsupportable to him.

She watched him with grave, musing eyes. She was moved, startled, softened to a profound pity for him, and filled with a wondering of regret; yet a strong emotion of relief, of pleasure, rose above these.

"What is it you fear from Philip?" she asked him, at last, when she had waited vainly for him to break the silence. "You can remember him but ill if you think that there will be anything in his heart save joy when he shall know that you are living. You little dream how dear your memory is to him——"

He paused before her abruptly.

"Hush, hush! or you will kill me! Why!—three nights ago I fled the camp as men flee pestilence, because I saw his face in the light of the bivouac-fire and dreaded that he should so see mine!"

She gazed at him in troubled amaze; there was that in the passionate agitation of this man who had been serene through so much danger, and unmoved beneath so much disaster, that startled and bewildered her.

"You fled from Philip? Ah, how you must wrong him! What will it matter to him whether you be prince or trooper, wear a peer's robes or a soldier's uniform? His friendship never yet was given to externals. But—stay!—that reminds me of your inheritance. Do you know that Lord Royallieu is dead? that your younger brother bears the title, thinking you perished at Marseilles? He was here with me yesterday; he has come to Algeria for the autumn. Whatever your motive may have been to remain thus hidden from us all, you must claim your own rights now. You must go back to all that is so justly yours. Whatever your reason be to have borne with all the suffering and the indignity that have been your portion here, they will be ended now."

"Why do you not answer me?" she pursued, while she leaned nearer with wonder, and doubt, and a certain awakening dread shadowing the blue luster of her eyes that were bent so thoughtfully, so searchingly, upon him. "Is it possible that you have heard of your inheritance, of your title and estates, and that you voluntarily remain a soldier here? Lord Royallieu must yield them in the instant you prove your identity, and in that there could be no difficulty. I remember you well now, and Philip, I am certain, will only need to see you once to——"

"Hush, for pity's sake! Have you never heard—have none ever told you——"

"What?"

Her face grew paler with a vague sense of fear; she knew that he had been equable and resolute under the severest tests that could try the strength and the patience of man, and she knew, therefore, that no slender thing could agitate and could unman him thus.

"What is it I should have heard?" she asked him, as he kept his silence.

He turned from her so that she could not see his face.

"That, when I became dead to the world, I died with the taint of crime on me!"

"Of crime?"

An intense horror thrilled through the echo of the word: but she rose, and moved, and faced him with the fearless resolve of a woman whom no half-truth would blind, and no shadowy terror appall.

"Of crime? What crime?"

Then, and then only, he looked at her, a strange, fixed, hopeless, yet serene look, that she knew no criminal ever would or could have given.

"I was accused of having forged your brother's name."

A faint cry escaped her; her lips grew white, and her eyes darkened and dilated.

"Accused. But wrongfully?"

His breath came and went in quick, sharp spasms.

"I could not prove that."

"Not prove it? Why?"

"I could not."

"But he—Philip—never believed you guilty?"

"I cannot tell. He may; he must."

"But you are not!"

It was not an interrogation, but an affirmation that rang out in the silver clearness of her voice. There was not a single intonation of doubt in it; there was rather a haughty authority that forbade even himself to say that one of his race and that one of his Order could have been capable of such ignoble and craven sin.

His mouth quivered, a bitter sigh broke from him; he turned his eyes on her with a look that pierced her to the heart.

"Think me guilty or guiltless, as you will; I cannot answer you."

His last words were suffocated with the supreme anguish of their utterance. As she heard it, the generosity, the faith, the inherent justice, and the intrinsic sweetness that were latent in her beneath the negligence and the chillness of external semblance rose at once to reject the baser, to accept the nobler, belief offered to her choice. She looked at him now, and stretched her hands out toward him with a royal and gracious gesture of infinite eloquence.

"You are guiltless, whatever circumstance may have arrayed against you, whatever shadow of evil may have fallen falsely on you. Is it not so?"

He lifted his head and looked her full in the eyes; her own closed involuntarily, and filled with tears. She felt that the despair and the patience of that look would haunt her until her dying day.

"I was guiltless; but none could credit it then; none would do so now; nor can I seek to make them. Ask me no more; give me your belief, if you can—God knows what precious mercy it is to me; but leave me to fulfill my fate, and tell no living creature what I have told you now."

"Tell no one!" she echoed. "What! not Philip even? not your oldest friend. Ah! be sure, whatever the evidence might be against you, his heart never condemned you for one instant."

"I believe it. Yet all you can do for me, all I implore you to do for me, is to keep silence forever on my name. To-day, accident has made me break a vow I never thought but to keep sacred. When you recognized me, I could not deny myself, I could not lie to you; but, for God's sake, tell none of what has passed between us!"

"But why?" she pursued—"why? You lie under this charge still—you cannot disprove it, you say; but why not come out before the world, and state to all what you swear now to me, and claim your right to bear your father's honors? If you were falsely accused, there must have been some guilty in your stead; and if——"

"Cease, for pity's sake! Forget I ever told you I was guiltless! Blot my memory out; think of me as dead, as I have been, till your eyes called me back to life. Think

that I am branded with the theft of your brother's name;
think that I am vile, and shameless, and fallen as the lowest
wretch that pollutes this army; think of me as what you will,
but not as innocent!"

"I hear you," she answered him gently; "but I do not
believe you, even against yourself. The man whom Philip
loved and honored never sank to the base fraud of a thief."

His eyes met hers full, and rested on them without
wavering; his head was raised, and his carriage had a fearless dignity.

"No. I was innocent. But in honor I must bear the yoke
that I took on me long ago; in honor I can never give you
or any living soul the proof that this crime was not mine.
I thought that I should go to my grave without any ever
hearing of the years that I have passed in Africa, without any ever learning the name I used to bear. As it is,
all I can ask is now—to be forgotten."

"You ask what will not be mine to give," she answered
him, while a great weariness stole through her own words,
for she was bewildered, and pained, and oppressed with a
new, strange sense of helplessness before this man's nameless
suffering. "Remember—I knew you so well in my earliest
years, and you are so dear to the one dearest to me. It
will not be possible to forget such a meeting as this. Silence,
of course, you can command from me, if you insist on it;
but——"

"I command nothing from you; but I implore it. It
is the sole mercy you can show. Never, for God's sake!
speak of me to your brother or to mine."

"Do you so mistrust Philip's affection?"

"No. It is because I trust it too entirely."

"Too entirely to do what?"

"To deal it fruitless pain. As you love him—as you
pity me—pray that he and I never meet!"

"But why? If all this could be cleared——"

"It never can be."

"Lord Royallieu," she said softly, at length, while she
rose and moved toward him; and at the old name, uttered
in her voice, he started, and turned, and looked at her as
though he saw some ghost of his past life rise from its
grave. "Why look at me so?" she pursued ere he could
speak. "Act how you will, you cannot change the fact that
you are the bearer of your father's title. So long as you
live, your brother Berkeley can never take it legally. You

may be a Chasseur of the African Army, but none the less are you a Peer of England."

"What matters that?" he muttered. "Why tell me that? I have said I am dead. Leave me buried here, and let him enjoy what he may—what he can."

"But this is folly—madness——"

"No; it is neither. I have told you I should stand as a felon in the eyes of the English law; I should have no civil rights; the greatest mercy fate can show me is to let me remain forgotten here. It will not be long, most likely, before I am thrust into the African sand, to rot like that brave soul out yonder. Berkeley will be the lawful holder of the title then; leave him in peace and possession now."

He spoke the words out to the end—calmly, and with unfaltering resolve. But she saw the great dews gather on his temples, where silver threads were just glistening among the bright richness of his hair, and she heard the short, low, convulsive breathing with which his chest heaved as he spoke. She stood close beside him, and gazed once more full in his eyes, while the sweet, imperious cadence of her voice answered him:

"There is more than I know of here. Either you are the greatest madman, or the most generous man that ever lived. You choose to guard your own secret; I will not seek to persuade it from you. But tell me one thing—why do you thus abjure your rights, permit a false charge to rest on you, and consign yourself forever to this cruel agony?"

His lips shook under his beard as he answered her.

"Because I can do no less in honor. For God's sake, do not you tempt me!"

A quick, deep sigh escaped her as she heard; her face grew very pale, as it had done before, and she moved slightly from him.

"Forgive me," she said, after a long pause. "I will never ask you that again."

She could honor honor too well, and too well divine all that he suffered for its sake, ever to become his temptress in bidding him forsake it. She stood silent long, leaning against the oval of the casement, with the sun shed over the glowing cashmeres that swept round her. He stood apart in silence also. What could he say to her? His whole heart longed with an unutterable longing to tell her the truth, and bid her be his judge between him and his duty; but his promise hung on him like a leaden weight. He must remain speechless—and leave her, for doubt to assail her, and scorn to follow it in her thoughts of him, if so they would.

Through the yellow sunlight without, over the barren, dust-strewn plains, in the distance there approached three riders, accompanied by a small escort of Spahis, with their crimson burnous floating in the autumnal wind. She started, and turned to him.

"It is Philip! He is coming for me from your camp to-day."

His eyes strained through the sun-glare.

"Ah, God! I cannot meet him—I have not strength. You do not know——"

"I know how well he loved you."

"Not better than I him! But I cannot—I dare not. Unless I could meet him as we never shall meet upon earth, we must be apart forever. For Heaven's sake promise me never to speak my name!"

"I promise until you release me."

"And you can believe me innocent still, in face of all?"

She stretched her hands to him once more. "I believe. For I know what you once were."

Great, burning tears fell from his eyes upon her hands as he bent over them.

"God bless you! You were an angel of pity to me in your childhood; in your womanhood you give me the only mercy I have known since the last day you looked upon my face! We shall be far sundered forever. May I come to you once more?"

She paused in hesitation and in thought a while, while for the first time in all her years a tremulous tenderness passed over her face; she felt an unutterable pity for this man and for his doom. Then she drew her hands gently away from him.

"Yes, I will see you again."

So much concession to such a prayer Venetia Corona had never before given. He could not command his voice to answer, but he bowed low before her as before an empress —another moment, and she was alone.

She stood looking out at the wide, level country beyond, with the glare of the white, strong light and the red burnous of the Franco-Arabs glowing against the blue, but cloudless sky; she thought that she must be dreaming some fantastic story born of these desert solitudes.

Yet her eyes were dim with tears, and her heart ached with another's woe. Doubt of him never came to her; but there was a vague, terrible pathos in the mystery of his fate that oppressed her with a weight of future evil, unknown, and unmeasured.

"Is he a madman?" she mused. "If not, he is a martyr; one of the greatest that ever suffered unknown to other men."

In the coolness of the late evening, in the court of the caravanserai, her brother and his friends lounged with her and the two ladies of their touring and sketching party, while they drank their sherbet, and talked of the Gérôme colors of the place, and watched the flame of the after-glow burn out, and threw millet to the doves and pigeons straying at their feet.

"My dear Venetia!" cried the Seraph, carelessly tossing handfuls of grain to the eager birds, "I inquired for your Sculptor-Chasseur—that fellow Victor—but I failed to see him, for he had been sent on an expedition shortly after I reached the camp. They tell me he is a fine soldier; but by what the Marquis said, I fear he is but a handsome blackguard, and Africa, after all, may be his fittest place."

She gave a bend of her head to show she heard him, stroking the soft throat of a little dove that had settled on the bench beside her.

"There is a charming little creature there, a little fire-eater—Cigarette, they call her—who is in love with him, I fancy. Such a picturesque child!—swears like a trooper, too," continued he who was now Duke of Lyonnesse. "By the way, is Berkeley gone?"

"Left yesterday."

"What for?—where to?"

"I was not interested to inquire."

"Ah! you never liked him! Odd enough to leave without reason or apology?"

"He had his reasons, doubtless."

"And made his apology to you?"

"Oh, yes!"

Her brother looked at her earnestly; there was a care upon her face new to him.

"Are you well, my darling?" he asked her. "Has the sun been too hot, or la bise too cold for you?"

She rose, and gathered her cashmeres about her, and smiled somewhat wearily her adieu to him.

"Both, perhaps. I am tired. Good-night."

CHAPTER XXII.

THE GIFT OF THE CROSS.

ONE of the most brilliant of Algerian autumnal days shone over the great camp in the south. The war was almost at an end for a time; the Arabs were defeated and driven desertwards; hostilities irksome, harassing, and annoying, like all guerrilla warfare, would long continue; but peace was virtually established, and Zaraila had been the chief glory that had been added by the campaign to the flag of Imperial France.

The whole of the Army of the South was drawn up on the immense level of the plateau to witness the presentation of the Cross of the Legion of Honor.

It was full noon. The sun shone without a single cloud on the deep, sparkling azure of the skies. The troops stretched east and west, north and south, formed up in three sides of one vast, massive square. The battalions of Zouaves and of Zephyrs; the brigade of Chasseurs d'Afrique; the squadrons of Spahis; the regiments of Tirailleurs and Turcos; the batteries of Flying Artillery, were all massed there, reassembled from the various camps and stations of the southern provinces to do honor to the day—to do honor in especial to one by whom the glory of the Tricolor had been saved unstained.

The red, white, and blue of the standards, the brass of the eagle guidons; the gray, tossed manes of the chargers; the fierce, swarthy faces of the soldiery; the scarlet of the Spahis' cloaks, and the snowy folds of the Demi-Cavalerie turbans; the shine of the sloped lances, and the glisten of the carbine barrels, fused together in one sea of blended color, flashed into a million prismatic hues against the somber, bister shadow of the sunburned plains and the clear blue of the skies.

The drums rolled out their long, deep thunder over the wastes, and the shot-torn standards fluttered gayly in the breeze blowing from the west; and the clear, full music of the French bands echoed away to the dim, distant, terrible south, where the desert-scorch and the desert-thirst had murdered their bravest and best—the Army was en fête. En fête, for it did honor to its darling. Cigarette received the Cross.

Mounted on her own little, bright bay, Étoile-Filante, with tricolor ribbons flying from his bridle and among the glossy fringes of his mane, the Little One rode among her Spahis. A scarlet képi was set on her thick, silken curls, a tricolor sash was knotted round her waist, her wine-barrel was slung on her left hip, her pistols thrust in her ceinturon, and a light carbine held in her hand with the butt-end resting on her foot. With the sun on her childlike brunette face, her eyes flashing like brown diamonds in the light, and her marvelous horsemanship showing its skill in a hundred désinvoltures and daring tricks, the little Friend of the Flag had come hither among her half-savage warriors, whose red robes surrounded her like a sea of blood.

And on a sea of blood she, the Child of War, had floated; never sinking in that awful flood, but buoyant ever above its darkest waves; catching ever some ray of sunlight upon her fair young head, and being oftentimes like a star of hope to those over whom its dreaded waters closed. Therefore they loved her, these grim, slaughterous, and lustful warriors, to whom no other thing of womanhood was sacred.

In the fair, slight, girlish body of the child-soldier there lived a courage as daring as Danton's, a patriotism as pure as Vergniaud's, a soul as aspiring as Napoleon's.

The Army looked on her with delight now. There was not one in all those hosts whose eyes did not turn on her with gratitude, and reverence, and delight in her as their own.

Not one; except where her own keen, rapid glance, far-seeing as the hawk's, lighted on the squadrons of the Chasseurs d'Afrique, and found among their ranks one face, grave, weary, meditative, with a gaze that seemed looking far away from the glittering scene to a grave that lay unseen leagues beyond, behind the rocky ridge.

"He is thinking of the dead man, not of me," thought Cigarette; and the first taint of bitterness entered into her cup of joy and triumph, as such bitterness enters into most cups that are drunk by human lips. A whole army was thinking of her, and of her alone; and there was a void in her heart, a thorn in her crown, because one among

that mighty mass—one only—gave her presence little heed,
but thought rather of a lonely tomb among the desolation of
the plains.

But she had scarce time even for that flash of pain to
quiver in impotent impatience through her. The trumpets
sounded, the salvoes of artillery pealed out, the lances and
the swords were carried up in salute; on to the ground rode
the Marshal of France, who represented the imperial will
and presence, surrounded by his staff, by generals of division
and brigade, by officers of rank, and by some few civilian
riders. An aid galloped up to her where she stood with the
corps of her Spahis, and gave her his orders. The Little
One nodded carelessly, and touched Étoile-Filante with the
prick of the spur. Like lightning the animal bounded forth
from the ranks, rearing and plunging, and swerving from
side to side, while his rider, with exquisite grace and address,
kept her seat like the little semi-Arab that she was, and with
a thousand curves and bounds cantered down the line of
the gathered troops, with the west wind blowing from the
far-distant sea, and fanning her bright cheeks till they wore
the soft, scarlet flush of the glowing japonica flower. And
all down the ranks a low, hoarse, strange, longing murmur
went—the buzz of the voices which, but that discipline
suppressed them, would have broken out in worshiping ac-
clamations.

As carelessly as though she reined up before the Café door
of the As de Pique, she arrested her horse before the great
Marshal who was the impersonation of authority, and put
her hand up in the salute, with her saucy, wayward laugh.

The Marshal, in advance of all his staff, doffed his plumed
hat and bowed to his saddle-bow as he faced her. He knew
her well by sight, this pretty child of his Army of Africa,
who had, before then, suppressed mutiny like a veteran,
and led the charge like a Murat—this kitten with a lion's
heart, this humming-bird with an eagle's swoop.

"Mademoiselle," he commenced, while his voice, well skilled
to such work, echoed to the farthest end of the long
lines of troops, "I have the honor to discharge to-day the
happiest duty of my life. In conveying to you the expression of the Emperor's approval of your noble conduct
in the present campaign, I express the sentiments of the
whole Army. Your action on the day of Zaraila was as
brilliant in conception as it was great in execution; and
the courage you displayed was only equaled by your

patriotism. May the soldiers of many wars remember and emulate you. In the name of France, I thank you. In the name of the Emperor, I bring to you the Cross of the Legion of Honor."

And as she heard, her face became very pale, her large eyes grew dim and very soft, her mirthful mouth trembled with the pain of a too intense joy. She lifted her head, and all the unutterable love she bore her country and her people thrilled through the music of her voice.

"Français!—ce n'était rien!"

In that moment she touched the full sweetness of a proud and pure ambition, attained and possessed in all its intensity, in all its perfect splendor. In that moment she knew that divine hour which, born of a people's love and of the impossible desires of genius in its youth, comes to so few human lives—knew that which was known to the young Napoleon when, in the hot hush of the nights of July, France welcomed the Conqueror of Italy. And in that moment there was an intense stillness; the Army crowned as its bravest and its best a woman-child in the springtime of her girlhood.

Then Cigarette laid her hand on the Cross that had been the dream of her years since she had first seen the brazen glisten of the eagles above her wondering eyes of infancy, and loosened it from above her heart, and stretched her hand out with it to the great Chief.

"M. le Maréchal, this is not for me."

"Not for you! The Emperor bestows it——"

Cigarette saluted with her left hand, still stretching to him the decoration with the other.

"It is not for me—not while I wear it unjustly."

"Unjustly! What is your meaning? My child, you talk strangely. The gifts of the Empire are not given lightly."

"No; and they shall not be given unfairly. Listen." The color had flushed back, bright and radiant, to her cheeks; her eyes glanced with their old daring; her contemptuous, careless eloquence returned, and her voice echoed, every note distinct as the notes of a trumpet-call, down the ranks of the listening soldiery. "Hark you! The Emperor sends me this Cross; France thanks me; the Army applauds me. Well, I thank them, one and all. Cigarette was never yet ungrateful; it is the sin of the coward. But I say I will not take what is unjustly mine, and this preference to me is unjust. I saved the day at Zaraila? Oh, hé! grande chose ça! And how?—by scampering fast on my mare, and asking for a squadron or two of my Spahis—that was all. If I had not done so much—I, a soldier of Africa—why, I should have deserved to have been shot like a cat—bah! should I not? It was not I who saved the battle. Who was it? It was a Chasseur d'Afrique, I tell you. What did he do? Why, this. When his officers were all gone down, he rallied, and gathered his handful of men, and held the ground with them all through the day—two—four—six—eight—ten hours in the scorch of the sun. The Arbicos, even, were forced to see that was grand; they offered him life if he would yield. All his answer was to form his few horsemen into line as well as he could for the slain, and charge—a last charge in which he knew not one of his troop could live through the swarms of the Arbis around them. That I saw with my own eyes. I and my Spahis just reached him in time. Then who is it that saved the day, I pray you?—I, who just ran a race for fun and came in at the fag-end of the thing, or this man who lived the whole day through in the carnage, and never let go of the guidon, but only thought how to die greatly? I tell you, the Cross is his, and not mine. Take it back, and give it where it is due."

The Marshal listened, half amazed, half amused—half prepared to resent the insult to the Empire and to discipline, half disposed to award that submission to her caprice which all Algeria gave to Cigarette.

"Mademoiselle," he said, with a grave smile, "the honors of the Empire are not to be treated thus. But who is this man for whom you claim so much?"

"Who is he?" echoed Cigarette, with all her fiery disdain for authority ablaze once more like brandy in a flame. "Oh, hé! Napoleon Premier would not have left his Marshals to ask that! He is the finest soldier in Africa, if it be possible for one to be finer than another where all are so great. They know that; they pick him out for all the dangerous missions. But the Black Hawk hates him, and so France never hears the truth of all that he does. I tell you, if the Emperor had seen him as I saw him on the field of Zaraila, his would have been the Cross, and not mine."

"You are generous, my Little One."

"No; I am just."

The Marshal listened gravely, the groups around him smilingly. If it had been any other than the Little One, it would have been very different; as it was, all France and all Algeria knew Cigarette.

"What may be the name of this man whom you praise so greatly, my pretty one?" he asked her.

"That I cannot tell, M. le Maréchal. All I know is he calls himself here Louis Victor."

"Ah! I have heard much of him. A fine soldier, but——"

"A fine soldier without a 'but,'" interrupted Cigarette, with rebellious indifference to the rank of the great man she corrected, "unless you add, 'but never done justice by his Chief.'"

As she spoke, her eyes for the first time glanced over the various personages who were mingled among the staff of the Marshal, his invited guests for the review upon the plains. The color burned more duskily in her cheek, her eyes glittered with hate; she could have bitten her little, frank, witty tongue through and through for having spoken the name of that Chasseur who was yonder, out of earshot, where the lance-heads of his squadrons glistened against the blue skies. She saw a face which, though seen but once before, she knew instantly again—the face of "Miladi." And she saw it change color, and lose its beautiful hue, and grow grave and troubled as the last words passed between herself and the French Marshal.

"Ah! can she feel!" wondered Cigarette, who, with a common error of such vehement young democrats as herself, always thought that hearts never ached in the Patrician Order, and thought so still when she saw the listless, proud tranquillity return, not again to be altered, over the perfect features that she watched with so much violent, instinctive hate. "Did she heed his name, or did she not? What are their faces in that Order? Only alabaster masks!" mused the child. And her heart sank, and bitterness mingled with her joy, and the soul that had a moment before been so full of all pure and noble emotion, all high and patriotic and idealic thought, was dulled and soiled and clogged with baser passions. So ever do unworthy things drag the loftier nature earthward.

She scarcely heard the Marshal's voice as it addressed her with a kindly indulgence, as to a valued soldier and a spoiled pet in one.

"Have no fear, Little One. Victor's claims are not forgotten, though we may await our own time to investigate and reward them. No one ever served the Empire and remained unrewarded. For yourself, wear your Cross proudly. It glitters above not only the bravest, but the most generous, heart in the service."

The eyes of Venetia Corona followed her with something of ineffable pity. "Poor little unsexed child!" she thought. "How pretty and how brave she is! and—how true to him!"

The Seraph, beside her in the group around the flagstaff, smiled and turned to her.

"I said that little Amazon was in love with this fellow Victor; how loyally she stood up for him. But I dare say she would be as quick to send a bullet through him, if he should ever displease her."

"Why? Where there is so much courage there must be much nobility, even in the abandonment of such a life as hers."

"Ah, you do not know what half-French, half-African natures are. She would die for him just now very likely; but if he ever forsake her, she will be quite as likely to run her dirk through him."

"Forsake her! What is he to her?"

There was a certain impatience in the tone, and something of contemptuous disbelief, that made her brother look at her in wonder.

"What on earth can the loves of a camp concern her?" he thought, as he answered: "Nothing that I know of. But this charming little tigress is very fond of him. By the way, can you point the man out to me? I am curious to see him."

"Impossible! There are ten thousand faces, and the cavalry squadrons are so far off."

She spoke with indifference, but she grew a little pale as she did so, and the eyes that had always met his so frankly, so proudly, were turned from him. He saw it, and it troubled him with a trouble the more perplexed that he could assign to himself no reason for it. That it could be caused by any interest felt for a Chasseur d'Afrique by the haughtiest lady in all Europe would have been too preposterous and too insulting a supposition for it ever to occur to him. And he did not dream the truth—the truth that it was her withholding, for the first time in all her life, any secret from him which caused her pain; and it was the fear lest he should learn that his lost friend was living thus which haunted her with that unspoken anxiety.

He, in his place among those squadrons, knew her, though so far distant, and endured the deadliest trial of patience which had come to him while beneath the yoke of African discipline.

As it was, he sat motionless as a statue in his saddle, and never looked westward to where the tricolors of the flag-staff drooped above the head of Venetia Corona.

Thus, he never heard the gallant words spoken in his behalf by the loyal lips that he had not cared to caress. As she passed down the ranks, indeed, he saw and smiled on his little champion; but the smile had only a weary kindness of recognition in it, and it wounded Cigarette more than though he had struck her through the breast with his lance.

The moment that he dreaded came; the troops broke up and marched past the representative of their empire, the cavalry at the head of the divisions. He passed among the rest; he raised his lance so that it hid his features as much as its slender shaft could do; the fair and noble face on which his glance flashed was very pale and very grave; the one beside her was sunny and frank, and unchanged by the years that had drifted by, and its azure eyes, so like her own, sweeping over the masses with all the swift, keen appreciation of a military glance, were so eagerly noting carriage, accouterment, harness, horses, that they never once fell upon the single soldier whose heart so unutterably longed for, even while it dreaded, his recognition.

Venetia gave a low, quick breath of mingled pain and relief as the last of the Chasseurs paced by. The Seraph started, and turned his head.

"My darling! Are you not well?"

"Perfectly!"

"You do not look so; and you forgot now to point me out this special trooper. I forgot him too."

"He goes there—the tenth from here."

Her brother looked; it was too late.

"He is taller than the others. That is all I can see now that his back is turned. I will seek him out when——"

"Do no such thing!"

"And why? It was your own request that I inquired——"

"Think me changeable as you will. Do nothing to seek him, to inquire for him——"

"But why? A man who at Zaraila——"

"Never mind! Do not let it be said you notice a Chasseur d'Afrique at my instance."

The color flushed her face as she spoke; it was with the scorn, the hatred, of this shadow of an untruth with which she for the sole time in life soiled her lips. He, noting it, shook himself restlessly in his saddle. If he had not known her to be the noblest and the haughtiest of all the imperial women who had crowned his house with their beauty and their honor, he could have believed that some interest, degrading as disgrace, moved her toward this foreign trooper, and caused her altered wishes and her silence.

CHAPTER XXIII.

THE DESERT HAWK AND THE PARADISE-BIRD.

SOME way distant, parted by a broad strip of unoccupied ground from the camp, were the grand marquees set aside for the Marshal and for his guests. They were twelve in number, gayly decorated—as far as decoration could be obtained in the southern provinces of Algeria—and had, Arab-like, in front of each the standard of the Tricolor. Before one were two other standards also: the flags of England and of Spain. Cigarette, looking on from afar, saw the alien colors wave in the torch-light flickering on them. "That is hers," thought the Little One, with the mournful and noble emotions of the previous moments swiftly changing into the violent, reasonless, tumultuous hatred at once of a rival and of an Order.

Cigarette was a thorough democrat, and the sight alone of those lofty standards, signalizing the place of rest of the "aristocrats," while her "children's" lowly tents wore in her sight all the dignity and all the distinction of the true field, would have aroused her ire at any time. But now a hate tenfold keener moved her.

Now, she acted on her impulse; her impulse of open scorn of rank, of reckless vindication of her right to do just whatsoever pleasured her; and she went boldly forward and dashed aside, with no gentle hand, the folds that hung before the entrance of the tent, and stood there with a gleam of the starry night and the glow of the torches behind her, so that her picturesque and brightly colored form looked painted on a dusky, lurid background of shadow and of flame.

The action startled the occupants of the tent, and made them both look up; they were Venetia Corona and a Levantine woman, who was her favorite and most devoted attendant, and had been about her from her birth. Venetia hesitated a moment in astonished wonder; then, with the grace and the courtesy of her race, rose and approached the entrance of her tent, in which that figure—half a soldier, half a child—was standing, with the fitful, reddened light behind. She recognized whose it was.

"Is it you, ma petite?" she said kindly. "Come within. Do not be afraid——"

"Fear!" she cried, with a camp oath, whose blasphemy was happily unintelligible to her listener. "Fear! You think I fear you!—the darling of the army, who saved the squadron at Zaraila, who has seen a thousand days of bloodshed, who has killed as many men with her own hand as any Lascar among them all—fear you, you hothouse flower, you paradise-bird, you silver pheasant, who never did aught but spread your dainty colors in the sun, and never earned so much as the right to eat a piece of black bread, if you had your deserts! Fear you—I! Why! do you not know that I could kill you where you stand as easily as I could wring the neck of any one of those gold-winged orioles that flew above your head to-day, and who have more right to live than you, for they do at least labor in their own fashion for their food, and their drink, and their dwelling? Dieu de Dieu! Why, I have killed Arabs, I tell you—great, gaunt, grim men—and made them bite the dust under my fire. Do you think I would check for a moment at dealing you death, you beautiful, useless, honeyed, poisoned, painted exotic, that has every wind tempered to you, and thinks the world only made to bear the fall of your foot!"

The fury of words was poured out without pause, and with an intense passion vibrating through them.

"Child, are you mad?" she said gravely. "Brave natures do not stoop to assassination, which you seem to deify. If you have any reason to feel evil against me, tell me what it is. I always repair a wrong, if I can. But as for those threats, they are most absurd if you do not mean them; they are most wicked if you do."

The tranquil, unmoved, serious words stilled the vehement passion she rebuked with a strange and irresistible power;

under her gaze the savage lust in Cigarette's eyes died out, and their lids drooped over them; the dusky, scarlet color faded from her cheeks; for the first time in her life she felt humiliated, vanquished, awed.

The rebuke was gentle, but it was all the more severe for its very serenity. It cut Cigarette to the quick; it covered her with an overwhelming sense of mortification and of failure.

The inborn truth within her, the native generosity and candor that soon or late always overruled every other element in the Little One, conquered her now. She dashed down her Cross on the ground, and trod passionately on the decoration she adored.

"I disgrace it the first day I wear it! You are right, though I hate you, and you are as beautiful as a sorceress! There is no wonder he loves you!"

"He! Who?"

There was a colder and more utterly amazed hauteur in the interrogation than had come into her voice throughout the interview, yet on her fair face a faint warmth rose.

The words were out, and Cigarette was reckless what she said; almost unconscious, indeed, in the violence of the many emotions in her.

"The man who carves the toys you give your dog to break!" she answered bitterly. "Dieu de Dieu! he loves you. When he was down with his wounds after Zaraila, he said so; but he never knew what he said, and he never knew that I heard him. You are like the women of his old world; though through you he got treated like a dog, he loves you!"

"Of whom do you venture to speak?"

"Sacré bleu! of him, I tell you, who was made to bring his wares to you like a hawker. And you think it insult, I will warrant!—insult for a soldier who has nothing but his courage, and his endurance, and his heroism under suffering to ennoble him, to dare to love Mme. la Princesse Corona! I think otherwise. I think that Mme. la Princesse Corona never had a love of so much honor, though she has had princes and nobles and all the men of her rank, no doubt, at her feet, through that beauty that is like a spell!"

"You speak idly and at random, like the child you are," the grande dame answered her with chill, contemptuous rebuke. "I do not imagine that the person you allude to made you his confidante in such a matter?"

"He!" retorted Cigarette. "He belongs to your class,

Miladi. He is as silent as the grave. You might kill him, and he would never show it hurt. I only know what he muttered in his fever."

"When you attended him?"

"Not I!" cried Cigarette, who saw for the first time that she was betraying herself. "He lay in the scullion's tent where I was; that was all; and he was delirious with the shot-wounds. Men often are——"

"Wait! Hear me a little while, before you rush on in this headlong and foolish speech," interrupted her auditor, who had in a moment's rapid thought decided on her course with this strange, wayward nature. "You err in the construction you have placed on the words, whatever they were, which you heard. The gentleman—he is a gentleman —whom you speak of bears me no love. We are almost strangers. But by a strange chain of circumstances he is connected with my family; he once had great friendship with my brother; for reasons that I do not know, but which are imperative with him, he desires to keep his identity unsuspected by everyone; an accident alone revealed it to me, and I have promised him not to divulge it. You understand?"

Cigarette gave an affirmative gesture. Her eyes were fastened suddenly, yet with a deep, bright glow in them, upon her companion; she was beginning to see her way through his secret—a secret she was too intrinsically loyal even now to dream of betraying.

"You spoke very nobly for him to-day. You have the fealty of one brave character to another, I am sure!" pursued Venetia Corona, purposely avoiding all hints of any warmer feeling on her listener's part, since she saw how tenacious the girl was of any confession of it. "You would do him service if you could, I fancy. Am I right?"

"Oh, yes!" answered Cigarette, with an over-assumption of carelessness. "He is bon zig; we always help each other. Besides, he is very good to my men. What is it you want of me?"

"To preserve secrecy on what I have told you for his sake; and to give him a message from me."

Cigarette laughed scornfully; she was furious with herself for standing obediently like a chidden child to hear this patrician's bidding, and to do her will. And yet, try how she would, she could not shake off the spell under which those grave, sweet, lustrous eyes of command held her.

"Pardieu, Miladi! Do you think I babble like any young blue drunk with his first measure of wine? As for your message, you had better let him come and hear what you have to say; I cannot promise to remember it!"

"Your answer is reckless; I want a serious one. You spoke like a brave and a just friend to him to-day; are you willing to act as such to-night? You have come here strangely, rudely, without pretext or apology; but I think better of you than you would allow me to do, if I judged only from the surface. I believe that you have loyalty, as I know that you have courage."

Cigarette set her teeth hard.

"What of that? I have them en militaire, that is all."

"This of it. That one who has them will never cherish malice unjustifiably, or fail to fulfill a trust."

Cigarette's clear, brown skin grew very red.

"That is true," she muttered reluctantly. Her better nature was growing uppermost, though she strove hard to keep the evil one predominant.

"Then you will cease to feel hatred toward me for so senseless a reason as that I belong to an aristocracy that offends you; and you will remain silent on what I tell you concerning the one whom you know as Louis Victor?"

Cigarette nodded assent.

"He is of your Order, then?" she asked abruptly.

"He was—yes."

"Oh, hé!" cried Cigarette, with her old irony. "Then he must be always, mustn't he? You think too much of your blue blood, you patricians, to fancy it can lose its royalty, whether it run under a King's purple or a Roumi's canvas shirt. Blood tells, they say! Well, perhaps it does. Some say my father was a Prince of France—maybe! So, he is of your Order? Bah! I knew that the first day I saw his hands. Do you want me to tell you why he lives among us, buried like this?"

"Not if you violate any confidence to do so."

"Pardieu! he makes no confidence, I promise you. Not ten words will Monseigneur say, if he can help it, about anything. He is as silent as a lama; it is populacier to talk! But we learn things without being told in camp; and I know well enough he is here to save someone else, in someone's place; it is a sacrifice, look you, that nails him down to this martyrdom."

"Look you, Miladi," said Cigarette, half sullenly, half passionately, for the words were wrenched out of her generosity, and choked her in their utterance, "that man suffers; his life here is a hell upon earth—I don't mean for the danger, he is bon soldat; but for the indignity, the subordination, the license, the brutality, the tyranny. He is as if he were chained to the galleys. He never says anything. Oh, no! he is of your kind, you know! But he suffers. Mort de Dieu! he suffers. Now, if you be his friend, can you do nothing for him? Can you ransom him in no way? Can you go away out of Africa and leave him in this living death to get killed and thrust into the sand, like his comrade the other day?"

Her hearer did not answer; the words made her heart ache; they cut her to the soul.

Cigarette's flashing, searching eyes bent all their brown light on her.

"Mme. Corona, you are courageous; to those who are so, all things are possible."

"A great fallacy! You must have seen many courageous men vanquished. But what would you imply by it?"

"That you can help this man, if you will."

"Would that I could; but I can discern no means——"

"Make them."

Even in that moment her listener smiled involuntarily at the curt, imperious tones, decisive as Napoleon's "Partons!" before the Passage of the Alps.

"Be certain, if I can, I will. Meantime, there is one pressing danger of which you must be my medium to warn him. He and my brother must not meet. Tell him that the latter, knowing him only as Louis Victor, and interested in the incidents of his military career, will seek him out early tomorrow morning before we quit the camp. I must leave it to him to avoid the meeting as best he may be able."

Cigarette smiled grimly.

"You do not know much of the camp. Victor is only a bas-officier; if his officers call him up, he must come, or be thrashed like a slave for contumacy. He has no will of his own."

Venetia gave an irrepressible gesture of pain.

"True; I forgot. Well, go and send him to me. My brother must be taken into his confidence, whatever that confidence reveals. I will tell him so. Go and send him to me; it is the last chance."

"Tell him to come here to me," repeated Venetia, with the

calm decision of one to whom any possibility of false inter-
pretation of her motives never occurred, and who was habituated to the free action that accompanied an ·unassailable
rank. "My brother must know what I know. I shall be
alone, and he can make his way hither, without doubt, unobserved. Go and say this to him. You are his loyal little
friend and comrade."

"If I be, I do not see why I am to turn your lackey,
Madame," said Cigarette bitterly. "If you want him, you
can send for him by other messengers!"

Venetia Corona looked at her steadfastly, with a certain
contempt in the look.

"Then your pleading for him was all insincere? Let the
matter drop, and be good enough to leave my presence,
which, you will remember, you entered unsummoned and
undesired."

The undeviating gentleness of the tone made the rebuke
cut deeper, as her first rebuke had cut, than any sterner censure or more peremptory dismissal could have done. Cigarette stood irresolute, ashamed, filled with rage, torn by
contrition, impatient, wounded, swayed by jealous rage and
by the purer impulses she strove to stifle.

The Cross she had tossed down caught her sight as it
glittered on the carpet strewn over the hard earth; she
stooped and raised it; the action sufficed to turn the tide
with her impressionable, ardent, capricious nature; she would
not disgrace that.

"I will go," she muttered in her throat; "and you—you—
O God! no wonder men love you when even I cannot hate
you!"

CHAPTER XXIV.

ORDEAL BY FIRE.

AMID the mirth, the noise, the festivity, which reigned
throughout the camp as the men surrendered themselves to
the enjoyment of the largesses of food and of wine allotted
to them by their Marshal's command in commemoration of
Zaraila, one alone remained apart; silent and powerless to
rouse himself even to the forced semblance, the forced endurance, of their mischief and their pleasure. They knew
him well, and they also loved him too well to press such

participation on him. They knew that it was no lack of sympathy with them that made him so grave amid their mirth, so mute amid their volubility. Some thought that he was sorely wounded by the delay of the honors promised him. Others, who knew him better, thought that it was the loss of his brother-exile which weighed on him, and made all the scene around him full of pain. None approached him; but while they feasted in their tents, making the celebration of Zaraila equal to the Jour de Mazagran, he sat alone over a picket-fire on the far outskirts of the camp.

The voice of Cigarette broke on his musing.

"Beau sire, you are wanted yonder."

He looked up wearily; could he never be at peace? He did not notice that the tone of the greeting was rough and curt; he did not notice that there was a stormy darkness, a repressed bitterness, stern and scornful, on the Little One's face; he only thought that the very dogs were left sometimes at rest and unchained, but a soldier never.

"For what?"

She stood looking at him without replying; her mouth was tightly shut in a hard line that pressed inward all its soft and rosy prettiness. She was seeing how haggard his face was, how heavy his eyes, how full of fatigue his movements. Her silence recalled him to the memory of the past day.

"Forgive me, my dear child, if I have seemed without sympathy in all your honors," he said gently, as he laid his hand on her shoulder. "Believe me, it was unintentional. No one knows better than I how richly you deserved them; no one rejoices more that you should have received them."

The very gentleness of the apology stung her like a scorpion; she shook herself roughly out of his hold.

"Point de phrases! All the army is at my back; do you think I cannot do without you? Sympathy too! Bah! We don't know those fine words in camp. You are wanted, I tell you—go!"

"But where?"

"To your Silver Pheasant yonder—go!"

"Who? I do not——"

"Dame! Can you not understand? Miladi wants to see you; I told her I would send you to her. You can use your dainty sentences with her; she is of your Order!"

"What! she wishes——"

"Go!" reiterated the Little One with a stamp of her

boot. "You know the great tent where she is throned in honor—Morbleu!—as if the oldest and ugliest hag that washes out my soldiers' linen were not of more use and more deserved such lodgment than Mme. la Princesse, who has never done aught in her life, not even brushed out her own hair of gold! She waits for you. Where are your palace manners? Go to her, I tell you. She is of your own people; we are not!"

The vehement, imperious phrases coursed in disorder one after another, rapid and harsh, and vibrating with a hundred repressed emotions. He paused one moment, doubting whether she did not play some trick upon him; then, without a word, left her, and went rapidly through the evening shadows.

He knew the password; that was sufficient. The Levantine waiting near the entrance drew the tent-folds aside and signed to him to enter. Another moment, and he was in the presence of her mistress, in that dim, amber light from the standing candelabra, in that heavy, soft-scented air perfumed from the aloe-wood burning in a brazier, through which he saw, half blinded at first, coming from the darkness without, that face which subdued and dazzled even the antagonism and the lawlessness of Cigarette.

He bowed low before her, preserving that distant ceremonial due from the rank he ostensibly held to hers.

"Madame, this is very merciful! I know not how to thank you."

She motioned to him to take a seat near to her, while the Levantine, who knew nothing of the English tongue, retired to the farther end of the tent.

"I only kept my word," she answered, "for we leave the camp to-morrow; Africa next week."

"So soon!"

She saw the blood forsake the bronzed fairness of his face, and leave a dusky pallor there. It wounded her as if she suffered herself. For the first time she believed what the Little One had said—that this man loved her.

"I sent for you," she continued hurriedly, her graceful languor and tranquillity for the first time stirred and quickened by emotion, almost by embarrassment. "It was very strange, it was very painful, for me to trust that child with such a message. But you know us of old; you know we do not forsake our friends for considerations of self-interest or outward semblance. We act as we deem right; we do not heed untrue constructions. There are many things I desire to say to you——"

She paused; he merely bent his head; he could not trust the calmness of his voice in answer.

"First," she continued, "I must entreat you to allow me to tell Philip what I know. You cannot conceive how intensely oppressive it becomes to me to have any secret from him. I never concealed so much as a thought from my brother in all my life, and to evade even a mute question from his brave, frank eyes makes me feel a traitress to him."

"Anything else," he muttered. "Ask me anything else. For God's sake, do not let him dream that I live!"

"But why? You still speak to me in enigmas. To-morrow, moreover, before we leave, he intends to seek you out as what he thinks you—a soldier of France. He is interested by all he hears of your career; he was first interested by what I told him of you when he saw the ivory carvings at my villa. I asked the little vivandière to tell you this, but, on second thoughts, it seemed best to see you myself once more, as I had promised."

"That French child," she went on rapidly, to cover both the pain that she felt and that she dealt, "forced her entrance here in a strange fashion; she wished to see me, I suppose, and to try my courage too. She is a little brigand, but she has a true and generous nature, and she loves you very loyally."

"Cigarette?" he asked wearily; his thoughts could not stay for either pity or interest for her in this moment. "Oh, no! I trust not. I have done nothing to win her love; and she is a fierce little condottiera who disdains all such weakness. She forced her way in here? That was unpardonable; but she seems to bear a singular dislike to you."

"Singular, indeed! I never saw her until to-day."

He answered nothing; the conviction stole on him that Cigarette hated her because he loved her.

"And yet she brought you my message?" pursued his companion. "That seems her nature—violent passions, yet thorough loyalty. But time is precious. I must urge on you what I bade you come to hear. It is to implore you to put your trust, your confidence, in Philip. You have acknowledged to me that you are guiltless—no one who knows what you once were could ever doubt it for an instant—then let him hear this, let him be your judge as to what course is right and what wrong for you to pursue.

It is impossible for me to return to Europe knowing you are living thus and leaving you to such a fate. What motive you have to sentence yourself to such eternal banishment I am ignorant; but all I ask of you is, confide in him. Let him learn that you live; let him decide whether or not this sacrifice of yourself be needed. His honor is as punctilious as that of any man on earth; his friendship you can never doubt. Why conceal anything from him?"

His eyes turned on her with that dumb agony which once before had chilled her to the soul.

"Do you think, if I could speak in honor, I should not tell you all?"

A flush passed over her face, the first that the gaze of any man had ever brought there. She understood him.

"But," she said, gently and hurriedly, "may it not be that you overrate the obligations of honor? I know that many a noble-hearted man has inexorably condemned himself to a severity of rule that a dispassionate judge of his life might deem very exaggerated, very unnecessary. It is so natural for an honorable man to so dread that he should do a dishonorable thing through self-interest or self-pity, that he may very well overestimate the sacrifice required of him through what he deems justice or generosity. May it not be so with you? I can conceive no reason that can be strong enough to require of you such fearful surrender of every hope, such utter abandonment of your own existence."

Her voice failed slightly over the last words.

He started from her side as he heard, and paced to and fro the narrow limits of the tent like a caged animal. For the first time it grew a belief to him, in his thoughts, that were he free, were he owner of his heritage, he could rouse her heart from its long repose and make her love him with the soft and passionate warmth of his dead Arab mistress—a thing that had been as distant from her negligence and her pride as warmth from the diamond or the crystal. He felt as if the struggle would kill him. He had but to betray his brother, and he would be unchained from his torture; he had but to break his word, and he would be at liberty. All the temptation that had before beset him paled and grew as naught beside this possibility of the possession of her love which dawned upon him now.

She, knowing nothing of this which moved him, believed only that he weighed her words in hesitation, and strove to turn the balance.

"Hear me," she said softly. "I do not bid you decide; I only bid you confide in Philip—in one who, as you must well remember, would sooner cut off his own hand than counsel a base thing or do an unfaithful act. You are guiltless of this charge under which you left England; you endure it rather than do what you deem dishonorable to clear yourself. That is noble—that is great. But it is possible, as I say, that you may exaggerate the abnegation required of you. Whoever was the criminal should suffer. Yours is magnificent magnanimity; but it may surely be also false justice alike to yourself and the world."

He turned on her almost fiercely in the suffering she dealt him.

"It is! It was a madness—a Quixotism—the wild, unconsidered act of a fool. What you will! But it is done; it was done forever—so long ago—when your young eyes looked on me in the pity of your innocent childhood. I cannot redeem its folly now by adding to its baseness. I cannot change the choice of a madman by repenting of it with a coward's caprice. Ah, God! you do not know what you do—how you tempt. For pity's sake, urge me no more. Help me—strengthen me—to be true to my word. Do not bid me do evil that I may enter paradise through my sin!"

He threw himself down beside her as the incoherent words poured out, his arms flung across the pile of cushions on which he had been seated, his face hidden on them. His teeth clinched on his tongue till the blood flowed; he felt that if the power of speech remained with him he should forswear every law that had bound him to silence, and tell her all, whatever the cost.

She looked at him, she heard him, moved to a greater agitation than ever had had sway over her; for the first time the storm winds that swept by her did not leave her passionless and calm; this man's whole future was in her hands. She could bid him seek happiness, dishonored; or cleave to honor, and accept wretchedness forever.

It was a fearful choice to hold.

"Answer me! Choose for me!" he said vehemently. "Be my law, and be my God!"

She gave a gesture almost of fear.

"Hush, hush! The woman does not live who should be that to any man."

"You shall be it to me! Choose for me!"

"I cannot! You leave so much in darkness and un-told——"

"Nothing that you need know to decide your choice for me, save one thing only—that I love you."

She shuddered.

"This is madness! What have you seen of me?"

"Enough to love you while my life shall last, and love no other woman. Ah! I was but an African trooper in your sight, but in my own I was your equal. You only saw a man to whom your gracious alms and your gentle charity were to be given, as a queen may stoop in mercy to a beggar; but I saw one who had the light of my old days in her smile, the sweetness of my old joys in her eyes, the memories of my old world in her every grace and gesture. You forget! I was nothing to you; but you were so much to me. I loved you the first moment that your voice fell on my ear. It is madness! Oh, yes! I should have said so, too, in those old years. A madness I would have sworn never to feel. But I have lived a hard life since then, and no men ever love like those who suffer. Now you know all; know the worst that tempts me. No famine, no humiliation, no obloquy, no loss I have known, ever drove me so cruelly to buy back my happiness with the price of dishonor as this one desire—to stand in my rightful place before men, and be free to strive with you for what they have not won!"

As she heard, all the warmth, all the life, faded out of her face; it grew as white as his own, and her lips parted slightly, as though to draw her breath was oppressive. The wild words overwhelmed her with their surprise not less than they shocked her with their despair. An intense truth vibrated through them, a truth that pierced her and reached her heart, as no other such supplication ever had done. She had no love for him yet, or she thought not; she was very proud, and resisted such passions; but in that moment the thought swept by her that such love might be possible. It was the nearest submission to it she had ever given. She heard him in unbroken silence; she kept silence long after he had spoken. So far as her courage and her dignity could be touched with it, she felt something akin to terror at the magnitude of the choice left to her.

"You give me great pain, great surprise," she murmured. "All I can trust is that your love is of such sudden birth that it will die as rapidly——"

He interrupted her.

"You mean that, under no circumstances—not even were I to possess my inheritance—could you give me any hope that I might wake your tenderness?"

She looked at him full in the eyes with the old, fearless, haughty instinct of refusal to all such entreaty, which had made her so indifferent—and many said so pitiless—to all. At his gaze, however, her own changed and softened, grew shadowed, and then wandered from him.

"I do not say that. I cannot tell——"

The words were very low; she was too truthful to conceal from him what half dawned on herself—the possibility that, more in his presence and under different circumstances, she might feel her heart go to him with a warmer and a softer impulse than that of friendship. The heroism of his life had moved her greatly.

His head dropped down again upon his arms.

"O God! It is possible, at least! I am blind—mad. Make my choice for me! I know not what I do."

He had suffered silently; endured strongly; fought greatly; these were the only means through which any man could have ever reached her sympathy, her respect, her tenderness. Yet, though a very noble and a very generous woman, she was also a woman of the world. She knew that it was not for her to say even thus much to a man who was in one sense well-nigh a stranger, and who stood under the accusation of a crime whose shadow he allowed to rest on him unmoved. She felt sick at heart; she longed unutterably, with a warmer longing than had moved her previously, to bid him, at all cost, lay bare his past, and throw off the imputed shame that lay on him. Yet all the grand traditions of her race forbade her to counsel the acceptance of an escape whose way led through a forfeiture of honor.

"Choose for me, Venetia!" he muttered at last once more.

She rose with what was almost a gesture of despair, and thrust the gold hair off her temples.

"Heaven help me, I cannot—I dare not! And—I am no longer capable of being just!"

There was an accent almost of passion in her voice; she felt that so greatly did she desire his deliverance, his justification, his return to all which was his own—desired even his presence among them in her own world—that she could no longer give him calm and unbiased judgment. He heard, and the burning tide of a new joy rushed on him, checked almost

ere it was known, by the dread lest for her sake she should
ever give him so much pity that such pity became love.

He started to his feet and looked down imploringly into
her eyes—a look under which her own never quailed or
drooped, but which they answered with that same regard
which she had given him when she had declared her faith
in his innocence.

"If I thought it possible you could ever care——"

She moved slightly from him; her face was very white
still, and her voice, though serenely sustained, shook as it
answered him.

"If I could—believe me, I am not a woman who would bid
you forsake your honor to spare yourself or me. Let us
speak no more of this! What can it avail, except to make
you suffer greater things? Follow the counsels of your
own conscience. You have been true to them hitherto; it
is not for me, or through me, that you shall ever be turned
aside from them."

A bitter sigh broke from him as he heard.

"They are noble words. And yet it is so easy to utter, so
hard to follow them. If you had one thought of tenderness
for me, you could not speak them."

A flush passed over her face.

"Do not think me without feeling—without sympathy—
pity——"

"These are not love."

She was silent; they were, in a sense, nearer to love than
any emotion she had ever known.

"If you loved me," he pursued passionately—"ah, God!
the very word from me to you sounds insult; and yet there
is not one thought in me that does not honor you—if you
loved me, could you stand there and bid me drag on this
life forever; nameless, friendless, hopeless; having all the
bitterness, but none of the torpor of death; wearing out the
doom of a galley slave, though guiltless of all crime?"

"Why speak so? You are unreasoning. A moment ago
you implored me not to tempt you to the violation of what
you hold your honor; because I bid you be faithful to it,
you deem me cruel!"

"Heaven help me! I scarce know what I say. I ask you,
if you were a woman who loved me, could you decide thus?"

"These are wild questions," she murmured; "what can they
serve? I believe that I should—I am sure that I should. As
it is—as your friend——"

"Ah, hush! Friendship is crueller than hate."

"Cruel?"

"Yes; the worst cruelty when we seek love—a stone proffered us when we ask for bread in famine!"

There was desperation, almost ferocity, in the answer; she was moved and shaken by it—not to fear, for fear was not in her nature, but to something of awe, and something of the despairing hopelessness that was in him.

"Lord Royallieu," she said slowly, as if the familiar name were some tie between them, some cause of excuse for these, the only love words she had ever heard without disdain and rejection—"Lord Royallieu, it is unworthy of you to take this advantage of an interview which I sought, and sought for your own sake. You pain me, you wound me. I cannot tell how to answer you. You speak strangely, and without warrant."

He stood mute and motionless before her, his head sunk on his chest. He knew that she rebuked him justly; he knew that he had broken through every law he had prescribed himself, and that he had sinned against that code of chivalry which should have made her sacred from such words while they were those he could not utter, nor she hear, except in secrecy and shame. Unless he could stand justified in her sight and in that of all men, he had no right to seek to wring out tenderness from her regret and from her pity. Yet all his heart went out to her in one irrepressible entreaty.

"Forgive me, for pity's sake! After to-night I shall never look upon your face again."

"I do forgive," she said gently, while her voice grew very sweet. "You endure too much already for one needless pang to be added by me. All I wish is that you had never met me, so that this last, worst thing had not come unto you!"

A long silence fell between them; where she leaned back among her cushions, her face was turned from him. He stood motionless in the shadow, his head still dropped upon his breast, his breathing loud and slow and hard. To speak of love to her was forbidden to him, yet the insidious temptation wound closer and closer round his strength. He had only to betray the man he had sworn to protect, and she would know his innocence, she would hear his passion; he would be free, and she—he grew giddy as the thought rose before him—she might, with time, be brought to give him other tenderness than that of friendship.

"Wait," she said softly, with the old imperial command of her voice subdued, though not wholly banished. "I think you have mistaken me somewhat. You wrong me if you think that I could be so callous, so indifferent, as to leave you here without heed as to your fate. Believe in your innocence you know that I do, as firmly as though you substantiated it with a thousand proofs; reverence your devotion to your honor you are certain that I must, or all better things were dead in me."

Her voice sank inaudible for the instant; she recovered her self-control with an effort.

"You reject my friendship—you term it cruel—but at least it will be faithful to you; too faithful for me to pass out of Africa and never give you one thought again. I believe in you. Do you not know that that is the highest trust, to my thinking, that one human life can show in another's? You decide that it is your duty not to free yourself from this bondage, not to expose the actual criminal, not to take up your rights of birth. I dare not seek to alter that decision. But I cannot leave you to such a future without infinite pain, and there must—there shall be—means through which you will let me hear of you—through which, at least, I can know that you are living."

She stretched her hands toward him with that same gesture with which she had first declared her faith in his guiltlessness; the tears trembled in her voice and swam in her eyes. As she had said, she suffered for him exceedingly. He, hearing those words which breathed the only pity that had never humiliated him, and the loyal trust which was but the truer because the sincerity of faith in lieu of the insanity of love dictated it, made a blind, staggering, unconscious movement of passionate, dumb agony. He seized her hands in his and held them close against his breast one instant, against the loud, hard panting of his aching heart.

"God reward you! God keep you! If I stay, I shall tell you all. Let me go, and forget that we ever met! I am dead—let me be dead to you!"

With another instant he had left the tent and passed out into the red glow of the torchlit evening. And Venetia Corona dropped her proud head down upon the silken cushions where his own had rested, and wept as women weep over their dead—in such a passion as had never come to her in all the course of her radiant, victorious, and imperious life. Her tranquillity was broken down; her pride was abandoned; her heart, at length, was reached and sorely wounded. The only man she had ever found, whom it would have been possible to her to have loved, was one already severed from her by a fate almost more hideous than death.

Outside her tent there was a peculiar mingling of light and shadow; of darkness from the moonless and now cloud-covered sky, of reddened warmth from the tall, burning pine-boughs thrust into the soil in lieu of other illumination. The atmosphere was hot from the flames, and chilly with the breath of the night winds; it was oppressively still, though from afar off the sounds of laughter in the camp still echoed, and near at hand the dull and steady tramp of the sentinels fell on the hard, parched soil. Into that blended heat and cold, dead blackness and burning glare, he reeled out from her presence; drunk with pain as deliriously as men grow drunk with raki. The challenge rang on the air:

"Who goes there?"

He never heard it. Even the old, long-accustomed habits of a soldier's obedience were killed in him.

"Who goes there?" the challenge rang again.

Still he never heard, but went on blindly. From where the tents stood there was a stronger breadth of light through which he had passed, and was passing still—a light strong enough for it to be seen whence he came, but not strong enough to show his features.

"Halt, or I fire!" The sentinel brought the weapon to his shoulder and took a calm, close, sure aim. He did not speak; the password he had forgotten as though he had never heard or never given it.

Another figure than that of the soldier on guard came out of the shadow, and stood between him and the sentinel. It was that of Châteauroy; he was mounted on his gray horse and wrapped in his military cloak, about to go the round of the cavalry camp. Their eyes met in the wavering light like the glow from a furnace-mouth: in a glance they knew each other.

"It is one of my men," said the chief carelessly to the sentinel. "Leave me to deal with him."

The guard saluted, and resumed his beat.

"Why did you refuse the word, sir?"

"I did not hear."

"And why did you not hear?"

There was no reply.

"Why are you absent from your squadron?"

There was no reply still.

"Have you no tongue, sir? The matraque shall soon make you speak! Why are you here?"

There was again no answer.

Châteauroy's teeth ground out a furious oath; yet a flash of brutal delight glittered in his eyes. At last he had hounded down this man, so long out of his reach, into disobedience and contumacy.

"Why are you here, and where have you been?" he demanded once more.

"I will not say."

The answer, given at length, was tranquil, low, slowly and distinctly uttered, in a deliberate refusal, in a deliberate defiance.

The dark and evil countenance above him grew livid with fury.

"I can have you thrashed like a dog for that answer, and I will. But first listen here, beau sire! I know as well as though you had confessed to me. Your silence cannot shelter your great mistress' shame. Ah, ha! la Faustine! So Mme. votre Princesse is so cold to her equals, only to choose her lovers out of my blackguards, and take her midnight intrigues like a camp courtesan!"

Cecil's face changed terribly as the vile words were spoken. With the light and rapid spring of a leopard, he reached the side of his commander, one hand on the horse's mane, the other on the wrist of his chief, that it gripped like an iron vise.

"You lie! And you know that you lie. Breathe her name once more, and, by God, as we are both living men, I will have your life for your outrage!"

And, as he spoke, with his left hand he smote the lips that had blasphemed against her.

It was broken asunder at last—all the long and bitter patience, all the calm and resolute endurance, all the undeviating serenity beneath provocation, which had never yielded through twelve long years, but which had borne with infamy and with tyranny with such absolute submission for sake of those around him, who would revolt at his sign and be slaughtered for his cause. Rank, duty, bondage, consequence, all were forgotten in that one instant of insult that mocked in its odious lie at her purity. He was no longer the soldier bound in obedience to submit to the indignities that his chief chose to heap on him; he was a gentleman who defended a woman's honor, a man who avenged a slur on the life that he loved.

Châteauroy wrenched his wrist out of the hold that crushed it, and drew his pistol. Cecil knew that the laws of active service would hold him but justly dealt with if the shot laid him dead in that instant for his act and his words.

"You can kill me—I know it. Well, use your prerogative; it will be the sole good you have ever done to me."

And he stood erect, patient, motionless, looking into his chief's eyes with a calm disdain, with an unuttered challenge that, for the first moment, wrung something of savage respect and of sullen admiration out from the soul of his great foe.

He did not fire; it was the only time in which any trait of abstinence from cruelty had been ever seen in him. He signed to the soldiers of the guard with one hand, while with the other he still covered with his pistol the man whom martial law would have allowed him to have shot down, or have cut down, at his horse's feet.

"Arrest him," he said simply.

Cecil offered no resistance; he let them seize and disarm him without an effort at the opposition which could have been but a futile, unavailing trial of brute force. He dreaded lest there should be one sound that should reach her in that tent where the triad of standards drooped in the dusky distance. He was content with what he had done—content to have met once, not as soldier to chief, but as man to man, the tyrant who held his fate.

For once, beneath the spur of that foul outrage to the dignity and the innocence of the woman he had quitted, he had allowed a passionate truth to force its way through the barriers of rank and the bonds of subservience. Insult to himself he had borne as the base prerogative of his superior, but insult to her he had avenged with the vengeance of equal to equal, of the man who loved on the man who calumniated her.

And as he sat in the darkness of the night with the heavy tramp of his guards forever on his ear, there was peace rather than rebellion in his heart—the peace of one heartsick with strife and with temptation, who beholds in death a merciful ending to the ordeal of existence. "I shall die in her cause at least," he thought. "I could be content if I were only sure that she would never know."

For this was the chief dread which hung on him, that she should ever know, and in knowing, suffer for his sake.

The night rolled on, the army around him knew nothing of what had happened. Châteauroy, conscious of his own coarse guilt against the guest of his Marshal, kept the matter untold and undiscovered, under the plea that he desired not to destroy the harmony of the general rejoicing. The one or two field-officers with whom he took counsel agreed to the wisdom of letting the night pass away undisturbed. The accused was the idol of his own squadron; there was no gauge what might not be done by troops heated with excitement and drunk with wine, if they knew that their favorite comrade had set the example of insubordination, and would be sentenced to suffer for it. Beyond these, and the men employed in his arrest and guard, none knew what had chanced.

None knew; not even Cigarette. She sat alone, so far away that none sought her out, beside the picket-fire that had long died out, with the little white dog of Zaraila curled on the scarlet folds of her skirt.

She had the Cross on her heart—the idol of her long desire, the star to which her longing eyes had looked up ever since her childhood through the reek of carnage and the smoke of battle; and she would have flung it away like dross, to have had his lips touch hers once with love.

"Que je suis folle!" she muttered in her throat; "que je suis folle!"

And she knew herself mad; for the desires and the delights of love die swiftly, but the knowledge of honor abides always. Love would have made her youth sweet with an unutterable gladness, to glide from her and leave her weary, dissatisfied, forsaken. But that Cross, the gift of her country, the symbol of her heroism, would be with her always, and light her forever with the honor of which it was the emblem; and if her life should last until youth passed away, and age came, and with age death, her hand would wander to it on her dying bed, and she would smile, as she died, to hear the living watchers murmur: "That life had glory—that life was lived for France."

She knew this; but she was young; she was a womanchild; she had the ardor of passionate youth in her veins, she had the desolation of abandoned youth in her heart. And honor looked so cold beside love!

She rose impetuously; the night was far spent, the camp

was very still, the torches had long died out, and a streak of dawn was visible in the east. She stood a while, looking very earnestly across the wide, black city of tents.

"I shall be best away for a time. I grow mad, treacherous, wicked here," she thought. "I will go and see Blanc-Bec."

Blanc-Bec was the soldier of the Army of Italy.

In a brief while she had saddled and bridled Étoile-Filante, and ridden out of the camp without warning or farewell to any; she was as free to come and to go as though she were a bird on the wing. Thus she went, knowing nothing of his fate. And with the sunrise went also the woman whom he loved—in ignorance.

CHAPTER XXV.

THE VENGEANCE OF THE LITTLE ONE.

THE warm, transparent light of an African autumnal noon shone down through the white canvas roof of a great tent in the heart of the encamped divisions at the headquarters of the Army of the South. In the tent there was a densely packed throng—an immense, close, hushed, listening crowd, of which every man wore the uniform of France, of which the mute, undeviating attention, forbidden by discipline alike to be broken by sound of approval or dissent, had in it something that was almost terrible, contrasted with the vivid eagerness in their eyes and the strained absorption of their countenances; for they were in court, and that court was the Conseil de Guerre of their own southern camp.

The prisoner was arraigned on the heaviest charge that can be laid against the soldier of any army, and yet, as the many eyes of the military crowd turned on him where he stool surrounded by his guard, his crime against his chief was forgotten, and they only remembered—Zaraila.

He preserved entire reticence in court. The instant the acte d'accusation had been read to him, he had seen that his chief would not dare to couple with it the proud, pure name he had dared to outrage; his most bitter anxiety was thus at an end. For all the rest, he was tranquil.

No case could be clearer, briefer, less complex, more entirely incapable of defense. The soldiers of the guard gave

evidence as to the violence and fury of the assault. The
sentinel bore witness to having heard the refusal to reply;
a moment after, he had seen the attack made and the blow
given. The accuser merely stated that, meeting his sous-
officier out of the bounds of the cavalry camp, he had asked
him where he had been, and why he was there, and, on
his commanding an answer, had been assaulted in the manner
described, with violence sufficient to have cost his life had
not the guard been so near at hand. When questioned as
to what motive he could assign for the act, he replied that
he considered his corporal had always incited evil feeling and
mutinous conduct in the squadrons, and had, he believed,
that day attributed to himself his failure to receive the Cross.
The statement passed without contradiction by the prisoner,
who, to the interrogations and entreaties of his legal dé-
fenseur, only replied that the facts were stated accurately as
they occurred, and that his reasons for the deed he declined
to assert.

When once more questioned as to his country and his past
by the president, he briefly declined to give answer. When
asked if the names by which he was enrolled were his own,
he replied that they were two of his baptismal names, which
had served his purpose on entering the army.

That was all which he answered, and neither his counsel
nor his accusers could extort another syllable from him.

He knew that what he had done was justified to his own
conscience, but he did not seek to dispute that it was un-
justifiable in military law.

He had kept faith to a woman whom he had known heart-
less and well-nigh worthless.

All through the three days that the conseil sat his look
and his manner never changed—the first was quite calm,
though very weary; the latter courteous, but resolute, with
the unchanged firmness of one who knew his own past
action justified.

He never moved once while the decree of death was read
to him; and there was no change in the weary calmness of
his eyes. He bent his head in acquiescence.

"C'est bien!" he said simply.

It seemed well to him. Dead, his secret would lie in the
grave with him, and the long martyrdom of his life be ended.

In the brightness of the noon Cigarette leaned out of her
little oval casement that framed her head like an old black

oak carving—a head with the mellow bloom on its cheeks, and the flash of scarlet above its dark curls, and the robin-like grace of poise and balance as it hung out there in the sun.

Cigarette had been there a whole hour in thought; she who never had wasted a moment in meditation or reverie, and who found the long African day all too short for her busy, abundant, joyous life.

The touch of a bird's wing brushing her hair brought her dreaming to her wandering thoughts. She started and lifted her head; it was a blue carrier-pigeon, one of the many she fed at that casement, and the swiftest and surest of several she sent with messages for the soldiers between the various stations and corps. She had forgotten she had left the bird at the encampment.

She caressed it absently, while the tired creature sank down on her bosom; then only she saw that there was a letter beneath one wing. She unloosed it, and looked at it without being able to tell its meaning; she could not read a word, printed or written. Military habits were too strong with her for the arrival not to change her reverie into action; whoever it was for, it must be seen. She gave the pigeon water and grain, then wound her way down the dark, narrow stairs, through the height of the tower, out into the passage below.

She found an old French cobbler sitting at a stall in a casement, stitching leather; he was her customary reader and scribe in this quarter. She touched him with the paper. "Bon Mathieu! wilt thou read this to me?"

"It is for thee, Little One, and signed 'Petit Pot-de-terre.'"

Cigarette nodded listlessly.

"'Tis a good lad, and a scholar," she answered absently. "Read on!"

And he read aloud:

"'There is ill news. I send the bird on a chance to find thee. Bel-à-faire-peur struck the Black Hawk—a light blow, but with threat to kill following it. He has been tried, and is to be shot. There is no appeal to the Conseil de Révision. The case is clear; the Colonel could have cut him down, were that all. I thought you should know. We are all sorry. It was done on the night of the great fête. I am thy humble lover and slave.'"

So the boy-Zouave's scrawl, crushed, and blotted, and written with great difficulty, ran in its brief phrases that the slow muttering of the old shoemaker drew out in tedious length.

Cigarette heard; she never made a movement or gave a sound, but all the blood fled out of her brilliant face, leaving it horribly blanched beneath its brown sun-scorch; and her eyes—distended, senseless, sightless—were fastened on the old man's slowly moving mouth.

"Shot!" she said vacantly. "Shot!"

Her vengeance had come without her once lifting her hand to summon it.

The old man rose hurriedly.

"Child! art thou ill?"

"The blow was struck for her!" she muttered. "It was that night, you hear—that night!"

"What night? Thou lookest so strangely! Dost thou love this doomed soldier?"

Cigarette laughed—a laugh whose echo thrilled horribly through the lonely Moresco courtway.

"Love? love? I hated him, look you! So I said. And I longed for my vengeance. It is come!"

She was still a moment; her white, parched mouth quivering as though she were under physical torture, her strained eyes fastened on the empty air, the veins in her throat swelling and throbbing till they glowed to purple. Then she crushed the letter in one hand, and flew, fleet as any antelope, through the streets of the Moorish quarter, and across the city to the quay.

Once only in her headlong career through the throngs she paused; it was as one face, on which the strong light of the noontide poured, came before her. The senseless look changed in her eyes; she wheeled out of her route, and stopped before the man who had thus arrested her. He was leaning idly over the stall of a Turkish bazaar, and her hand grasped his arm before he saw her.

"You have his face?" she muttered. "What are you to him?"

He made no answer; he was too amazed.

"You are of his race," she persisted. "You are brethren by your look. What are you to him?"

"To whom?"

"To the man who calls himself Louis Victor? a Chasseur of my army?"

Her eyes were fastened entirely on him; keen, ruthless,

fierce, in this moment as a hawk's. He grew pale and murmured an incoherent denial. He sought to shake her off,
first gently, then more rudely; he called her mad, and tried to
fling her from him; but the lithe fingers only wound themselves closer on his arm.

"Be still—fool!" she muttered. "You are of his people;
you have his eyes, and his look, and his features. He dis-
owns you, or you him. No matter which. He is of your
blood; and he lies under sentence of death. Do you know
that?"

With a stifled cry the other recoiled from her; he never
doubted that she spoke the truth; none could who had looked
upon her face.

"Do not lie to me," she said curtly. "It avails you nothing.
Read that."

She thrust before him the paper the pigeon had brought;
his hand trembled sorely as he held it; he believed in that
moment that this strange creature—half soldier, half woman,
half brigand, half child—knew all his story and all his shame
from his brother.

"Shot!" he echoed hoarsely, as she had done, when he had
read on to the end. "Shot! Oh, my God! and I——"

She drew him out of the thoroughfare into a dark recess
within the bazaar, he submitting unresistingly. He was filled
with the horror, the remorse, the overwhelming shock of his
brother's doom.

"He will be shot," she said with a strange calmness. "We
shoot down many men in our army. I know him well. He
was justified in his act, I do not doubt; but discipline will not
stay for that——"

"Silence, for mercy's sake! Is there no hope—no possibility?"

Her lips were parched like the desert sand as her dry, hard
words came through them. "None. His chief could have
cut him down on the instant. It took place in camp. You
feel this thing; you are of his race, then?"

"I am his brother!"

"You are his brother," she said slowly, so much as an affirmation that his belief was confirmed that she had learned
both their relationship and their history from Cecil. "You
must go to him, then."

He shook from head to foot.

"Yes, yes! But it will be too late!"

She did not know that the words were cried out in all the

contrition of an unavailing remorse; she gave them only their literal significance, and shuddered as she answered him.

"That you must risk. You must go to him. But, first, I must know more. Tell me his name, his rank."

He was silent; coward and egotist though he was, both cowardice and egotism were killed in him under the overwhelming horror with which he felt himself as truly by moral guilt a fratricide as though he had stabbed his elder through the heart.

"Speak!" hissed Cigarette through her clinched teeth. "If you have any kindness, any pity, any love for the man .of your blood, who will be shot there like a dog, do not waste a second—answer me, tell me all."

He turned his wild, terrified glance upon her; he had in that moment no sense but to seize some means of reparation, to declare his brother's rights, to cry out to the very stones of the streets his own wrong and his victim's sacrifice.

"He is the head of my house!" he answered her, scarce knowing what he answered. "He should bear the title that I bear now. He is here, in this misery, because he is the most merciful, the most generous, the most long-suffering of living souls! If he die, it is not they who have killed him; it is I!"

"Settle with yourself for that sin," she said bitterly. "Your remorse will not save him. But do the thing that I bid you, if that remorse be sincere. Write me out here that title you say he should bear, and your statement that he is your brother, and should be the chief of your house; then sign it, and give it to me."

He seized her hands, and gazed with imploring eyes into her face.

"Who are you? What are you? If you have the power to do it, for the love of God rescue him! It is I who have murdered· him—I—who have let him live on in this hell for my sake!"

"For your sake!"

She flung his hands off her and looked him full in the face; that glance of the speechless scorn, the unutterable rebuke of the woman-child who would herself have died a thousand deaths rather than have purchased a whole existence by a single falsehood or a single cowardice, smote him like a blow, and avenged his sin more absolutely than any public chastisement. The courage and the truth of a girl scorned his timorous fear and his living lie. His head sank, he seemed to shrink under her gaze; his act had never looked so vile to him as it looked now.

"Monsieur, I do not know your story; I do not want to know. I am not used to men who let others suffer for them. What I want is your written statement of your brother's name and station; give it me."

He made a gesture of consent; he would have signed away his soul, if he could, in the stupor of remorse which had seized him. She brought him pens and paper from the Turk's store, and dictated what he wrote:

"I hereby affirm that the person serving in the Chasseurs d'Afrique under the name of Louis Victor is my elder brother, Bertie Cecil, lawfully, by inheritance, the Viscount Royallieu, Peer of England. I hereby also acknowledge that I have succeeded to and borne the title illegally, under the supposition of his death.

(Signed)
"BERKELEY CECIL."

He wrote it mechanically; the force of her will and the torture of his own conscience driving him, on an impulse, to undo in an instant the whole web of falsehood that he had let circumstance weave on and on to shelter him through twelve long years. He let her draw the paper from him and fold it away in her belt. He watched her with a curious, dreamy sense of his own impotence against the fierce and fiery torrent of her bidding.

"What is it you will do?" he asked her.

"The best that shall lie in my power. Do you the same."

"Can his life yet be saved?"

"His honor may—his honor shall."

"Stay!—stay! One word——"

She flung him off her again.

"This is no time for words. Go to him—coward!—and let the balls that kill him reach you too, if you have one trait of manhood left in you!"

Then, swiftly as a swallow darts, she quitted him and flew on her headlong way, down through the pressure of the people, and the throngs of the marts, and the noise, and the color, and the movement of the streets.

The sun was scarce declined from its noon before she rode out of the city, on a half-bred horse of the Spahis, swift as the antelope and as wild, with her only equipment some pistols in her holsters, and a bag of rice and a skin of water slung at her saddle-bow.

She had a long route before her; she had many leagues to travel, and there were but four-and-twenty hours, she knew well, left to the man who was condemned to death.

The horse was reeking with smoke and foam, and the blood was coursing from his flanks, as she reached her destination at last, and threw herself off his saddle as he sank, faint and quivering, to the ground. Whither she had come was to a fortress where the Marshal of France, who was the Viceroy of Africa, had arrived that day in his progress of inspection throughout the provinces. Soldiers clustered round her eagerly beneath the gates and over the fallen beast; a thousand questions pouring from their curious tongues. She pointed to the animal with one hand, to the gaunt pile of stone that bristled with cannon with the other.

"Have a care of him; and lead me to the chief!"

She spoke quietly; but a certain sensation of awe and fear moved those who heard. She was not the Child of the Army whom they knew so well. She was a creature, desperate, hard-pressed, mute as death, strong as steel; above all, hunted by despair.

They hesitated to take her message, to do her bidding. The one whom she sought was great and supreme here as a king; they dreaded to approach his staff, to ask his audience.

Cigarette looked at them a moment, then loosened her Cross and held it out to an adjutant standing beneath the gates.

"Take that to the man who gave it me. Tell him Cigarette waits; and with each moment that she waits a soldier's life is lost. Go!"

The adjutant took it, and went. Over and over again she had brought intelligence of an Arab movement, news of a contemplated razzia, warning of an internal revolt, or tidings of an encounter on the plains, that had been of priceless value to the army which she served. It was not lightly that Cigarette's words were ever received when she spoke as she spoke now; nor was it impossible that she now brought to them that which would brook neither delay nor trifling.

A few minutes and the decoration was brought back to her, and her demand granted. She was summoned to the Marshal's presence. She was taken within the casemate of the fortress. It was the ordnance room, a long, vast, silent chamber filled with stands of arms, with all the arts and appliances of war brought to their uttermost perfection, and massed in all the resource of a great empire against the sons of the desert, who had nothing to oppose to them save the despair of a perishing nationality and a stifled freedom.

The Marshal, leaning against a brass field-piece, turned to her with a smile in his keen, stern eyes.

"You, my young décorée! What brings you here?"

She came up to him with her rapid leopard-like grace, and he started as he saw the change upon her features. She was covered with sand and dust, and with the animal's blood-flecked foam. The beating of her heart from the fury of the gallop had drained every hue from her face; her voice was scarcely articulate in its breathless haste as she saluted him.

"Monseigneur, I have come from Algiers since noon——"

"From Algiers!" He and his officers echoed the name of the city in incredulous amaze; they knew how far from them down along the sea-line the white town lay.

"Since noon, to rescue a life—the life of a great soldier, of a guiltless man. He who saved the honor of France at Zaraila is to die the death of a mutineer at dawn!"

"What!—your Chasseur?"

"Mine!—since he is a soldier of France; yours, too, by that title. I am come here, from Algiers, to speak the truth in his name, and to save him for his own honor and the honor of my Empire. See here! At noon, I have this paper, sent by a swift pigeon. Read it! You see how he is to die, and why. Well, by my Cross, by my Flag, by my France, I swear that not a hair of his head shall be touched, not a drop of blood in his veins shall be shed!"

He looked at her, astonished at the grandeur and the courage which could come on this child of razzias and revelries, and give to her all the splendor of a fearless command of some young empress. But his face darkened and set sternly as he read the paper; it was the greatest crime in the sight of a proud soldier, this crime against discipline, of the man for whom she pleaded.

"You speak madly," he said, with cold brevity. "The offense merits the chastisement. I shall not attempt to interfere."

"Wait! you will hear, at least, Monseigneur?"

"I will hear you—yes, but I tell you, once for all, I never change sentences that are pronounced by conseils de guerre; and this crime is the last for which you should attempt to plead for mercy with me."

"Hear me, at least!" she cried, with passionate ferocity— the ferocity of a dumb animal wounded by a shot. "You do not know what this man is—how he has had to endure; I do. I have watched him; I have seen the brutal tyranny of his chief, who hated him because the soldiers loved him. I have seen his patience, his obedience, his long-suffering beneath insults that would have driven any other to revolt and murder. I have seen him—I have told you how—at Zaraila, thinking never of death or life, only of our Flag, that he has made his own, and under which he has been forced to lead the life of a galley slave——"

"The finer soldier he be, the less pardonable his offense."

"That I deny! If he were a dolt, a brute, a thing of wood, as many are, he would have no right to vengeance; as it is, he is a gentleman, a hero, a martyr; may he not forget for one hour that he is a slave? Look you! I have seen him so tried that I told him—I, who love my army better than any living thing under the sun—that I would forgive him if he forgot duty and dealt with his tyrant as man to man. And he always held his soul in patience. Why? Not because he feared death—he desired it; but because he loved his comrades, and suffered in peace and in silence lest, through him, they should be led into evil——"

His eyes softened as he heard her; but the inflexibility of his voice never altered.

"It is useless to argue with me," he said briefly; "I never change a sentence."

"But I say that you shall!" As the audacious words were flung forth, she looked him full in the eyes, while her voice rang with its old imperious oratory. "You are a great chief; you are as a monarch here; you hold the gifts and the grandeur of the Empire; but, because of that—because you are as France in my eyes—I swear, by the name of France, that you shall see justice done to him; after death, if you cannot in life. Do you know who he is—this man whom his comrades will shoot down at sunrise as they shoot down the murderer and the ravisher in their crimes?"

"He is a rebellious soldier; it is sufficient."

"He is not! He is a man who vindicated a woman's honor; he is a man who suffers in a brother's place; he is an aristocrat exiled to a martyrdom; he is a hero who has never been greater than he will be great in his last hour. Read that! What you refuse to justice, and mercy, and courage, and guiltlessness, you will grant, maybe, to your Order."

She forced into his hand the written statement of Cecil's name and station. All the hot blood was back in her cheek, all the fiery passion back in her eyes. She lashed this potent ruler with the scourge of her scorn as she had lashed a drunken horde of plunderers with her whip. She was reckless of what she said; she was conscious only of one thing—the despair that consumed her.

The French Marshal glanced his eye on the fragment, carelessly and coldly. As he saw the words, he started, and read on with wondering eagerness.

"Royallieu!" he muttered—"Royallieu!"

The name was familiar to him; he it was who, when he had murmured, "That man has the seat of the English Guards," as a Chasseur d'Afrique had passed him, had been ignorant that in that Chasseur he saw one whom he had known in many a scene of Court splendor and Parisian pleasure. The years had been many since Cecil and he had met, but not so many but that the name brought memories of friendship with it, and moved him with a strange emotion.

He turned with grave anxiety to Cigarette.

"You speak strangely. How came this in your hands?"

"Thus: the day that you gave me the Cross, I saw Mme. la Princesse Corona. I hated her, and I went—no matter! From her I learned that he whom we call Louis Victor was of her rank, was of old friendship with her house, was exiled and nameless, but for some reason unknown to her. She needed to see him; to bid him farewell, so she said. I took the message for her; I sent him to her." Her voice grew husky and savage, but she forced her words on with the reckless sacrifice of self that moved her. "He went to her tent, alone, at night; that was, of course, whence he came when Châteauroy met him. I doubt not the Black Hawk had some foul thing to hint of his visit, and that the blow was struck for her—for her! Well; in the streets of Algiers I saw a man with a face like his own; different, but the same race, look you. I spoke to him; I taxed him. When he found that the one whom I spoke of was under sentence of death, he grew mad; he cried out that he was his brother and had murdered him—that it was for his sake that the cruelty of this exile had been borne—that, if his brother perished, he would be his destroyer. Then I bade him write down that paper, since these English names were unknown to me, and I brought it hither to you that you might see, under his hand and with your own eyes, that I have uttered the truth. And now, is that man to be killed like a mad beast whom you fear? Is that death the reward France will give for Zaraila?"

Her eyes were fixed with a fearful intensity of appeal upon the stern face bent over her; her last arrow was sped; if this failed, all was over. As he heard, he was visibly moved; he remembered the felon's shame that in years gone by had fallen across the banished name of Bertie Cecil; the history seemed clear as crystal to him, seen beneath the light shed on it from other days.

His hand fell heavily on the gun-carriage.

"Mort de Dieu! it was his brother's sin, not his!"

There was a long silence; those present, who knew nothing of all that was in his memory, felt instinctively that some dead weight of alien guilt was lifted off a blameless life forever.

She drew a deep, long, sighing breath; she knew that he was safe. Her hands unconsciously locked on the great chief's arms; her eyes looked up, senselessly in their rapture and their dread, to his.

"Quick, quick!" she gasped. "The hours go so fast; while we speak here he——"

The words died in her throat. The Marshal swung around with a rapid sign to a staff officer.

"Pens and ink! instantly! My brave child, what can we say to you? I will send an aid to arrest the execution of the sentence. It must be deferred till we know the whole truth of this. If it be as it looks now, he shall be saved if the Empire can save him!"

She looked up in his eyes with a look that froze his very heart.

"His honor!" she muttered; "his honor—if not his life!"

He understood her; he bowed his haughty head low down to hers.

"True. We will cleanse that, if all other justice be too late."

The answer was infinitely gentle, infinitely solemn. Then he turned and wrote his hurried order, and bade his aid go with it without a second's loss. But Cigarette caught it from his hand.

"To me! to me! No other will go so fast!"

"But, my child, you are worn out already."

She turned on him her beautiful, wild eyes, in which the blinding, passionate tears were floating.

"Do you think I would tarry for that? Ah! I wish that I had let them tell me of God, that I might ask Him now to bless you! Quick, quick! Lend me your swiftest horse! one that will not tire. And send a second order by your aid-de-camp; the Arabs may kill me as I go, and then they will not know!"

He stooped and touched her little, brown, scorched, feverish hand with reverence.

"My child, Africa has shown me much heroism, but none like yours. If you fall, he shall be safe, and France will know how to avenge its darling's loss."

She turned and gave him one look, infinitely sweet, infinitely eloquent.

"Ah, France!" she said, so softly that the last word was but a sigh of unutterable tenderness. The old, imperishable early love was not dethroned; it was there, still before all else. France was without rival with her.

Then, without another second's pause, she flew from them, and vaulting into the saddle of a young horse which stood without in the court-yard, rode once more, at full speed out into the pitiless blaze of the sun, out to the wasted desolation of the plains.

The order of release, indeed, was in her bosom; but the chances were as a million to one that she would reach him with it in time, ere with the rising of the sun his life would have set forever.

There were eight hours' hard riding before her, at the swiftest pace her horse could make; and she was already worn by the leagues already traversed.

Hour on hour, league on league, passed away; she felt the animal quiver under the spur, and she heard the catch in his panting breath as he strained to give his fleetest and best, that told her how, ere long, the racing speed, the extended gallop at which she kept him, would tell, and beat him down, despite his desert strain.

What she dreaded came.

Midway in her course, when, by the stars, she knew midnight was passed, the animal strained with hard-drawn, panting gasps to answer the demand made on him by the spur and by the lance-shaft with which he was goaded onward. In the lantern light she saw his head stretched out in the racing agony, his distended eyeballs, his neck covered with foam and blood, his heaving flanks that seemed bursting with every throb that his heart gave; she knew that, half a league more forced from him, he would drop like a dead thing never to rise again.

Her gaze, straining through the darkness, broken here and there by fitful gleams of moonlight, caught sight in the distance of some yet darker thing, moving rapidly—a large cloud skimming the earth. She let the horse, which had paused the instant the bridle had touched his neck, stand still a while, and kept her eyes fixed on the advancing cloud till, with the marvelous surety of her desert-trained vision, she disentangled it from the floating mists and wavering shadows, and recognized it, as it was, a band of Arabs.

If she turned eastward out of her route, the failing strength of her horse would be fully enough to take her into safety from their pursuit, or even from their perception, for they were coming straightly and swiftly across the plain. If she were seen by them, she was certain of her fate. She was known throughout the length and the breadth of the land to the Arabs; she was neither child nor woman to them; she was but the soldier who had brought up the French reserve at Zaraila; she was but the foe who had seen them defeated, and ridden down with her comrades in their pursuit in twice a score of vanquished, bitter, intolerably shameful days. Some among them had sworn by their God to put her to a fearful death if ever they made her captive, for they held her in superstitious awe, and thought the spell of the Frankish successes would be broken if she were slain. She knew that; yet, knowing it, she looked at their advancing band one moment, then turned her horse's head and rode straight toward them.

"They will kill me, but that may save him," she thought. "Any other way he is lost."

So she rode directly toward them; rode so that she crossed their front, and placed herself in their path, standing quite still, with the cloth torn from the lantern, so that its light fell full about her, as she held it above her head. In an instant they knew her.

"I surrender," she said briefly; she had never thought to say these words of submission to her scorned foes; she would not have been brought to utter them to spare her own existence. Their answer was a yell of furious delight, and their bare blades smote each other with a clash of brutal joy. They had her, the Frankish child who had brought shame and destruction on them at Zaraila.

"I surrender," she said, with the same tranquillity. "I have heard that you have sworn by your God and your Prophet to tear me limb from limb because that I—a child, and a woman-child—brought you to shame and to grief on the day of Zaraila. Well, I am here; do it. You can slake your will on me. But that you are brave men, and that I have ever met you in fair fight, let me speak one word with you first."

Through the menaces and the rage around her, fierce as the yelling of starving wolves around a frozen corpse, her clear, brave tones reached the ear of the chief in the lingua sabir that she used. He was a young man, and his ear was caught by that tuneful voice, his eyes by that youthful face. He signed upward the swords of his followers, and motioned them back as their arms were stretched to seize her, and their shouts clamored for her slaughter.

"Speak on," he said briefly to her.

"You have sworn to take my body, sawn in two, to Ben-Ihreddin?" she pursued, naming the Arab leader whom her Spahis had driven off the field of Zaraila. "Well, here it is; you can take it to him; and you will receive the piasters and the horse, and the arms that he has promised to whosoever shall slay me. I have surrendered; I am yours. But you are bold men, and the bold are never mean; therefore, I will ask one thing of you. There is a man yonder, in my camp, condemned to death with the dawn. He is innocent. I have ridden from Algiers to-day with the order of his release. If it is not there by sunrise he will be shot; and he is guiltless as a child unborn. My horse is worn out; he could not go another half league. I knew that, since he had failed, my comrade would perish, unless I found a fresh beast or a messenger to go in my stead. I saw your band come across the plain. I knew that you would kill me, because of your oath and of your Emir's bride; but I thought that you would have greatness enough in you to save this man who is condemned, without crime, and who must perish unless you, his foes, have pity on him. Therefore I came. Take the paper that frees him; send your fleetest and surest with it, under a flag of truce, into our camp by the dawn; let him tell them there that I, Cigarette, gave it him. He must say no word of what you have done to me, or his white flag will not protect him from the vengeance of my army—and then re-

ceive your reward from your chief, Ben-Ihreddin, when
you lay my head down for his horse's hoofs to trample into
the dust. Answer me—is the compact fair? Ride on with
this paper northward, and then kill me with what torments
you choose."

As they heard, silence fell upon the brutal, clamorous herd
around—the silence of amaze and of respect. The young
chief listened gravely; by the glistening of his keen, black
eyes, he was surprised and moved, though, true to his teach-
ing, he showed neither emotion as he answered her.

"Who is this Frank for whom you do this thing?"

"He is the warrior to whom you offered life on the field
of Záraila because his courage was as the courage of gods."

She knew the qualities of the desert character; knew how
to appeal to its reverence and to its chivalry.

"And for what does he perish?" he asked.

"Because he forgot for once that he was a slave; and
because he has borne the burden of a guilt that was not his
own."

"And you have given yourself up to us that, by your
death, you may purchase a messenger from us for this
errand?" pursued their leader.

She held the paper out to him, with a passionate entreaty
breaking through the enforced calm of despair with which
she had hitherto spoken.

"Cut me in ten thousand pieces with your swords, but
save him, as you are brave men, as you are generous
foes!"

With a single sign of his hand their leader waved them
back where they crowded around her, and leaped down from
his saddle, and led the horse he had dismounted to her.

"Maiden," he said gently, "we are Arabs, but we are not
brutes. We swore to avenge ourselves on an enemy; we
are not vile enough to accept a martyrdom. Take my horse
—he is the swiftest of my troop—and go you on your errand.
You are safe from me."

"You play with me!" she murmured, while her lips grew
whiter and her great eyes larger in the intensity of her
emotion. "Ah! for pity's sake, make haste and kill me, so
that this only may reach him!"

The chief, standing by her, lifted her up in his sinewy
arms, up on to the saddle of his charger. His voice was very
solemn, his glance was very gentle; all the nobility of the
highest Arab nature was aroused in him at the heroism of a

child, a girl, an infidel—one, in his sight abandoned and shameful among her sex.

"Go in peace," he said simply; "it is not with such as thee that we war."

Then, and then only, as she felt the fresh reins placed in her hand, and saw the ruthless horde around her fall back and leave her free, did she understand his meaning; did she comprehend that he gave her back both liberty and life, and, with the surrender of the horse he loved, the noblest and most precious gift that the Arab ever bestows or ever receives. The unutterable joy seemed to blind her, and gleam upon her face like the blazing light of noon, as she turned her burning eyes full on him.

"Ah! now I believe that thine Allah rules thee, equally with Christians! If I live, thou shalt see me back ere another night; if I die, France will know how to thank thee!"

"We do not do the thing that is right for the sake that men may recompense us," he answered her gently. "Fly to thy friend, and hereafter do not judge that those who are in arms against thee must needs be as the brutes that seek out whom they shall devour."

Then, with one word in his own tongue, he bade the horse bear her southward, and, as swiftly as a spear launched from his hand, the animal obeyed him and flew across the plains.

And, borne by the fleetness of the desert-bred beast, she went away through the heavy, bronze-hued dullness of the night. Her brain had no sense, her hands had no feeling, her eyes had no sight; the rushing of waters was loud on her ears, the giddiness of fasting and of fatigue sent the gloom eddying round and round like a whirlpool of shadow. Yet she had remembrance enough left to ride on, and on, and on without once flinching from the agonies that racked her cramped limbs and throbbed in her beating temples; she had remembrance enough to strain her blind eyes toward the east and murmur, in her terror of that white dawn, that must soon break, the only prayer that had been ever uttered by the lips no mother's kiss had ever touched:

"O God! keep the day back!"

CHAPTER XXVI.

IN THE MIDST OF HER ARMY.

SUNRISE and solitude: they were alike chosen, lest the army that honored, the comrades that loved him, should rise to his rescue; casting off the yoke of discipline, and remembering only that tyranny and that wretchedness under which they had seen him patient and unmoved throughout so many years of servitude.

He stood tranquil beside the coffin within which his broken limbs and shot-pierced corpse would so soon be laid forever.

When they came near to bind the covering over his eyes, he motioned them away, taking the bandage from their hands and casting it far from him. "Did I ever fear to look down the depths of my enemies' muskets?"

It was the single outbreak, the single reproach, that escaped from him—the single utterance by which he ever quoted his services to France. Not one who heard him dared again force on him that indignity which would have blinded his sight, as though he had ever dreaded to meet death.

Over the slope of brown and barren earth—at the very moment that the ramrods were drawn out—there came a single figure—tall and lithe. The newcomer (who was his old friend the Seraph) went straight to the adjutant in command and asked for permission to speak with the prisoner, which was granted.

After some minutes the clear voice of the officer in command rang shrilly through the stillness.

"Monseigneur, make your farewell. I can wait no longer."

The Seraph started, and flung himself round with the grand challenge of a lion, struck by a puny spear. His face flushed crimson; his words were choked in his throbbing throat.

"As I live, you shall not fire! I forbid you! I swear by my honor and the honor of England that he shall not die like a dog. He is of my country; he is of my Order. I will appeal to your Emperor; he will accord me his life the instant I ask it. Give me only an hour's reprieve—a few moments' space to speak to your chiefs, to seek out your general——"

"It is impossible, monseigneur."

The curt, calm answer was inflexible; against the sentence and its execution there could be no appeal.

Cecil laid his hand upon his old friend's shoulders.

"It will be useless," he murmured. "Let them act; the quicker the better."

"What! you think I would look on and see you die?"

"Would to Heaven you had never known I lived——"

The officer made a gesture to the guard to separate them. "Monsieur, submit to the execution of the law, or I must arrest you."

Lyonnesse flung off the detaining hand of the guard, and swung round so that his agonized eyes gazed close into the adjutant's immovable face, which before that gaze lost its coldness and its rigor, and changed to a great pity for this stranger who had found the friend of his youth in the man who stood condemned to perish there.

"An hour's reprieve; for mercy's sake, grant that!"

"I have said, it is impossible."

"But you do not dream who is——"

"It matters not."

"He is an English noble, I tell you——"

"He is a soldier who has broken the law; that suffices."

"O Heaven! have you no humanity?"

"We have justice."

"Justice! If you have justice, let your chiefs hear his story; let his name be made known; give me an hour's space to plead for him. Your Emperor would grant me his life, were he here; yield me an hour—a half hour—anything that will give me time to serve him——"

"It is out of the question; I must obey my orders. I regret you should have this pain; but if you do not cease to interfere, my soldiers must make you."

Where the guards held him, Cecil saw and heard. His voice rose with all its old strength and sweetness.

"My friend, do not plead for me. For the sake of our common country and our old love, let us both meet this with silence and with courage."

"You are a madman!" cried the man, whose heart felt breaking under this doom he could neither avert nor share. "You think that they shall kill you before my eyes?—you think I shall stand by to see you murdered? What crime have you done? None, I dare swear, save being moved, under insult, to act as the men of your race ever acted! Ah, God! why have lived as you have done? why not have trusted my faith and my love? If you had believed in my faith as I believed in your innocence, this misery never had come to us!"

"Hush! hush! or you will make me die like a coward."

He dreaded lest he should do so; this ordeal was greater than his power to bear it. With the mere sound of this man's voice a longing, so intense in its despairing desire, came on him for his life which they were about to kill in him forever.

The words stung his hearer well-nigh to madness; he turned on the soldiers with all the fury of his race that slumbered so long, but when it awoke was like the lion's rage. Invective, entreaty, conjuration, command, imploring prayer, and ungoverned passion poured in tumultuous words, in agonized eloquence, from his lips; all answer was a quick sign of the hand; and, ere he saw them, a dozen soldiers were round him, his arms were seized, his splendid frame was held as powerless as a lassoed bull; for a moment there was a horrible struggle, then a score of ruthless hands locked him in as in iron gyves, and forced his mouth to silence and his eyes to blindness. This was all the mercy they could give—to spare him the sight of his friend's slaughter.

Cecil's eyes strained on him with one last, longing look; then he raised his hand and gave the signal for his own death-shot.

The leveled carbines covered him; he stood erect with his face full toward the sun. Ere they could fire, a shrill cry pierced the air.

"Wait! in the name of France."

Dismounted, breathless, staggering, with her arms flung upward, and her face bloodless with fear, Cigarette appeared upon the ridge of rising ground.

The cry of command pealed out upon the silence in the voice that the Army of Africa loved as the voice of their Little One. And the cry came too late; the volley was fired, the crash of sound thrilled across the words that bade them pause, the heavy smoke rolled out upon the air; the death that was doomed was dealt.

But beyond the smoke-cloud he staggered slightly, and then stood erect still, almost unharmed, grazed only by some few of the balls. The flash of fire was not so fleet as the swiftness of her love; and on his breast she threw herself, and flung her arms about him, and turned her head backward with her old, dauntless, sunlit smile as the balls pierced her bosom, and broke her limbs, and were turned away by that shield of warm young life from him.

Her arms were gliding from about his neck, and her shot limbs were sinking to the earth as he caught her up where she dropped to his feet.

"O God! my child! they have killed you!"

He suffered more, as the cry broke from him, than if the bullets had brought him that death which he saw at one glance had stricken down forever all the glory of her childhood, all the gladness of her youth.

She laughed—all the clear, imperious, arch laughter of her sunniest hours unchanged.

"Chut! It is the powder and ball of France! that does not hurt. If it was an Arbico's bullet now! But wait! Here is the Marshal's order. He suspends your sentence; I have told him all. You are safe!—do you hear?—you are safe! How he looks! Is he grieved to live? Mes Français! tell him clearer than I can tell—here is the order. The General must have it. No—not out of my hand till the General sees it. Fetch him, some of you—fetch him to me."

"Great Heaven! You have given your life for mine!"

The words broke from him in an agony as he held her upward against his heart, himself so blind, so stunned, with the sudden recall from death to life, and with the sacrifice whereby life was thus brought to him, that he could scarce see her face, scarce hear her voice, but only dimly, incredulously, terribly knew, in some vague sense, that she was dying, and dying thus for him.

She smiled up in his eyes, while even in that moment, when her life was broken down like a wounded bird's, and the shots had pierced through from her shoulder to her bosom, a hot, scarlet flush came over her cheeks as she felt his touch, and rested on his heart.

"A life! Tiens! what is it to give? We hold it in our hands every hour, we soldiers, and toss it in change for a draught of wine. Lay me down on the ground—at your feet —so! I shall live longest that way, and I have much to tell. How they crowd around me! Mes soldats, do not make that grief and that rage over me. They are sorry they fired; that is foolish. They were only doing their duty, and they could not hear me in time."

But the brave words could not console those who had killed the Child of the Tricolor; they flung their carbines away, they beat their breasts, they cursed themselves and the

mother who had borne them; the silent, rigid, motionless
phalanx that had stood there in the dawn to see death dealt
in the inexorable penalty of the law was broken up into a
tumultuous, breathless, heart-stricken, infuriated throng, maddened with remorse, convulsed with sorrow, turning wild
eyes of hate on him as on the cause through which their
darling had been stricken. He, laying her down with unspeakable gentleness as she had bidden him, hung over her,
leaning her head against his arm, and watching in paralyzed
horror the helplessness of the quivering limbs, the slow
flowing of the blood beneath the Cross that shone where
that young heroic heart so soon would beat no more.

"Oh, my child, my child!" he moaned, as the full might
and meaning of this devotion which had saved him at such
cost rushed on him. "What am I worth that you should
perish for me? Better a thousand times have left me to my
fate! Such nobility, such sacrifice, such love!"

The hot color flushed her face once more; she was strong
to the last to conceal that passion for which she was still
content to perish in her youth.

"Chut! We are comrades, and you are a brave man. I
would do the same for any of my Spahis. Look you, I never
heard of your arrest till I heard, too, of your sentence——"

She paused a moment, and her features grew white and
quivered with pain and with the oppression that seemed to
lie like lead upon her chest. But she forced herself to be
stronger than the anguish which assailed her strength; and
she motioned them all to be silent as she spoke on while her
voice still should serve her.

"They will tell you how I did it—I have not time. The
Marshal gave his word you shall be saved; there is no
fear. That is your friend who bends over me here?—is it
not? A fair face, a brave face! You will go back to your
land—you will live among your own people—and she, she will
love you now—now she knows you are of her Order!"

Something of the old thrill of jealous dread and hate
quivered through the words, but the purer, nobler nature vanquished it; she smiled up in his eyes, heedless of the tumult
round them.

"You will be happy. That is well. Look you—it is nothing
that I did. I would have done it for any one of my soldiers.
And for this"—she touched the blood flowing from her side
with the old, bright, brave smile—"it was an accident; they
must not grieve for it. My men are good to me; they will

feel much regret and remorse; but do not let them. I am glad to die."

The words were unwavering and heroic; but for one moment a convulsion went over her face; the young life was so strong in her, the young spirit was so joyous in her, existence was so new, so fresh, so bright, so dauntless a thing to Cigarette. She loved life: the darkness, the loneliness, the annihilation of death were horrible to her as the blackness and the solitude of night to a young child. Death, like night, can be welcome only to the weary, and she was weary of nothing on the earth that bore her buoyant steps; the suns, the winds, the delights of the sights, the joys of the senses, the music of her own laughter, the mere pleasure of the air upon her cheeks, or of the blue sky above her head, were all so sweet to her. Her welcome of her death-shot was the only untruth that had ever soiled her fearless lips. Death was terrible; yet she was content— content to have come to it for his sake.

There was a ghastly, stricken silence round her. The order she had brought had just been glanced at, but no other thought was with the most callous there than the heroism of her act, than the martyrdom of her death.

The color was fast passing from her lips, and a mortal pallor settling there in the stead of that rich, bright hue, once warm as the scarlet heart of the pomegranate. Her head leaned back on Cecil's breast, and she felt the great burning tears fall, one by one, upon her brow as he hung speechless over her; she put her hand upward and touched his eyes softly.

"Chut! What is it to die—just to die? You have lived your martyrdom; I could not have done that. Listen, just one moment. You will be rich. Take care of the old man— he will not trouble long—and of Vole-qui-veut and Étoile, and Boule Blanche, and the rat, and all the dogs, will you? They will show you the Château de Cigarette in Algiers. I should not like to think that they would starve."

She felt his lips move with the promise he could not find voice to utter; and she thanked him with that old child-like smile that had lost nothing of its light.

"That is good; they will be happy with you. And see here—that Arab must have back his white horse; he alone saved you. Have heed that they spare him. And make my grave somewhere where my army passes; where I can hear the trumpets, and the arms, and the passage of the troops—O

God! I forgot! I shall not wake when the bugles sound. It will all end now; will it not? That is horrible, horrible!"

A shudder shook her as, for the moment, the full sense that all her glowing, redundant, sunlit, passionate life was crushed out forever from its place upon the earth forced itself on and overwhelmed her. But she was of too brave a mold to suffer any foe—even the foe that conquers kings—to have power to appall her. She raised herself, and looked at the soldiery around her, among them the men whose carbines had killed her, whose anguish was like the heart-rending anguish of women.

"Mes Français! That was a foolish word of mine. How many of my bravest have fallen in death; and shall I be afraid of what they welcomed? Do not grieve like that. You could not help it; you were doing your duty. If the shots had not come to me, they would have gone to him; and he has been unhappy so long, and borne wrong so patiently, he has earned the right to live and enjoy. Now I—I have been happy all my days, like a bird, like a kitten, like a foal, just from being young and taking no thought. I should have had to suffer if I had lived. It is much best as it is——"

Her voice failed her when she had spoken the heroic words; loss of blood was fast draining all strength from her, and she quivered in a torture she could not wholly conceal. He for whom she perished hung over her in an agony greater far than hers. It seemed a hideous dream to him that this child lay dying in his stead.

"Can nothing save her?" he cried aloud. "O God! that you had fired one moment sooner!"

She heard; and looked up at him with a look in which all the passionate, hopeless, imperishable love she had resisted and concealed so long spoke with an intensity she never dreamed.

"She is content," she whispered softly. "You did not understand her rightly; that was all."

"All! O God, how I have wronged you!"

The full strength, and nobility, and devotion of this passion he had disbelieved in and neglected rushed on him as he met her eyes; for the first time he saw her as she was; for the first time he saw all of which the splendid heroism of this untrained nature would have been capable under a different fate. And it struck him suddenly, heavily, as with a blow: it filled him with a passion of remorse.

"My darling! my darling! what have I done to be worthy

of such love?" he murmured, while the tears fell from his blinded eyes, and his head drooped until his lips met hers. At the first utterance of that word between them, at the unconscious tenderness of his kisses that had the anguish of a farewell in them, the color suddenly flushed all over her blanched face; she trembled in his arms; and a great, shivering sigh ran through her. It came too late, this warmth of love. She learned what its sweetness might have been only when her lips grew numb, and her eyes sightless, and her heart without pulse, and her senses without consciousness.

"Hush!" she answered, with a look that pierced his soul. "Keep those kisses for Miladi. She will have the right to love you; she is of your 'aristocrates,' she is not 'unsexed.' As for me—I am only a little trooper who has saved my comrade! My soldiers, come round me one instant; I shall not long find words."

Her eyes closed as she spoke; a deadly faintness and coldness passed over her; and she gasped for breath. A moment, and the resolute courage in her conquered; her eyes opened and rested on the war-worn faces of her "children"—rested in a long, last look of unspeakable wistfulness and tenderness.

"I cannot speak as I would," she said at length, while her voice grew very faint. "But I have loved you. All is said!"

All was uttered in those four brief words. "She had loved them." The whole story of her young life was told in the single phrase. And the gaunt, battle-scarred, murderous, ruthless veterans of Africa who heard her could have turned their weapons against their own breasts, and sheathed them there, rather than have looked on to see their darling die.

"I have been too quick in anger sometimes—forgive it," she said gently. "And do not fight and curse among yourselves; it is bad amid brethren. Bury my Cross with me, if they will let you; and let the colors be over my grave, if you can. Think of me when you go into battle; and tell them in France——"

For the first time her own eyes filled with great tears as the name of her beloved land paused upon her lips. She stretched her arms out with a gesture of infinite longing, like a lost child that vainly seeks its mother.

"If I could only see France once more! France——"

It was the last word upon her utterance; her eyes met Cecil's in one fleeting, upward glance of unutterable tenderness, then, with her hands still stretched out westward to where her country was, and with the dauntless heroism of her smile upon her face like light, she gave a tired sigh as of a child that sinks to sleep, and in the midst of her Army of Africa the Little One lay dead.

In the shadow of his tent, at midnight, he whom she had rescued stood looking down at a bowed, stricken form before him with an exceeding, yearning pity in his gaze.

The words had at length been spoken that had lifted from him the burden of another's guilt; the hour at last had come in which his eyes had met the eyes of his friend, without a hidden thought between them. The sacrifice was ended, the martyrdom was over; henceforth this doom of exile and of wretchedness would be but as a hideous dream; henceforth his name would be stainless among men, and the desire of his heart would be given him. And in this hour of release the strongest feeling in him was the sadness of an infinite compassion; and where his brother was stretched prostrate in shame before him, Cecil stooped and raised him tenderly.

"Say no more," he murmured. "It has been well for me that I have suffered these things. For yourself—if you do indeed repent, and feel that you owe me any debt, atone for it, and pay it, by letting your own life be strong in truth and fair in honor."

And it seemed to him that he himself had done no great or righteous thing in that servitude for another's sake, whose yoke was now lifted off him for evermore. But, looking out over the sleeping camp where one young child alone lay in a slumber that never would be broken, his heart ached with the sense of some great, priceless gift received, and undeserved, and cast aside; even while in the dreams of passion that now knew its fruition possible, and the sweetness of communion with the friend whose faith had never forsaken him, he retraced the years of his exile, and thanked God that it was thus with him at the end.

CHAPTER THE LAST.

AT REST.

UNDER the green, springtide leafage of English woodlands, made musical with the movement and the song of innumerable birds that had their nests among the hawthorn boughs and

deep, cool foliage of elm and beech, an old horse stood at
pasture. Sleeping—with the sun on his gray, silken skin, and
the flies driven off with a dreamy switch of his tail, and the
grasses odorous about his hoofs, with dog-violets, and cow-
slips, and wild thyme—sleeping, yet not so surely but at one
voice he started, and raised his head with all the eager
grace of his youth, and gave a murmuring noise of welcome
and delight. He had known that voice in an instant, though
for so many years his ear had never thrilled to it; Forest
King had never forgotten. Now, scarce a day passed but
what it spoke to him some word of greeting or of affection,
and his black, soft eyes would gleam with their old fire, because its tone brought back a thousand memories of bygone
victory—only memories now, when Forest King, in the years
of age, dreamed out his happy life under the fragrant shade
of the forest wealth of Royallieu.

With his arm over the horse's neck, the exile, who had returned to his birthright, stood silent a while, gazing out over
the land on which his eyes never wearied of resting; the
glad, cool, green, dew-freshened earth that was so sweet and
full of peace, after the scorched and blood-stained plains,
whose sun was as flan e, and whose breath was as pestilence.
Then his glance came back and dwelt upon the face beside
him, the proud and splendid woman's face that had learned its
softness and its passion from him alone.

"It was worth banishment to return," he murmured to her.
"It was worth the trials that I bore to learn the love that I
have known——"

She, looking upward at him with those deep, lustrous, imperial eyes that had first met his own in the glare of the
African noon, passed her hand over his lips with a gesture
of tenderness far more eloquent from her than from women
less proud and less prone to weakness.

"Ah, hush! when I think of what her love was, how
worthless looks my own! how little worthy of the fate it
finds! What have I done that every joy should become mine,
when she——"

Her mouth trembled, and the phrase died unfinished;
strong as her own love had grown, it looked to her un-
proven and without desert, beside that which had chosen to
perish for his sake. And where they stood with the future as
fair before them as the light of the day around them, he
bowed his head, as before some sacred thing, at the whisper
of the child who had died for him. The memories of both

went back to a place in a desert land where the folds of the
Tricolor drooped over one little grave turned westward toward the shores of France—a grave made where the beat
of drum, and the sound of moving squadrons, and the ring of
the trumpet-call, and the noise of the assembling battalions
could be heard by night and day; a grave where the troops,
as they passed it by, saluted and lowered their arms in tender
reverence, in faithful, unasked homage, because beneath the
Flag they honored there was carved in the white stone one
name that spoke to every heart within the army she had
loved, one name on which the Arab sun streamed as with a
martyr's glory:

"CIGARETTE,

"ENFANT DE L'ARMÉE, SOLDAT DE LA FRANCE."